TIGHTROPE

TIGHTROPE

MARNIE RICHES

First published in Great Britain in 2019 by Trapeze Books,
an imprint of The Orion Publishing Group Ltd
Carmelite House, 50 Victoria Embankment,
London EC4Y 0DZ

An Hachette UK company

1 3 5 7 9 10 8 6 4 2

A CIP catalogue record for this book is
available from the British Library.

ISBN (mass market paperback) 978 1 4091 8194 1
ISBN (eBook) 978 1 4091 8195 8

Typeset by Born Group

Printed and bound in Great Britain by Clays Ltd, Elcograf S.p.A.

www.orionbooks.co.uk

For my darling Natalie and Adam, the loves of my life. I apologise for your genetic predisposition for filth and swearing. Soz, not soz.

PROLOGUE

The Wolf

Pinned beneath him on the leather chaise, the girl stares up into the gaping maw of the latex wolf mask he is wearing. Despite the alcohol and cocktail of drugs they forced her to take to make her relaxed and pliant, the terror is evident in her eyes.

'You know what I'm going to do?' His voice is muffled as he speaks – hollow and otherworldly. It excites him to tell her what he has in store for her, adopting the role as narrator in this climactic scene of her own personal horror story. It is being filmed, after all. 'I'm going to squeeze the life out of you, because that's what your sort deserves.'

Her expression freezes for a brief moment. Perhaps she is deciphering the unfamiliar English. Suddenly, her face crumples into a look of sheer despair. She shakes her head from side to side. 'No! I don't like,' she says. 'Stan. Where is? I need to talk.' Her words are vodka-slurred, making her Russian accent unguent and treacly. Tears track down the sides of her face as she turns to the cameraman for a reaction. 'Please make stop.' She says something in her mother tongue. The imploring tone in her high-pitched whimper makes her sound like the little girl she really is beneath the heavy make-up.

But her needs are not The Wolf's concern, and the camera keeps rolling. He digs his knees into those slender haunches to limit her movements. Pinions her skinny arms above her head to stop her from lashing out in defence. He calls to the others to hold her down, and like her, they comply with his demands.

'No! No!' she cries, wriggling uselessly against them. 'It hurt. Where Dmitri? Get Stan! Stan! Help!'

'Stan's not here,' he says, almost whispering in her ear. 'Dmitri's busy. And so are we.'

She screams, loud enough to distort the soundtrack.

The Wolf looks up at the other men. There are five in total, all naked but for their masks. A pig. A bulldog. A horse. A cockerel. He stars as The Wolf. It is hard to infer the others' moods at this point, but they are all still visibly aroused, queuing up for a second bite of this ripe cherry.

Right now, however, it is The Wolf's turn.

He reaches over to the coffee table. Snatches up the ball gag, which he straps around her head with practiced ease, despite her wriggling. The only sounds of protest she can emit now is the gurgle of her choking on her own saliva.

'That's better. You talk too much.'

He puts his hand around the naked girl's neck and squeezes while he rides her. Invincible. In charge of her destiny, as he'd witnessed his own father, all those years ago, masterfully controlling the babysitter, the cleaner's daughter, his younger sister. The girl – silenced now; red-faced with the sheer effort of clinging to life – writhes beneath him in a bid to break free. There is pleading in her wide eyes, the veins in her forehead standing proud. She mouths the word, 'Nyet!' but the sound never quite breaks free of her compromised gullet.

The others have started shouting at him, shouting over each other. Their noise is such that it is difficult to tell if they are egging him on or protesting. But with the smell of fresh meat in his nostrils, The Wolf does not care.

When the girl's body finally lies still and her head lolls to one side, the bulldog speaks:

'Jesus! She's gone limp. Is she dead?' He approaches, pressing two fingers to her neck. 'I can't find a pulse! Am I pressing in the right place?' Unbuckling the leather straps of the gag and prising the red plastic ball from her mouth, he cocks his head and holds his ear close to her lips. 'I can't hear her breathing.'

'Try her wrist,' the horse says. He approaches and feels along the inside of her wrist for a pulsating vein. 'Nothing.' Lifting the girl's eyelids, he uselessly waves his hand in front of her glazed eyes. 'You've fucking killed her, haven't you?' he says to The Wolf. 'You absolute knob. We're buggered.' His voice is tremulous. He backs away from the scene, covering his waning erection with both hands as if he finally knows shame.

The Wolf, however, has no such compunction. Sated, he dismounts the teenage prostitute. She is nothing more to him than a spent horse after a long, hard ride. His work is done.

This is why he is the star of this little home movie, which Stan's sweaty coke-head of a cameraman is still discretely shooting.

The girl's limbs hang around her at odd angles like the arms of a broken clock, which is fitting as time no longer matters to her now.

The pig tugs at his mask as though he wants to remove it. He seems to think better of it, though. 'Why the hell did you strangle her? You prat. This is going to come back on us. My wife will find out. We'll all get nicked as accessories to murder. Christ's sake, you brutal bastard! We're ruined.' Both anger and terror are audible in his voice.

'Can you just stop panicking for five minutes?' The cockerel speaks quickly to the pig. He turns to The Wolf. 'We can't just leave her like this . . . can we? We should at least find out who she is.' He snatches up the girl's handbag, perching it on his paunch. Starts to rummage through it. Clearly agitated, he empties it out onto the coffee table of the stylish apartment, rifling through the pile of contents. Painkillers. Phone. Lipstick. Lube. Condoms. A tampon. Purse.

The Wolf picks up what appears to be ID but it is only an Oyster Card. 'Fake,' he says. He holds the photocard up. Compares the smiling girl in the photograph to the anguished death mask of the under-aged prostitute. 'Emma Davies? Not bloody likely. This silly little bitch was Russian. She's just another of Dmitri's trafficked whores. Let's face it, boys, nobody's going to miss her.'

'Look, you did this,' the horse tells The Wolf, his voice sounding nasal as it filters down the long nose of the mask. 'This is your problem.' He holds his hands up, taking a step backwards. Shaking his head. 'I'm off. I'm not getting involved. We were supposed to come here for a bit of fun. Let off some steam. But this . . .? You're on your own, bud. I've got a family. A reputation . . .'

The bulldog pulls his foreskin back over his deflating penis, his doggy head cocked to one side as he contemplates the girl. His disbelief is audible in the high pitch of his speech. 'The only way this disappears is if *she* disappears. You're going to have to get rid of her. What are you going to do with her body?'

The Wolf turns to him. 'What am *I* going to do with it? You mean, what are *we* going to do? We're all in this together, remember?'

As the others start to back away from the body and the camera, covering themselves with cushions and items of clothing that they'd discarded gleefully only minutes earlier, The Wolf moves with stealth into the kitchen. He reappears, carrying a butcher's knife block and a roll of black bin liners. Sets the block down onto the coffee table, knocking the girl's things to the floor. He pulls out a meat cleaver and a bread knife, staring down at the glinting blades through the eyeholes of his wolfish mask. Still bearing a sizeable, angry erection.

'I know exactly how to get rid of this little problem.'

The film clip ends.

The appeal of watching it over and over again in the privacy of his office never wanes, though he knows that it is now on the Dark Net for every Tom, Dick and Harry to savour too, provided they can get themselves beyond the paywall. Masturbating himself slowly, gripping the rosewood tabletop of his desk with his free hand, he muses that it makes him some sort of celebrity. He certainly feels like one, every time that piece of footage flickers into life on his laptop's screen. He is The Wolf. Everyone else is an incidental character in that unfolding drama; that perfect world, where he was the King of Everything in a penthouse in West London.

When the footage runs out, it freezes mid frame with an outstretched palm in close-up. His hand. He'd turned to Stan's cameraman, telling him to switch it off and destroy the film. Except the money-grubbing moron had done no such thing. At Stan's suggestion, to compensate for the lost income from his dead whore, he'd uploaded it onto the net instead where it could be monetised. At first, The Wolf had felt like the skies were about to collapse in on him. But they hadn't. He has nothing to fear from the authorities or that scumbag, Stan. Time has elapsed, and still, nobody knows who was responsible for the appearance of the mystery girl, bagged in pieces in the butcher's bin along with the other rotten meat. A broken Russian doll.

Cleaning himself up, he now prepares for another day as a man of unimpeachable standing. He is honourable and trustworthy and liked, just as his father was. They do not know about his starring role as The Wolf. That knowledge remains a secret which he is certain will be carried to the graves of all concerned. In those fleeting minutes captured on film, he will forever more be God's own emissary on earth, dispensing judgement and death according to his whim.

He tucks himself back in, washes his hands and checks his reflection in the mirror. All is silent but for his footfalls and the persistent voice in his head that not even the clip can drown out:

'No thanks. You're not what I'm looking for.'

Her voice on a deafening loop. The time she rejected him and humiliated him publicly. But that is nothing compared to the gargantuan lie she has been telling for more than a decade. The woman he pictures in his mind's eye has committed the ultimate act of betrayal. She has stolen from him in the worst way imaginable. But he will have his revenge.

The Wolf is watching her. He is hungry. And waiting.

CHAPTER 1
Bev

'Balls to Dr Mo and his group-therapy cobblers,' she said, savouring the sight of the object of her desire. Endorphins fizzed in her bloodstream. The rush of a conquest was always a narcotic, numbing the jab, jab, jab of her conscience that insisted she was derailing her own fast-train back to a future worth having. With a quick glance up the double-parked street of elegant Edwardian brick terraces, she negotiated a traffic hump. The car shuddered and her teeth clacked. OK, perhaps she was going a little too fast. Eyes back on the prize. 'Oh, Mama. I *cannot* wait to get you home and rip off your—'

When the 4x4 ploughed into her at speed, Beverley Saunders' little VW Polo lurched improbably to the right, missing the parked Audi on the opposite side of the road by only inches.

Her airbag inflated immediately.

'Jesuf pft.' A muffled outcry was all she could manage until the bag deflated, leaving her gripping the steering wheel with white-knuckled, shaking hands. Stunned, she stared at the bag that now looked like an oversized, spent johnny. 'What bastard . . .?'

Flushed through with adrenaline, she applied her hand-brake, punched her hazard warning lights into life and stepped out of the car. The culprit was looking down at her from the elevated vantage point of an Overfinch Range Rover. Staring directly at Bev open-mouthed as though she couldn't quite believe what had just come to pass.

Bev took in the devastation wrought on her beloved little VW by the unforgiving bulk of this pimped-up Chelsea Tractor – or rather, Hale Tractor in this overpriced pocket of Cheshire. Enraged, she marched up to the driver's side window of the 4x4, expecting to find some washed up soap actress or footballer's wife.

'Get out of the fucking car, lady!' she yelled.

The woman raised her hand to her mouth, but otherwise didn't move.

She didn't seem to be a celebrity, but Bev knew her type well. High blonde ponytail. Pearl earrings. Expensive-looking fur gilet that showed off the owner's reed-like arms, accented with a shitty taupe silk scarf that chimed in perfect harmony with the Farrow and Ball-painted doors and window frames of the surrounding houses. Rocks on those bony fingers that could fund a developing country. That much she could see through the glass.

'Entitled shitbag. I'm talking to you!'

Bev eyed the stoved-in passenger side of her Polo, noticing how the tyre was facing inwards at an untenable angle. A flicker of guilt strobed at the back of her mind, telling her that a crash was karmic payback for being weak. But that didn't excuse this stupid cow. She thumped the bonnet of the Range Rover.

'You killed my car!'

Shutters were twitching either side of the street. Cleaners and nannies peered out at the scene, no doubt making morality judgements as Bev cursed and the blonde finally emerged, tugging at the ties of her gilet.

'I'm so, so sorry. My foot slipped and I just shot out.' The blonde looked back regretfully at the give-way markings on the road.

'I take it *you're* not hurt.' Bev eyed the pristine white Range Rover. It didn't have a single dent in it. Naturally. And those gleaming black alloys were intact. Naturally. Only the Polo looked like it had been in a fight with Godzilla. 'Details!' Her heartbeat was thunderous as she proffered the brown envelope from a recent, terrifying HMRC communiqué and a pencil she'd stolen from IKEA. 'I think we've got to call the police, get a reference number or something, but first, we exchange details.'

'Yes. Of course.' The blonde dithered, clearly looking for something to lean on. Opted for her bonnet. She wrote, 'Angela Fitzwilliam' in a shaky hand.

The crash threatened to send Bev careening to the rock bottom of a cliff face she had already been struggling to cling to, let alone scale. She was just about to subject the woman to another tirade of expletives, when the guilt flickered on again; brighter and steadier, this time, like a searchlight shining on her shortcomings. She privately acknowledged that she hadn't really been paying attention either. Too busy staring at the extremely rare, mint origami kit she'd bought off the old guy in Rusholme. A moment of eBay madness, indulging in the very compulsion she had sworn she would eschew. Dr Mo would remind her that she had taken four steps backwards in the board game of her life, sliding down yet another damned snake at a point where she'd hoped to climb the next ladder. Well, the self-appointed saviour of the obsessive, the compulsive and the habitually disorderly would have to damn well find out first.

Maybe she *was* equally to blame for being unobservant. But this woman looked loaded. She could almost certainly afford to lose her no claims bonus and pay the excess. Bev, on the other hand, had a stack of unopened bills waiting on the side in her crappy flat, not to mention the tax demand. Screw it.

'So, you admit, it was your fault?'

The woman closed her large, deep-set eyes and held up hands that were beautifully manicured. 'Oh, absolutely. Mine entirely.'

A fixed-up car, a month or two of lovely physio, being pummelled with warm oils by some beefcake – the nearest Bev would get to a massage now that she was permanently broke. A couple of grand in damages would clear some of those debts. Bish, bash, bosh. Bev mentally rubbed her hands together and thanked God for silver linings.

Driving the Polo back to the flat was a challenge. She crawled along at 5mph, rehearsing what she would say to her insurer on the phone: *The other driver wasn't watching where she was going; my car's had it; will her insurance pay for a quality hire car? Can I have an Alfa Romeo please?*

Barely managing to turn into Sophie's gravelled driveway before her car breathed its last, Bev balked at the sight of the Range Rover already parked up outside the detached Victorian villa. A white Overfinch with black alloys. All thoughts of retiring to her mildewed basement to console herself with the rare origami contraband were long, long gone.

'You are bloody kidding me. What the hell . . .?'

Upstairs, the stained-glass front door swung open. Sophie appeared in the doorway, a pearly grin plastered on her beautiful face. She draped a territorial arm around the shoulder of her guest who trotted forwards like a shy Bambi, with those skinny fawn-like legs and that expensive

10

pelt on her back. 'Bev, meet my friend, Angela Fitzwilliam. She's the wife of one of Tim's colleagues from way back. Angie, meet my oldest college pal and PI extraordinaire, Beverley Saunders.'

Angela Fitzwilliam looked as though she'd seen a ghost. '*You?*'

'I've already had the pleasure,' Bev said, grimacing pointedly at her mangled car. 'What do you want, Sophie? I've got no wheels, thanks to *her*. How am I supposed to stake out cheating scumbags without a bloody car? I might have a job on in Warrington next week.'

'Come on, Bev. There's no need to be so unfriendly,' Sophie said.

'Oh, there's every need.'

Learn to walk away from stressful situations when they threaten to overwhelm you, Dr Mo had told her. *Don't resort to your bad habits to regain control. Remember what's at stake.*

She needed to get out of there.

Pushing past both women, she picked her way around the pushchair, car seats and kid-paraphernalia that littered the otherwise pristine period chic of Sophie's spacious hallway, and descended the narrow stone stairs to her poky basement flat. Sophie had deigned to rent to it to her at an only slightly discounted mates' rates. Bev couldn't stick her key in the lock quickly enough. She slammed the door behind her, praying that even someone as single-minded as her oldest friend would realise Bev was in no mood to make small talk with the reckless cow who had ruined her day.

Flinging herself onto the sofa, choking back a sob, she examined the origami kit. Obviously, once the delicate structure was complete, she would plonk it with the thousands of other cranes, flowers, dragons that were gathering dust on her display shelving. The itch would be scratched. She'd be back to buckling beneath the weight of disappointment, with the zero in her thirty years of age representing the emptiness of an existence where she felt distinctly sub-prime in the prime of her life; where she'd failed with aplomb.

With determined fingers, she started to tear at the cellophane.

There was a knock at the door, leaving her poised mid-rip. Sophie shouted through from the other side. Her voice sounded tinny in the claustrophobic subterranean space at the bottom of the stairs, which constituted a vestibule of sorts.

'Are you OK, sweets? Can we come in?'

Hiding her new acquisition in plain sight among the clutter on her coffee table, Bev opened the door. Both of them were standing there, a picture of *Harper's Bazaar* perfection.

'What do you want?' she asked, suddenly feeling cheap and scruffy in supermarket jeans that were worn at the knees and a rower's top from college that was stained on the belly. 'I already gave her my details.' She leaned against the architrave, arms folded. Legs crossed. 'I'm busy.'

'Oh, don't be like that. Let us in.' Sophie winked. Strong-armed her way past Bev as though she owned the place, which of course, she did. 'Angie needs to talk to you.'

'No! No, it's fine,' Angie said, folding her arms and turning to leave. 'Let's forget it.'

'Nonsense.' Sophie reached back and yanked her friend inside.

The dark, one-bedroomed flat felt overstuffed with three people in it. Bev waited for the kettle to boil, watching Angie through the crack in the kitchenette door. The two women were pointing at Bev's origami collection, nodding and cooing over the delicate creations. But

Bev could see them exchange a glance and wrinkle their noses. She was certain she heard the word, 'dusty' said by one of them.

'Stinks in here, doesn't it?' she said, emerging with a cafetière of coffee and three cups on a tray. A packet of digestives that she knew only she would eat, judging by the telltale thick hair that grew on Angie's forearms – a classic symptom of anorexia. And Sophie didn't do carbs. 'That's because I collect black mould as well as origami. Tim won't tank the basement properly. You're married to a slum landlord, Soph. Ha ha.'

Dr Mo had told her to try to let go of her bitterness, thereby freeing up more positive energy with which to improve her life. But Mo hadn't been taken for a ride by a disease like her ex, Rob. Mo wasn't fighting to make ends meet. Mo wasn't under the scrutiny of social services.

Ignoring the pointed comment, Sophie motioned regally that Angie should sit. Both of them perched gingerly on the edge of the sofa, like glittering Lalique vases wedged amongst the junk in a high street thrift shop.

Sipping her black coffee, Sophie waited until all eyes were on her. Then, finally, she revealed the reason for the visit. 'Angie needs your help. Don't you?'

Bev was surprised when tears started to fall freely from this stranger's perfectly made-up eyes. The Bev of old would have clucked around her, knowing instinctively how to cope with this outpouring. But then, her former self wouldn't have felt such an outsider in her own home. Who the hell was this woman, with her beige Gucci loafers and her silk scarf wrapped artfully around her neck? She looked as if she'd just come from a yoga session in some pocket-Ashram above an organic butchers or artisan bakery.

13

Whipping her new origami set from under her cup and replacing it with an unopened overdue gas bill, Bev offered her visitor the last tissue from a Kleenex box.

'I'm so sorry,' Angie said. 'You don't even know me and . . .' She shook her head.

'Jerry's a bully,' Sophie said. 'Angie's husband . . . he watches their bank account like a hawk, doesn't he, Ange? And Angie's certain he plays away when he's down in London. Maybe up here, too.' She turned to Bev, her porcelain cheeks flushed with the enthusiastic glow of a gossip who was on fire. Patted Angela's leg as if she was a child who needed nothing more than a good bit of advocacy from a grown-up who knew best. 'He's a dog and she needs to put him down.'

Angie toyed with her rings. 'Hang on a minute, Soph. I wouldn't say that—'

But Sophie wasn't listening. 'Jerry used to work on the trading floor with Tim at Lieberman Brothers. The boys were so close, they got a pied-à-terre together, didn't they, Angie?' Her eyes were glassy as though she'd just hoovered a line of coke, though Sophie had always been steadfastly anti-drugs. She always got like this when she was on a mission. She'd been no different at college. Save the Children fund; Oxfam; Antonia on the ground corridor whose dad was being a pig. Do-gooding Sophie to the rescue with her sponsored walks and her Kum-Ba-Ya positivity and her leaflet-distributions. Tea, chat and a damp basement flat. 'The two of them fast-tracked from being *the* hotshot new grad-trainees to masters of the universe in next to no time. They were quite the dream team. Before it all went . . .' Her carefully shaped eyebrows bunched together as if in disbelief that those particular tits should have gone quite so spectacularly up in the period following

14

the crash of 2009. 'Jerry's always been *such* an alpha. I'm not surprised Angie wants to make a break.'

'What *do* you want, Angela?' Bev watched the visitor's spine curve like a whippy branch bent in a stiff wind. 'You want a divorce?'

Those beautifully made-up eyes darted from Sophie to the iPhone she'd set down amongst the detritus on Bev's coffee table. Her voice was small when she spoke. 'Well, yes.' A blotchy rash had started to crawl its way out of the bounds of the silk scarf and up towards her chin. She scratched the pad of her index finger with her thumbnail. Scratching. Scratching.

'Angie needs to get irrefutable grounds for divorce. Dig up dirt on Jerry. That sort of thing.' Sophie nudged her friend. 'Show her the picture!'

Looking at the photo that Angie pushed into her hands, Bev studied Jerry Fitzwilliam's face. Instant recognition. 'The bloody shadow Science Minister? Are you kidding me?' She started to laugh. 'He was on breakfast telly this morning! The toast of Westminster and Labour's great white hope? He's our local MP too, isn't he?' She shook her head vociferously, imagining being revenge-stalked by some terrifying goon from MI5 or MI6 or whatever the hell it was. 'I'm not poking my long-range lens anywhere near this guy. It's beyond me. Seriously, Angela. I'm flattered you thought I'd be able to help, and God bless Sophie for believing in me. But I'm a marketing wonk who turned to a bit of PI work because . . . let's just say, circumstances demanded it. Long story. Seriously. Get a pro with an expenses account and a five-star rating on Trustpilot. Actually, just get a bloody divorce lawyer like everyone else and get on with it.'

Angie reached out and snatched up her phone. Barely glancing at Bev. 'I never should have come here. I'm sorry. It's not as if I can pay you, anyway.'

15

'*You can't pay?*' Bev was on her feet, now. What kind of bullshit had Sophie brought to her door? A woman with fashionably jutting hips and a high-profile husband who lacked the gumption to stand on her own two pedicured feet.

She ushered the two towards the front door. 'Do me a favour, Soph. Don't bring potential clients to me if they're looking for a freebie. I can't pay my bills with goodwill.'

'She can pay, Bev!' Sophie clearly wouldn't admit defeat. Blustering like a WI federation leader. 'Stop being so mean. You must help her. The impact that this is bound to be having on Angie's children is just—'

'Will you please *not* speak about me as if I'm not in the room?' Angie said with a sudden acidity to her voice that seemed to change the pH value in the room. 'That's exactly the sort of thing Jerry does all the time. I'm quite capable of telling Bev myself.'

Feeling whiplash from the crash really starting to bite into her shoulder muscles, Bev just wanted to be alone. Two painkillers and a kip before Molly Peters, a paying client, turned up at 2 p.m. to see the photos Bev had taken of her shitehawk of a husband, holding hands with his pert work colleague in Blackpool Starbucks. Maybe the rescue truck would show up to take her broken car in the interim. That was the extent of her ambition.

She held the front door open. 'Look, Angela. I take happy snaps of snogging builders and IT bods when they're bonking in Travelodges. But digging up dirt about someone in the public eye? For free? You're on your own. I'm sorry.'

16

CHAPTER 2
Angie

The warm sun streaming in through the shutters meant it was a good day to ask for a divorce. Didn't it? The paparazzi were outside. Sure. Poppy's eczema had flared up again. Well, that was par for the course. Benjy was throwing his nibbled toast across the kitchen like a broken boomerang, screaming when he didn't get it back. But Angie had been waiting for the right moment for weeks, before Sophie had put the idea of 'making a case' into her head. Today was the first day the rain had finally stopped. It was a sign. She'd do it now. She didn't need Beverley Saunders.

'Don't want toast!' Benjy yelled, banging his balled fist onto the table. 'Benjy wants choccy. Get me choccy, Mummy.'

With a quailing heart, she took in the sight of her five-year-old son's bright-red face. Her eyes. Her length of limb. Her platinum blonde hair. The temper was all his father's.

'No, darling.' She picked the soggy, masticated toast up off the floor, hoping Jerry wouldn't kick up a stink again that grease marks had permeated the wood. Reclaimed parquet from a French chateau needed to be treated with respect, he'd said. Why the hell couldn't she just put a mat beneath the children when they ate? She'd conceded it was a fair point and had apologised. Now, here she was again, caught in the same predicament. Angry Benjy who hated the mat because it made him feel like a baby. Sneering Jerry, who couldn't see why the hell she failed to mother her own children properly.

She sighed, rinsing out the cloth and cursing softly when she noticed the shellac polish on her nails had chipped.

The doorbell rang. Reporters, clamouring to get the press conference started. Jerry was keeping them waiting. Jolly whistling coming from the en suite as he prepared for the glare and flash of the cameras. If she asked quickly, he'd be so busy, he might not even process her request until the evening, giving him time to respond calmly, in a considered manner. *I want a divorce*, she'd say. *It's not you. It's me. Let's do this like civilised adults.*

'Choccy! Benjy wants choccy.' Her son threw his plate at her head. 'Get Benjy choccy, bitch!'

Poppy started to laugh hysterically at her brother, scratching and scratching at the florid, scabbed crooks of her arms. 'You're naughty!'

Angela reached out to her daughter, silently processing what Benjy had just called her. 'Leave the scabs, darling. They'll bleed. Mummy will put cream on for you after breakfast.'

'I want Gretchen to do it,' Poppy said, snatching her arm away. Clawing at the rash. 'Where is she?'

'She's gone on holiday to Austria, sweetie, to see her family. Mummy will do your cream.'

Bitch. A spiteful word that made Angie's stomach twist into knots. Benjy had overheard his father using it. Maybe she had driven him to it. That had been his excuse. *Nagging bitch. Frigid bitch.* Maybe she was at fault and should just be thankful for this wonderful life he so generously funded and these children he had given her. Put her plans to start again on a back-burner indefinitely. Think of the children. They needed stability.

No.

She shook her head. Remembered Sophie's words of encouragement: *You can do it, Angie. Nobody should accept a life sentence of unhappiness. If you've given up on love, you've been looking for it in the wrong place. Do it when he's distracted and the nanny's not there. It will be fine. Jerry's a reasonable guy.*

Sophie had to be right. Sophie was always right, after all. Especially after a couple of gin and slims. And wasn't the sun streaming merrily through the kitchen shutters as though God had ordained that her fresh start should begin this very morning?

'Bitch! Bitch! Choccy, bitchy bitch!'

'Don't use that horrid word, Benjamin,' she said, cleaning the boy's hands with a wet wipe. 'That's really not a nice thing to call ladies, especially Mummy who loves you very much. Drink your milk please.'

'No! I can't have it.'

She wasn't sure which stung more – the fact that her son slapped her or that his blow fell on a bruised rib that still smarted. 'Oh, that's not very nice, Benjamin Fitzwilliam.'

'What's not nice?'

Jerry had appeared in the threshold to the kitchen, still fiddling with his tie. He smiled warmly but his eyebrow was raised. He expected a response.

'Just Benjy being silly, darling. I've made you a coffee.'

She smoothed her hair behind her ear and trudged over to the counter.

'You're walking like a hod carrier again, Angela.' Her husband strode over and slapped her on her cashmere, legging-clad bottom. 'A big filly like you should trot, not shuffle.' He laughed at his own joke. 'Think of the example you're setting Poppy.'

Big filly. Her stomach growled. She fingered the waistband of her size 0 leggings and acknowledged silently that they had grown tight of late. Today, she would only drink boiled water infused with lemon. Go to the gym once the kids were at nursery. Even if he agreed to divorce, she'd need to keep trim. She could hear the taunts of her old school pals from the tough teen years when she *had* been big. Angie the Arse. Bloater Bedford. She'd lost the weight and swapped the hurtful school pals for a husband who called her Fatty Fitzwilliam, though he swore blind to all their friends that it was merely, 'in an ironic way'.

The children were delighted to see their father, of course, unaware that each of his words cut into her carefully moisturised skin. They stretched out their little arms to him, wanting to be swept up and swung into the air. But Daddy was preparing for the camera, only doling out hair ruffles and a peck on the forehead this morning.

'What do you think of Daddy's tie, eh kids? Will it look good on the TV when I talk about my new proposed Green Paper?'

'Oh, Jerry, the children don't know what a Green Paper is.' Now was her chance. She turned to Poppy and Benjy, treating them to her most beatified smile, lest they cotton on to what was about to take place. It was important they knew as little as possible of any parental anguish or strife. Hadn't she been careful to give them the dream childhood? Organic food; designer clothes; music lessons; the best Austrian nanny money could fund; a packed schedule of exciting and improving activities. The least she owed them was carefully stage-managed change. 'Go and play, darlings. Mummy needs to talk to Daddy about boring grown-up things.'

Poppy led Benjy away from their undersized kiddy-table and chairs. They thundered off towards the playroom, oblivious to what was about to take place.

Angie's heart thudded against the prominent bones of her ribcage. She fingered her pearls, trying to appear calm and keep the tremor out of her voice.

Jerry had seated himself at the breakfast table and was scrolling through the messages on his phone. Slurping his coffee as though the world's press wasn't waiting outside for their favourite shadow Science Minister, about to pronounce on the latest opposition party line on renewable energy. He didn't have a clue, did he?

Now, they were alone. She took a deep breath and held it, poised to blurt out the lines she'd rehearsed over and over. Two years of desperate longing. Her head swam with a mixture of dread and adrenaline. Somewhere beneath that toxic cocktail lurked a base note of euphoria.

Standing in front of him, she said the introductory words quickly. 'Jerry, I'm unhappy.'

He kept scrolling. Thumbing that damned iPhone screen. Had he even heard?

'Did you hear me? I said I'm not happy, Jerry.' She took a seat opposite him. Splayed her reed-thin fingers wide on the glass tabletop. Felt her pulse flick-flickering into overdrive all over her body.

'I heard you,' he said, studiously failing to look up.

Should she blurt out the rest or wait for a response?

Finally, he put down his phone and stood up. 'I know Gretchen's being off must be difficult, darling.' His cheeks had coloured but still there was no real indication that he had read her thoughts and intentions. Reaching into his trouser pocket, he pulled out a roll of twenty-pound notes held together by a silver Asprey clip. Peeling off half of it, he

21

pushed the money towards her. Winked. 'Here. Get yourself a little treat. Go to the hairdresser and get some extensions. I like those. Or get a massage. Whatever will cheer you up.' He peeled off another few hundred. 'Oh, and get your teeth whitened too. The caps are beginning to discolour again.' He wrinkled his nose as if at the core of her very being there lingered a bad smell. 'Save me the receipts.'

'It's not about money, Jerry. You're always generous.' Those were the words that came out in a small voice. But what she'd intended to do was to yell that he was an insensitive, insulting bastard and that she was sick of having to ask him for cash. His generosity came in rare fits and starts and usually came with conditions attached that she should spend the money he deigned to give her on her appearance. She was still angry that he had insisted they close their joint account years ago, setting up a new one in his name only because she hadn't been able to justify the money she had withdrawn in Waitrose at the till during the weekly shop. Fed up to the back of her poor, decaying teeth that none of the utilities were in her name; none of the cars were registered to her and the house officially belonged to him and him alone. *Say the words, for God's sake!* Deep breath in. 'It's just that I've come to realise—'

Barely had she begun her grand speech, when he appeared behind her, massaging her shoulders with so much force that she squirmed with discomfort.

'Oh,' she said, placing her hand on his. Wanting to push him off. Feeling instinctively that she shouldn't.

Suddenly, those ham-like hands of his were around her neck. He dug his thumbs in at the nape. His fingers pressed on her windpipe. She started to kick. Panic rising in her throat but unable to escape. She felt the warmth of his cheek on hers. Smelled his early morning breath – a melange of coffee and minty toothpaste. His aftershave was overpowering. His voice was soft and deadly.

'I do hope you're not about to launch into some silly nonsense about how miserable you are in our marriage, Angela.' He kissed her ear as she fought for breath. 'Let me stop you before you even start, my love. Because we've had this chat before, haven't we?'

Though she felt her consciousness ebbing away, she forced herself to nod. Realised she had neither the physical strength nor the emotional energy to fight him off. Prayed the children wouldn't walk in on this nightmarish scene.

'Let me tell you again what will happen if you ever try to leave me . . .'

She felt him press up against the back of the chair and knew he'd be hard. At least the thick, bentwood structure saved her from having his erection pressing painfully into her shoulder blade. He wouldn't dare do his usual trick with all those reporters and photographers hanging around on the other side of the half-open shutters.

With his hands still around her throat, he continued to speak in a half whisper, too close to her ear for comfort.

'If you try to leave me and say I was a bad husband, nobody will trust a word you say. Because you're nothing but a silly, lying cunt and I'm a democratically elected Member of Parliament and a valued part of the shadow cabinet. If you try to divorce me, I'll refute any grounds you submit. Your name will be mud. You'll be broke. Every penny that comes into this house is mine and will remain mine. I'll cut you out of the kids' lives, because you're nothing but a fat, lazy bitch who relies on a nanny to bring her own children up. All that gin you sit swilling in the afternoon with your other show-pony pals – that won't look good for you when I have a word with my solicitor. Not one bit. None of it will.'

Scraping the chair against the wood floor, he man-oeuvred her around with ease, so that she faced him at crotch height. She gasped to refill her lungs with air now that he had finally released his grip on her. Desperate to check that the children weren't watching but unable to tear her gaze from his fingers as he undid the zip of his suit trousers. She knew exactly what was coming next. His party piece. The press gathered outside seemingly had no dampening effect on his ego whatsoever.

'Don't, Jerry. The children—'

'Open your mouth.'

He grabbed the back of her head with one hand and was freeing his erection from his trousers with the other.

As Angela Fitzwilliam did as she was told, the sun went in, plunging the kitchen into dismal shadow and snuffing out all hope of her fresh start.

Later, when Beverley Saunders answered the door of Sophie's house, Angela could barely speak for sobs that caught in her swollen throat.

'Jesus, Angie. What's wrong? Sophie's out, I'm afraid.'

'I'm h-here to see you,' she said, barely able to utter the words.

Bev frowned. 'You don't need me. I've already told you I can't . . .'

By way of explanation, Angie slowly unwound her silk scarf to reveal the newly developing bruises on her neck. Two sets of four perfect small circles in bright blue.

'I haven't been entirely honest with you, Bev,' she said haltingly, shivering with grief. 'Or Sophie, for that matter. Things are bad. *Very* bad. I'm so frightened. I can't take it any more. Please say you'll help.'

CHAPTER 3
Bev

The clock said 11.23 a.m. Squinting at the painfully bright digital display, Bev's hungover brain told her the clock was a liar and a cheat. How could it possibly be that late? The darkened room was still spinning slightly. But then, the smell of the stale wine glass on her nightstand reached her nostrils. Bev caught sight of the empty Chardonnay bottle beyond it, on her dressing table that doubled as a desk. Remnants of a night spent trying to kill the whiplash burn in her neck and shoulders; agonising over whether or not she'd done the right thing in saying yes to Angela Fitzwilliam.

'A Cabinet Minister!' she'd said, over and over, as a weeping Angie had worked her way through the box of tissues on her cluttered coffee table. 'They'll find my body in bits, zipped into a holdall like that spy guy in London.'

Angie had shaken her head, blinking away the tears. 'No, no, no! Please don't say that. You'll be fine. Jerry's not a criminal. And he's only in the shadow cabinet.'

But her bruised, waiflike body, folded up tightly like an upright foetus nestling into the womb of Bev's threadbare sofa, had told a very different story. Jerry Fitzwilliam was a domestic abuser and a liar, at best. Bev had felt danger register in her bones like the sudden onset of flu.

'I'm telling you, Angela. If he susses for one minute that I'm on his tail or threatening him in some way, he'll have some nutter from MI6 on my case. You think high-level spooks won't get on a train?'

'Please! I've got to get out before . . .' She touched her bruised neck. 'My children. What if . . .?'

She'd seen the desperation in Angie's bloodshot eyes, then – the fear that Bev might reconsider and back out at any moment, taking all hope with her. Lucky for Angie, setting up as a PI had not gone as smoothly as anticipated, and for Bev, even the vague promise of income was better than no income at all. 'Dry your eyes,' she'd said. 'Get your make-up back on. He can't know that the game has changed. Act normal.'

'But I already told him I want a divorce. Sort of.'

'Un-tell him then!'

Angie had startled. Fresh tears in her eyes.

Too brusque. Bev had tried to soften her voice. 'Look. I realise it's difficult for you, but just try to make nice. Apologise like your life depends on it.' She'd patted Angie's arm in a placatory fashion but had hastily withdrawn as her jittery new client had flinched at the contact. 'Leave the rest to me.'

Now, here Bev was, hungover and staring at the spoils of last night's emotional war, where she had started to Google Jerry Fitzwilliam and realised just what she was letting herself in for. The headlines in the newspapers said it all:

Hydrogen Hero – Shadow Science Minister pledges clean cars for all in next 5 years.

Shadow Science Minister vows funding for UK medical research.

Fitzwilliam gives Chinese run for their money in global biotech race.

Even the red tops adored him, it seemed:

Jerry and his pacemaker – shadow cabinet Minister fights Tories' threat to put UK science coffers under cardiac arrest.

It seemed Jerry Fitzwilliam could do no wrong in the media's eyes. Right wing or left wing – it didn't matter. They all had the hots for this apparent man of the people who was nothing more than a charmer with a knack for promising things that the country needed most. Easy when it coincided with a time when his governing opponent – tactless ball-breaking Tory, Maddie Chandler – was being routinely pilloried for some cock-up with the Chinese and a lost billion-pound investment in some new life-changing technology or other.

Clutching a coffee, clad in her underwear and a kimono that had been a gift from Rob, at a time in their doomed marriage when he'd still been making an effort, Bev took a seat at her dressing table. She avoided the reflection in the mirror that told her she had put on weight and had dark rings beneath her eyes.

'I must be mental,' she said, firing up her laptop. 'I'm digging myself deeper into the sodding hole I'm meant to be climbing out of.' She could visualise again the judge's granite-like face, which had loomed over her from the lofty vantage point of his bench. He had outlined the conditions of the court in a voice that had been entirely devoid of warmth: a clean bill of psychiatric health, domestic stability, financial independence. These were the things Beverley Saunders needed to prove if she wanted to get back that which was most dear to her and put her world back together. But then, wasn't Angela Fitzwilliam being destroyed in a similar way? Was it right to let another woman suffer, and possibly be beaten to death, when it was within Bev's power to help?

She brought up Facebook. It took only a flurry of clicks to find Jerry Fitzwilliam – two degrees of separation away, thanks to his friendship with Sophie's husband, Tim.

'Bingo.'

In fact, Jerry Fitzwilliam, self-described as, 'mouthpiece for the masses, social entrepreneur, Geek Lord' was friends with over three thousand people. His profile picture wasn't one of the professionally taken portraits that Bev had seen used in the newspapers – posing with a rictus grin and just a little shiny below the hairline. Neither was it a paparazzi snap of him leaving some high-level meeting in Westminster, chatting to a young female aide who wore a clinging skirt and heels. No. This was the sort of photo Bev had seen countless times on dating websites: an over-weight middle-aged guy on a tropical beach near sunset, sitting with legs akimbo, drink in hand, wearing shades. A cocky bastard, trying to look way cooler and younger than he was. No evidence whatsoever that he had a wife or children.

'Right, Mr Ego. Let's see how easy it is to enter your world.'

She set up a new profile, realising she couldn't use her own Facebook account. She'd abandoned that since her split with Rob the Knob and the ensuing social ice age which began when their fair-weather friends had frozen her out. What should she call this predatory female? Cat? Yes, it made sense. Cat . . . She spied a picture of her maternal grandmother on the bookshelf, alongside a row of yellowing origami frogs. Nana Thomson. Cat Thomson, then. That would do.

She pulled an old photograph of herself from the laptop's hard drive and stared wistfully at the younger, almost unrecognisable, Bev who gazed out at her. Challenging. Glamorous. Exactly the kind of woman Jerry Fitzwilliam might go for.

Sending friend requests to hundreds of people already connected to the shadow Cabinet Minister, reasoning that most people were vain or naïve enough to accept approaches from strangers as long as there was an apparent link to their other acquaintances, Cat Thomson quickly garnered enough friends to make her profile seem legitimate. Finally, after she'd sent Fitzwilliam himself a friend request, she tried to connect to him on LinkedIn as Cat Thomson, marketing exec from Belfry Automotive Engineers Ltd. Nothing to do now but wait.

The rumble of a truck heralded the arrival of Bev's temporary replacement car. She was standing on the driveway, scratching her head at the sight of the piss-stained driver's seat of the turd-brown Ford Fiesta when Sophie rolled her pushchair through the gate. Beatrice stood on the buggy-board and Finn was strapped in.

'Aunty Bev!' their little voices shrieked.

Sticky little hands covered hers, as the two children broke free of the pushchair and grabbed at her. High as kites on organic blueberry muffins, judging by their juice-stained faces. Bev swung them up into the air, blowing raspberries into their necks until they squealed. Savouring the close contact with such tiny, unconditionally loving beings.

'New car! New car!' Beatrice shouted.

Before Bev could protest, the pre-schooler had opened the unlocked rear door and was climbing in and out the other side, with her tiny brother Finn hot on her Lelli Kelly heels.

'Ah. Soph. Just the woman. I've been looking for you.'

Sophie was all am-dram enthusiasm and googly-eyed wonderment. 'Angie told me the terrific news. Well, well done, Bev! You really are a superstar.' She eyed the Fiesta. 'Replacement car? Cool. Can you just make sure you park it right behind the rhododendrons, darling? You know how Tim . . .?'

She didn't finish the sentence. She didn't need to. A crappy loan car didn't add to the house's kerb appeal, unlike his BMW 6 series and Sophie's Lexus hybrid. Bev knew Tim allowed her to rent the basement flat only because Sophie had nagged the hell out of him to offer her loser friend a roof that didn't require a deposit and a month's rent up front.

She moved the Fiesta off the kerb, onto the drive and out of view, knowing complaint would be futile. Climbed out with a sigh, readying herself to tackle her landlady.

'Lend us a couple of hundred, will you?' Bev asked, lugging Beatrice's pushchair and several bags of shopping up the steep stairs.

But Sophie was preoccupied, dragging a reluctant pre-schooler and toddler away from a squirrel they'd spotted. It was climbing the cedar of Lebanon, whose canopy fanned out like a dark green awning over the Victorian gentleman's residence. 'Please, Beatrice! It's time for lunch. Leave Mr Squirrel and come inside. Finn! Stop throwing stones at Aunty Bev's new car.'

Dumping the cumbersome pushchair in the hall, and lugging the shopping into the bespoke grandeur of Sophie's prized Martin Moore kitchen, Bev felt suddenly like an unpaid skivvy. There was always a price to be paid for

Sophie's generosity. Right now, though, Bev needed that generosity to be a sub of the cash-money variety.

'It's just until Angie comes through with her first payment,' she said.

'What?' Sophie looked flustered. She was emptying a fresh bag of quinoa into a Tupperware container; shoving cartons of almond milk into the Sub-Zero fridge. Busy, busy, busy, with a loose strand of perfect golden hair falling free from her chignon to hang over her prominent cheekbones.

'Two hundred quid. I've taken Angie on but I've got no money to float the job. Come on, Soph. It was your idea!'

Sophie beamed at her and straightened up. Her feline form was clad in silk palazzo pants and a tiny spaghetti-strapped vest today. She was so Selfridges food hall. Made Bev feel like a sack of spuds from Lidl. 'Sorry, darling. I don't have a single bean left 'til you give Tim your rent. He texted me earlier to remind you that you're two months overdue. It's not a problem is it?' She clicked her fingers. 'Put the kettle on will you, sweets? I've just bought some amazing amaretto-flavoured coffee.'

Amaretto-flavoured coffee. At least £6 a throw, and yet Sophie didn't have a bean. Aw, poor lamb. Here Bev was, broke and trying to peel herself off rock bottom by asking her wealthy friend for a sub, and the only response that came back was a rent-demand. What crap! Bev chewed the inside of her cheek and considered her new job. Prospect of getting paid – low. Prospect of ending up in a holdall – medium. Prospect of getting beaten to a pulp by a vengeful MP – high. The vibes were all wrong with this case, she was certain. She made a mental note to discuss trusting her instincts at the next therapy session. See what Mo said about being taken for granted.

Trudging back down to the murky, mildewed dive she called home, she was just about to indulge in an afternoon on Porn Hub when she decided to check Facebook, see how her alter ego, Cat Thomson, was doing. Her friend request had still not been accepted. Would she have fared better through LinkedIn? She opened a new tab and loaded the site.

The notification glowed on her screen.

You and Jerry Fitzwilliam are now connected.

She was in! A message from him was sitting in her inbox, and she could barely believe what he'd written.

CHAPTER 4

Boo

'Are you sure you love me, Boo Boo?' Mitch asked, coiling himself around her in the narrow bed. He spoke loud enough to be heard above the music – her ambient playlist that was designed to relax, not agitate.

'How many times do I have to tell you the same thing? Yes!'

"Cause you say you do, but I've seen you down the bar, when you thought I was in town, draping yourself around Steve Pritchard; letting Jake Sewell tap you up.'

'Hey! That's not fair. I was just talking to them.' Boo tried to wriggle free from his stifling embrace. 'You really need to stop worrying. I'm not interested in other blokes. I told you.'

'But I've heard the other girls talking.' His lips pressed together in a mean line. His pallor gave him a cold-blooded, almost reptilian air, a look exacerbated by the pinpricks that were his pupils. 'You think what goes on tour, stays on tour? Well, don't kid yourself, Boo. Your inability to keep your legs together is the talk of the bloody college. And I'm the laughing stock.'

'Oh, here we go again! For fuck's sake, Mitch,' Boo said, swinging her legs out of bed and crossing the room just to put some distance between her and the emotionally volatile guy she called a boyfriend. She pulled her worn-out terry towelling dressing gown over her large breasts. Tied the belt, feeling unattractive and lumpen. 'Just chill out, will you? People gossip. And if they haven't got anything real to talk about, they make it up. You're being ridiculous.' Finding a tinny on her bookshelf that still had some foul-smelling stale lager sitting in the bottom, Boo took a swig. She felt instantly dirtied by it and flung the can into an already overflowing bin which attested to last night's excess. She moved to her desk, grabbing her old plastic kettle.

'Ridiculous, am I? Well, I think I love you more than you love me. I'm in danger of getting my heart broken here. Can I trust you with my heart, Boo? Can I trust you with all those other guys?'

'Oh, shut your face. I'm going to fill the kettle.' She felt vulnerable and exposed, despite having covered her nakedness. 'And keep your voice down! I bet Holy Jo can hear every bloody word.'

'I couldn't give a monkey's flying arsehole about Holy Jo.'

'Well, I could. She's my neighbour. I've got to live on this corridor. Anyway, you've just got a paranoid head on. You smoked too much.'

'I didn't smoke enough.' Mitch pressed his eyes with the palms of his shaking hands. 'Skin up, will you?'

Wanting to placate him, Boo considered that maybe there was something worth smoking in one of the butts in the ashtray. She was sure there had been a good chunk of hash left. Where was it now? Rifling through the remnants, she spied nothing but relics of their drug-fuelled indulgence: burnt out tobacco and lipstick-stained roaches. There were two wine glasses on the desk, next to the ashtray. Hers. Mitch's. Souvenirs of the start of the evening, when everything had been a riot and a blast. Scroll forward six hours and they still hadn't been to sleep, though the wintry sun had risen enough to cast its dim light onto the blanket of snow that covered the college grounds.

'Let me make a brew first.'

She slid her phone into her dressing gown pocket and closed the door of her college room behind her before Mitch could interrogate her yet again.

In the shared kitchen, beneath the unforgiving strip light that she knew made her look as much like death as she felt, she filled the kettle. Swallowing down tears along with her pride, the desperate need to hear a familiar voice that didn't belong to Mitch surged within her. She picked her phone out of her pocket and dialled home. Expecting to be redirected to voicemail to hear the comforting rumble of her father's voice on the recorded message, she was surprised when her mother picked up. The instant cold comfort coming down the line made her shiver.

'What do *you* want?' the old lady said by way of greeting.

'You're awake? This early?'

'I haven't been to bed yet. Now, what do you want?'

'I'm homesick,' Boo said in a small voice. 'I know I said I'd be back for Dad's birthday, but I need to come home earlier. Please.'

'Running back to your parents every time you get homesick is not the point of going away to university, young lady. You need to learn self-reliance if you're ever going to grow up.'

'What skin is it off your nose if I'm at home a few days longer?'

'Please yourself. Do what you want. Come home or don't come home.'

Her mother's indifference bit deep. 'Lend us some money for the train fare, then. I'll have to change my ticket and I'm skint.'

The old lady scoffed. 'You've got some fucking cheek, you have.'

'Well, if you can't send me the money, can you come and get me?' Boo asked, clutching the phone to her ear. Her headache was registering a 7.5 on the hangover Richter scale. Today of all days, she really didn't need this. Not after such a heavy night.

'How many times do I have to tell you? I can't just drop everything.' Her mother was being unnecessarily shrill, which meant she was still tanked from the previous day. Hell, perhaps she'd already had her early sharpener. Breakfast in their house. Every time she shrieked down the line, Boo felt the voice stab at the back of her eyes.

'You're drunk, aren't you?' Boo leaned on the water-splashed Formica worktop, tracing her finger dolefully along the grout between the standard-issue tiles of the splashback.

'I don't see that that's any of your business, young lady.' She was over-enunciating, as well as high-pitched. Definitely drunk. 'If you must know, I'm preparing for my exhibition. I've got forty-eight hours before the doors open. Alasdair said he's expecting some serious buyers on opening night, so I can't let the ball drop.'

'Please!' Boo momentarily lost her balance, her elbow slipping from its anchor on the wet worktop. Her stomach lurched from the sudden movement. 'I can't stay here a minute longer.' She softened her voice, hoping to appeal to whatever shred of maternal instinct still lurked inside her mother's vodka-pickled husk of a body. The sudden tears took her by surprise, and Boo sensed the swell of the deep river of melancholy and loneliness flowing within her. 'I need my mum.'

But the hatchet-faced old cow was having none of it. 'I'm not haring down the motorway to rescue you and five suitcases full of dirty washing just because lover-boy's gone weird on you *again*.'

Boo wiped her eyes roughly on the sleeve of her shabby dressing gown. The heavy, organic smell of last night's Super Skunk clung to it. Cheap, strong lager was still pungent in her hair, where Mitch had thrown his drink on her. 'He hasn't gone weird. It's just that . . . Please. Get Dad to come.' Under the stark kitchen light, she felt just as small and lost as she had as a little girl on those nights when a tempest had raged between her parents, just on the other side of her flimsy bedroom door. She started to hiccough with tears. 'I just want to come home.'

'You're hungover. That's all. Get some chips down you, for God's sake. And in future, learn to hold your drink or don't bother,' her mother said.

Boo's head pounded, as if the old lady had driven an axe into her skull. The cold sweat on her skin made her shiver. 'Well, Jesus, Sylvia! Thanks for the sympathy.' She knew her mother hated it when she used her first name but the old cow's indifference to her suffering stung. 'Do you really want me to be stuck here?' A glance out of the window confirmed that it had started to snow again, hard. The weather was unforgiving this far north, cutting off roads and closing motorways, as though Durham was a psychopathically possessive host that didn't want any of its visitors ever to leave. The urban warmth of home felt like a world away. 'The snow's so thick, if it keeps going at this rate, I could miss Dad's big day!'

'Your dad's in one of his funks. He hasn't got out of bed for four days. I doubt he cares two hoots whether you miss his birthday or not. And if those mates of yours are so bloody wonderful, why don't you tap them up for cash? That Klingon of a boyfriend of yours is always declaring his undying love for you. Let him put his money where his mouth is.'

Boo's rage was ignited by the realisation that she was nothing more than a handy whipping boy for people around her. Making her suffer somehow compensated for their substandard lives. 'Why do you have to be so nasty?' she shouted.

'Why do you have to be such a disappointment?'

Enough. Boo felt like an avatar in a martial arts arcade game that had just taken a lethal kick, draining her life force to zero. She ended the call, throwing the phone against the wall. Its back came apart and the lithium battery went scudding across the floor. 'Cow!'

Padding back along the deserted corridor, carrying the full kettle, she was surprised to find Mitch in a state of obvious agitation, rifling through the flotsam and jetsam on her desk.

'Bert's coming with McIntyre,' he said. 'Your God-bothering arsehole of a neighbour dobbed us in. You need to clean up. Now!'

Boo felt the blood drain from her lips and the heat leech from her body. 'Are you shitting me?'

He shook his head. 'She just knocked on and said she'd had enough. They're on their way.' Though his face was the colour of dirty snow with a fine sheen of sweat that screamed hungover, coming down and exhausted, the truth was clear in those bloodshot eyes. She closed the door.

'You do the ashtrays,' she said. 'Empty them in the bin on the corridor below. I'll get the empties and clear the glass.'

'Get some fresh air in here,' he said. 'You can smell the weed right down the corridor.' He flung the windows wide open, letting an icy blast and a flurry of fat snowflakes inside. Peered below. 'I can see them. They're crossing the courtyard. Quick.' Mitch whipped the stinking ashtray off the desk, sweeping the empty packaging from Rizlas and tobacco and the damning piece of cling film in which the Super Skunk had been wrapped onto the top of the other detritus. 'Downstairs kitchen, yeah?'

She nodded. They were a crack clean-up team, now, working together to head off a disaster. If she got kicked out of college for possession, she'd never hear the end of it from her mother. Apocalyptic scenarios played out in her mind's eye: facing Dad's terminal sorrow as he picked her up and carried her cases on the walk of shame to the car park, every step taking her away from the bright future she'd planned and back towards the wasteland of home. Dad's unshaven face, bearing its trademark hangdog expression and the pyjama top he never seemed to take off. His eyes, dulled with medication, but still acutely aware of his daughter's failure. Back to the old soak and her 'atelier' that took up half the lounge and the constant influx of weirdo pals – locusts who picked the place clean of food and drink, leaving nothing behind but the resonance of empty laughter; cigarette burns in the settee.

Was she turning out any different?

'Don't let this happen, Boo. You can't become her.' As she spoke, she eyed the photograph in the dusty IKEA frame of the three of them. Sylvia, Dad, her. She deliberately placed it face-down. 'Focus!'

Trying to juggle empty cans and bottles was no mean feat with shaking hands. Boo failed to swallow down the dry sobs that forced their way out of her sore, swollen gullet.

'Bin bags. Bin bags! I've got no bloody bin bags.' Blind panic. There were too many cans, spilling from the top of her wastepaper basket with a metallic clatter, covering her feet in splashes of stale lager. Hearing the fire door squeak and clang as it was pushed open at the end of the corridor, she looked around the cramped room in desperation.

Footsteps click-clacked towards her door in a rhythm that meant business. She knew it was McIntyre, the accommodation manager and Bert, the caretaker. Closer and closer, their military march coming to a halt outside her door. At least they'd knock.

Holding the bin full of spent cans in one hand, she threw back her duvet with another, poised to spread the evidence over her crumpled bedsheet and cover it over. Air freshener. Where was the air freshener? The place still stank. She spied her deodorant on the bookshelf next to her hand-crafted decorations. Bin or spray? There was time to deal with both, wasn't there? They'd knock.

But they didn't knock. Boo froze when she heard the key in the door. Yelped when she spied the large remnant of skunk, wrapped in cling film, sitting next to her purple cycle helmet. Master key in the lock. The door swung open.

CHAPTER 5
Bev

> Hey, Cat. How lovely to connect with you on LinkedIn. You
> look just like my sort of voter and what impressive
> credentials, you have.
>
> J

Staring at the screen, Bev couldn't help but feel a thrill
that Jerry Fitzwilliam had just held open the virtual door
to his world and invited her to walk through. She sank
back against the headboard and grinned.

'Beverley Saunders, come on down!' she said, reading
through his LinkedIn profile that listed his various professional achievements, from his years in banking in the City
to his stratospheric rise in the world of politics.

Next, she headed for Facebook, where her friend request
had so far been ignored. She clicked through the various
Facebook tabs to see what had been posted on his timeline
and what kind of a story his photos told.

Everything that had a 'public' status update was
extremely formal and clearly focused on his political career.

> This is what you won't see reported on the television.
> Labour MPs out in force to support the NHS along with
> you, the public.
> What a brilliant day I had, visiting Jaguar Land Rover in

Castle Bromwich to see new car manufacturing innovation. We want British engineering to show the world how it's done!

The feed included numerous photos of him pressing the flesh with workers, nurses, members of the public, children, teachers . . . There was nothing evidently personal from his account. No 'likes' for films, music, hobbies, books. Only photos and status updates that felt like professional transmissions, the conversation threads beneath revealing a polite and chatty relationship with his adoring voters, but little else. No innuendo. No indication that he was anything other than squeaky clean and a consummate performer.

'He keeps his private life very private,' Bev reasoned aloud. She dug a spoon into a new jar of peanut butter and sucked the greasy clump off, savouring the cloying texture against the roof of her mouth. 'This is no bloody good. I need *some* dirt.'

Scrolling way back through several years, she eventually came to some posts from 2009, before he'd got into politics.

'Aha! He's forgotten to hide his past posts,' she told the origami model of a frog on her dressing table.

Finally, here were some clues as to who Jerry Fitzwilliam was. There was a series of photos of him with Angie. She wore only her gobstopper of an engagement ring on her wedding finger. The two were locked in an easy embrace, posing around a table with none other than Sophie and Tim. The status said it was Tim's birthday dinner at some upmarket brasserie in Alderley Edge – all teak tables, luxuriously upholstered seating and minimalist lighting. The kind of place that was normally frequented by the region's premiership footballers and *Coronation Street* stars. It was clearly the time when Jerry and Tim had worked together in finance, both commuting to the City of London for a working week spent in a shared flat in Clapham, according to Sophie.

Birthday dinner with my brother-from-another-mother and our womenfolk.

'Quite the bromance,' she said.

Bev wondered how she'd been unaware of the close friendship, despite decades of knowing Sophie. But then, hadn't she and Sophie been estranged from one another for all those years because of her intense dislike of Rob? And hadn't Sophie always quietly kept her as her 'walk-on-the-wild-side friend'? Novelty Bev, who was always getting it wrong and who desperately needed fixing; who made Sophie feel better about her own slavish adherence to 'normal'; Bev, who wasn't stylish enough to parade in front of those facsimile-glitterati friends?

'Let go of the bitterness,' Bev said, repeating Dr Mo's mantra. She exhaled deeply, massaging her burning shoulders and neck until her thumbs ached. Rammed another spoonful of peanut butter into her mouth, stuffing her hurt feelings back down as she swallowed. 'Focus!' Back to Facebook.

Scrutinising the photo of Angie, Bev was surprised to see that she had been rail thin back then. Had Jerry been abusing her from the outset? Or had Angie come to the relationship with problems surrounding her body weight and eating? Not that that mattered. If Angie was already emotionally vulnerable, it made sense that an abuser of women would have sought her out as an easy victim, on hand whenever he needed a sadistic ego-boost.

Scrolling further back into the past, Bev could find nothing more. Frustrated, she searched for Angela

Fitzwilliam and was surprised to see her client wasn't on Facebook at all. The only people Bev knew in her own age group who refused to tweet or post about themselves were people like her therapy-group buddy, Doc. People who were painfully shy, ferociously private or those who had something to hide.

'How's about we try your "brother-from-another-mother", then, Jerry?'

She brought up Tim's Facebook page. That was more revealing. The Fitzwilliams had been tagged in a number of posts from four years earlier, when Jerry had already left the City and just started in local politics, if his Wikipedia page was to be believed. There were Tim and Sophie – the bride and groom, sitting on their top table wearing beatified grins. Next to Tim, Jerry stood in his tailcoat and cravat, reading from a sheet. Mr Best Man. Photo after photo revealed the guests, including a beaming Angie, sitting at a table near the top with her infant son in a high chair.

'And where were we on the big day, Soph?' Bev said, acknowledging a sudden stab of resentment. She recalled how she and Rob hadn't even been invited to the grand celebration at a castle in Cheshire, popular with the local new money.

Everybody looked happy. Even where the Fitzwilliams featured in more recent photos, Bev couldn't spot any indicators that either of them were anything but blissfully happy. No telling sideways glances that hinted at private anguish. No apparent stiff body language that pointed to an emotional gulf between them. It was all cuddles and smiles and shiny eyes.

'What the hell is going on here?' Bev wondered aloud. 'Nobody's that good at acting. Are they?' But then she remembered the bruising around Angie's neck. The woman had been petrified. Of that, Bev was certain. And she had sworn Bev to secrecy over the violence. Not even Sophie knew about it. She couldn't find out the extent of Jerry's abuse! No matter how tempting it would be to sound Sophie out, Bev had had to agree a moratorium on quizzing their mutual friend.

Needing to hear the sincerity in her client's voice to remind herself that she wasn't on a fool's errand, she dialled her number. Angie picked up on the third ring, the sound of crying children in the background.

'Bev! How are you getting on?' There was an edge to her voice, as though she didn't want her own children to eavesdrop.

'I need cash, Angela,' Bev said. 'I can't follow a man who has two homes in opposite ends of the country without so much as petrol money.'

'I can get you £30.' Her voice was a near whisper. 'Maybe next week.'

Bev bit back a that's-no-damned-good retort. 'Is it really that bad?' she asked.

'Yes. He did give me some money but I had to spend it on my teeth. Sorry. You will get paid eventually, though. He's sitting on a fortune.'

'You need to search the places where he might write sensitive information down. Has he got a study?'

'Yes.'

'Look for passwords. Pin codes. Anything that might get you into his online banking.'

'How would I even know where he banks now?'

'You're kidding me, right?'

There was a pause on the other end of the phone that was filled with the sound of small children's squealing laughter. Angie's voice became tight and squeaky, breaking up in parts where she sounded like she was choking back tears. 'I know it sounds ridiculous, but for years he's just . . .'

Come on, Bev, she thought, fighting back the urge to scoff. *You of all people should know the corners that bad people back their partners into. Don't traumatise the poor cow.* 'Listen, Angie. He'll have cards in his wallet and *some* paperwork somewhere. He's sure to. And try to get evidence of his maltreatment of you. Shitty texts. Nasty emails. Take snaps of your bruises. Look out for any photos or correspondence that might prove infidelity. That sort of stuff. Dirt that a divorce lawyer is going to love.'

The call ended. Bev felt no better. This was the trickiest job she had ever taken on.

'Why the hell are you doing this, you berk? Just walk away! You're not her mother,' angry, cynical Bev told a younger, naïve version of herself, who was hiding beneath the layers of bluff and bluster that had become her armour since her divorce.

But the mental image of that bruising wouldn't leave her. Beverley Saunders was no longer Rob's passive, pleasing wife. She was now a woman who wouldn't take any more shit, helping other women who weren't yet strong enough to fight their own battles. And didn't she still have the biggest battle of her own to fight? This job could give her the financial security and professional standing she so desperately needed to convince the judge she was back on track and a responsible adult.

Picking up the phone, she dialled an ally she hadn't spoken to in some years. Wondering if he'd even take her call, she was pleased that his secretary put her straight through.

'Beverley,' her old boss said. His voice had aged audibly. Near to retirement, now. 'What a blast from the past. To what do I owe this pleasure?'

'Graham,' Bev said, not hiding the gratitude in her voice for the man who had given her her very first proper job. They exchanged pleasantries while she mentally rehearsed her pitch. Best not to skirt around the issue with an old-school, no-nonsense sort like Graham. 'I'm looking for some freelance work. Copywriting, if you've got it or some print management.'

'I thought you'd left marketing for good after that sticky business at BelNutrive.'

'None of that was down to me, you know.' She bit her lip. Realised she was holding her breath. Silence on the other end.

'Of course, my dear. I know slander when I hear it. How on earth did you get yourself into such a mess?'

'Look, it's a long story,' Bev said, swallowing hard as she remembered the feel of her skin crawling as she'd faced the BelNutrive death squad in the directors' boardroom. 'I'll tell you over a coffee if you can find me some hours. Please, Graham. I wouldn't ask if I didn't need it. I could mainly work from home. Even if I'm down in London a couple of times per month for meetings . . .' She quickly thought of the best way to spin the financial sting of claiming travel expenses from Graham's charity. 'I'll work out cheaper than a salaried marketeer or a consultant. You know I'll more than pay for myself.'

'Actually, our marketing girl has just gone on maternity leave . . . just at a point when we need to design and print the annual report. We need a new legacy marketing leaflet putting together too. A cinch for an old hand like you, eh?'

Ending the call, Bev discovered she was breathless and dizzy as conflicting emotions did battle beneath her apparent composure. She was going back to London, however temporarily, and to a career she'd been forced to leave behind. All with the intention of helping a stranger. It felt good to make things happen. It felt dreadful to dredge up the past. But the old Bev would never entirely go away, she realised.

She channelled that old Bev now, as she wrote a LinkedIn message to Jerry Fitzwilliam.

Hi Jerry. Thanks for accepting my connection request. I saw you on breakfast TV the other day, delivering that speech about the future of British science education, which was utterly captivating. At Belfry Automotive Engineers, we want to start a mentoring scheme for local schoolchildren who might consider careers in engineering. Can I pick your brains? I think we could work together.
Cat x

Pinging off the missive, she swapped her formal business profile photo for a coquettish snap of her former self – chewing seductively on her glossy bottom lip, a knowing twinkle in her eyes, with the camera angled down from on high, so that her cleavage was in the frame too. It was the photo she'd used to good effect online – during her single years. It had always worked. Would it work this time? Would it pique the shadow cabinet minister for Science's interest?

CHAPTER 6
Angie

'Coffee darling?' Angie asked, standing in the doorway to Jerry's office with a thudding heart she was certain he could hear.

'Hmm.' He was seated behind his desk, facing her. His large computer monitor obscured what he was doing, though he was looking down at something. Presumably preoccupied by his phone, judging by his movements. No difference there, Angie realised. Except . . . her gaze wandered over the desktop. She could see the corner of his iPhone peeking out from beneath a pile of paperwork.

Almost as if he'd only just registered she was watching him, he looked up swiftly. Red in the face.

'Don't sneak up on me like that, for Christ's sake. You nearly gave me a heart attack.' As he spoke, it was apparent from his upper arm movements that he was slipping something into the drawer.

Angie could hear Bev's words resounding in her memory. *Make nice. Get him onside. Pretend the whole divorce thing has all blown over.* Forcing a benign smile onto her face, she avoided making eye contact. 'So sorry, darling. I just wanted to know if you fancied a coffee. I'm making a fresh pot.' She could hear the tremor in her own voice.

Swallowing hard, the bruising around her neck ached as though her husband's hands were still on her.

He sized her up and the silence between them was so thick, it was almost tangible. Was he trying to read her mind or was he genuinely considering his coffee options?

'Forget it,' he said, checking his watch and standing abruptly. He plonked his briefcase onto the desk and started to stuff paperwork into it. 'I've got to go into the office for my surgery. I've got to see a pile of nimbies moaning about the HS2 rail thing before I head back down to London tomorrow.'

This was her chance. If Jerry got wind that she had Bev snooping around, it would take very little for him to whisk any banking paperwork down to London in that big briefcase of his. She couldn't wait for tomorrow to sneak a peak in those desk drawers. Gretchen might finally be back from her trip home to Austria. This morning though, Benjy was on a playdate with a little pal from Montessori. Poppy was taking a nap. It was now or never.

'Shall I make you a sandwich to take with?'

He pulled a laptop out of one of his drawers and slid it into his briefcase. Was that the glint of a key between his fingers? Yes.

'I'll grab a bite while I'm out,' he said.

She couldn't see what he was doing from her vantage point, but she could hear him turning the key in the desk-drawer lock. What would he do with the key? Had he pocketed a second phone? Suddenly, Angie found herself wondering if he'd deliberately rigged his desk up with piles of books, a row of family photos and a giant monitor to conceal from her view everything that went on behind it.

Find out what cash cards he's got. Bev's instructions. *If you know where he banks and you can make a note of his account numbers and sort codes, you've got a cat-in-hell's chance of getting your mitts on your fair share of the money. Paying solicitors' bills and funding your new-found independence won't come for free, love. Find any confidential documents, anything that might help us. You need proof that he's a liar, a cheat and a bully. Dick pics on a second phone. Love letters. Anything.*

Angie stood her ground and waited until her husband was almost upon her. Silently, she prayed that the sexual favours she'd extended to him last night and the heartfelt faux admission that she'd made, proclaiming her demand for a split had merely been a terrible hormonal-led mistake, would be enough to keep him calm and unsuspecting. 'Before you go, can I have some money, please, darling? I've got to go to Waitrose.'

He frowned. Her pulse quickened. All she could hear was the blood rushing in her ears. Was he irritated that she was barring his easy exit? Instinctively, when he set his briefcase down, she flinched, waiting for a slap or more.

'You're out of cash already?' He reached into his trouser pocket and pulled out his wallet. 'Jesus, Ange. Are you trying to bankrupt us?'

She put her arms around his thick middle as though she was hopelessly in love. Planted a kiss on his florid cheek. How had she ever found him attractive? At what point had she started to find him repulsive? 'I wanted to make your favourite tonight just to show you how very sorry I am and how much I love you.'

'Fillet steak and chips?' He grinned. 'Good girl.' Slapped her bottom before extricating himself from her embrace. 'No chips for you though, eh?' He unfastened the press-stud on his wallet. Still staring at her with narrowed eyes that seemed full of suspicion, though his thin lips curved up into a smile.

51

Don't let him know you're interested in the cash cards. Bev's advice. Angela forced herself to meet his gaze right up until the moment he glanced down to open his wallet. Then, she drank in as much visual information as she could, scrutinising the colours on the plastic. Trying to place them. But the cards were all rammed too deeply into their slots to show any logos.

'Forty do?' Jerry shoved two blues at her, though she could see the section for paper money was fat with notes.

'Perfect.' Now was not the time to draw attention to herself. She'd failed this time on the wallet front but there would be other opportunities. Perhaps when he was sleeping. The main thing was to get him out of the house. 'What time will you be home?'

He glanced at his watch. The wallet was back in his trouser pocket now. He was picking up his briefcase. Silently, Angie prayed Poppy would sleep on long enough to give her the opportunity to have a good half hour's rifle through Jerry's office.

'Couple of hours, depending on the turnout.'

As he shooed her out of the doorway, Angie could feel an itchy rash creeping beyond her collar, up towards her neck. She pulled her silk scarf up. Deflated to see Jerry pull out the key to the mortice and lock it, as usual. Today of all days, she would have appreciated him slipping in his routine, but such a lucky break wasn't forthcoming.

He plopped the mortice key into the breast pocket of his jacket and, zipping it shut, winked at her.

Did he anticipate her ham-fisted sleuthing attempt? Or was she being paranoid?

When she closed the front door behind him, Angie exhaled heavily and stood with her back against the stained glass, considering her next move. She waited for the engine of his car to spark into life. Tears rolled unbidden down her cheeks as tension sapped the strength from her body. But this was not a time for weeping. It was a time for action.

Advancing along the wood-panelled hallway, praying Poppy would sleep on, she tried the handle of Jerry's study. How sturdy would a Victorian lock really be? After peering to see if there was a gap between the door and the architrave, she retrieved her Costa coffee loyalty card from the kitchen drawer and tried to slide the card between the two surfaces. She remembered forgetful students breaking into their own rooms in halls by doing a similar thing with their cashpoint cards. She tutted. It was apparent the gap was too tight to breach, and anyway, she realised that the bank-card trick only worked on latchlocks, didn't it? And if she forced the lock, he'd know.

'Come on, Ange. Hold it together,' she whispered beneath her breath.

After five minutes, she was out of ideas. Damn this. *Maybe I should just get out of the marriage and take my chances. Run away with the children. Start again. Do I really need the money? I'll get a job in admin or some temping work.* But then she considered how Jerry had only managed to build his profitable career thanks to her efforts in holding hearth and home together. Half of that money was hers! And hadn't he threatened to deny her access to the kids? He'd come after her; expending every effort to blacken her name publicly and make her life a waking nightmare. No. She had no option but to go for broke, and the only way she could do that was to gather intel like a low-rent spy, to demonstrate what a bullying manipulator she'd married. She rang Bev, who suggested trying to climb in through the sash window. Had Jerry locked that too?

Hooking the baby monitor onto the waistband of her jeans, Angie padded into the garden, carrying a basket of washing. She glanced around to check she wasn't being observed by the neighbours.

Setting the basket down, she looked up at the study window. She could see there was a gap of about half an inch where she could perhaps get her fingers in. If only she could reach it. Pursing her lips, she examined her beautifully manicured nails. They wouldn't last long. Wishing she were stronger, she lugged a cast-iron garden chair to the window, wincing when it scraped noisily against a flagstone. She held her breath. Would Poppy wake? No sound from the baby monitor.

Angela stood in her Gucci loafers on the chair and started to hoist the window up with all the might she could muster. The sinews in her forearms stood out like ropes as she edged the peeling wood upwards. It was back-breaking work, as the pulley mechanism had been painted over so many times and was stiff. But inch by inch, she managed to lever the window open by a good twelve inches before it jammed. She said a silent prayer of thanks to the Goddess of Desperate Housewives that Jerry had forgotten to shut and lock it properly. At that moment it was clear to her that in locking his office, his aim was to keep his wife out, rather than any burglar with a penchant for government white papers.

'Bastard,' she muttered.

Being thin had its advantages. She clambered up onto the sill; wriggled until she had squeezed herself through the gap. Dropping down to the stripped and polished floorboards, her breath ragged, she looked around the study. First, she made for the desk, tugging at the drawers. No use. They were locked. She picked up a brass letter-opener and tried to slot the tip of the blade into the keyhole of the central drawer where she felt certain Jerry had stashed another phone from view.

'Damn it.'

Angie realised she had no way of breaking into the desk without causing damage. The deep drawers on either side were also locked. Her husband was a man who liked to maintain control over what he kept secret and what he made public. Spotting his smug face grinning out from the largest of the family photos, she spat on the glass, savouring the sight of her gob of mucus rolling from his forehead onto the chin. 'Filthy pig!' Reluctantly, she wiped it off.

Next, she padded over to the filing cabinet. Surely he left something unlocked. Tugging at the handles, she realised quite how careful he was.

Turning slowly in the room, she pondered where her husband might leave the key to a filing cabinet. If it was on his keyring, her efforts would be scuppered. But if he'd hidden it somewhere in here . . .

Could he have tucked it among the political tomes and James Patterson novels on the bookshelves that lined the alcoves either side of the chimney breast? Nothing was evident lower down. Feeling on the higher shelves, she found only dust among the leather spines. Next, she eyed the fireplace and noticed the silver art-nouveau candle-sticks, plant pots containing orchids and elegant nick-nacks she'd thoughtfully arranged on the mantel in a bid to feminise the masculine space. They had always hidden the spare key to the house under the plant pot by the front door. Perhaps Jerry had lacked the imagination to find a better hiding place for his filing cabinet key.

Sighing, it felt like a fool's errand as she lifted the plant pot holders, one by one. As she held the third aloft, she gasped. The object that lay beneath glinted in the light, as though winking at her in collusion. It was the key to the filing cabinet – of that she was certain.

As Angie pulled the top drawer of the filing cabinet open, she was so thrilled by her own skulduggery that she failed to notice the thrum of an engine – the engine of a powerful car. Rummaging through the hanging files, she saw documents for their house insurance, car insurances, BUPA plans . . . She was so beside herself with excitement when her fingers happened upon a file hidden beneath the other mountain of documentation, right at the back, that she didn't immediately recognise the telltale crunch of gravel as Jerry's Jag pulled onto the driveway. In fact, her husband's early return didn't register with Angie at all until the baby monitor picked up the front door slamming and Poppy starting to cry as her sleep was disturbed.

The key being inserted into the lock on the other side of the study door gave Angie no more than a five second countdown before she was discovered, clutching a sheaf of correspondence from Coutts & Co bank.

Four seconds: she shut the filing cabinet.

Three seconds: she darted to the window.

Two seconds: the handle turned and Angie was faced with a choice – to hide or to attempt escape.

The door opened and Jerry walked in.

CHAPTER 7
Bev

Hello Cat
My, how lovely it is to speak to someone so enthused about science and engineering. Thanks for your kind words. You're clearly a woman of taste! Ha. Are you a voter in my Cheshire seat? I hold a surgery where I can meet constituents face-to-face.
Regards
Jerry

Bev read the LinkedIn message again, trying to decide if there was an undertone of flirtation in Jerry Fitzwilliam's words or not. He had taken less than thirty minutes to come back to her. Was that normal for a busy shadow cabinet minister whose days ought to be diarised to the nines, from waking to sleeping? Thirty minutes. With a prompt for further contact, though he hadn't studied her fake LinkedIn profile carefully enough to read that the fictitious Belfry Automotive Engineers Ltd was in the Midlands.

'Have you got something to share with the group, Beverley?' Mo asked.

Her shrink was sitting at the head of their circle in his flowery armchair; a quizzical smile on his face.

Shit. Why the hell had she checked her phone during a session? Her compatriots looked at her expectantly.

'Sorry,' she said, shaking her head. 'I'm waiting for an important text. Work. You know?'

In a safe space where honesty ruled supreme and everyone was supposed to pay attention to the person speaking, out of respect, her excuse rang with insincerity. Big Debbie, who had been describing how she'd been unable to make an important doctor's appointment because she kept getting her home security ritual wrong, glared at her.

'What makes you think your obsessive collecting bullshit is more important than my problems?' she said, sitting bolt upright in a chair that looked uncomfortably too small for her. Folding her meaty arms.

The rest of the group followed suit, one by one, in a Mexican wave of uptight body language. All except her unlikely friend, Doc, who slouched with his arms hanging by his sides, as usual. He wore a nonchalant smirk on his face. Rolling his eyes at Big Debbie, who was easy to insult at the best of times.

'Put the phone away please, Beverley,' Mo said. 'I think you owe Debbie an apology.'

Bev slid the phone into the pocket of her hoodie. Wishing she were anywhere at that moment but in a health-centre meeting room that smelled of cheap floral disinfectant . . . or was it the sickly-sweet stink of Mo's psychiatric goodwill wafting off his trim little body?

She felt the phone vibrate twice. Another LinkedIn notification. Had Jerry Fitzwilliam followed up his first response with a prompt? Should she play hard to get?

'Now, Beverley.' Mo leaned forwards and smiled. Hands on his knees. 'You seem preoccupied this week. Do you want to share what's on your mind with the group?'

She realised she needed to give him something. Mo knew her too well.

All eyes were on her. Gordon, the Klepto, who seemingly never washed. Neil, the gym addict, who looked like the picture of health but whose continual twitching said his mental well-being was precarious at best. Wanda, the compulsive eater, who dieted constantly and never lost weight thanks to the heavy bag of snacks she carted around in the secret compartment of her handbag. The new guy whose name she couldn't remember, whose health anxiety saw him knock back thirty different vitamin supplements per day. Big Debbie, with her repetitive door-slamming and repeated setting and unsetting of her alarm. Sam, the clean-freak. Doc, the tech nerd with a similar collecting compulsion to hers and her only real ally in the group. None of the others had any idea how the connection between her and Doc had grown outside their therapy setting, morphing into something akin to a business partnership. His skills were an invaluable resource to have at her disposal in her new career as a PI.

'Well?'

'I bought another origami kit.' Bev examined her nails and blushed, though she knew this was only half of it. She felt a twinge in her groin when she privately considered the other addiction which she hadn't revealed.

'Oh, you didn't!' Gordon said. 'And after all that guilt-tripping you laid on me last session.'

She stared blankly into the serial shoplifter's doughy face and feigned contrition. 'I know. I'm really sorry for that. I don't know what came over me.' Flashbacks to the skinny man with the giant cock who had come over her in a rather different sense of the word. She'd sneaked him from the local nightclub back down to her basement flat a few nights earlier. Remembering the conquest, her cheeks felt like they were being superheated on the inside, flashing red to alert the therapy group to her lies. 'It's been a really tough week. I was in a car crash.' That would do the trick.

The flurry of concerned voices came all at once. Was she OK? Was it her fault? Did the car get totalled?

'My Polo might get written off,' she said. Caught Doc's eye but focused on Big Debbie to deflect attention. 'Some silly cow in a Range Rover just came out of nowhere.' She rubbed her left shoulder and grimaced, conscious that her phone was pinging and buzzing away in her pocket. 'I've got rotten whiplash.'

But Mo wasn't that easily fobbed off. 'So you consoled yourself by indulging in the very habit you'd sworn off?' He sighed. 'Oh, Bev. How long had it been since your last origami purchase? Three months?'

Bev chewed the inside of her cheek, already bored by the cross-examination and wanting to check her phone. 'Three months, two weeks and five days. It was a rare kit.'

'How did you feel afterwards?'

'Dissatisfied. Dirty. Like a failure.' That much, at least, was the truth. It had felt the same after skinny, clubbing wang-man. She didn't need Dr Mo to tell her why she did these crazy things, of course. Everybody needed a panacea to life's miserable challenges and disappointments, didn't they? It was just that some panaceas were more socially acceptable and practically workable than others. And thanks to Rob's spiteful flapping tongue and his solicitor's £300 per hour legal vitriol, the judge had declared that her particular addictions were utterly unacceptable and impractical, given her aspirations for the future. Without attending the court-ordered weekly therapy to quash her compulsive behaviour and to demonstrate her fitness as a responsible adult, Bev's dream of righting all the wrongs was just that – a flight of fancy. *Bastards, the lot of them,* she mused.

'Jesus, Bev,' Doc said. 'Stop beating yourself up. You're only human. Next time, just give one of us a call.'

She could see him checking the time on the clock behind her. He too had itchy feet today.

The hour was up. Grabbing her parka, Bev hung back near the toilets, waiting for Doc to fall into step with her. What on earth was he doing? Talking to Mo, wearing his most earnest expression. Nodding.

Itching to know if Jerry Fitzwilliam had pinged her again, she thumbed through her notifications. There it was:

> Tell me more about yourself then, Cat. How did a woman like you get into the automotive industry? Judging by that photo, you certainly don't look the type to spend your day around grease monkeys!

He's flirting, Bev thought. *Not overtly, but it's there. Either he's a fanny merchant and just trying to be charming, or else he's got an eyeful of my tits in that old photo, taken in flattering light!* She knew she used to scrub up well enough before the divorce, but she wasn't labouring under any illusion that she was some long-limbed beauty. She had legs like bananas and a chest that was far too big for anything but porn, which she mainly hid beneath baggy jumpers. Her subtle catfishing definitely had him on the hook, though. Flattery. Curiosity. Where should she go from here? She didn't have anything like enough evidence for Angie yet.

'Wanna go for a coffee then?' Doc asked, suddenly at her side, peering over her shoulder in a bid to read the phone's screen. He flicked his lank fringe out of his eye. Shoved his bony hands deep into the pockets of stonewashed jeans that were yellowing at the knee. 'You can tell me what all that crap was about in there.'

Bev hastily put her phone away. 'Shut up, will you? Mo will hear.' She dragged him into the car park, bundling him past the parked vehicles and down towards a row of run-down shops that were a precursor to Sale's tiny high street. They found a cramped café near the Waterside, opposite the town hall. Inside, it smelled of frying sausages – the evidence of a brisk breakfast trade that was only just petering out thanks to a late influx of hungry builders.

With a mug of strong tea steaming before her on the smeary table, Bev told Doc about her latest job.

'I need to get access to his emails. Bank statements, texts, whatever I can dig up.'

He shook his head; blond eyebrows arched in disbelief above heavy-lidded eyes with livid purple shadows beneath, attesting to late nights spent staring at a screen. 'Are you mental?'

'We're both mental, Doc. But that's beside the point. Come on. When I get paid, there's a wad of cash with your name on it.'

'You want me to get up in the shadow Science Minister's shit? No fucking way. I bet the secret service has beaten me to it, anyway. Are you telling me they don't keep tabs on high profile MPs? Especially the opposition.' He gripped the tabletop and rocked back on the chair.

Bev looked down at his grubby fingernails, inwardly wincing. She was partial to strong hands. Doc's never did anything more action-packed than hammering a games console or rattling across a keyboard as he surfed the Dark Net for its sordid secrets. 'Come on, for Christ's sake!' she said. She downed her tea. Slammed the cup onto the table. 'This is what you're brilliant at. This is what *we're* brilliant at. Details. Pernickety little things that normal people overlook.'

'What, like the details of a public figure's finances? Can't you go through his bins like a normal PI?'

'Don't be facetious.' Bev glanced over at the cakes displayed in a glass cabinet. Remembered she was already having to undo the top button of her jeans and turned away. 'Everything's online now, and a man like Jerry Fitzwilliam is hardly going to cob his highly confidential mail into the paper recycling bin, is he?' As Doc's hand swooped down to retrieve his espresso, she snatched it up. Clammy and weak. Her mother had called hands like his, 'wet kippers'. But she clung on nevertheless. 'This is what you do for a living, Doc, and you're damned good at it. You wanna proper job? Go ahead. See if some bank or law firm in Spinningfields will take you on as their IT manager.' She let go of his hand. 'I'm sure they'd happily turn a blind eye to your record.'

Doc rocked back on his chair, looking up at the ceiling so that his Adam's apple protruded as though he'd swallowed a small wireless mouse. 'You're a piece of work. Do you know that?'

'I wasn't the one caught running a phishing scam—'

'I was fresh out of college. I was wet behind the ears!'

'Oh. And the small matter of the weed farm in your roof void? I bet the jury loved you when you appeared before the judge. Long hair and shitty trainers, trying to look respectable by wearing your dad's oversized tweed suit. Ha!' Was he weakening? Bev couldn't be sure if her tactics would draw him in or push him away.

Biting his lower lip, Doc's nostrils flared. The fine blue veins were more visible than usual beneath the almost translucent white skin on his temples. He was agitated.

'Gen-pop doesn't care much for Oxford grads,' he said. 'Especially not computer-science geeks. I was dead in the water before I even got in the dock. It was intellectual discrimination that got me a year inside. If I'd been a hard-working electrician with a sob story, I'd have got away with it.'

Bev laughed. She screwed up her napkin and threw it playfully at his Iron Maiden *Aces High* T-shirt, hitting the sinister zombie icon, Eddie, squarely between his gleaming satanic eyes. 'Give over with the "year inside" crap, you melodramatic dick! You got community service. What did they have you doing? Picking up litter from motorway sidings.'

Doc drained his espresso and stared dolefully into his empty cup. 'I've still got a record, though.'

Now, she had him. 'Precisely! So, how the hell can you turn me down, when a job like this is a walk in the park for you? It's easy money. It's no different from what you did for me last time.'

'The guy was a curtain and blind salesman, Bev. Not a top politician.'

Bev's phone buzzed twice. She withdrew it and gasped when she saw there was yet another message from Jerry Fitzwilliam.

Hey, Cat. If you're a floating voter, how about I win you over with a drink and we can discuss your campaign tactics?

She shared the thread with Doc. 'This guy's a sleaze and a wife beater.' She googled a photo of her target in all his pink-faced, chalk-stripe-suited glory. 'I know you can't stand prats like this.'

'College was full of them. Rugger-buggers from public school. Big thick, arrogant twats.'

Bev found a photo of Angie on Facebook. 'Think of those shovels Jerry Fitzwilliam calls hands wrapped around his Mrs's skinny little gullet. Because that's the bullying arsehole I'm dealing with, here.'

Doc was gnawing at his lip again. Narrowed eyes locked onto the phone's screen.

'Come on! Think of it as earning karma points. He needs taking down and we're the team to do it.' She sensed success, only a final slurp of tea away. 'I'm nothing without a good IT man.'

'I'll hack his cloud first,' Doc said. 'Let's take it from there.'

CHAPTER 8
The Wolf

The Wolf is standing on the other side of the road, observing through the large window of the café how she is talking to her lanky idiot friend. Is she fucking him? He looks like a heavy metal throwback from the 1980s. They are deep in discussion about something or other, but there is no erotic promise or chemistry apparent in their body language. Good.

How dearly he would like to know what plans they are hatching, or what confidences they are sharing, in that café. Perhaps he could walk straight in and sit behind them, covering his face with a menu, should she look his way. Of late, he has been fantasising a great deal about getting closer to her. If he's to make her pay and get away with it, it will be essential to know the finer details of her life.

Being a busy man makes it difficult to track someone like Bev Saunders. She darts to and fro in the world like a dragonfly – fragile, mysterious and difficult to catch but a glimpse of her true colours at any one time. He has seen her in that basement flat, coming and going at unpredictable times of the day and night. These days, she most often wears a harried, grey-faced expression, looking like a sack of potatoes in that androgynous scruffy garb she insists on wearing. She's put on weight. Occasionally, though, she is dressed to kill, as she used to be. He knows where she's going with all that make-up and those heels on. The Wolf remembers the glow of her porcelain-perfect skin beneath the harsh lights of the city's fleshpots. He imagines the pain she still inflicts on other hapless men who only want to please her but whom she dismisses as though they were shit on her spike-heeled shoe. He feels their exquisite agony. This bitch needs to be punished and The Wolf is the man to do it. He is the bringer of death and hellfire. He is the tamer of wanton women who don't know their place. Again he remembers the Russian and smiles.

Suddenly, the greasy-haired boyfriend stands and slings a rucksack on his back. They are emerging from the café together in the drizzle. Both pull the hoods of their anoraks up. His, over his tracts of mousy hair. Hers, over her thick, dark braid. They look like young people with old faces. He's downwind of them, but their chatter is still swallowed by the swish of cars' tyres over the wet asphalt. Though they leave the café together, they then go their separate ways, with Bev walking towards Waterside multi-storey car park and the man disappearing in the direction of the tram.

The urge to know the nature of their relationship bites deep. He'd like to spend more time observing her and deciding how best to have his revenge for what she's done. But the only windows of opportunity he has in which he can indulge in voyeurism like this are the occasional snatched half hours in between meetings, appointments and family commitments. He makes a mental note to find a way of eavesdropping on her conversations. Perhaps if he places a bug in her car, he'll be able listen in on the phone calls she'll inevitably have during those lengthy stakeouts that are part of her new job. It would be less risky than installing a camera in her home, though he's giving that thought too.

As the rocker boyfriend disappears from view, he follows Bev towards her car. She pays for her parking, validating a ticket. He is careful to hang back behind a ragged privet bush while she does this, lighting a cigarette and pretending to check his phone. Up the ramp she goes. He moves off again, dogging her every step some fifty paces behind. What would she say if she turns around and discovers him? How long would it take him to squeeze the life out of her? She's no physical match for him but she's a grown woman – certainly able to put up more of a fight than the Russian whore.

Aware that he's becoming aroused, The Wolf lengthens his stride. She's fumbling in her bag, now. Still not aware of his presence. The distance between them is shortening and he realises that he can take her now. There is nobody else in the car park – certainly not on this deserted third floor. Only row after row of parked cars which he can duck behind. He is stalking his prey.

He reaches out. She is mere feet away.

CHAPTER 9
Boo

'Go on, Boo. Have a go. You'll love it,' Antonia said, collapsing backwards against the wall and sliding down until she was sitting on the floor, legs splayed at awkward angles. She held her hand in front of her face and started to laugh uncontrollably. Showed her palm to Boo as though a thing of wonder were visible. Then pulled what appeared to be a small Post-it note or a large stamp from her pocket. There were tiny, brightly coloured cartoons on it. A clown with googly eyes.

Acid. Boo wasn't a stranger to it though she had not yet dropped any herself. She'd witnessed her mother tripping with some friends when she was only twelve. It had been frightening to see the old lady out of control; standing there in the nip, wielding a paintbrush and a palette like some fucking mad Spanish surrealist, transposed into a damp British terrace, being groped from behind by some wanker with an acoustic guitar called Chet.

'I'll give it a miss, thanks.' Boo watched Monty as he bowled along the corridor, arms outstretched as though he was a Spitfire on a bombing raid. Eton's finest, tripping off his tits. 'It was a close shave with McIntyre and Bert. They've got my ticket. I'd better keep my nose clean or I'm out, thanks to that grassing little Holy Jo next door.' She remembered the burning embarrassment when the accommodation manager and caretaker discovered a veritable mattress of empty lager cans, hastily hidden beneath her duvet. Copping to a drink problem had been the perfect tactic to divert their attention away from the big ball of super-skunk only feet from where they had been standing. Amazing what a quick squirt of deodorant and a blast of Durham fresh air could mask.

'Don't be such a boring cow,' Antonia said, holding the tab out. 'Feel the fear and do it anyway, Boo. We'll have an amazing time.'

Every fibre of Boo's being wanted to join her friends. More of them burst through the fire door at the end, clearly already high. Mitch was among them, not so much as stealing a glance her way.

'Forget it. I'm not getting involved if *he's* with you.' Boo folded her arms tightly across her chest in a bid to hold in her mixed feelings for this on-off Casanova. He made her feel like she was the centre of his universe, one day and a black-hole wasteland, another.

Antonia got to her feet. 'I thought you guys were good. Suit yourself.' She pelted down the corridor after the others, whooping with glee.

Boo retreated inside her room, fully intending to tackle the essay on Nietzsche that was already two weeks late. With night falling outside, she drew the curtains and put on her desk lamp, cocooning herself in a womb of dated soft furnishings and blond-wood standard-issue furniture. Now this modest space, that doubled as home, was clean of all drugs paraphernalia and booze, she could finally breathe. And it had been far easier to clean up than to do the essay and tackle the issues of her folks.

She sat at her desk, picked up the letter yet again and read her mother's sloping, looping hand, inviting her home, when previously she'd told Boo to stay away. Explaining that the enclosed cheque for fifty quid and the change of heart was down to her dad's worsening depression, ' . . . *which you're so much better at dealing with than me*'. There was no affection in or between the lines.

Boo sighed. Folded the letter and shoved it into her pen pot. The banks were shut until Monday anyway and her essay crisis had reached fever pitch. Time to knuckle down.

Just as she put pen to paper, there was a knock at her door.

'I'm busy!' she shouted, irritation making her skin feel too tight for her body.

'It's me.'

She broke out in a sudden sweat as she realised who her visitor was. Mitch. The bad boyfriend whose overbearing attentions made her feel like she actually mattered. The good lover whose mind games made her feel so worthless and hollowed out. She'd seen him only days ago, and they'd parted on bad terms that had left her in tears. *Screw him. Don't answer the door.*

Boo glanced down at her essay and felt her resolve melt away. She never had been good at playing hard to get. Games weren't her thing.

Knowing she'd regret it later, sensing the butterflies in her stomach take flight, she opened the door. Mitch was standing before her with a lopsided smile on his face. The tiny pupils in his long-lashed doe-eyes, just visible in the murk of the lamplight cast from her darkened room, were unequivocal proof that he was high.

He stroked her face and leaned in for a kiss. 'Why won't you join in the fun, Boo Boo?'

Offering him her cheek, she found herself repelled by the smell of booze on his breath. Too reminiscent of her mother. 'I'm busy. Leave me be, Mitch. I can't do this.'

His hand enveloped hers. His palms and fingertips were dry and warm; the connection, electrifying.

'I miss you, Boo,' he said. 'You're the love of my life.' There was sincerity in his handsome face. Wasn't there? Or was it just the acid kicking in? Didn't you love everyone if you were having a good trip?

Boo felt the visceral ache of needing his embrace. Mitch hadn't been her first by any stretch of the imagination, but he'd been the first to tell her he loved her. He was the only person in her eighteen years who'd looked her in the eye and promised her the world. How she needed to believe him.

She pushed him gently backwards into the corridor. 'It's OK you saying that, but what happens the next time I say something that upsets you or I accidentally look at another guy the wrong way? I feel like I'm treading on eggshells all the time with you.'

Mitch reached out and stroked her cheek with his left hand. Pulled from his jeans pocket the brightly coloured sheet of acid tabs with his right. 'All work and no play makes Boo a dull girl, right? And I need you to take this trip with me. You make me feel safe.'

With her essay abandoned, negotiating the draughty corridors of St Mary's on wobbly legs, Boo felt time slowed and space stretched as she followed Mitch on his narcotic journey. Wired with the thrill of a new experience and the rush of love for this narcotically addictive bad boy who meant well, her every emotion felt heightened. As if painted in the same bright technicolours as the paper that held the acid. The smell of dust and paint on the walls stung in her nostrils. She was aware of the buzz of electricity all around her, as if she could hear it thrumming through the cables beneath the plaster of the walls and ceilings. She imagined the blood coursing around his body, his life force connected to hers through shimmering ripples of energy in the air.

All laughing like drains and talking absolute crap, the five of them had already been ejected from Mary's Bar by the grumpy barman, Thom, who had a zero-bullshit policy when dealing with unruly undergrads. Now, Antonia was cartwheeling outside Holy Jo's room.

'Give it a rest,' Boo said, feeling like her voice was being beamed from the fluorescent lights overhead. 'I don't want any hassle off that nosy bitch.'

Sure enough, her neighbour emerged from her room, surveying the situation with a judgemental look on her perky little face. Clearly wondering what Jesus would do when faced with a gang of marauding stoners; stiff body language beneath the preppy skirt and twin set.

'Look, Boo. If you don't tell your friends to keep it down, I'll have to call Bert,' Holy Jo said. 'You're all being really selfish. I'm trying to read.'

Boo scrutinised her adversary. Grim determination written into every taut muscle and the flinching sinew of her jaw. 'Mind your own business, you hypocrite.'

'What do you mean?' The indignation in her voice raised her pitch by almost an octave.

'It's OK when you wake me up at 5.30 a.m. every fucking morning to go rowing?'

Holy Jo had no answer for that, apparently. 'I'll pray for you.'

'Don't. You know what you need to do?' Boo moved in towards her, but the girl stood her ground. She seemed to grow in stature while Boo could feel herself shrinking. 'You need to take the stick out of your arse, you do. Now, get back in your room and stop pissing on our parade. We're not doing you any harm, are we?'

Mitch started to sprint towards them, a look of fury on his face.

'Why do you have to be such a grass?' His voice was so rough with hostility that the colour drained instantly from Holy Jo's face. 'Are you jealous that Boo knows how to enjoy herself? Is that it? You're taking it out on her because you've got nothing else in your life? You're a boring, nosy, uptight little virgin with nothing better to do. Get back to reading your Bible and mind your own business!'

She stepped wordlessly back over the threshold to her room and slammed the door in his face. He thumped the wood so hard that the door shook in its frame.

'Leave it, Mitch,' Boo said, pulling him away, startled by his sudden mood swing towards aggression. 'I don't need you fighting my battles. You're making it worse.'

This time, he kicked the door. 'Cow!'

The other occupants of the corridor started to poke their heads out of their rooms to see what was going on.

Clutching her well-worn chunky cardigan close – a gift that her dad had knitted for her during one of those agoraphobic spells when he'd not felt able to leave the house – Boo finally managed to wrestle Mitch into the shared kitchen, where they sat down at a small table. The others were gone, now. Moved on to someone's room to finish their psychedelic adventure beyond prying eyes, and where Jimi Hendrix could be readily brought back to life on someone's sound system. But here, beneath the harsh flickering light, with the stink of grease in their nostrils, Mitch was starting to twitch and peer round nervously. There were deep shadows beneath his eyes.

The light flickered off.

The light flickered on.

His love flickered off.

74

His love flickered on.

Boo watched her boyfriend move from good trip to bad trip beneath the glare. She reached out to take his hand and offer him comfort.

'How much did you take, Mitch?'

He was scratching at his arm. Staring at the skin, now. Horror etched deep into the contours of his sweat-drenched face.

'Get it off me. Get it off, Boo.' His voice was small now, like a boy in the grip of a nightmare.

'There's nothing there. Chill out, love.'

'The blisters. Can't you see them? I'm contaminated. I know it.' His focus shifted to her and the look of fear transformed into a thunderous scowl. 'You. It's all you, isn't it? You made this happen.' He reached out and took a swipe at her. 'You're breathing poison into the air.'

Boo shuffled hastily backwards in her seat, tensing as the chair toppled almost in slow motion, and crashed to the ground. The tiles rippled beneath her with the impact. Or did they? She felt no pain but the agony of Mitch's accusations that she was a pollutant. It was a searing poker, stoking memories of her mother bawling her out, telling her that she always ruined everything.

'Fuck you!' she shouted, scrambling to her feet as he lurched out of his chair towards her.

Breathing raggedly, Boo pushed Mitch out of the way and ran.

Swallowing back the tears, sensing the fuzzy edges around normality as she started to come down, she sought safety in the company of others in the bar. Boo sat in a corner, sipping a pint of cider while she watched the rugby players sloshing their drinks around and filling the already choking air with sweat, testosterone and their sickly-sweet exhalation of beer fumes on a high tide of raucous song.

Mitch is no good for me. I've got to ditch him, she thought. *Holy Jo said he was a bad influence and she was right, for all she's a square and a grass. He's just too much. I wanted to get away from Mum and her boozing and drugs, but Mitch is turning me into a carbon copy of the old bag. And he's suffocating me. This is my only chance to make a new life for myself and I'm fucking it up.*

The more of her cider she drank, the colder the bar suddenly felt. The warm light and laughter of the others felt grey, thin and disingenuous. It was time to go. And yet, could she go back to her room when Mitch was still hanging around, nearby?

'Mind if I sit here?'

Boo looked up to find one of the rugby players staring down at her with a grin on his square-jawed face. It seemed charming one moment, leering the next. Flickering on. Flickering off.

'Suit yourself.'

His gaze was fixed on her chest. She looked down to see that her top had torn, gaping open at the cleavage. Suddenly, she was acutely aware of the naked flesh of her legs, barely covered by her denim hot pants. She stretched her cardigan over her knees. But the guy's eyes steadfastly followed the contours of her breasts beneath the yellow silk blouse.

'Buy you a drink?' he asked.

Say no. You don't need this. Not when you're coming down. This guy's not right for you.

He was big for a fresher – muscular and tall, already with the facial hair of a man in his late twenties. What was his name? Did it matter? She knew his room was as far away from hers as it was possible to get. Far enough away from Mitch to buy her a night of safety.

'Yeah. Go on. Mine's a cider.'

76

CHAPTER 10

Bev

'Who's there?' Bev shouted in the dim light of the car park, her voice echoing off the concrete walls and floor.

Her skin puckered into goosebumps. She felt eyes on her. But looking around the murky, vast space, she could see only cars parked like silent sentries. She could hear only the Mancunian rain pattering in earnest outside.

'I know you're there!' she shouted, the bravado almost sticking in her throat. She clutched her bag tightly across her body, acutely aware of the hairs on her arms standing on end and the tingling sensation of adrenaline coursing around her body. 'I'm calling the police.'

Yeah. After I'm in the bloody car, she thought, trying desperately to get the key in the door's lock and failing thanks to her shaking hand.

Footsteps. One, two, three. She was certain she had heard them just then. But still, Bev could see nothing in the industrial concrete space which was deserted except for her and the empty, alarmed vehicles with their immobiliser lights winking red in silence. Feeling like she was going mad, she was just about to look beneath her car to see if she could spot a pair of feet, when she heard several women noisily ascending the ramp to her level, chatting animatedly among themselves.

'Come on, come on, come on,' she said, finally sliding the key home in the lock.

She'd never clambered into a car and locked the doors so quickly in her life. As she pulled out of her space, she glanced through her rear-view mirror. Saw a man standing against the wall in the shadows, watching her. So, she'd been right. Who the hell was it? A mugger? Another driver? Was his appearance a coincidence? Perhaps her overwrought imagination was playing tricks on her.

A horn honked. Her attention was diverted to a car coming down the ramp from the level above. Flashing headlamps. Honking again. Bev slammed on the courtesy car's brakes, coming to a juddering halt. An angry-looking man in the driver's seat of the other car, was shaking his fist at her and mouthing what was clearly 'stupid bitch' through the windscreen.

'Fuck you, pal!' Bev shouted, offering him the finger. But privately admitting he'd had right of way. She glanced in her rear-view mirror once more. Her imagined pursuer had gone. She shook her head.

Feeding her ticket into the machine and escaping onto Sale's shining wet streets, she exhaled heavily. 'I think the mildew's gone to my brain. I'm losing the plot.'

Driving back through the leafy boulevard of Brooklands Road towards Hale, Bev admired the large 1930s houses. Wished she hadn't let Rob the Knob bully her during their divorce negotiations into handing over all the equity from their London home. Not that she'd had much choice after he'd blackened her name professionally with trumped-up allegations of sleeping her way through the staff list, fiddling her expenses and suffering from ropey mental health. Judges weren't too impressed by those kinds of things, it turned out, and Rob was very, very good at lying.

After they'd split and sold up to move North, where the cost of living and the pace of working life was more palatable for newly single Rob with leisure time on his mind, he'd bought himself a new super-pad in Didsbury. She'd ended up in a damp rented basement flat and subject to psychiatric scrutiny. Laughably, with the help of his top-drawer solicitor and the hindrance of her own bargain-basement legal loser, Rob had made her feel like he was doing her a favour. And she'd just swallowed his shit wholesale, fearing Hope would be beyond her reach entirely if she complained.

Deep in resentful thought, Bev was startled when her phone rang. Angie's name on the screen. Glancing around to ensure there were no police patrol cars knocking around, she answered and pressed the phone to her ear.

'Go on. What is it?'

Angie sounded jittery on the other end. 'You won't believe what just happened to me.'

'Did you find anything?'

'Yes. But not before Jerry nearly found me, hiding behind the sofa bed in his office. I can't stop shaking. Can you pop over?'

Coming to a halt at the roundabout, Bev caught sight of a cop car to her right. 'I'm driving. Can't talk. Gotta go to the vacuum shop in Hale.' She ended the call abruptly and flung the phone onto the passenger seat. Realised there had been a message from someone. Surely not another reply from her target?

Pulling into Hale village, she navigated her way past the Maseratis, Ferraris and plain old BMWs, waiting to park in the scant number of spaces available. Bev skirted in front of some yummy mummy in an Audi Q8 to steal a space outside Costello's electrical shop. She ignored the woman's passive-aggressive smile and hand gestures that she could go right ahead and cut her up. Stuff her. Bev needed her repaired vacuum cleaner back and she was damned if she was going to walk quarter of a mile, carrying an old Dyson the length of the village.

But first, the message. It wasn't via LinkedIn. With a thudding heart, she pressed on the Messenger app's icon. It was Tim.

Rent? That was it. No, 'Hello Bev, how are you?' No please or thank you.

Heated by a sudden flash of anger, so that she imagined she could see steam rising from the car's wet bonnet, she thumbed back a curt reply.

Mould? Fishing among the detritus in her anorak pocket, she took out a crumpled receipt for the haul of cough medicines, painkillers and throat sweets she'd recently bought in the local chemist. She straightened it out and photographed it, attaching the snap to her message. Next, she took a screengrab of a local solicitors' firm that firmly believed, 'Where there's blame, there's a claim' and attached that. Just because he was married to her best friend and she was living in their basement, didn't mean she had to take his crap. The wanker could wait for his money.

She rubbed her burning, stiff shoulders, and considered her response, or rather, Cat Thomson's response to Jerry Fitzwilliam's enthusiastic correspondence.

You had such a commanding presence when I saw you on breakfast TV. Your opponent went away with her tail truly between her legs, but I'll bet your bark is worse than your bite! I think it wouldn't be too hard for you to win this cat over! Why don't you try? Let's meet to discuss how we can help each other. When and where suits?

Scattered throughout the missive, Bev included several emojis. Laughter, winkie, dancing girl, cat, kissing face. She had a fine line to tread between encouraging flirtation and avoiding frightening him off.

Within twenty minutes, he'd messaged back.

Might you be in London at any point in the next couple of weeks?

Jx

Once in the electrical repair shop, she pushed all thoughts of the Fitzwilliams out of her mind.

'I've come to pick up my Dyson,' she told the old guy behind the counter.

The shelves in there were lined with electrical oddities and other people's repaired appliances. The air smelled of old carpet and dust. It reminded her of a typewriter repairs place her mother had taken her to as a kid by the tall Co-op Insurance building. The old lady had wanted to collect machine parts from Underwood typewriters destined only for the scrapyard. Eccentric old bugger.

With heaviness in her heart at the bittersweet memory, she gave the owner her receipt. He came out from behind the counter, trying to match Bev's job number to her vacuum cleaner. But she had already spotted the first-edition Dyson with its grey plastic body and yellow trim. The vacuum for which she had fought for custody.

'All back to normal?' she asked.

The guy laughed but there was no real humour in his voice. He dragged the Dyson to towards the till, beckoning her to follow. 'Let me show you something,' he said.

Perplexed, Bev frowned. Retrieved her purse from her bag just wanting to pay up. 'You serviced it, right? It's working again?'

'Do you want to know why it got bunged up in the first place? Eh? It jammed. Do you want to see what I pulled out from the pipes?'

She shook her head. Shrugged. 'Not really.'

With a look of pure disgust on his face, the repair guy pulled out a clear plastic bag full of grey fluffy junk.

'Yeah? And?' Bev said. Checked her watch impatiently.

Massaging the plastic, he moved the fluff aside to reveal cigarette butts galore and three used condoms. 'The Dyson DC01 was not designed to vacuum up debauchery, young lady. It plays havoc with the dual cyclone.'

She peeled an extra ten pounds from her purse. Half of her food budget for the week. Her cheeks felt like they might blister up with heat at any moment. Holding the note out to the repair man, she couldn't bring herself to make eye contact.

'Save your money,' he said, waving it away. 'Pay for some lessons on basic hygiene.'

'I had a visitor . . .' Bev recalled the circumstances under which her design classic vacuum cleaner had been abused. She'd woken late the following morning, too hungover and too short on time to deal with the mess properly. Her client – the wife of a serially unfaithful curtain salesman – had turned up only twenty minutes later, forcing her to push her visitor out of the bedroom's patio doors and into the garden. He'd been encouraged to use his initiative with regard to Sophie and Tim's high fencing and just make himself scarce, pronto. 'I'm sorry,' she said in a small voice.

He pushed the bag into her hand 'Well, you can take your intimate muck with you.'

'So is the vacuum . . . you know? Sucking again?' She could feel a giggle welling up inside her as though she was some idiot schoolgirl. *Get lost, giggle. This is not the time or place. This guy hates you.*

'I wouldn't be giving it back if it wasn't—'

Her phone vibrated in her pocket. She checked the screen. It was Angie calling.

'Bev!' There was urgency in her client's voice. 'I need to speak to you in person. I'm parked across the road.'

Bev glanced outside and noticed the Range Rover parked in a bay alongside the bowling green.

'Not here,' Bev said. 'Meet me in Altrincham Aldi, on the odds and sods aisle.'

The disgust was evident from Angie's tone. '*Aldi?* No! Odds and *what*? Why not Waitrose?'

'Aldi. Follow me there. And wear a hat.'

'I haven't got a hat to hand.'

Bev thought about the knitted fashion disaster that was sitting in the hire car's glovebox – her go-to headwear for masking her identity during stakeouts. 'I'll lend you a sodding hat.'

Cutting Angie off and not staying to listen to any more of the repair guy's lecture, Bev wheeled the Dyson rapidly out of the shop.

CHAPTER 11
Bev

'I don't know why we couldn't have met somewhere more civilised,' Angie said, pulling the bright green bobble hat further down over her ears. She was wearing sunglasses too and was beginning to attract the attention of the till staff. She wrinkled her nose at a poorly dressed old man who was examining a nylon striped doormat with interest.

'Look, Angie. We've got to be careful that we're not seen together in public by anyone in your social circle,' Bev said, eyes darting up and down the jumbled aisle of miscellaneous marked-down merchandise. 'Jerry doesn't know what I look like, right? It needs to stay that way.'

'Can I take this hat off? It's itchy. And green's not my colour. It makes me look jaundiced.'

'You'll look fucking jaundiced if your husband finds out I'm catfishing him under a pseudonym. Look, Angie. What have you found that can't wait for half an hour?'

Jerry Fitzwilliam's battered wife shoved a piece of paper into her hands. 'A bank statement,' she said. 'I managed to break into his office but he came back home to get something. I nearly died. I can't believe he didn't notice the open window. I thought he'd catch me, but I managed to—'

Bev set her shopping basket on the ground and snatched

the statement from her. Examined the logo on the quality paper. 'Coutts & Co? Nice. They don't let you bank there if you're stacking shelves in Asda.' She grinned. 'This is a good start. Well done.' Scanning the transactions, she could see the current account was over quarter of a million in the black some two weeks ago, but that the money had been transferred out. It was not immediately obvious where to. 'There's a few listings of an account number registered to a company named Spartacus Holdings. Does that ring any bells?'

Scratching gingerly at her forehead beneath the green, rough wool hat, Angie shook her head. 'No.'

'Does Jerry have any business interests or jobs outside of his political work?'

'Not that I know of. He gave up his City job. He was stressed. We've been living off savings, he said, and then his MP's salary, once he was elected.'

'Let me show this to a friend,' she said, folding the statement carefully in half. 'Try to have another dig around his office next time he's out. Look for laptops, USB sticks, phones or statements for phone accounts you didn't know about. They might list numbers he's dialled . . . get more financial information like this.' She waved the Coutts statement. Slipped it into her handbag. 'Anything you can lay your hands on. Look for keys to furniture that's locked. People lock things for a reason.'

'Like his desk drawers?'

Bev's response was fully formed and waiting on the tip of her tongue to be shared with Angie, when she swallowed the words back down to join the sinking feeling in the pit of her stomach. Standing only three feet away was Rob. Rob the Knob, who had crept up on her like the sneaky shit he was.

'Hello, Bev.' Carrying a plastic basket laden with shopping. He glanced into her basket, empty but for a pack of heavy-flow sanitary towels and two bottles of cooking wine. 'I see you're eating well.'

'What the fuck are you doing in Altrincham, Robert? Didsbury's your patch.' How much of her conversation with her new client had this destroyer of worlds heard? She appraised his shiny grey suit trousers that were befitting of an office junior – not a thirty-year-old marketing manager. Noticing the small paunch that had recently appeared above his belt, she curled her lip. 'Skiving? Been sacked?'

'Afternoon off. I needed a new curtain pole from Homebase for my *magnificent* home and thought I'd nip in here for some bits.' He smiled the smile of a boxer who'd just delivered a sucker punch to an opponent. 'Is that OK with you or do you have to consult your solicitor for an opinion?'

'Yeah, *magnificent* with my hard-earned cash. Shove it up your arse, Rob. And fuck off while you're doing it, or I'll call security and tell them you're a sex pest.'

Rob glanced disparagingly at Angie's snot-green bobble hat, failing to look directly at her, as if Bev was a contagious disease, easily spread to anyone she talked to. 'You'd know all about sex pests, Beverley. Pulling in Aldi's a bit of a low for you, though, isn't it?' Finally he addressed Angie directly. Still staring at the hat. 'She's got a fanny like a fire bucket, this one. Are you one of her wingmen, or is she doing you?'

Angie merely stared at him, open-mouthed.

'That's it,' Bev shouted. 'Security! Guard! Help!'

Laughing as though he'd said something hilarious, Rob scuttled off towards the tills, dumping his basket on a chocolate display and exiting empty-handed.

Breathing deeply and slowly to calm herself after the altercation, Bev turned back to Angie, picking up their conversation anew, as if a run-in with the man who'd ruined her life had never happened. It didn't do to share her drama with a client who had enough of her own to contend with.

'Yes. Desk drawers. Exactly. Check them if you can,' she said. Keeping the adrenaline and cortisol out of her voice. Calmer, calmer, calm. 'Look through the pages of books for illicit photos or hidden documents. Check the pockets of his suits. And I need money to float this job, Angie. If you think he's messing around but can't find evidence of an affair, I'll need to honeytrap him.'

'Oh,' Angie said, the furrows on her brow deepening. 'Really?' Clearly she had no interest in bringing up the subject of Rob. Good.

'You want grounds? Infidelity is a biggie. I pretend to be sexually interested in him. If he tries to put the moves on me and we get evidence of that . . . I've already arranged to meet with him in London. Get as much evidence as I can.'

Angie pulled her purse out of her Mulberry handbag, opening the notes section.

Bev could see only a fiver in there. No sign of any credit cards whatsoever. She sighed, thinking of her share of the water bill that Sophie had recently dropped into her lap. A nasty addition to the pile of brown paper envelopes that were stacking up on the coffee table. Demands for thousands of pounds' worth of payments she knew she couldn't make. Utilities. Credit card bills. The dreaded tax demand. Not to mention the rent she owed. 'Is that all you've got in the world?'

Angie bit her lip. Tears standing in her blue eyes. 'For now . . . Sorry.'

Bev waved her hand dismissively, though the worry of her own financial meltdown was not so easily wafted away. But asking clients for money up front was the element of self-employment that she struggled with most. 'Forget it. Give me some cash next time. Leave it with me. But Angela, do me a favour. Don't come chasing after me in public. We're damned lucky Jerry's never met me before, given his connection with Tim. And what would have happened if Rob knew Jerry and had recognised you? If Jerry gets wind of what's going on, we're both in a mountain of bother. Right?'

CHAPTER 12

Bev

'Can I get you a drink, madam?' the waiter asked.

Bev clenched her fists, pressing her fingernails into her palms until it hurt. Forced a smile onto her face. 'A Hendricks and tonic, thanks.' Glancing down at the drinks menu, she realised too late that she couldn't actually afford a drink that was approaching £15. *Shit*. But she had to blend in, here in the busy bar of this Michelin-starred restaurant that felt like a memory from her past.

'Cucumber?'

'Yes please.'

Perched on the bar stool, she smoothed down her uncomfortably tight dress, pulling the fabric towards her knees. Hooked her stiletto heels over the footrest, feeling the sting in her feet that had grown unaccustomed to glamour, having spent the last year mainly in trainers. Beyond the packed bar, she spied tables full of elegantly dressed Sloane Rangers and their moneyed husbands. Funny how wealthy women so frequently wore pale colours, as though they were boasting by means of their Max Mara cashmere that no dirt would ever besmirch them.

What the hell was she doing? Her heart was thundering away to the point where she felt it might give out entirely. Agreeing to meet Jerry Fitzwilliam for a drink and nibbles felt like a step too far in her shitty career as a private investigator.

'Breathe,' she counselled herself, practicing the techniques Mo had taught her. Breathe in for four, hold for two, out for six. Repeat.

As she tried to calm her heart rate, she considered the last few days. Already wound tight enough to snap, there had been another incident where she'd been sure she was being followed – on the way back from a late-night trip to Hale Tesco Express for two pints of milk and a bag of custard doughnuts. The shadow Science Minister had finally accepted her friend request on Facebook, resulting in some back and forth between her – masquerading as Cat Thomson – and him on Messenger. She had ramped up the flirting to a level where, worryingly for this job's prospects, he'd accused her of being a journalist, digging for scandal. Naturally, she had denied it. She'd asked Doc to put together a suitably boring corporate website for a spoof engineering company, listing her as the marketing manager on the, 'meet the team' page. Catherine Thomson, with the winsome smile and the tits to die for, who had been with the firm for five years. She'd sent Jerry the link, challenging him to see for himself if she was for real or if she was, indeed, a hack on the hunt for an exposé.

Maybe he got a mate to look into it, she thought, twisting and twisting at a napkin. *Maybe he's got contacts in HMRC or wherever it is they hold National Insurance records. Those bastards would know in a click of the mouse if Cat Thomson is a fake ID or not. Shit, shit, shit. He might be coming here with the police to have me arrested. Maybe that's why he's late. Maybe there are cops outside with guns, waiting to take me down like some terror suspect. Christ. What the hell are you doing, you berk?*

'Your Hendricks and tonic, madam,' the waiter said, laying down a paper coaster and a bowl of nuts. Setting her drink on the bar with some ceremony.

Bev nodded. Forced another smile. 'Ta. I mean, thanks.' She gulped down half of the double gin in one hit. Registered the alcohol flowing through her veins like quicksilver. It should have served to bolster her confidence. She had nothing to worry about. Not really. Didn't she? Fitzwilliam had seemed to accept Doc's website as the real deal, after all. And though he hadn't exactly reciprocated her amorous advances in the universal languages of emoji and innuendo, neither had he closed her down, which implied tacit encouragement. He had been the one to chase her for a London meet, though he had only suggested a drink in this very public place. Would he take her bait or play it straight?

Bev reached into her handbag, switching on the tiny recording device just poking out beneath the lid. She said a silent prayer that the equipment would pick up all sound and hopefully, feed a half decent picture back to Doc's laptop in Manchester.

'Cat?' A warm palm on the small of her back.

She started. Jerry Fitzwilliam was standing before her, now, grinning, all chalk-stripe suiting and shiny shoes.

Did he see me fiddling with the camera? I bloody hope not. Flirt, you daft cow.

'Jerry. My, my.' She held out her hand, expecting him to kiss her knuckles. Instead, he encased it in his giant pink fist and shook it energetically as though she were a male colleague at the office.

'Thanks for coming all this way,' he said, casting a fleeting eye over her and immediately moving his focus onto the restaurant beyond. A man with better things to do than this.

'How nice to meet you in the flesh,' Bev said, trying to switch on her inner seductress. *Don't say pig. Don't say pork. My God, he's got a sty in his left eye. Eeuw.* Every muscle in her body tensed up anew, shrinking away from the contact. This was going to be tough. She batted her eyelashes.

But her greeting was lost as a maître d' swept up to them.

'Mr Fitzwilliam!' All smiles and sycophantic bowing. 'Your private dining awaits.'

'Private?' Bev said, almost losing her footing as she slid off her bar stool. 'What? You mean on our own? Oh. Right. Fine.' She pictured Angie's bruised neck and swallowed hard.

'I took the liberty of booking a delightful space away from prying eyes. We can hear each other in there.' Fitzwilliam's hard blue stare was fixed on her, then.

He gestured that she should follow the maître d', past all those sophisticated diners who couldn't hear her anguished silent cry for help. Private.

They were led to an exquisitely decorated room where some top-end interior designer had gone mad with taupe velvety finishes, leather and mirrored this and that. It had been set up for dining à deux. There were no windows. The chaise longue against the back wall sent images flickering through Bev's brain of the email thread she'd been sent anonymously only days ago. Snippets made to look like clippings from newspaper articles.

Beverley Saunders slept her way to the top.
A regular on the CEO's casting couch.
How else do you think someone like her ended up the marketing director?
Saunders is a slag.

And now she was being shut inside a room with a strange, apparently violent man, where the chaise implied that she may well end up the desert course in a Michelin-starred taster menu.

Come on, woman. Be a professional PI. You're Cat Thomson. Hot to trot; paid by the hour to dig for dirt.

She set her bag on a mirrored console table that held the most enormous arrangement of tropical flowers in a giant glass vase. The bag would be easily overlooked at the side of that floral confection, she reasoned. She needed her connection with Doc more than ever in this overly intimate space.

Her date helped her into her seat, loosened his tie and undid the top button of his blue shirt. He sat facing her at the table. Watching her. The waiting staff fussed around them both, handing them each a large menu. Then, they left, and the silence in the room was deafening.

'It's good to have a little privacy.' He finally said, the glistening tip of his pink tongue flashed over his thin bottom lip.

Bev laughed coquettishly. 'Oh, it wouldn't do for a man like you to be seen with a young marketing exec like me. What would people think?' She leaned forwards, letting him get a good look at her cleavage in the Karen Millen wiggle dress she'd bought off eBay from Partygrrl24. It had allegedly been worn only, 'a handful of times for weddings. Has been dry-cleaned.' The dried-in stain on the lining said otherwise. Bev was wearing a Monica Lewinsky moment in pre-owned fashion. Would she fall prey to her own Clinton cock-clinch with her client's husband?

'They'll think I'm chatting with a representative of an engineering company that has the future of the country's talent pool at heart,' he said, no trace of the Lothario in his deadpan delivery. 'I am the shadow Science Minister, after all. And you're involved in just the sort of engineering company that can help deliver my vision for science education.' He punctuated his gentle slap-down with a polite smile, not a leer.

Bev was disappointed. Was Jerry Fitzwilliam really the cartoon villain Angie had painted him as? His online flirtation and willingness to meet her suggested sexual interest, but the frost emanating from him at that moment said otherwise. Her concern started to mount anew. Could the shadow Science Minister have access to a register of every legitimate engineering company in the UK? Might he know that Belfry Automotive Engineers Ltd was a figment of her imagination?

Get him to proposition you for the camera and then get the hell out.

'Ooh! I feel like a naughty schoolgirl, being told off for being frivolous in lessons. Come on, then. Give me a good grilling about my experience with hot rods!' She drained the rest of her gin noisily through her straw, trying to look as suggestive as possible. Making eye contact, though she felt stripped naked in doing so.

Her innuendo bounced off him, his attention never diverting from the menu. No heightened colour in his cheeks. But Bev saw a flicker of a smile again flash across his lips. Perhaps some calculation behind his eyes. 'Let's get champagne! I do love a good bottle of Veuve Clicquot.'

There was a surprise. Party petrol. Perhaps Mr Minister wasn't quite as all business, as he seemed to be.

Her date buzzed for service, requesting a magnum of fizz to be brought straight away. With their glasses charged, they filled the excruciating minutes with tedious, in-depth conversation about the future of Britain's automotive industry – something Bev knew little about, though she managed to busk it. In any case, it turned out Jerry Fitzwilliam was like most men in wanting to hog the conversation and demonstrate quite how knowledgeable he was. He was staring at the ceiling, trotting out party lines as if he'd had them written for him and then learned them by heart. Blinking, blinking earnestly. Chugging his champers. Barely making eye contact with her. She was starting to doubt that he would take her bait.

'Of course, the research that has gone into the hydrogen fuel cell will revolutionise . . .'

He poured himself a second glass swiftly. As he droned on about his big plans for an educational initiative designed to get school-aged children interested in environmentally friendly technologies, Bev's attention started to wane. She stifled a yawn. Studied his hands. Were those big pink hams really the hands that had wrapped around Angie's slender neck and squeezed tightly? Was this smartly dressed, businesslike man really a domestic abuser and player? He downed his second glass, topping them both up again.

Three rapidly-drunk glasses in, and Jerry Fitzwilliam's behaviour started to change subtly. He'd opened another button on his shirt and was leaning in towards her. His smiles were more frequent and seemed to come more easily. His perfect diction started to soften around the edges. But he was still Mr Serious.

Come on, you stubborn bastard, she thought, staring at the coffee stains on the underside of his bottom teeth as he chatted away. *Show your true colours. Why else would you take me to dinner and ply me with booze unless you were scoping me out as an extra-marital shag-prospect? Just drop your guard for the camera and let me go home.*

Deciding to push her dinner date, she allowed her knee to brush his beneath the table. 'Tell me, Jerry, doesn't your wife mind you wining and dining strange women?' She chewed her little finger coquettishly, expecting him to bat her question aside and continue with the science talk.

Fitzwilliam was suddenly a different beast entirely. He trotted out a response straight away, as though years of practice had worn down the rough edges from the corny lines, leaving their delivery automatic and silky smooth. 'Listen, Cat. My wife's two hundred miles away, but you and I are here in London with a wealth of chemistry between us.' He reached over and ran a finger the length of her hand. 'What are we doing here if not studying the science of attraction?'

She withdrew her hand rapidly, startled by his change in tack. *Woah. Dr Jekyll can't take his loon-juice. Maybe now's my chance. Say something, Goddammit! Encourage him! You're here to honeytrap. So, trap his fucking honey!* Bev gripped the underside of her chair, searching in vain for a suitable response. All she could manage was a coquettish giggle.

Another glass down, and her date slammed his menu onto the table triumphantly. 'I'm having the steak,' he declared. 'Are you a carnivore, Cat? The sausage on offer is particularly meaty.' He winked. Played footsie with her under the table.

'Oh, Jerry! You are a one!' she managed, praying Doc was getting an earful and eyeful of this sleaze. Jesus. Bev now saw a predator on the other side of the table. She'd need to keep her wits about her in this windowless room – no mean feat when the trek down from the north, coupled with her first working day as a freelance copywriter for her old boss, had left her body and mind heavy with fatigue. Worse still, with no money for a hotel, she had no option but to drive all the way back to Cheshire that night.

Bev found herself yawning.

'Ready for bed so soon?' he said, looking pointedly at the chaise longue with a hungry expression on his porcine, flushed face. 'Perhaps you can have a lie-down, Cat. Does pussy like being stroked?'

This chump had to dial it down again. Maybe she could cool some of his ardour by boring the pants back on him. 'I've had a really busy day at work. It's not easy being a marketing guru. My diary's been back-to-back meetings!'

'Time for a little front-on-front action then,' he said, locking eyes with her over the top of his menu.

Bev felt the heat creep into her cheeks. Saw Angie in her mind's eye, weeping and desperate on her doorstep. 'So, Jerry. You seem like a fascinating man with the perfect life. What makes a guy like you want to hook up with a girl like me, when you've got everything you need at home?'

He leaned forward and pushed her menu down. 'What makes you think my needs are met at home?'

'I didn't . . . I don't—'

'Doesn't a desirable woman like you have someone waiting for you at home too?'

'No. I'm single. I like to keep things uncomplicated.' She thought about her squalid flat and the bed that always felt too big and too cold for her since her split with Rob. She thought about the even greater, cavernous gap in her life that only a court order in her favour, and a clean bill of mental health from Mo, would fix.

'Strings-free, eh? I'm rather a fan of strings-free, too.' He winked. 'As far as I'm concerned, marriage is just a domestic arrangement. Don't you agree?'

She wanted to say no. She wanted to yell that if he wasn't happy with his wife, he should do the honourable thing and cut her loose so they could both begin again.

97

She wanted to slap his face and tell him that she'd forced herself to believe in her own marriage like a religion – accepting of its flaws, iniquities and confines as was demanded of the long-suffering devout – feeling utterly stripped of her faith on that day she'd found out what Rob had really been doing. It was only then that she'd realised the Bev of old had been supplanted by a brain-washed drone who hadn't been able to function without her husband's approval. And then, somehow managing to blame her for his years of gaslighting, controlling her and screwing anything that moved, he'd disbanded the Cult of Rob and Bev and had ushered in her own personal End of Days. *Forget about Rob, for God's sake. This is work. Act like a pro!* 'I wouldn't know,' she said. She ran her finger seductively around the rim of her champagne flute. 'But you're a big boy. I'm sure you can tell right from wrong all by yourself. I guess nothing's ever as simple as it seems. Especially not for a complicated man like you.'

'Do you have multiple orgasms?' Another comment that caught her off guard. This was next level talk. He was topping himself up yet again but splashed some of the champagne onto the tablecloth.

I do, but not with you, dickhead. 'Maybe I do. Maybe I don't,' she tittered. 'My word. You're forward, Jerry Fitzwilliam. What a naughty boy you are!'

'I think you're a tease. I'm not sure about you.' He seemed to scan through her make-up and skin to the true intent beneath. 'Maybe I should check you for a wire. Shall I have a look through your handbag and see there's no snooping equipment inside?' He licked his lips. Raised an eyebrow and turned around to the console table. Reaching out for the handbag. Snatching it up; opening the front flap, he peered inside . . .

CHAPTER 13
Bev

Holding her breath, Bev's mouth opened and closed as she watched him rummaging in the front of the bag, unaware that the recording equipment was in the back pocket. She was just about to distract him with the desperate measure of a kiss when there was a knock on the door.

'Sir, Madam, are you ready for your entrées?'

Fitzwilliam dumped the bag back onto the console, forgetting his suspicions. It was difficult to tell if the camera was still focused on the correct spot. The main thing, though, was that Bev hadn't been discovered.

The waiting staff bustled in, carrying dishes of steaming food. Bev's stomach growled loudly enough to be audible, had a young waiter not jostled the champagne bottle inside its silver bucket full of rattling ice cubes.

'This is empty, sir. Shall I bring you another?'

'Yes. I'm trying to get this young lady tipsy,' Fitzwilliam slurred. 'She thinks I'm going to sleep with her later. Ha ha.' The champagne had definitely smothered his misgivings, as well as any inhibitions, in an alcoholic fog.

Bev pursed her lips and wrung the tablecloth with sweaty hands, out of sight. Her innards were in knots.

The waiting staff had barely exited the private dining

room when her date blurted out, 'Do you shave? I like a woman who waxes.'

How tempted was she to tell him that she had an unapologetic 1970s style Brian Blessed in her pants, and that he could imagine whatever topiary he wanted, because he was never getting to see hers? 'Would you like me to pour you some water?' She snatched up the carafe. Holding it above his water glass. Desperately wanting to throw it in his face.

His hand slid over the rim. 'Are you trying to put my fire out, Cat? Don't be a spoilsport.'

It was then that she noticed the difference in skin colour on his knuckles, presumably where scabs had recently fallen off. Was it evidence of him having thumped Angie? Surely he hadn't hit her hard enough to draw blood. A smooth operator like Jerry Fitzwilliam would be careful to inflict damage where it could be easily concealed. Or was he the kind of psycho who hit walls in a temper when he'd exhausted all the soft-tissue options on his wife? Yes. Bev could imagine that.

She ate quickly. 'I like a strong man,' she said. 'I like to feel like a woman. I bet you take charge in your house.'

'Oh, you'd be surprised,' he said. 'My wife's a ball-breaker. She skins me alive for money, and I have to do as I'm told at home. Honestly. She wears the trousers. I can never do right for doing wrong. All the hours I work, trying to put food on the table and keep a good roof over our heads, but it's never enough for her. You should hear the vicious bile that comes from her mouth too. And then there's the thing of no sex. All work and no play makes Jerry a dull boy. I need to be loved, Cat. Do you think you can do that for me?'

There seemed to be tears in his eyes. What was this nonsense? She'd met Angie and knew a petrified victim when she saw one. He was pulling the same table-turning nonsense Rob had tried on her. Men like Jerry Fitzwilliam never took the blame.

When the first course was done, he left the room with the ghost of an erection clear through his chalk-stripe trousers. His jacket hung on the back of his chair. Bev checked her watch – 9.30 p.m. He was on his sixth glass of champagne. She was on her fourth, though she felt almost sober. But full of enough Dutch courage to dart around to the other side of the table and check his pockets.

A quick pat-down revealed he had two phones. A Blackberry, perhaps for work. A Samsung, presumably for play. She had his private phone number on Cat Thomson's new burner. Made a mental note to get Doc to pull what he could from the fun-phone's call log – he'd assured her that if the phone's Bluetooth connection was active, it was a possible, remote way in for malware. But Fitzwilliam's wallet must have been in his trouser pocket. How she would have liked to get a glimpse of his credit and debit cards.

Footsteps outside, she threw herself back onto her chair, resolving to wrap this up as quickly as possible.

When Fitzwilliam came back in, he was sniffing hard and waxy-faced. Was that a glimmer of white powder she spied just below his right nostril?

'I'm so sorry, Jerry, but I'm going to have to go in a minute.' She laced her fingers together, closing the window of opportunity for debate. Certain there was anger beneath his look of disappointment.

He glanced at the giant Breitling bin-lid on his wrist. 'Oh, you're kidding me. But the night's young, and I'm at your beck and call for the entire evening.'

She stood, smoothing her dress down slowly and suggestively. Let him think there was still the possibility of a tryst somewhere down the line.

'Here. You've missed some crumbs,' he said, moving into her space and brushing down her hips.

Pushing him away with a fingertip, she giggled. 'Now, now, Jerry. I'm the sort of cat who likes to get to know a boy before she lets him stroke her.'

His hand moved down to her groin but she took a swift step backwards, circling the table to grab her bag.

'Oh, that's a shame,' he said, placing himself between her and the door.

Bev angled her handbag so that the camera was hopefully right on him.

He caressed her face with sweaty fingertips. She could smell the champagne on his breath. 'I thought I was going to get a feel of your pussy then. You're such a tease.'

Her index finger trembled as she touched his chin, but she assessed he was too drunk to pick up on her fear. He merely took her finger into his mouth and sucked it.

Wincing inwardly, she kept her voice deliberately soft and suggestive. 'Next time. If you're a good boy, I'll get my claws into you then. I bet you'd like that.'

Get out of the damned room before he shoves you on that chaise longue and forces himself on you. You're playing a ridiculous, risky game here.

When he grabbed her around the middle, she yelped. 'I really must go, Jerry.' Pushed him away, half-laughing. Trying to work out if the butter knife was within reach, should she need it.

Knocking at the door dispelled the tension immediately. Bev's heart galloped away at such a pace, she could barely speak.

'Come in!' she managed.

The waiting staff slipped inside to clear the plates, and with a wink and a kiss blown in the shadow Science

102

Minister's direction, Bev strutted as fast as she could away from the room and down the stairs. Outside, she hastened down the street, not daring to look back in case he was following her.

Spotting an Uber that was dropping two women off outside a wine bar, Bev click-clacked along the pavement, weaving her way past a parked-up pizza delivery moped. She ran after the old Skoda, shouting frantically.

'Wait! Tell the cabbie to wait,' she implored the disembarking women.

But they ignored her and marched purposefully into the bar, laughing, as though Bev was just some novelty drunken spectacle in a high-end part of town.

Only a couple of hundred yards away, Jerry had appeared in the restaurant's doorway and was starting to lumber towards her, swaying on legs that appeared full of champagne. Waving at her.

Bev hammered on the Uber's window and the driver lowered it by mere inches.

'Please. I need a cab urgently.'

The driver looked her up and down. Adjusted his pristine white mosque hat and thumbed his beard. 'Sorry, love. I'm Uber, innit? You got an account? You've got to book it through the app or I'm not insured. And I've got another fare—'

'There's a man. He's drunk and he's hassling me. I need to get away from him. I'll bung you extra.' She spoke quickly.

His expression softened and the doors unlocked. 'Go on. Get in.'

Amid a flurry of, 'Thank you, thank you, thank you,' Bev folded herself into the back seat. Breathed a sigh of relief when the doors locked. She jumped when Jerry suddenly slapped a hand on the passenger window, shouting something incoherent to her through the glass. Blowing him a kiss and miming that she'd call him, she caught the cabbie's eye in the rear-view mirror. 'Just drive.'

He pulled away from the kerb with a squeal of rubber, leaving swaying Jerry Fitzwilliam standing on the kerbside like an oversized abandoned child.

'As long as you pay me in cash, love, I'll take you wherever you want. Where to?'

The adrenaline was coursing around Bev's body, mingling with alcohol she shouldn't have drunk. She realised how desperately close she'd come to being discovered, or else pinned down and raped by a man who clearly wasn't used to taking no for an answer. And yet, she'd succeeded, hadn't she? She'd caught her client's husband in the act of extra-marital seduction. The melange of slowly abating panic and euphoria whipped up a storm inside her that only one thing could quell.

She felt the bite of her other compulsion – the most intense one that she never brought up in therapy; the one that was as close as she could get to trepanning to release the pressure inside her. Better than drugs. Better than origami. It was the perfect way to celebrate her small triumph. She couldn't get back behind the wheel until she'd sobered up anyway. What the hell . . .

'Earl's Court, please. I'll give you directions when we get nearer.'

They sped away down Chelsea's empty backstreets. She was heading for somewhere she hadn't visited in a long, long time. But she'd checked online only days ago and knew it was still operating.

'Live over that way, do you?' the driver asked.

'No. I'm going to a kind of club,' Bev said. 'Members only.'

'Oh yeah? That feller's face not fit?' Eyes on the road. Eyes on her reflection. He was grinning. Was it conceivable that a devout Muslim man knew exactly the sort of things that went on inside the unassuming-looking, four-storey house on an unremarkable, double-parked street in backpacker-land?

'I've got a birthday party to go to,' she lied. '*He's* certainly not invited. He's just some drunken pest I went on a date with who forgot his manners.'

She handed over her money as the Uber idled outside the Victorian terrace, where it looked for all the world as though nobody was home. Bev stared at the black, anonymous-looking door with nervous anticipation and a sizeable dollop of excitement.

CHAPTER 14
Bev

The password had changed but Bev was not stalled at the front door for long.

'Well, well, well.' The tubby proprietor gestured to the young bouncer that he should step aside and let her in. 'It's a good long while since you last darkened the X-S Club's doorstep. To what do I owe the pleasure?'

Bev gave Phillipe d'O a peck on the cheek. 'You've barely changed,' she said, linking arms with him. 'You still look like Salvador Dali ate too many pies.'

He twirled his moustache archly and raised an eyebrow. Slapped her bottom. 'Looks like you've been on the pies yourself, hot stuff. Look at that arse! You're going to be popular tonight.'

'Everyone wanted size zero when I was last here.' She strutted through to the back of the house, grabbing a carnival mask from the girl in the cloakroom. He followed.

'Haven't you heard? It's all bootylicious these days, darling, thanks to Beyoncé. Anyway, why are you here? Is the North West too soggy even for you?' He slid his hand between her legs. She pushed him away, laughing. Feeling like she was already playing her favourite role in a game where she was in charge. The perfect narcotic antidote to Jerry Fitzwilliam's unwanted sexual aggression. She pulled at the plunging neckline of her dress so that her breasts jiggled. 'No, Phillipe. There's a positive drought up there. Come on. Let me get out of this lot and you can show me the fresh meat.'

The X-S club was busy. High with anticipation, Bev eyed the clientele in the warren of rooms that the house boasted. Music played at just the right volume in the expertly soundproofed house, so that people could hear each other's safe word and sex noises. Everyone wore masks, stripped naked in the main but for the odd piercing or item of fetish-wear. Bev had opted for nudity, not having planned to be here in advance. The only thing she carried with her was her phone.

She stood in a doorway momentarily, watching a woman astride a man with a large gut. Judging by the slight sag of the woman's flesh and the silver web of stretch marks that spanned her belly and hips, she was middle-aged. Her conquest, on the other hand, looked like an overweight younger man. She was riding him slowly, while a second man sucked her right nipple and masturbated himself.

It wasn't Bev's scene. She continued into the house's main salon, past rooms where it was man on man, girls kissing, cosy threesomes. She smiled. Anything went in here.

'Hello. What's your name?' A man padded down the stairs. His head was clean-shaven with the ghost of male-pattern baldness showing on the shining scalp, but his body was covered in dark hair. He had a great body at that. Toned, but not muscle-bound. And a giant erection that bobbed about before him like it was a buoy, keeping him afloat in the house's sea of depravity.

'Whatever you want it to be,' Bev said.

It had been a week since her last conquest. Too long. She could smell lube and promise on this stranger, who'd clearly already been indulging elsewhere in the house. Pumped full of Viagra he may be, but he was the opposite of Jerry Fitzwilliam.

Approaching him, she ran her finger the length of his torso, following the chevron of naval hair to his groin. 'Want to go join the others in the lounge?' she asked, looking up into the carnival mask. Amazing what you couldn't tell about a person when their face was covered. He might have come across as a doped-up waster, or a lying, spineless idiot like Rob, without the mask on, but none of that mattered here. Everyone was in this club for the physical solace and release the other members offered, strings free. Nothing more. Here, you could be as ugly as a mule and still get laid. Here, you were desired without any conditions attached. Here, nobody judged your compulsion. And besides, she liked the set of this man's chin and his clean, straight teeth.

His caress felt good. 'I don't think I can wait.'

No kissing. No information. No games. Just how Bev liked it.

Within a handful of easy foreplay moves, she was being screwed from behind on the stairs, revelling in the other partygoers ascending and descending at their side, pausing to watch before moving on to their own adventure. She enjoyed the conquest and the thought of what they were doing more than the deed itself. Sexual daring, voyeurism and power were narcotic. They would have been enough to get her off had her phone not started to ring, vibrating between her elbows on the step.

'Oh, I don't believe this,' she said, spying Doc's name flashing on the screen.

'Just turn it off,' her partner said, still humping away at her rear.

'Yeah. Sorry.'

Bev prodded at the icon to reject the call, but her lover's thrust was so enthusiastic that her hand slipped. Inadvertently, she found herself in conversation with Doc.

'What the hell are you doing?!' he shouted, his voice emanating from the phone, tinny and full of concern. 'Did you know you were still filming after you'd ditched Fitzwilliam?'

'Doc, I've got to go.' Bev teetered between laughter and mortification that Doc might have seen her entering the world of X-S. Was her secret out?

'Where the hell are you? Are you in . . . a sex club? There's knobs! And boobs! Shitting Nora, Bev. There was a man . . . and his wang was—'

Yes. Doc knew. Damn it.

Ending the call, Bev bit her lip. *Shelve it. It's none of his business. You're a grown woman and it's your choice to share your body with who the hell you like.* She focused anew on the important work of anonymous sex with a hot stranger.

In the main reception room, she enjoyed an encore with a girl who had the perkiest breasts she'd ever seen and two men who'd leave her sore for days. With every hole given due attention except the one in her heart, she got all the way to her parked car in an Archway side street before checking her voicemails. Six of them – all from Doc.

'Jesus, Bev. Are you OK? I can't believe that creep, Fitzwilliam. Call me back. There's a problem with the footage.' His concern for her was audible.

Half an hour later.

'It's me again. Bev . . .' Hesitation. What was he trying to say? *Come on, Doc. Out with it.* She realised, then, that this message had been left on her arrival at the club. 'I think you need to turn the camera off. I mean, what are you up to? Are you safe?!'

More messages, following the call she'd accidentally picked up:

'Crikey, Bev.' Crikey! Who on earth said, 'crikey' any more? 'You never told me you had another problem apart from origami. Why've you never brought this up at therapy? You're a sex addict, right? The guy who opened the door knew you. I googled him. It said he's called Phillipe d'O, O short for orgasm! You nutter. Hit me back. I'm worried about you.'

The final voicemail yielded a rather stern-sounding Doc. 'Hey. When you've finished shagging yourself into next Wednesday, I've got news. I've found something out about Spartacus Holdings. You'll not believe this. Call, dammit!'

She was torn between wanting to hear his news and needing to treat his proprietorial judgement of her private life with the silence it warranted. Whatever it was, she decided it could wait.

Bev knew she was doing wrong when she switched on the engine and tried to reverse out of the parking spot. Her spatial awareness wasn't what it should be thanks to the alcohol. She was misjudging the unfamiliar car's size and turning capacity. It took her a full five minutes to be free of the tight squeeze between a souped-up Subaru and a clapped-out combi van.

'If you get pulled over, you're in deep shit,' she told herself, crawling up the A1. 'You should go back. Sleep it off in the car.'

And yet, she kept going. Bev felt the insistent urge to get as far away as possible from London and Jerry Fitzwilliam and the X-S Club. Normality. That's what she needed. And familiarity, though it currently manifested itself as a mildewed, mouldy basement flat in someone else's house.

At 2 a.m. the roads were dead. No sign of the police – not that they'd be interested in a turd-brown Fiesta, trundling along the inside lane doing 65 mph. Two hours' drive gave her liver time enough to process the alcohol. The last hour passed in a whirl of heavy eyelids, trying to sing along to PJ Harvey playing on her phone in a bid to stay awake. She grappled with jumbled recollections of Jerry Fitzwilliam – the professional politics-bore who quickly turned into a sex pest with one sniff of the proverbial barman's apron.

She pulled off the M56 near Manchester airport and crawled her way home past the mansions of the nouveau riche, the white-collar criminals and the quinoa brigade who, like Sophie, wished they were living in Fulham or Belgravia or some place with capital cachet. All she wanted to do was fall into bed and forget. She clenched her numb buttocks in a bid to kickstart the flow of blood to them. She tried to loosen her pants. The cystitis that had flared up since her visit to X-S demanded a couple of painkillers and a large glass of cranberry juice. To make matters worse, when she tried to pull onto the gravel driveway, her space had been taken by an old Volvo. She was forced to park badly by the kerbside.

Almost falling out of her car, barefoot and clutching her killer heels, Bev was surprised to hear voices on the still night air.

'Bev? Is that you?' Giggling. The clickety-click of quality shoes.

'Sophie? Tim?' They were walking arm in arm. Or rather, weaving down the street. As they got closer, Bev could see Tim had had a skinful, to the point his eyes were slightly unfocused.

'Have you just got back from London?' Sophie asked, pulling her keys from her Mulberry bag with a perplexed look on her perfectly made-up face.

'Who's looking after the kids?' Bev asked, deciding her comings and goings were none of her friend's business.

'My mum,' Sophie said. 'It's date night. We've just been to a terrific dinner party at Abigail Gosport's on Carrwood.' Her voluble booze-fuelled response gushed forth. 'She's got a massive bloody house and the best live-in chef ever.' She paused to look Bev up and down. 'Gosh. You look . . .'

Tim stumbled up to the doorstep. 'Do us a favour, Bev. There's a good girl. Don't let the neighbours see you dressed like that, will you?' He hiccupped. 'You know how they gossip round here.'

Wanker. Cheeky bloody . . . aaaagh. Even in her head, Bev didn't have the right words for Tim's put-down. She could see tacit agreement with his sentiments in Sophie's well-meaning nod, too. What a pair. Best left until morning.

They parted company in the hall, where her path led towards the mildew stink and down the cold-stone steps. Theirs led up, to the family area that smelled of wood floor polish and wealth.

Once inside, Bev's flat was cold. She shivered, but it was not just because the heating had been off for two days. It felt like somebody had been inside her personal space. Moving from room to room, she examined the positions of her origami models – always arranged in a specific way and in a specific relationship to one another that only Bev could know. One of her cranes – a delicate bird in flight that had special significance for her – hadn't just been moved. It was missing.

CHAPTER 15
Bev

The smell of Doc's flat drifted out to greet her before she'd even stepped inside the cramped hallway. Feet. WD40. Old pizza. B.O. beneath a top note of cheap deodorant – the kind the adverts insisted made you irresistible to the pneumatic, up-for-it members of the opposite sex.

'You're gross. Do you know that?' Bev said, looking around at the trail of devastation that was his living room.

'And you're a hypocrite. Do you want a bag of Quavers? I've only got flat Dandelion and Burdock and Quavers. Soz.'

'No, ta.'

On his coffee table was a large cut-glass ashtray full of evidence. 'You still growing weed in your loft space?'

He grinned in answer. 'Let me show you something.' Flung himself onto a dog-eared typing chair. It was at a desk that was almost invisible beneath computer hardware that must have cost him a fortune, Bev assessed. While he tapped away, her eye wandered over the empty Pot Noodle packaging and abandoned pepperoni pizza boxes to a wall of colour.

'Is this your collection, then?' Shelf after shelf at the far end of the living room was filled with Lego models. Sports cars. Star Wars figures. Entire scenes, carefully built on green flat bases.

'That's nothing,' he said, never taking his eyes from his giant computer screen. 'Check out my spare room.'

Wandering down the hall, Bev spied a bathroom that smelled of poor ventilation and strong toilet cleaner. Next to it was, she presumed, Doc's bedroom. She walked quickly past that, unwilling to more than glance at his unmade bed and the mountain of clothes on a wicker chair. Finally, at the end, she found a closed door. She opened it to reveal a single bedroom crammed with display cabinets that sported not a speck of dust. Their glass had been polished until it shone, without a single fingerprint to mar the overall effect. Inside them, Lego creations had been arranged artfully. From the ceiling, there hung a giant Lego Star Wars X-Wing, the Millennium Falcon and several other airborne models, including a dragon and a rocket ship. Bev was surprised by an intense rush of happiness, as though she had stepped into a pristine, magical children's museum that conjured the joy of her own innocent years. An enormous build – the kind you saw in the windows of Lego stores – took pride of place on the floor. Two life-sized Lego children were kneeling in a flower-strewn garden, also made from bricks. Together, they were constructing an ingenious mill house with a large waterwheel by a river. Bev spied a switch on the periphery of the display. When she flipped it, the house lit up, the wheel started to turn and the blue plates of Lego that comprised the river started to move, as if attached to a hidden conveyor belt. Just like water.

'Jesus, Doc,' she shouted down the hallway. 'You're a genius! No word of a lie. Never mind Oxford and therapy and this foetid dump you call home in the arse end of Manchester. You should be in Denmark, being a Lego Jedi Master, getting paid by head office for designing their displays.' She reached out to touch one of the little boy's ears and balked when it came away in her hand. Desperately trying to fix it as she spoke. 'I've been past the Lego shop in London and there was nothing this good in the window.' Damn it. How the hell was she going to reattach the ear without causing more damage?

'What?' Doc's voice from the living room. He hadn't heard a single word of what she'd said. 'Are you OK in there?'

Bev could hear footsteps, advancing to where she knelt, desperately pressing the ear to its anchor on the side of the child's face. Praying she wouldn't make it worse.

'Give me that!'

Doc marched towards her from the doorway, holding his hand out for the dismembered body part. 'I said you should check it out. I didn't say you could maul it. Don't touch my things, please.'

It took him only seconds to reattach the ear. He flipped the switch, bringing the mill wheel and river to a standstill.

The hurt and irritation was evident in the set of his jaw. Bev had been poised to repeat her high praise, but damn him, the silly prick.

'You know, this stuff's meant to be played with,' she said. 'I loved it as a kid.'

'Yes. I've seen *Lego Movie*. I don't need a lecture.'

'Eh? There's no need to be an arsehole.'

'How would you like it if I came round your place and started messing with your origami models?' He was glaring at her now. 'I bet you've got them arranged just so. And they're delicate like this.' He waved a hand at his opus in brightly coloured plastic.

Should she tell him how panic had gripped her when she'd realised the crane was missing? To most people it would be just a dusty folded bird, but for her it held a special memory of her father. A gift from him that could never be replaced. No. Maybe she'd imagined it was gone. She'd been in a bad way when she got home. It made sense to double check she hadn't moved it absent-mindedly before raising the alarm that someone was trying to freak her out or keep tabs on her.

'Sorry,' she said. 'It's really impressive though. And tactile. I didn't mean—'

'Come on. I'll show you those bank records and then we can run through yesterday's footage.'

'So, Spartacus Holdings,' he said, pointing at the screen.

Bev sat on an old dining chair at his side, her battered nether regions stinging thanks to the almost non-existent upholstery. 'What of it?'

'Big chunks of money come in from various companies, yeah? Just over a quarter of a mill, in six months. I googled those companies, right?'

Bev scanned the generic-sounding names. They looked like corporates. 'Maybe he does consultancy work on the side. A lot of these MPs supplement their income with private work. They sit on boards. He does have twenty years' of banking experience behind him.'

'No! Listen! All of those companies. Data International Ltd, Fisher, Fraser and Delaware. Cranbourne Consulting. All of them . . . they're owned by one guy. A business magnate called Matthew Stephens, right? And guess what?' He brought up a different tab that showed an article in the *FT*.

Scanning the contents, Bev started to nod.

Owner of Stephens Biotech plc was delighted today when his company's stock soared after parliament greenlit funding for research into the editing of human genes. The groundbreaking research, developed to help eliminate hereditary disease, has been championed by the Chinese, but shadow Minister for Science, Jerry Fitzwilliam, said it was high time the UK reclaimed its mantle as a leading . . .

'Oh, I get it,' Bev said, smiling wryly. 'Cash for questions, or whatever they call it. That sort of thing.'

'And cop this,' Doc said, bringing up another screen from a leading science journal. He poked at a paragraph of densely written text. 'Stephens Biotech has been done for fudging research in the past when the company had its main labs overseas. Their lead researcher retracted six articles from scientific journals after he was rumbled for paying for fake reviews. The researcher was sacked, so Matthew Stephens brushed the dirt right off himself and his company. But I'll bet this guy's not so clean.'

'Certainly not if he's bunging a politician backhanders to influence parliament and make it rain millions of quid's worth of funding,' Bev said. 'Where does all this dodgy cash go then? Into Spartacus Holdings? What is that?'

Doc raised an eyebrow. 'Offshore account in the Bahamas,' he said. 'Angela Fitzwilliam's down as the director. Clever.'

The hairs stood up on Bev's arms. 'Angie? But she claims not to know a thing about their money set-up. She's done nothing but cry poverty. That's why she's got me working on a promise. Apparently, she's lucky if Jerry gives her enough cash for the shopping.'

Folding one long, spidery leg over another, Doc stretched and yawned. 'Well, she could be feeding you a line – maybe she wants to bring him down, get him out of the picture and walk off into the sunset with her tennis instructor and Fitzwilliam's hard-embezzled cash. Or else he's nominated her as a director without her knowledge, to keep the heat off him. Which sounds more likely to you?'

Shrugging, Bev bit her lip. 'I think she's straight. But my ex took me to the cleaners, I just don't trust anyone.'

There was that hurt expression on his face again. A tautness in his features. Narrowed eyes. Surely he wasn't going to cry.

'I trust *you*, like,' she added. 'Obviously.'

'Do you?' He snatched up a sponge stress ball and started to squeeze it until the skin covering his knuckles bleached out. 'Is that why you didn't tell me you're a sex addict?' Clicking his mouse, he started to run the shaky, muffled footage from the X-S Club. There was a glimpse of Phillipe d'O, grabbing her crotch. There were the other members, screwing in the hallway. There was a tiny man being fellated by a giant of a woman. The film sputtered out when her handbag and clothes were finally stashed in the cloakroom, but not before the camera had caught a brief shot of her, topless and grinning.

'I've told you. My private life has nothing to do with you.'

'You're ill and you've not told Mo about this. This is way more than an origami habit, Bev! For Christ's sake! You could get murdered. Is this why Rob ditched you?'

But Bev was not going to engage with this intrusive crap. 'Show me what you've got from the dinner date. Have I got enough to show to Angie? I don't want to have to go through that again with her sleaze of a husband.'

'Are you going to ignore me?' Doc asked, scrolling backwards to footage of the private room in the fine-dining establishment.

Balling her fist, grinding her teeth, Bev wrestled with her emotions. Indignant outrage; guilt; the need to confess.

'Rob didn't ditch me because of anything *I* did, you twat.' Her angry words tumbled from her mouth like speeding molten lava. 'Don't pass judgement on something you know nothing about.' She poked her friend hard in his pigeon chest, watching him deflate as though he'd been punctured by her touch. 'I've had my entire world destroyed by my shit of an ex, right? Like gaslighting and controlling me for years wasn't enough! He stole everything from me. *Everything!* And ever since, he's been blowing my hard-earned cash on cheap slags and living high off the hog.' She thought, then, about Jerry Fitzwilliam's hog-like features and found she was shaking with anger; choking back tears, not just for herself but for Angie Fitzwilliam and all other wronged women. 'I didn't feel strong enough to fight. All I could do was accept my fate for the time being. Crawl under a stone and hope, over time, I could lick my wounds, regroup, come back at him when I've sorted myself out. The only means of survival I had left after he'd ruined me were these two hands.' She held her hands aloft. Pointed to her head. 'This brain, and the ability to graft. But even then my options are limited, because of what he did. I can't go back to a marketing director's salary and perks. He had me blackballed. So, now I'm a two-star budget PI. I'm struggling to stay afloat because the man I trusted most robbed all my money *and* my reputation, and took from me the one beautiful, precious thing in my life that I thought was mine unconditionally. So don't lecture me about my behaviour. Whatever I've done, Rob's done far worse.'

Doc was all awkward arms and legs, folded into his typing chair. His lips were trembling and almost pale blue, as though he were allergic to conflict. It didn't stop him, though. 'You lied to me.'

'I didn't lie. I was economical with the truth. It's *my* business and mine alone what I do when the sun goes down. I don't need a father, James Shufflebotham. One was enough. I'm a big girl now. So how about you keep your well-meaning neb out of my shit and just show me that footage from the restaurant? The sooner we give Angie what she needs, the sooner we both get paid.'

Doc pressed play on the filmed evidence. As she watched, Bev's own discomfort was instantly forgotten. In tampering with her handbag, Jerry had inadvertently knocked the recording equipment so that the sound was muffled and the camera had only recorded great shots of the empty chaise longue. She felt the blood drain from her lips, leaving them prickling with ill portent. 'I don't believe it. We've got nothing. I'm gonna have to meet him again.'

'Listen. You're on your own, now,' Doc said, holding his hands up. 'This guy's too well-connected for my liking. I'm not saying I don't need the money, but you can't even pay me more than twenty at a time.'

'Hey! I'm giving you what I can, when I can, right? I've got to cover the travel to London. I need to eat! Twenty's all I can manage for now. Angie promised there'll be cash. If they're as loaded as that Coutts account suggests, she'll be able to pay, once she's got her hands on it.'

'Yeah. Right. Assuming the cops don't freeze their assets. And it's not just about the money. I've got a criminal record, Bev. If Fitzwilliam gets wind that I'm hacking his shit, what's the bet I'll get my collar felt? I'll go down. Imagine what all those meatheads in prison will do to a streak of piss like me. They'll eat me for breakfast! Imagine what my arsehole folks will say!'

'Please, Doc!' Bev could see her opportunity to pay off her credit card debts and settle the mounting bills slipping away with every word that came from her friend's downturned mouth.

He merely shook his head. 'Sorry. I'm out.'

CHAPTER 16
Doc

The knocking on his front door was insistent. But not the pounding he would expect if it were bad news or heavies in the employ of Jerry Fitzwilliam, waiting to chop his hacking fingers off. Doc looked through the spyhole, his heart a-flutter, and opened the door. Bev was standing before him, carrying a box.

She pushed past him, advancing down the hall and into his living room. 'Get a brew on and get the Jaffa Cakes out. You're gonna need sustenance when you see this.'

Pulling his bedroom door shut, praying she hadn't seen the mess, he called out after her. 'You've been dodging my calls for three bloody days. I thought you were sulking because I said I wouldn't do any more snooping. Now you show up all Mrs Chirpy? You been off on a sex-bender again?'

'Shut your face, Doc. I was sourcing something.' Bev sat on the sagging sofa. Pushed the computer magazines and marijuana paraphernalia on his coffee table aside, laying the box down reverentially. It was wrapped in brown paper. 'If this doesn't convince you of my good intentions, I don't know what will.' That smile was still there.

With a tingle of anticipation, Doc took a seat next to her, staring at the package.

'Go on,' she said.

Frowning, Doc's nimble fingers made short shrift of the poorly wrapped gift. But it didn't matter that it hadn't been expertly presented with bows and ribbons. He gasped, feeling suddenly light-headed. He could feel an asthma attack coming on. Rifled through the mess for his inhaler and took a sharp toot on the Ventolin. 'Oh my God. Oh. My. God.' Gazing at the image of Star Wars' Darth Maul – head and neck, rendered faithfully in black and red Lego on the cover of the box, complete with tribal Sith markings and horns. 'This is the motherlode of all Star Wars Lego, man. Do you realise that? I mean . . .' He opened and closed his mouth several times, trying to find the words. Savouring the endorphins that rushed around his body, making him feel like a King of Men, or at least, he acknowledged, a Lord Among Dorks. 'How the hell did you afford this? I thought you were stony broke. This is, like—'

'Sophie and Tim can wait for their rent,' Bev said, sinking back into the sofa's squishy cushions. 'I whacked in an invoice for some work I've been doing for my old boss and asked him to push through payment. It's my way of investing in this case. Speculating to accumulate, and all that. Investing in me and you.' She nudged him and winked. 'Was I on the money, then?'

Doc put his hand over his mouth, grinning beneath it. 'A Darth Maul bust. An actual limited edition, rare-as-fuck Darth Maul bust. Jesus. You've just given a Lego addict the equivalent of a junkie getting the keys to a Colombian coke lab. You're the bomb, Bev.' He desperately wanted to lean in and kiss her on the cheek for this literally breathtaking show of generosity. But, of course, he never would. And as he studied the light that shone in her eyes, he privately admitted that she hadn't even needed to bribe him. He would have relented in the end, he knew, simply because he wanted more than anything to make Bev happy. He would never have let her tread a dangerous path alone. But, of course, he'd never tell her any of these things because Bev wore knackered old trainers and jeans for him, not stilettos and a tight skirt.

'Now, will you please hack that bastard's cloud? I had a rendezvous with her in Altrincham Aldi. Angie, I mean,' Bev continued. 'She had fresh bruising on her back, Doc. He'd punched her in the—'

'Yeah, yeah.' Taking another shot from his inhaler, Doc imagined Bev taking this rare Lego kit he'd coveted for years away from him, along with her friendship. He couldn't let either of those things happen. He held his hands up. Itching to get started on those polythene bags full of black and red bricks. 'Whatever, man. I'll do it.'

Three hours later, when his legs and bottom had gone quite numb and he'd smoked his way through three strong joints, he realised he was desperate for a pee, something to eat and a break from his new obsession. Doc sat at his desk with a party-sized bottle of Dandelion and Burdock and a cold Cornish pasty. Feeling that it would be worth every night spent sleeping in a cell if he got caught, providing he could keep his new Lego prize, he started to reach through his keyboard into the secret back alleys of the information superhighway. The firewalls of Jerry Fitzwilliam's internet provider were flame retardant to the uninitiated, but Doc was no hacking virgin.

By the time he'd finished his pasty, two bags of Quavers and a packet of Maltesers for pudding, he'd accessed Fitzwilliam's entire electronic world – or at least, the world contained on his laptop and home computer, connected to the cloud.

As he downloaded every email exchange, every photo, every document and spreadsheet onto a USB hard drive plugged into his own machine, he sang at the top of his voice about blazing torches and sacred chants, as the hordes worshipped the beast. Iron Maiden's finest moment perfectly described this desk-based IT triumph.

'666 . . .' Heavy metal fingers bent into devil's horns, Doc told the screen that he had the fire, the force and the power to make his evil—

'Fuck! No!'

Just as he removed the USB stick from his machine's port, his screen started to flash in bright shades of neon, showing strings of corrupted code spooling ever down, down, down. Symbols. Letters. Worse than the number of the beast.

'Shit!' Switching his machine off, Doc panted heavily, feeling the warmth drain from his face. Switched it back on again, praying for a normal reboot. But there was the code, still whizzing down his screen. Lights flashing.

He unplugged his machine from the wall, staring at the keyboard as though an assassin had doused it liberally with anthrax.

Throwing clothes into a rucksack, he pinned his phone between his shoulder and ear. 'Pick up for Christ's sake.'

Bev answered just before her voicemail message kicked in. All bright and breezy and, 'How's it going, partner?'

'I'm in deep shit, Bev. Shut up and listen. I've just hacked Fitzwilliam's cloud. He has malware installed on his devices that are designed to infect anybody hacking his shiz. Don't ask me how. It's beyond even me how he's bypassed the cloud. I'm guessing this is some high-level spy-type crap.' He was struggling to breathe. Feeling light-headed again. Where was his inhaler?

'Slow down, Doc. Have you been smoking too much?'

'Nah, man. I'm outa here. I bet they're tapping this bloody phone already.' He could hear his own voice, amping up into hyperdrive; rattling the words off as fast as they popped into his head. 'Be careful, Bev.'

Ending the call, after explaining to her he'd send the USB, he broke apart his phone and destroyed the SIM card in his microwave. The last things he packed into a separate holdall were the Darth Maul kit, a bag of home-grown and his limited edition vinyl pressing of Iron Maiden's *Killers*. Even his favourite Slipknot CDs were surplus to requirement. *Some MI6 ninja could kick down the door at any moment. Come on, Doc! Get a wriggle on, man.*

Before he headed off to hitch the first ride he could get down the M6, hoping to make it to his folks' place in the home-counties cultural dust bowl of Chalfont St Giles, he placed the USB hard drive into a Jiffy bag and addressed the package to Bev. Placing every stamp he had in his wallet on the front, praying it would be virus-free and would get to her – providing her post wasn't being intercepted and read – he slid the package into the postbox at the end of the street. Looked up, to see if there were any CCTV cameras in sight.

'Oh, you're kidding,' he said, gazing into the lens of one that was hanging from the nearest lamp post. It seemed to be focused directly on him.

Sirens wailed on the air, suddenly, coming swiftly closer. Were they coming for him? He started to walk briskly in the direction of Washway Road, where he might find an accommodating van driver heading south, via the M60.

Sticking out his thumb. Heart pounding. Chest tightening.

The police cars came into view. Swung a right into the main road, blues and twos flashing. A dizzying din. And they were speeding straight for him.

CHAPTER 17
Boo

'*I'm* moody?' Mitch said, slamming down his pint so that his stout sloshed out, drowning the cardboard coaster beneath. '*Difficult?* Are you kidding me?' He angled his body away from her. Pointedly looked through the window at the view of the river and the castle above. 'How is adoring you difficult behaviour?'

Though she didn't even have a hangover, Boo's head throbbed. And the lime and soda wasn't quelling the constant waves of nausea, exacerbated by the pub's smell of second-hand alcohol and roast dinners.

'Look, I didn't mean to insult you.' She reached over to rub his upper arm in a show of contrition. Wishing she could unsay those accusatory words. Hating herself for managing this badly.

He jerked his arm away. Still staring up at the castle. 'Well, you're doing a good enough job. First you accuse me of eyeballing those girls at the bar, when I clearly wasn't. Now, I'm moody and difficult.' Finally, he turned to her with glassy eyes. 'That cuts me to the core, when all I want to do is make you happy.'

'I'm sorry,' Boo said, feeling like an old car, jammed in reverse. Her frustration came unstuck all of a sudden. A defensive barrage shooting past her inner censor. 'But

I saw you smiling at the blonde one, for fuck's sake. You winked at her!'

'I didn't. You imagined it.'

'Come on, Mitch. You did! You were leering at her legs.'

He rubbed her arm and smiled at her hopefully, like a puppy dog wanting to regain the trust of its owner. 'The only legs I have eyes for are yours, Boo Boo. I'm so sorry if you're unhappy. That's the last thing I want for you.' He took a swig from his stout. Already on his third pint with sobriety several hours away. 'But it makes me sad that you've called me a liar.'

Boo started to breathe faster to match the pace of her pulse. Cortisol rapidly chilling the blood in her veins. She felt suddenly light-headed. Clenched and unclenched her hands, trying to stop her fingertips from prickling. Why did this have to happen now? Like things weren't stressful enough.

Stand up to him, she counselled herself. *He can't keep pulling this stunt.* And yet, the enormity of her situation loomed large in the forefront of her overburdened mind. She wanted to yell, 'You *are* a difficult, moody bastard and you *were* giving her the eye, right in front of me. You're full of crap and you're suffocating me.' But instead, Boo simply said, 'I'm sorry. I know you're not a liar. Of course I know. Look, I am really really sorry. OK?' She put her hand on his, knowing she had to break the news and break it fast. Maybe a shock like that would put paid to this bickering.

He pulled his hand away. 'You make me feel bad, Boo. You can be so cruel. And all I want to do is—'

'Love me. Right. Yeah. Listen, Mitch.' *Here I go. Come on, Boo. Spit it out.* 'I'm pregnant.'

Mitch's face crumpled up into a quizzical frown. 'What?' He was looking so directly at her now, his gaze seemed to penetrate skin and bone to find her soul beneath. 'How?'

She shrugged. 'Happy accident.'

Would he buy it?

Boo cast her mind back to the one-night stand with the rugger bugger from the college bar. What was his name? Had his eyes been brown or blue? It had hardly mattered at the time. He'd bought her a drink. They'd chatted briefly about themselves, revealing that they'd had nothing in common whatsoever beyond a shared love of an HBO cop series. She'd known that the rugger bugger had been all wrong for her, but she'd seen him weeks earlier when she'd been orientating herself in her new academic home-from-home. A fresher like her, he'd been clutching his kettle in his doorway, on a corridor that was as far away from her own room as she could get. Away from Mitch.

Sitting in the pub now, overlooking the river, Boo felt heat in her cheeks as she recalled that, what had begun as a fun grapple on the guy's bed, as she'd been coming down from acid, had quickly turned into something more sinister. Overwhelmed by his sheer bulk, the strange chemical smell emanating from his pores and the realisation that she hadn't wanted sex, even in exchange for safety from Mitch in the throes of a bad trip, she'd said no. No, I'm sorry. No, I've changed my mind. But her conquest hadn't seemed to hear her. He'd pressed on – not violent, per se, but still forcing himself on her, apparently oblivious to her protestations or lack of desire. She'd fallen silent once he'd prized her legs apart and entered her. In any case, it had seemed pointless, given her size, to fight against a giant like that. Staring at the ceiling, Boo had heard her mother berating her, loud enough to be standing in a corner of that room, watching. *You should be flattered that a feller like that should want a girl like you. You always were ungrateful.* Or had that just been the LSD-fallout talking?

Five minutes of Boo gritting her teeth and it had all been over. She'd lain in whatever-his-name-was's bed until 5 a.m., unable to find sleep as he'd snored beside her.

Having decided that Mitch would have crawled back to his own hole by that time, she'd dressed hastily and fled back to her room. Only realising once she'd burrowed inside her poorly made bed that she had no memory of the rugger bugger having used a condom. Damn it.

As Boo sat there, waiting for Mitch's reaction to the news, she admitted to herself that she'd failed to take the morning-after pill because she'd wanted this baby. She'd wanted a fresh start and someone to love unconditionally, no matter who his or her father might be. It was a need that now consumed all the other ambitions she had harboured at the start of her university life.

After an agonising minute, Mitch's look of utter confusion gave way to a timorous smile, like the morning sun daring to peak through the night's heavy storm clouds as dawn broke. He swaddled her in an embrace, their conflict instantly forgotten. Hot tears leaking onto her neck as he held her tight.

'Oh, that's amazing, Boo. Amazing. Christ. I'm gonna be a dad. I'm the happiest man alive.'

They parted momentarily. Boo felt relief and abject terror curdle inside her abdomen, as though the foetus growing within was now the epicentre of her gut feelings. Mitch was bad for her. Mitch made her feel alive. Mitch was the making of her. Mitch was her ruination and downfall.

'Will you marry me, Boo?'

The following weekend, Boo returned to her parents' house. Dreading breaking the news to them that their eighteen-year-old only child was up the duff and engaged to a hedonist whom she loved and feared in equal measure.

The train slowed, grinding and squealing its way past derelict factories, lumber yards and part-worn tyre warehouses. These gave way to the blackened red-brick walls of a neglected station, in the one-eyed hole of a town Boo called home.

She disembarked, lugging her case onto the platform, wishing that her pregnancy was already showing enough to arouse sympathy in the male travellers who might offer to help. No such luck only a month in. Beyond swollen ankles and constant nausea, Boo looked the same as ever. Whey-faced and poorly dressed in Primark jeans that would no longer fasten and a bobbled old black coat from Top Shop that just about fastened across her chest.

Hastening to the taxi rank, she watched her fellow travellers being collected at the main entrance by enthusiastic relatives and friends.

'Thirty-eight Milltown Street please, and can you give us a lift putting my case in the boot? I'm pregnant.' It was the first time she'd told anyone apart from Mitch. Now she'd confessed her deepest secret to a taxi driver whose ID badge declared he was Aleksander.

Aleksander looked her up and down, making silent judgements, of course. Under different circumstances, Boo might have found him attractive, with his Eastern European high cheekbones and green eyes. But it was all she could do to stop herself from vomiting in the back of his old Mazda.

Home looked the same as ever. A two-up-two down on a gardenless street, where the neighbours who worked in factories, on building sites, in supermarkets couldn't quite fathom how a nice, quiet tiler like Boo's father had come to be with a loud, drunk woman who said she was an artist and who spoke, 'with plums in her gob'. As ever, a dreamcatcher was visible in the lounge window and the retro floral curtains were wonkily drawn in the main bedroom above.

Left alone on the doorstep, Boo slipped her key in the lock and opened the door to the smell of turps, oil paint and cigarette smoke. No welcoming committee for her. No, 'Boo, darling! Come in and I'll get the kettle on. We've missed you so much.' That sort of reception was for other girls.

'Hello?' she shouted.

No response. Though she knew there was somebody home because she could hear the familiar dash-dash-smush sound of her mother's paintbrush, daubing a canvas in the back room.

Standing in the middle of the shabby, hippy-trail throwback of a through-lounge, wondering how long it would take her to realise her daughter had arrived, Boo watched the old lady at work. Dressed in paint-smudged overalls, her bleached hair, yellowed with nicotine and scraped into a high ponytail, she was clutching a palette in her left hand, stabbing colour onto a large canvas with a long brush held in her right. How did she not see Boo, standing there? Her easel had been placed against the neighbouring wall, meaning the front lounge was certainly in her peripheral vision. How the hell did you not notice a five-foot-three girl enter the room?

No need to ponder further. Boo spied a tray on the sideboard, sporting a half-empty bottle of budget vodka and a full glass, smudged with greasy-looking turpentine fingerprints and a waxy neon pink lipstick mouth-mark. It was only two in the afternoon. The first half of the bottle would have been breakfast. The Olympic-standard lush was drunk, as usual, or perhaps simply winding her daughter up. Hadn't Boo texted from the station? Announced her arrival as she'd opened the door? And yet, her mother painted on, seemingly oblivious to anything beyond her own tiny world, there in the back lounge, in the space she liked to call her, 'atelier'.

'Oh, there you are!' Finally, the old cow turned around, brush in hand. She opted to snatch up her V&T, rather than offer Boo an embrace. Of course. 'Get the kettle on.' Her bleary eyes were devoid of warmth. Her lips, thinned to a pruned pink line where the neon pink pigment of her lipstick had feathered upwards onto the crepe of her skin. 'Your dad's not had a drink since breakfast. We don't want him dehydrating, do we?'

At that moment, Boo knew she'd made a mistake coming home. The rest and solace she sought would not be found here. Not in her mother. But perhaps in Dad, if he was speaking . . .

Carrying a mug of strong tea upstairs, Boo could already smell the bedroom where her dad had been holed up for weeks, according to her mother. Stale breath. Unwashed body in bedding that hadn't seen the washing machine for a month. Poor ventilation. The cowbag's caring ministrations were clearly almost non-existent.

'Hey, Dad. I'm home. I've brought you a cuppa.'

The loud floral curtains let little light in beyond an orangey glow. Boo could see her father's dark hair peeking out above the duvet. Bottles of his medication next to the bed. Was he asleep?

She set the tea down. 'Dad,' she said, sitting on the edge of the bed and cupping his shoulder gently. He was wearing the same old U2 T-shirt he'd been wearing when she'd left for the start of the new term. She leaned over. Kissed his stubbled cheek. 'It's me. Boo.'

As he opened his eyes slowly, she saw a sharpness in his focus that said he'd not been taking the meds. He smiled. Stirred beneath the bedclothes and shuffled into a sitting position, 'Oh, it's smashing to see you, love. I have missed you.' His voice sounded hoarse from disuse. He held his arms out. 'I know I pong, but come and give your old Dad a hug.'

It was exactly what Boo needed. She allowed him to wrap her in his strong, hairy arms, only holding her breath slightly against his sweaty odour. The tears started to flow immediately as she let out all the tension that had accrued over the past few weeks. The break-up. The make-up. The drugged-up, boozed-up bust-up. Getting knocked-up. She told him everything, apart from the details of her sort-of date rape. Then, she told him about the baby.

'You're kidding?' he said, sipping his tea. His hazel eyes looking even wider than usual behind the thick lenses of his tortoiseshell glasses. 'A baby? How far along are you? Is it a boy or a girl? Jesus, Boo!'

Pulling a tissue from the box at the side of the bed, Boo dried her eyes. 'I won't know for ages, Dad. It's still very early days.'

'Are you going to keep it?' He blinked fast. Dark shadows beneath his eyes meant he'd slept little, despite his refusing to get out of bed for weeks. How long had he been off the meds?

'Yep. I don't know how I'll manage with uni and that.'

He squeezed her hand. 'We'll make it work, kiddo. Daddy's here for his little Boo Boo no matter what scrapes she gets into. We're a team, me and you. Right?'

'You bet.'

She nestled against her father's warm body, no different to the way they'd snuggled when she'd been a small girl.

'What do you think?' she asked after a while, looking up at his bristled face.

He peered down at her, smiling properly so that his crow's feet crinkled up. She hadn't seen that in a long, long while.

'I think it's smashing, love,' he said, treating her to a gap-toothed grin, then. 'A baby in the family. Fancy that! It's grand.'

That night, despite sharing a soul-destroying Chinese takeout with her mother downstairs, listening to the witch talk incessantly about herself, when she wasn't admonishing Boo for being a 'dozy tart' for getting knocked-up, Boo slept deeply in her childhood bed. Knowing Dad was on her side was exactly what she'd wished for. Perhaps having a grandchild to fuss over would pull him out of his funk of despair once and for all.

She revisited her childhood in her dreams – a time when her father had been happy. A master tiler, working to build his own business; providing. Always available to talk to or play with, thanks to starting work at the crack of dawn and finishing early. He'd had self-respect and a goal in life. He'd always been the one to give a shit.

On waking, Boo sprang out of bed, patting her stomach. 'It's all gonna be smashing, babba,' she told her stomach. 'Dad's going to get well and I'll marry Mitch and fatherhood will straighten the bugger out. We'll be fine. Maybe I'll be able to stay at college too. Take you with me to lectures.'

Sensing from the silence below that she was the first one up, she crept downstairs, ravenously hungry for breakfast.

Her father's feet were the first thing she saw from the stairs, swinging round from back to front. Then, as she descended slowly, barely able to breathe, with icy dread all but paralysing her, she saw his legs, clad in tartan pyjama bottoms. Finally, standing in the doorway to the lounge, she beheld the horror of it all. Noticed the overturned chair beneath the body of her beloved father. Already grey-skinned, he hung limply from a complex rig-up of electrical cable. He'd somehow strung it around the supporting wooden beam that bisected the through-lounge. A white envelope perched centrally on the mantelpiece with 'Boo' written on the front in his distinctive capitals.

Her champion, her best friend, the only parent she'd ever loved, was gone.

CHAPTER 18

Bev

'It's all lies!' Bev shouted, waking herself up from the too vivid dream – a recurring nightmare of her dismissal at BelNutrive, where each time, she faced the board of directors wearing only her oversized period knickers and a bobble hat.

Wiping the drool from her mouth, she rubbed her head where it had been uncomfortably pressed against the chilly car window, for the best part of . . . She checked her watch . . .

'Five hours?! Oh, you're kidding me.'

She wiped the fogged up windows, struggling to see clearly the suburban 1930s semi she'd followed Jerry Fitzwilliam to. Bev smacked her lips. Adjusted the red wig that now hung crookedly over her left eye, as though it too had fallen asleep unexpectedly. Desperate for coffee and the toilet. She checked her scribblings in her notebook to see if she'd been hit by the genius stick at some point during the previous evening and tried to reconstruct the night's events:

During the late afternoon, Angie had texted her to say her husband had finally returned home from London. Bev had followed Fitzwilliam from the family home to the nerve centre of his Cheshire seat – an office above a health charity's second-hand furniture shop.

The shadow Science Minister had then left his campaign HQ in the early evening and headed north to what appeared to be the most boring street in Stockport, lined with uniform, well-kept red-brick houses. What had he been doing there? Who owned this house with its anonymous-looking venetian blinds and the overgrown bamboo in the front garden?

Got mistress?

That was all she'd written about the case, as she'd sat in the courtesy car on her stakeout. The rest was first-draft copy she'd penned for her new freelance marketing gig – four pages of heart-rending text for the charity's new annual report. She'd have to present it, along with visuals she'd commissioned, to Graham and his fundraising director when she was next in London. Hardly useful for the task currently in hand.

'Oh, Bev, Bev, Bev, you dopey-arsed tool!'

If Jerry Fitzwilliam had appeared at the semi's front bedroom window at any point during the night, in a clandestine clinch with some mistress, she'd completely missed it. *And* the opportunity to collect photographic evidence of his inability to keep his winkie in his Saville Row trousers. Had he left already? Walked or driven past and spotted her? Surely even if he had, he wouldn't have recognised her in the wig, slouched in the driver's seat of a fogged-up turd-brown Ford Fiesta. Especially not with her face well-scrubbed of any make-up.

She examined her reflection in the vanity mirror inset into the car's sun visor. Wiped her hands along her sallow cheeks, noting the dark circles beneath her eyes and the parallel furrows that had visibly deepened in her forehead, of late. 'What a mess. You look a million years old. But at least you look nothing like Cat Thomson.'

Shivering, she realised it was time to go home, where a hot shower and some breakfast beckoned. She pulled off the wig and scratched at her scalp, sighing. Yawning. Deepening those furrows on her forehead as she frowned. Two days had passed and Doc's phone was still out of order. Concern had started to niggle away at the back of her mind. The Jiffy bag he had promised was on its way had not shown up yet. Was it possible her post *was* being intercepted?

Hitting the M60, the landscape changed. Bev was glad to leave the cramped, steeply inclined streets of Stockport behind, with those hulking, sulking disused brick mills on the horizon that bore neglected, crumbling testament to the town's industrial past. She sped past the car dealerships and signs for Cheadle, turning onto the M56 that took her past the promise of the airport and the threat of Wythenshawe. Home. Not her own home, but it would do.

Pulling onto the drive, Bev caught sight of the postman in the distance in his hi-vis bib, carrying his red satchel down the street. *Is he coming or going? Has Doc's package showed up?* She climbed out of the car, grunting as she straightened up. The stiff muscles in her legs screaming.

'Out again?' Sophie asked.

Bev started and let out a small shriek. Clutched at her chest. Tittered nervously. 'Jesus, Soph. You gave me a fright. Where the hell did you come from?' She'd not noticed her friend and landlady, crouching in the flower bed that bordered the driveway, with a potted petunia plant in her hand. Next to it was a tray of identical brightly coloured plants.

Sophie pointed to the tray. 'An impulse purchase.'

'I thought you had a gardener,' Bev said.

'They're so colourful. I couldn't resist.' Sophie stood, stripped off her gardening gloves and brushed the non-existent soil from her pale pink cropped trousers. 'Tim's taken the children to the park and the weather's divine, so . . .'

'Divine, is it? I'm frozen to the marrow.' *Nobody gardens in pastel trousers,* Bev thought. *Is she seriously wearing Prada trainers?*

'Actually, you look like you're the one who's been gardening,' Sophie said, chuckling. Pointing at the coffee and chocolate stains on Bev's jeans.

'Stains come with the job,' Bev said, suppressing the urge to grimace at her friend.

'Shall I make us a coffee?' Sophie asked, untying her ponytail and pinning her blonde locks into a high bun. 'You still haven't told me where you went all dolled up the other night.'

But Bev switched off Sophie's gossip-hunting the moment she heard next door's letterbox squeak open and clatter shut. She spied the postman's head bobbing up and down beyond the bushes. He was moving towards them. Striding along the gravel driveway with his back bowed against the weight of his bulging red satchel.

'Morning, love! Got anything for me?' Bev asked. 'Basement flat.'

'Sorry, cocker. Not today.' He handed a sheaf of letters to Sophie.

'I'm expecting a package though. My mate posted it four days ago, first class. I should have had it by now.'

Rummaging inside his satchel, the postie shook his head. 'There's nowt else in here for you.' His eyes narrowed. 'I delivered a package yesterday, though. Basement flat. Wasn't that what you're waiting for?'

Bev frowned. 'Package? What package?'

The postie inclined his head towards Sophie. 'I gave it your flatmate.' He shrugged. 'Ta-ra!'

He loped quickly away leaving Bev alone with Sophie. 'You took in a package for me and didn't say anything?' She ground her molars together.

Sophie's porcelain complexion had flushed pink. 'I-it's in the kitchen. Sorry. I completely forgot.' Biting her lip. Blinking too fast.

'Do you think you might give it me? Now!'

Bev followed her friend up the steps to the main house and into the kitchen, where Sophie pulled a small Jiffy bag from her 'To Do' basket full of bills, business cards for workmen, school letters and other family-logistics-detritus. Snatching the small mustard-coloured padded pack from her, Bev saw that Doc's scrawl was on the front, together with far too many stamps.

She turned the packet over, spying the poorly stuck flap. 'You've opened this.' It was a statement, rather than a question. Sophie's reddened face told Bev all she needed to know. 'You opened my bloody post and didn't even have the good grace to pass it on?!'

Sophie turned away and poured coffee beans into the Gaggia machine. 'I'm sorry,' she said in a small voice. 'I thought it was for me.'

'Bullshit!' Bev thumped the marble worktop of the kitchen island. 'It's got Beverley Saunders written in giant capitals on the front, marked, "Private and Confidential". How can you stand there and tell me you thought it was for you? Admit it, you're nosing into my shit!'

But her friend still faced the gleaming glass splashback. 'I am not.'

'At least turn around when you're lying to me, Sophie! Look me in the eye and tell me you haven't been in my flat. You've had my origami crane, haven't you?'

Her friend was staring at her, finally, a hurt expression

puckering up her beautiful face. Incomprehension in the tightness around her eyes. 'I *haven't* been in your flat.' Shook her head. 'No way! Not without your invitation. I never have, I swear. And I haven't got your origami . . . thing. I admit, I did open your package *in error* and I'm sorry.' She folded her slender arms tightly. 'Forgetting to pass it on to you was a simple oversight and I apologise.'

'Liar!'

'Oh, that's nice! I offer you a home and a fresh start and bring paid work to your door, and this is what I get in thanks? Verbal abuse!'

The tears standing suddenly in Sophie's eyes took Bev aback. What was this nonsense?

'Stop crying!' she said, steeling herself not to put an arm around her friend, who was clearly vying for the sympathy vote in a bid to avoid Bev's further castigation. 'I overreacted. I believe you. OK?'

Sophie dabbed at her eyes with a piece of kitchen roll. 'It's bad enough having to keep secrets from Tim. He'd go spare if he thought I was helping Angie to leave his best friend. He'd see it as a betrayal of Jerry, and Tim's got very strong opinions on divorce. He's never got over his own parents' acrimonious split.' She whispered conspiratorially to Bev, 'My father-in-law was a terrible husband, by all accounts. And I mean, *terrible*!' Wide eyes implied a raft of the worst kind of marital misdemeanours.

Bev glimpsed the USB stick inside her packet. She decided that she really didn't need to stand in her friend-cum-landlady's designer kitchen, listening to how badly done-to poor old Timbo was and how wronged Sophie was feeling. 'Can we do this later, Soph? I've got work I need to be getting on with.'

'But your coffee!'

'Later. And don't even try to pump me for information about Angie's case. She's a client. Confidentiality and all that.'

'I'm not!'

'OK. Well, stop opening my post, then.'

Quickly descending the steep stone steps that led from the period splendour of the family home above to the cold, utilitarian gloom of her flat below, she burst through her front door and took out the stick.

'Bingo.' She held the unobtrusive chunk of plastic and metal before her reverentially, as if it were the Holy Grail. 'Oh, you beauty. Good on you, Doc.'

About to insert the stick into her laptop's USB port, she paused suddenly, wondering if she'd be infected with the same malware as Doc had been. If only the irritating sod was answering his phone. Knowing Doc with his love of a good conspiracy theory and hatred of authority, he'd already destroyed the SIM and his connectivity with it. She didn't even have a landline for his parents either, nor an address, assuming he had gone there.

For as long as it took to make herself a pot of coffee and two slices of toast and Vegemite, she pondered exactly what her laptop might contain that was irreplaceable. Concluded that she didn't really have anything that wasn't backed up. Even the laptop itself could be replaced on the insurance, if she accidentally on purpose dropped a full mug of coffee onto it or knocked it from her dressing table. All of it was expendable – especially if it meant she had the chance to access perhaps all the dirt she'd ever need on a corrupt wife-beating moron like Jerry Fitzwilliam.

'Feel the fear and do it anyway, Bev,' she said, shoving the stick into the port.

Bracing herself to contract a dramatic virtual plague, she was relieved to see nothing happened whatsoever.

143

Either her own anti-virus software had protected her from anything hidden in the stick's contents or the malware had bust its beans on Doc's machine.

'Don't question it, for God's sake.' She downed her scaldingly hot coffee. 'Sometimes the universe just provides, woman.'

And it had. Doc had been right. He'd stolen the map and found the buried treasure. Word files, spreadsheets and, most important of all, emails. At a glance, with a thudding heart, Bev worked out that Jerry also banked with the Halifax and Natwest. He had equity investments coming out of his nose – all legitimate, unless you questioned how an MP on his modest salary could afford to have several million in investments, as well as a mortgage the size of Texas on the family house in Hale.

'Spartacus Holdings, eh?'

Scanning through his emails, she found correspondence not only with Matthew Stephens from Stephens Biotech, but also with several other CEOs of science or engineering companies that were FTSE listed. A little light googling showed that all had been given lucrative government contracts to provide products to the military or else had been awarded enormous amounts of public funding for research projects. In every instance, Fitzwilliam had been the main advocate for them in parliament. But that felt like old news, since Doc had unearthed the Coutts statements. Bev's eye was caught by something else.

To: stan8055@gmail.com
From: jfitzw@yahoo.co.uk
Subject: shopping list
Hey, Stan. Thought I'd send through the list for the
weekend. We need a big bag of sugar and some spring lamb.

144

Make sure the lamb's nice and tender. Maybe two lambs, thinking about it. One of the guys has asked for dark meat. He's in the mood for something different. Deliver to the usual place.

J.

Every few weeks, Jerry had sent an email in a similar vein to somebody called Stan. Each time, he'd ask for sugar. The communiqués would always refer to fresh meat or spring lamb or a tender chicken.

Stan, please make sure the meat you send is as tender as possible. The last lot you sent was on the leathery side and gave us indigestion. Mutton's not my bag. We need nice racks of lamb and a mix of white and dark meat. Preferably plenty of greens.

'Girls,' Bev said. 'He's after underage prostitutes. Virgins, maybe? I bet they're trafficked. Ugh. Scumbag.'

She chewed on her toast, reading how in other emails he asked for Ernie to come along. Was that some euphemism for Ecstasy? The sugar was almost certainly cocaine. With years' of experience of attending the X-S Club and places like it, Bev knew code when she read it.

'You've got a bolthole in London, haven't you, you piece of filth?' she said, scrolling through his grand plans with Stan, the mystery dealer and pimp. Bev struggled to remember if Sophie had said whether or not Tim still owned his pied-à-terre in London that he'd bought together with Jerry, and made a note to quiz her. She also needed to make contact with Angie as soon as possible. Though if her client didn't even know where her husband banked, how likely was it that she'd have laid eyes on the deeds to a secret London pad? It might even be rented

145

through some Westminster civil service department as an MP perk.

The complexities of this damned case felt insurmountable at that moment to an exhausted, dishevelled Bev. More than anything, she wished she had Doc to moan to.

'You're on your own, kiddo,' she told herself, feeling loneliness and loss nibble away at her edges, threatening to devour her completely if her life didn't change soon.

Aware of the tears that stabbed at the backs of her eyes, she was about to close her laptop and head for the shower when she noticed the subject heading on one of the more recent emails to Stan.

Tatjana

It was flagged as high priority. She clicked the message open, feeling curiosity bite.

Stan
You're not answering my calls. What did they do with Tatjana? What happened to the film?
J

Bev had a gnawing feeling in the pit of her stomach. Rereading the words, she felt certain that Jerry Fitzwilliam was keeping an even darker, more ominous secret, and that somewhere, the evidence of it was just waiting to be uncovered.

CHAPTER 19
Angie

'So, Jerry owns a second home in London?' Bev asked, her voice cracking thanks to terrible phone reception. 'Is that where he stays when he's in parliament?'

'No, gosh. You must be joking,' Angie said. 'MPs only get a modest rental allowance nowadays, so he rents a tiny barge on the dock at Surrey Quays. It's an icebox in winter.'

'Jerry. Roughing it on a barge? You're kidding. Have you been there?'

'Once or twice,' Angie said, twirling a pearl on her necklace like a worry bead. She leaned forward, resting her elbows on the work-surface of her kitchen island, keeping her voice as low as possible, lest the children should hear. 'He says he doesn't need distractions while he's working, and to be honest, staying in a cramped, leaky tub is not my idea of minibreak heaven.'

'So, you never visit? It's London!'

'Of course I go down occasionally. Theatre. Shopping. Sightseeing with the children. But we stay at my friends' houses or in a hotel. The barge doesn't sleep more than two.' Angie felt agitation itching away beneath her skin. Glanced at the large clock on the wall. 10.30 a.m. She was running late for her meet with Sophie. 'Even when Jerry was in banking and shared the Clapham flat with Tim, it was the same. Work was work. Home was home. And never the twain shall meet.'

'Did he sell the flat with Tim?'

'Yes. I think so.'

'You think so?'

'Yes. I'm certain. I think.'

'He definitely doesn't own a second property in London, then? Are you absolutely certain? Co-own, maybe, with another old work colleague? Share with other MPs?'

'I told you. No!' she shouted. Then, in a smaller voice, 'No. Not that I know of. Why is this such a big deal? Do you think he owns property I don't know about?'

Bev hesitated on the line so long that Angie checked the bars on her phone to see if the signal had failed again. Finally, she spoke. 'Let's call it a hunch. OK? Can't you just ask him?'

'Don't be ridiculous.'

'You could just drop it into conversation, couldn't you? Especially if he controls the finances. Crack on thick! Say you were watching some housey-housey programme on daytime TV about second homes and casually ask if—'

'He'll smell a rat or think I'm making a pointed comment about his running of the family finances.'

'You're entitled to know if you own a damned flat in London. Ask!'

How the hell could a strident, independent ball-breaker like Bev comprehend what life for Angie was like, being married to a man like Jerry? Bev wouldn't have a clue!

'I daren't.' Angie clutched the phone to her ear, gently stroking a fine scar on her cheekbone. It was where Jerry had punched her in the late stages of her second pregnancy – his response when, bolstered by hormonal courage, she'd

148

demanded to know why he'd returned home one night at 3 a.m. reeking of perfume. That had been the turning point. She had realised then that, if Jerry Fitzwilliam was prepared to knock his pregnant wife to the floor for reasonably asking why he'd missed a booked trip to the cinema, and then gone AWOL for eight hours, she had to get out. The only saving grace had been that he'd paid to have the cut on her cheekbone stitched by a cosmetic surgeon.

The criticism and disbelief were gone from Bev's now-softened tone, thankfully. 'I'm just thinking of you, you know. Jerry's got a lot of money you never even knew about, and at least one company that's registered in your name. I'm assuming you didn't know about that, right? Anyway, it stands to reason that a man like him will have a bit of a property portfolio. I feel it in my water, Angie. If you can find the deeds to a second home, you've got a valuable asset you're entitled to half of, right there. Plus, I'm on my way to the Big Smoke now. I can go to the barge and anywhere else he lays his head. Get me addresses and it's very easy for me to go round and rifle through his paper recycling bin. If his guard is down when he's away from home, who knows what he throws away unwittingly? Deeds, Angie. Go through his filing cabinet again. Just to be sure.'

But Angie already knew that the door to Jerry's office was locked. Moreover, he'd now bolted the window shut from the inside. She was certain he was onto her.

She could ask Sophie. She might be able to help. But Tim was far more likely to know Jerry's secrets. Interrogating Tim was risky, though. Might Jerry have already confided in him that Angie had shown signs of discontent? If she started asking Tim questions, might he somehow intuit she was up to no good? She'd have to be stealthy and act natural. Drop it into conversation. Was she up to a task like that?

Angie stood there, surrounded by glossy magazine domesticity, staring blankly at her children in their corner play area. Poppy was sitting on her padded mat, chewing on a Duplo brick. Benjy was drawing all over the freshly painted walls with pink chalk, determinedly refusing to use his child-sized blackboard. Angie acknowledged silently that she had no control over her marriage, no control over her home and, with Gretchen still on leave, following her demand for an extension of her time off, no control even over her own children. Perhaps it was time to take back ownership of her destiny. Wasn't that why she was planning for a divorce?

Damn right!

Her head reeling, feeling like her legs might give way at any moment, Angie took a seat at the kitchen table and started to apply make-up thickly to cover her scar; the dark circles beneath her eyes from lying in bed at night, unable to find sleep; the ghost of the bruises on her jawbone and neck. Showtime.

The children were safely stowed at the stand-in childminder's. Having inveigled the information from Sophie over coffee that Tim was meeting friends for lunch in Carluccio's, ahead of the big Manchester United v. Liverpool showdown, Angie thundered around the M60 in the Range Rover. She prayed that she'd be able to find him before he disappeared into a seventy-five thousand-strong crowd of excitable football fans, dressed almost identically in red and white.

You can do this, Angie. The more you can help Bev, the better case she'll be able to build. And the sooner you'll be out of this waking nightmare.

More than an agonising forty minutes later, having crawled along with the other traffic bound for Old Trafford, or a hard afternoon's consumerism, she pulled into the car park of the Trafford Centre. It was laid out like a patchwork throw of coloured metal, beneath the blue dome, marble statuary and stucco of this cod-classical shopping mall masterpiece. Despair threatened to erase her resolve like a strong solvent. Would she really be able to find Tim at midday on a Saturday when the rest of the North West had descended on the place for the week's biggest shopping bonanza?

'Carluccio's,' she said, darting between the cars. Walking up the broad steps past the gaudy marble fountain. 'Soph definitely said he'd be in Carluccio's. Think positive, Angie.'

Standing in the gift shop area full of epicurean Italian eats, Angie hid behind some large bags of colourful speciality pasta, peeking through to the main restaurant. It was busier than usual – unsurprising, given there was a big match on down the road in an hour's time. *I need to make it look like a casual coincidence, but Sophie will know I was lying. Damn it. Why am I here? Why couldn't I have just waited?*

'Can I help you, madam?' A voice by her ear.

Angie spun around to see a shiny-faced and enthusiastic assistant.

'No, I'm looking for a friend.'

But Tim was nowhere to be seen. She was on a fool's errand. Might he be eating somewhere else in the vast food court? It was a two-storey space where restaurants from all corners of the world occupied ethnically appropriate stage set after stage set – New Orleans, Chinatown, a French backstreet, downtown Italy. What were the odds of him walking away in one direction as she approached from another? And if she happened upon him, would he mention to his wife and Jerry that he'd seen her?

Ascending the grand, marble staircase, that seemingly couldn't decide if it was deco or neo-classical, passing beneath the giant brass and glass bauble of a Moroccan chandelier, she peered below, scanning the eateries within sight. No Tim at the Tex-Mex or the burger joint. Making her way to the upper storey of the food court, which schizophrenically transformed into the upper deck of a cruise liner, she could spy him neither below, in the seating around the fake pool, nor at her level, which swarmed with Manchester's hungry and irritable.

The longer she searched, the more doubt dogged her steps. *I'll be rousing suspicion if I do find Tim. I can't just blurt out, 'Oh and by the way, do you and Jerry still have that flat and if so, where exactly is it?' And he'll tell Jerry, and it might be the tipping point. Jerry will put me in hospital again and this time, he'll take the children and kick me out of the house and I'll lose everything. And, and, and . . .*

She could barely breathe. The colours swirled around her in a dizzying vortex. The need to pee was suddenly pressing.

Turning to leave, she was just about to mount the escalator down when she spotted her quarry. There Tim was. He'd arrived at Carluccio's while she'd been seeking him elsewhere. Or had he been there all along and she'd simply been looking but not seeing?

From her elevated vantage point, she observed him, wearing a Manchester United top beneath a leather jacket. Sitting at a table, eating pasta. As Sophie had indicated, he was indeed in company. Except he was with not one, but two other men, similarly attired and ready for the match.

And Angie recognised them immediately. One from her trips to the medical centre where she attended therapy for her anorexia and the other from some months ago in Sophie's front garden, when the new female lodger who'd moved into the basement flat had been having a stand-up argument with a man. Tim's companions were Mo, the psychiatrist and a man she'd most recently seen in Aldi – Bev's ex, Rob.

CHAPTER 20
The Wolf

'Can I get you anything else, Sir?' the waitress asks, smiling. She is slender and looks far younger than her probable years. Firm flesh beneath her black uniform.

He smiles. 'Maybe later. Thanks.' Raises an eyebrow. Winks. Tips her a ten. 'For you.'

She stashes the money in the breast pocket of her blouse. Pats her chest. Her outpouring of gratitude is effusive. The evening ahead looks promising. But for now, he is busy with other matters.

It has been the best of days, with the welcome smell of victory in The Wolf's nostrils. He sits at the bar, sipping his fine brandy and demolishing his bowl of nuts, preferring to scroll through the bounty that his phone offers than to admire the views of the glittering urban sprawl many, many storeys below.

He is looking at several PDFs that he has managed to get hold of, showing column inches from old editions of a local newspaper. There are two sorry sob stories, both paired with photographs that feature that perfect bitch, Beverley Saunders. He reads the reports again, savouring the scandal and the pain those catastrophic life events had inevitably caused her. There is no way she can know he has dredged this up. Not yet. But soon, she will.

Breaking into her home has been child's play. Little does the object of his vengeful intentions realise how easy it is to gain access to that squalid little basement flat. He wonders if she's noticed how he has moved her things, just enough to make her doubt her own sanity.

He flicks to another tab where he is researching the logistics of installing internal CCTV without her knowledge. It would be so easy to tamper with her BT landline, sending in a bogus workman who could slip a fibre-optic camera in amongst the books that line the walls. He is The Wolf. He can make this happen. How quickly would she spot anything behind the hundreds of origami models that clutter every surface? How easy would it be to insert a tracking device on the phone that she so stupidly leaves unattended on a regular basis. Watching her over time has revealed much of her weakness and behavioural tics.

The Wolf sips his drink, flicking to the legal documents he also has stored on the phone. Here lies the real dirt. Beverley Saunders is so busy digging into other people's business, he muses. She has no inkling as to who might be compiling a dossier on her to use at a date in the very near future, with dire consequences. 'Know thine enemy and know thyself.' – so said Sun Tzu in *The Art of War*. Well, he knows Beverley Saunders, better than she could ever imagine. And he will have no compunction in spilling her blood, as he spilled the Russian whore's.

'Are you sure I can't get you anything else, Sir?' the waitress asks. 'Only I'm going off shift, now.' Her smile is pleasing and open. It is suggestive of more than just alcohol and bar snacks.

'What are you doing now?' he asks. 'Have you got plans?' He pointedly puts his wallet on the bar.

She seems to be assessing him, rubbing her glossy lips together. Her gaze wanders down to the wallet and clearly, she grasps what's on offer. Her expression alters subtly. Those reddening cheeks are almost certainly flushed with desire. She laughs coquettishly. 'Oh, yeah. No. Sorry. I'm meeting someone.'

He laughs. Wolfishly, of course. 'Yes. Me.' He reaches out to touch her in the same way he's done so many times with girls like her. They always succumb.

But she whips her hand swiftly away, and the smile is gone. Sounding flustered now, she stumbles over her words. 'I'm sorry. You're getting . . . You've got the, er, wrong end of the stick.'

He sips his brandy. Savours the sting at the back of his throat. 'Oh, don't be shy. I don't bite. Let's get out of here. We can party really *hard*.'

She has taken a step back. Holding a bottle opener in her hand like a threat. 'Sir. I'm flattered but I'm not interested. OK? I have a partner.' She pushes the wallet back towards him. 'And even if I didn't, I'm certainly not for sale just because I'm this side of the bar.'

The Wolf holds his hands up, barely able to disguise his mounting annoyance. 'My bad. Enjoy your evening.'

It feels as though flames of wrath are scorching the backs of his eyes. The scent in his nostrils is no longer that of victory but of his prey's fear. Abandoning his drink, he takes the lift down to the foyer and waits in the shadows of the concrete columns and leather sofas, pretending to take a call. The Wolf blends in in this sort of place. It was built to accommodate men of the world, just like him. Life's winners; the leaders of the pack.

Within fifteen minutes, the waitress appears, wearing an ugly anorak and carrying a rucksack. Her jaunty ponytail nods up and down, as if she's tacitly agreeing to what is about to befall her. She exits the skyscraper through the main doors, exchanging pleasantries with the security guards.

'Night!' They hold the door open for him too and he slips outside.

He has anticipated that the waitress's onward journey will involve public transport or a bicycle, given her age and level of income. Silently, as he stalks in her wake, he hopes it will be a cycle, tethered to a lamp post in a deserted back street. Successfully being The Wolf is predicated on knowing how his prey behaves.

He is so focused on the hunt that he trips over something. Looks down to find a homeless man, sitting at the foot of this glorious glass and steel monolith, his legs stuck out at an inconvenient angle.

'Spare change?' the hobo asks, holding his empty disposable coffee cup aloft. His rancid breath steams on the night air. The blanket that covers his legs is filthy and threadbare. At his side, a well-fed Staffordshire Bull Terrier is curled up on the piss-splattered paving slabs. Docile, showing no interest in defending its owner. It too knows The Wolf is top of the food chain.

Annoyed that this loser has slowed his progress, he mutters beneath his breath, 'Get a fucking job.' Circumnavigates the obstacle.

Happily, some way ahead, the waitress hangs a right into a narrow, cobbled side street. This must surely only contain the under-utilised service entrances for grand Victorian office blocks which are empty at this time of night. Perfect. Those places are littered with industrial sized wheelie bins and trash. Easy for The Wolf to hide his kills in.

She disappears from view but he can hear the jangle of keys. He was right. She's unlocking a bike. The distinctive dull rattle of a U-lock being taken apart in the dark.

As he turns the corner, there is only one sputtering street light at the end of the alley. The place where the waitress is bent over, fumbling with her locks, is enshrouded almost entirely in the black of night.

'What do you want?' She has turned her head in his direction, now, perhaps sensing that a predator is in her midst. Her lithe body straightens. She is poised to challenge him.

Good. He likes it this way. He knows Saunders will do the same when it is her turn.

He approaches. Holding the bent portion of the U-lock above her, the waitress strikes him, metal connecting with his jaw. He grabs her with a strong, practised right arm that is used to pinioning and restricting. With his left, he covers her mouth, undeterred by her attempts to bite him.

It is easy to drag her behind a large bin. Her muffled screams abate, giving way to pleas that are impossible to hear through his large, fleshy palms. He can almost taste her tears on the air.

The waitress is frightened and yielding, now. Not even trying to turn around to see his face.

'Do as I say, or I'll squeeze the life out of you. Would you like that?' Though the endorphins and adrenaline have really kicked in now, he keeps his voice even and hushed.

She tries one more time to kick out behind her, but he holds her tight against his body, seeking out her curves with his erect penis.

'If you make a sound, you'll be found in the morning by the cleaners, once the starving pigeons and rats have picked at your eyes. Now, are you going to be a good girl?'

Under cover of such impenetrable darkness – the sort that hides the city's grubbiest secrets – he knows she would never be able to ID him, though she might suspect he is the man from the bar. In this knowledge, with the young girl subdued in his grip, he savagely rips her jeans and pants from her and steals her happiness, her confidence, her plans for the future and her trust in men. It feels as though, in forcing himself upon her, he is absorbing all of her goodness, leaving but a terrorised husk.

This is a perk of being The Wolf.

But the greatest rush comes in knowing that it will be like this with Beverley Saunders. She will be next. And she won't even anticipate from which direction her nemesis is coming.

CHAPTER 21

Bev

'Who's Tatjana?' the woman sitting beside her asked.

Bev turned to her, shrugging off the fog of her reverie. 'Eh?'

They swayed together momentarily as the train traversed a set of points. The woman's ample bottom was encroaching on Bev's allotted space, in a carriage that was still stuffed with sweaty, bored commuters, though their end destination of Beaconsfield was not far now. Unusual for a London worker to make conversation with a stranger during a rush-hour journey.

'You said the name out loud four times,' the woman said, peering at her expectantly. Clutching her shopping bag close against her kagoule-clad bosom.

'Did I?' Bev chuckled nervously. Considered ways to shut her nosy travel companion down. 'Lyrics to a song I had in my head,' she said, pointedly turning to stare out of the window. The train rattled past the suburban Buckinghamshire idyll of Gerrards Cross, made up of outsized family homes and their perfectly manicured gardens. Like Hale, but without the northern honesty of the nouveau-chav footballing set.

As they chugged through the rolling green quilt of the Chilterns, Bev considered her situation. She had a day of exhausting marketing meetings under her belt, briefing

designers for the charity's annual report artwork and inter-
viewing social workers for case studies of their educational
endeavours with vulnerable children to be included in the
report. At least she'd got away fairly early. Now she needed
to make her trip down to the South East count. She still
had to get proof of Jerry's inclination to commit adultery
– enough to make Angie's divorce solicitor clap her hands
in glee and, in turn, make it rain cash for her and her satisfied client. But first she needed to make contact with Doc,
whom she hadn't heard from in a worryingly long time.

As the train slowed for the Beaconsfield approach, she
messaged Jerry Fitzwilliam yet again.

Hi J!
I'm in London til 2morrow. Wanna hook up?
Maybe I want to get my claws into you! ;)
Cat xx

Angie had already told her he was working in London,
though she still hadn't found proof of any property he
might stay at other than his barge. Getting off the train,
all Bev could do now was wait . . . and catch the bus to
Chalfont St Giles.

'Pick up, damn it!' she muttered, trying yet again to
call Doc. But dialling his old phone number yielded a
flatlining out-of-order tone. If he was contactable, he was
almost certainly using a burner, as though the Badlands of
Baltimore had somehow set up camp in that leafy commuter-
belt parish.

'Can you give us a shout when we get to Chalfont St
Giles, please?' she asked the driver as she boarded the 580
towards Uxbridge.

The handful of elderly passengers and commuters on board
stared at her with glum faces, sitting with their feet together

as the bus lurched over potholes. This was no friendly Mancunian free-for-all on the Metrolink tram from town – sharing your life story inside twenty-five minutes with some garrulous drunk from Stretford, who reeked of budget booze and decades spent propping up the bar in Yates's.

With no idea where she was going, she peered out as the bus trundled down the winding road, past hedgerows that hid nothing more than cultivated green fields beyond, wildlife and the odd grand house. The soft South. Memories of her life with Rob, living in Kent, came flooding back: their semi-detached in West Wickham. A functional family home where dysfunction reigned supreme behind closed UPVC doors. No real grasp of who their po-faced neighbours were on either side, though Rob had blamed Bev for their taciturn demeanour towards them.

She missed belonging with all her heart.

She didn't miss being pushed to the brink of mental ill health one iota.

Finally, her end destination came into view. A picture-postcard English village, where the flint church was presumably still well-attended, and where Morris Dancing on the village green during the Month of Maying replaced the rest of Britain's Bank Holiday addiction to Sky Sports and a 24-pack of lager.

Bev alighted, not having a clue where to start in her search. She felt tired, grubby and stupid, mindful of the fact that she didn't actually have anywhere to stay that night – a lack of planning and show of irresponsibility that Mo would question in the next therapy session.

The pub was her first port of call.

'Shufflebotham,' she said, bringing up a photo of Doc on her phone that had been lifted from an old *Manchester Evening News* article from some years ago. Doc in his police mugshot, which had accompanied an article about the Computer Science nerd turned scamming-scoundrel who had been busted for his phishing endeavours and weed farm. 'James Shufflebotham. His folks live round here,' she told the barman that presided over this eclectic mix of ye-olde wooden charm and semi-industrial gastropub style. 'Seen him in here?'

The barman nodded. Ran a hand through his carefully waxed hair. 'Yeah. He's been in here a couple of times with some guys. All look like heavy rock throwbacks. White socks and black trainers. They're hysterical.'

'That's the one,' Bev said, smiling, feeling the tension in her shoulders loosen for the first time in days. 'Know where he lives?'

'Who's asking?' The barman raised an eyebrow. 'Girlfriend?'

'No way!' Bev said, wrinkling her nose. Feeling suddenly like she was standing in the middle of a school playground, playing truth or dare.

The barman wasn't able to tell her where Doc's family home was. But it hadn't taken long to find an elderly local in the know, who was willing to part with the information in return for some help wheeling her laden shopping wagon to her own front door. Bev had admitted that the old lady's bunions looked painful and had absolved her of all guilt for giving the Shufflebotham family up so easily.

Now, she stood before a sprawling 1930s detached, part-timbered home that was as far away from Doc's squalid south-Manchester flat as it was possible to get. She looked down at the scrap of paper the old lady had handed to her. 73, Oak Avenue, written in a shaky leaning hand.

She made her way up the pitted tarmac drive, past an old Mercedes estate car and a knackered Volvo. The house must have been worth a couple of million but had clearly fallen somewhat into disrepair. Breathing deeply to slow her heartbeat, she crossed her fingers. Pressed on the doorbell.

A thin, short-haired woman in her sixties answered. 'Yes, dear?' She treated Bev to a kindly smile. Her eyes were Doc's.

'I'm here to see James. I'm his friend.'

The mother's face lit up, clearly identifying Bev as a girlfriend. 'Of course. You must come in! Come in, dear!'

Bev was ushered past a battered grand piano in the large panelled hall to the front room. She sat awkwardly, perched on the edge of an overstuffed, chintz sofa. Drank in the dusty, fusty smell of decades-old soft furnishings that had been bleached at the edges by the sun and which sported a top note of wet dog. The yellowing paint on the single-glazing had been peeling a good few years, by the looks of it, and the windowsill was a jungle of overgrown spider plants, maidenhair ferns and broad-leaved something or other, giving the room a green tinge. It felt like she was about to be grilled regarding her prospects and her intentions towards Doc, whilst being offered tea in the best china and a side plate of slightly bendy digestive biscuits. Or maybe there would be questions regarding her fertility and willingness to make small Shufflebothams. She shuddered at the thought.

'What the hell are you doing here?' Doc asked, appearing in the doorway. He wore a rictus grin that belied the panic in his eyes, his mother hovering just behind him in the hall. True to his sartorial form, he was clad in drainpipes and a Metallica T.

Bev was transfixed by his pale, bare feet. 'You have abnormally long toes. Do you know that?'

164

Doc's mother pushed him into the living room, all smiles and handwringing and, 'Well, well, well. James has never brought a lady friend home before.' Bev could see Doc squirming. Spying the shiny-eyed fervour in his mother's eyes, she didn't have the heart to put matters straight.

'Me and James have got some stuff to discuss, if that's OK, Mrs Shufflebotham. I'm sorry I came empty-handed. I would have brought flowers or chocs but I've had a long journey from Cheshire.' She was well-behaved Bev, now. The kind of woman who had shot to the top in the cut-throat world of big brand marketing, where likeability was as important as demonstrable skill and results. *Be a Lovely Girl. Don't sit like a builder. Put your hands on your lap and stop slouching.* 'This is kind of off the cuff. I really hope you don't mind.'

Of course Doc's mother didn't mind. Soon, they were ensconced in his attic with the obligatory tea and biscuits on a tray. Alone.

'Fucking hell, man. I'm supposed to be lying low.' Doc flung himself into an old captain's chair at a battered leather-topped desk. Spun around to the right. Spun around to the left. He stood up abruptly, almost hitting his head on the low ceiling. Scanned the world below the small attic window through what appeared to be a pair of stolen theatre binoculars. 'What if you've been followed by Fitzwilliam's feds?'

'You've ditched your phone, haven't you?' Bev asked, thinking that perhaps she'd made a mistake coming all this way out, hoping for her occasional business partner's co-operation and a free bed for the night. She conquered the urge to drag him back down into his seat and force him to look her in the eye. 'I've been trying to get hold of you. This is serious shit, Doc. I read Fitzwilliam's emails.'

Finally, Doc plonked his lanky frame back onto the chair, folding himself into an untenable shape, like human origami, put together by an amateur. He closed his eyes. 'I can't have anything to do with it, Bev. I thought I could step up and be . . . But that bastard killed my computer. I'm crapping my pants, Bev. I'm just biding my time, here, keeping my head down 'til he comes for me.'

'Do me a favour, you big banana,' Bev said, not bothering to hide the ridicule in her voice. 'The barman at the Merlin said you've been down the pub every night for the last week. Lying low? My arse.'

Even in the gloom of the attic, Bev could see her friend and ally colour up. The red in his cheeks was almost the same shade as the stripes on his now fully assembled Lego Darth Maul bust, which took pride of place on the desk.

He pressed his palms over his face. Groaned.

Leaning forward, Bev patted his bony knee. Determined to spare him the details of how some random pensioner had practically led her straight to his mother's front door. 'Cut yourself some slack, will you? I'm a PI ninja. It's my job to track down wily motherfuckers who have gone off grid.'

'Jesus. If I stay here much longer with the loser mates I grew up with, I'm going to vegetate. If I go home, MI6 will be waiting to serve me up a ricin kebab or rig a gas explosion. Either way, I'm a dead man walking. All because I let you drag me into this job!'

Bev ground her molars together. Chewed over her words before she blurted out a string of insults she wouldn't be able to take back. 'I didn't force your hand, Doc. Don't come that crap with me. Anyway, Fitzwilliam's secret service mugs will never come after you. They're just public school boys playing Action Man.'

'Why are you really here, Bev?' His blushes had subsided. His eyes locked with hers.

'I told you. I read Fitzwilliam's emails.' She held her hand up. 'Don't worry. I never got infected by that virus.'

'Whoopdedoo. Lucky you.'

'He's into other shady business with drugs and underage prostitutes from what I can tell. He orders them to a flat in London like pizza . . . from some guy called Stan. A dealer or pimp or both, I guess.'

'Well, that's only going to add weight to your case, isn't it?' Doc relit a half-smoked joint and inhaled deeply, wafting the pungent smoke out of the open window. Coughed. 'Your client can use that to prove he's not a fit father. But I'm guessing you haven't rocked up here because you missed me.'

'I've got a bad feeling,' Bev said, holding her hand out for the joint. Eyeing the Iron Maiden posters and tie-dye Indian wall hangings that covered up the cobweb-strung walls in this time warp of a bedroom. 'In one email, he mentions a prostitute called Tatjana. He asks this Stan what they did with her. He talks about a film.'

'Home-made skin flick with him as the star?' Doc asked.

'I guess so. Only I've googled the name, Tatjana and the word, "prostitute", together with "film" and just got page after page of porn. There must be a million ropey-looking Eastern European actresses out there with lopsided tit-jobs.'

'Porn Hub?'

'Trawled it. I got bupkis. Nada.'

'Maybe you found nothing because there's nothing to find.'

She shook her head vehemently. 'No. I can't explain it. This guy's a seedy bastard, right? He's a bent politician. He's a wife beater. He keeps asking this pimp for "spring lamb". Young girls. So, that means he's a kiddy-fiddler, too. Nope. I've got a horrible feeling a girl's got hurt and gone missing on Fitzwilliam's watch. And there'll be evidence out there on the Dark Net.'

With careful fingers, Doc retrieved the joint from her. His shoulders had already settled from their hunched position. He leaned back in his Captain's chair. Inhaled hard, held his smoke inside, exhaled it in a yellow-blue plume towards the ceiling. His voice buckled with the heat. 'But you're not getting paid to solve a missing person case. How come you care about some prostitute? Why d'you come all the way out here to find me?' He was contemplative; observing her through narrowed eyes.

'Well, I was worried about you and wanted to check you're still alive.'

'Bullshit.'

Bev exhaled heavily. 'It's not bullshit. I was worried. But yeah, I guess I also want to know who Tatjana is and what happened to her.' She could see the scepticism on Doc's face. 'Come on! It's the right thing to do. And Jerry could be involved. Some kid's gone missing . . . I think you're a good person and would wanna know too. And you're the best keyboard warrior I know. If there's evidence online of abuse or worse, you'll find it.'

'You think our shadow cabinet minister's a lady-killer?'

At that moment, Bev's phone erupted in a frenzy of buzzing and pinging in her pocket. She took it out and saw she had three Facebook messages from Jerry Fitzwilliam.

What's new, pussycat?
Fancy dinner this evening? Meet me at my club? There's a rooftop pool. Bring a bikini!
Jerry. Xx

She glanced at her watch – it was approaching six. Looked up at Doc. 'I'm about to find out. What time's the next train back to London?'

CHAPTER 22
Bev

'I'm meeting a friend here,' Bev told the hip young bearded man on reception. The stylish architectural lighting in the foyer of the private member's club was a triumph of form over function. But even in the murk, she could make out the look of disdain on his face. She didn't fit in here. Perhaps it was down to the hasty makeover she'd demanded from the Yves Saint Laurent girl in Debenhams, offering in return an empty promise to come back and drop a tonne of cash on cosmetics. She was catwalk hi-glamour, from the neck up; Blue Cross rummage-rack, in ill-fitting leopard-print polyester, from the neck down. 'Jerry Fitzwilliam. My name's Cat Thomson.'

Yeah, stick that in your pipe, you snotty little arse-wipe, Bev thought as the receptionist's expression changed from judgemental to surprised.

He scanned through the names in a visitors' log. Nodded and smiled. 'Ah yes. Mr Fitzwilliam is waiting for you by the pool, but we need to escort non-members upstairs. Someone will be with you shortly. Please take a seat.'

As she waited, Bev slid her fingers inside her handbag, checking for the fifth time that the filming and recording equipment was correctly arranged and ready to roll. She had brought it down from the north in the hope that exactly this kind of scenario would come up. With Doc's own computer zapped, and his entrenched reluctance to do anything on his parents' home PC, the equipment was set to record this time, rather than ping a live feed back to Doc's laptop via Wi-Fi. If the recording failed, Bev knew this would be another wasted evening, putting herself at unnecessary risk.

'Madam?' A woman wearing ugly black clothing, with too many pockets and inexplicable ruching, tapped her on the shoulder. She held a clipboard before her like a shield to fend off the uncool and deeply average. 'Follow me.'

Standing in the lift, staring blankly at the bad skin of the hostess's cheek, Bev's stressed bladder registered a mixture of relief that this would soon be over and trepidation that things could end very, very badly, should her seductive façade be torn down. Considering she'd been sharing a joint in Doc's attic room only two hours earlier, she was hardly mentally in gear to play Cat Johnson, flirtatious bit on the side.

The lift opened at the summit of the building. She was marched past a glazed wall, beyond which lay an open-air pool that glowed with azure, floodlit stripes. Fat businessmen were lounging on recliners around the edge in their trunks, as though this were the Bahamas, rather than London in April, with a nip in the air. A couple in the pool were drinking and talking but not moving enough to cause more than a mere ripple on the water's perfect surface. The light-spangled skyline of a nocturnal City of London blazed beyond. Places like this had given Bev a buzz in the past. Right now, her legs felt as though they might buckle beneath her at any moment.

Jerry Fitzwilliam was seated on a chair by the poolside. Manspreading, as if he suffered from hypermobility of the hips, his hands were behind his head, elbows wide as he gazed contemplatively into the pool. He wore blue shorts and a linen short-sleeved shirt, open at the collar. On his feet were pristine deck shoes. His face was lit from beneath by spotlights in the water, giving him a demonic appearance; his thoughtful composure looked entirely staged.

Bev was all smiles as she was led to him. 'Jerry!'

He rose to greet her, kissing her chastely on both cheeks. Shaking her hand formally. 'Cat! How lovely to see you again.' He waved to the chair on the other side of the low table by the pool, which was already laden with a bottle of champagne, two glasses and three small bowls containing queen olives, nuts and mixed nibbles.

With so many witnesses by the poolside, it dawned on Bev that her target might not behave inappropriately. Would her efforts at faux-seduction be thwarted?

'Isn't it fabulous that we both happened to be in London on the same evening? I'm *so* sorry I had to dash off last time.' She set her daytime handbag on the already cluttered table, suddenly aware of how large and clumsy it looked. Silently, she castigated herself for leaving the neat little evening bag on her bedside cabinet at home. An oversight that could cost her.

Her date's eyes transferred from her cleavage to the bag. The grin started to slide from his porcine face, giving way to a frown. The bag looked oversized and out of place. This wasn't going to work. Damn it! She moved the bag to the floor, placing it between her feet. Without the barrier between them, he perked up, leaning in towards her.

They exchanged small talk about work – Cat Thomson's ups and downs in the world of engineering, all a figment of Bev's imagination, of course. The champagne helped the lies to flow. She steered clear of technical detail. Mainly,

Jerry Fitzwilliam was happy to talk and talk and talk about himself. This deal he was brokering with big business. That law he was trying to get passed in parliament. Me, me, me, becoming louder and more animated with every glass he drained. Finally, his focus shifted.

'I've been thinking about you a lot, you know,' he said quietly, sizing up her thighs that were barely covered by her short dress. 'Thanks for all your messages. I would have responded but—'

'Were you too busy with your other admirers?' she asked, coquettishly popping an olive into her mouth.

He guffawed, then. Topped up their champagne. Seemed to fully let down his guard, at last. 'I realise I behaved like a bit of an oaf when we last met.'

'A misunderstanding,' Bev said, shaking her head. She needed the exact opposite to gentlemanly apologies if she was ever going to get paid. And she needed evidence of a secret London bolthole if she was going to do any kind of digging into his nefarious arrangements with a pimp called Stan.

'I got carried away. It's my wife, you see.' He cleared his throat. Paused between sips from his champagne flute. 'We haven't had sex in years. It's very hard on a full-blooded man like me.'

Ah. Here we go, Bev thought. *My wife won't fuck me. I have needs! Jesus, if I had a fiver for every time I've heard that line . . .* She prayed his words, at least, were being picked up by the tiny microphone.

'What about this swim you were promising me?' she said, two glasses of fizz in.

'Ah. That.' His hungry grin betrayed an increasingly drunk man with adultery on his mind. 'You brought your bikini, then?'

172

She crossed her legs slowly, treating him to a flash of her knickers. 'Your wish is my command.'

'Is it . . . scanty?'

Dabbing at the corners of her mouth with a napkin, she batted her lashes slowly. 'Very.'

In the ladies' changing room, Bev removed the hastily chosen new outfit, pulling it over her hair with a crackle of static electricity. The two-piece she'd flung into her basket had been designed to look amazing on a sylph-like eighteen-year-old. Now, Bev stood in front of the mirror, beholding her dimpled, overweight thirty-year-old's body in the unflattering light from an overhead spot. The bikini dug in in all the wrong places. Her cellulite beneath the tropical-patterned lycra put her in mind of an elephant that had been covered with brightly coloured bubble-wrap. At least it would be dark by the pool. And men like Jerry Fitzwilliam didn't look at the mantelpiece if there was the whiff of an opportunity to give the fire a good poke.

When she came out, the other businessmen who had been reclining on the loungers had mercifully left. But there Jerry was, already sitting on the side of the pool with his legs dangling in the water, sipping some ridiculous-looking cocktail. Slurring as he spoke. 'Aren't you a sight for sore eyes, young lady?'

A sore sight for young eyes, Bev thought, noticing how two of the hipster waiters who were collecting empties looked at her, sniggering and exchanging knowing glances. Or maybe they were looking at the shadow cabinet minister with his barrel chest full of blond hair. His big gut hung over the most revolting baggy swim trunks she'd seen since she and Rob had last gone for a miserable, argumentative, seemingly never-ending fortnight to the Algarve.

Setting her bag on her seat, so that the camera and microphone were surreptitiously pointed straight at her target, she slid into the pool. Gasped at the change in temperature.

'It's freezing!'

'Good for the circulation,' he said, slipping into the water alongside her.

It was reasonably shallow. Bev noticed him eyeing her nipples which protruded thanks to the cold. She sank further into the water.

'You'd win in a wet T-shirt competition,' he said, grabbing her around the waist.

She wriggled out of his grasp and swam to the opposite side and back, coming to rest conveniently close to her bag. 'Actually, it's quite refreshing once you get going.'

'You get me going.' He prized her hand free of the pool's edge and slid it onto his crotch.

Bev could feel his erection through the fabric. Felt her olives and nuts coming back up. Relieved that he had crossed the line now that they were practically alone and he was full of alcohol; needing him to say something irredeemably incriminating, she let her hand linger there. 'Wow. That's impressive in water this cold. I really do get you going, don't I? What are your intentions with me, Mr Fitzwilliam?' Giggling, to make it sound like flirtation.

He leaned in to kiss her. She offered him her neck. He sucked like her Dyson after its recent servicing. The skin would surely bruise. Arsehole. What would Mo say at group therapy if she turned up covered in love bites like a randy seventeen-year-old?

'I want to fuck you into next Wednesday,' he said. 'How about that?'

She could feel his fingers searching for the ties at the

side of her bikini bottoms. Had he spoken loud enough for the microphone? Could the waiters see what was going on?

'Cheeky!' she said, pushing him away playfully. 'What about your poor wife? Does she know you like to party when you're in London?'

'I don't want to talk about her. I want to talk about me and you, getting all down and dirty. Come back to my flat.'

That had definitely been loud enough. And he'd mentioned the flat. 'Where is it?'

'You'll see. The view from the living room's amazing.'

'Is it your place?'

'I share it with some friends. My, my.' He reached out to caress her breasts under the water. Was he too drunk to realise that somebody might see or did he simply not care, now she was on his members-only turf? 'Aren't you the inquisitive one?'

Bev was torn. A voice within her said she was overstepping a mark. Asking too many questions at once. But she wanted this over and if she were to succeed, she needed more information. She was certain he wasn't about to take her to his barge. At least if she discovered the address of his secret pad, she'd be able to make up some excuse and beat a hasty retreat back to safety.

She swam to the far side of the pool, climbed out, trying to appear as lithe and seductive as possible for a woman with big knees and breasts almost heavy enough to give her a stoop. Took a towel from the pool-guy. Turned back to her date. 'I can be dressed and ready to go in five.' In for a penny . . .

The journey out to Ealing took an hour in a cab. The shadow Science Minister's need to uphold a respectable public persona in front of a very chatty, Labour-voting cabbie saved Bev from being mauled mercilessly on the back seat. Clearly, he wasn't so drunk that he didn't know where the line was drawn.

Pulling up outside a high-rise that looked like some ex-local authority block, covered in the sort of cladding that had seen Grenfell go up in flames, Bev found she could barely bring herself to leave the safety of the cab.

'Are you coming then?' Jerry was holding the door open for her. An expectant look on his face, complete with raised eyebrow. 'For our marketing meeting.' Wink, wink.

She swallowed hard, clutching her bag that contained a wet bikini, wrapped in a stolen towel. The ends of her hair still dripped chlorinated water onto her crappy dress, rendering the fabric almost see-through. She felt just as transparent. What happened next? Should she take her chances inside with a man who didn't take no for an answer? She was well aware that having travelled all the way out here, sex would be an expectation. And though Bev was hardly averse to one-night stands now that she was single, this was business. A client's repulsive, violent husband humping away on top of her was the opposite of what she wanted and didn't even approach being professional conduct.

'Get your skates on, love!' the cabbie said, an impatient look on his face, visible in his rear-view mirror. 'I've got another fare to pick up.'

Stepping out into the night, standing alone in the harsh light emanating from the block's foyer, Bev reminded herself that she was no victim like Angie. She was not a vulnerable young girl like the prostitutes ordered from 'Stan'. Her days of being in thrall to and at the mercy of a man were over. If the need arose, she determined to clobber her way to freedom with her heavy handbag.

Fitzwilliam beckoned her inside, where there was no concierge but where they were followed by the whine and zoom of a CCTV camera, suspended by a bracket, high on the wall. In the lift, he inserted a key into the bank of numbered buttons and pressed P for penthouse. He leaned in for a kiss, but Bev pointed to another lens, spying on them from behind what appeared to be a shatterproof glass panel, mounted high in the corner of the cubicle.

'We've got an audience,' she said, wondering if any footage had been taken of 'spring lamb and sugar' coming to the flat. 'Slow down, cowboy.' She placed a firm hand on his chest, keeping distance between them.

He clasped her hand and kissed her knuckles.

She pulled away. 'Marketing meeting, remember?'

He backed off, nodding at her cleavage and smiled.

The lift doors opened to reveal a small, carpeted lobby with one solitary door facing them.

'Welcome to my modest little pleasure palace,' he said.

Fumbling momentarily with his keys, he unlocked the door to reveal a cramped hall, which led straight into a large living room. It was all parquet flooring and leather sofas. There was a glass coffee table, on which she imagined lines of coke would have been cut on many an occasion, waiting to be snorted up bent politicians' hairy nostrils through a twenty-pound note. A reproduction Mondrian on the walls. Through large ceiling-to-floor windows, the vista of a main Ealing thoroughfare – still busy though it was late – and the suburban roads beyond, was striking, if not stunning.

'Nice place. Must be expensive,' she said, staring down at the neon lights of an off-licence and the neighbouring kebab shop.

'Like I said, I share it with buddies.' He disappeared into the kitchen.

There was the sound of a cupboard opening. Glasses set on a worktop. The tinkle of ice.

'You're a gin drinker, aren't you?' He poked his head out of the door. A charming host, now, as if the watchful presence of the CCTV in the foyer and lift had pushed them both into the eye of his amorous storm.

'You bet.' Bev took her drink from him. Made a mental checklist: she now knew he did have an additional property, the details of which he hadn't disclosed to his wife; this was an interior to look out for in any dodgy videos they found online; decided on a sudden migraine as an excuse for a sharp exit. Just a few more questions, and she'd go . . .

They both took a seat on one of the sofas, her handbag and the camera within reach on the coffee table, facing them. He spread his free arm along the back, leaning in towards her. His shirt rode up, revealing that his flies were undone. She spied his erection peeping over the top of his underpants, thick and red with sexual intent. He reached out to caress her hair.

OK, lady. You're in danger. Do whatever it takes to get your footage and get the hell out of here. But Bev's gung-ho tongue had seemingly disengaged itself from her cautious brain. 'What else do you like to do when you let your hair down, Jerry? Does Charlie come to the party?' She raised her eyebrows suggestively. 'What about . . . Ernie?'

The temperature in the living room seemed to drop abruptly by several degrees.

'Hang on,' he said, backing away. 'I'm not sure I feel comfortable with where this conversation's going. You're starting to sound like some red-top hack on the hunt for scandal.' He grabbed her face, inclining her jaw so that she could see him only through her right eye.

'You're hurting me.' It was difficult to speak in his vice-like grip. 'Let go, Jerry. You've got me all wrong. I was . . . just curious.'

But he didn't let go. He held his face so close to hers that she could smell the champagne and gin on his breath; the chlorine in his hair. 'You know what curiosity did, don't you, *Cat*?' He said her name with exaggerated emphasis. 'If I find out you're spinning me a yarn, and it turns out you're actually an undercover reporter, you might find I pay you a visit in the middle of the night that you won't enjoy. How about that? Waking up to find me at the end of your bed in your basement flat.'

Enough. Bev pinched him hard on the inner thigh. How on earth did he know she lived in a basement flat? Had she slipped up in conversation? Did he know everything? It didn't matter. She'd spent her entire life being bullied. She wasn't about to let this evil chump join the list of her tormentors. 'Get your fucking hands off me, Jerry Fitzwilliam. I resent your accusation and I will not tolerate your threats.'

'And I won't tolerate blackmailing honeytrappers and gold-diggers.'

She stood, dizzy from the sudden rush of blood away from her brain. 'Enough of this crap. I'm off.' Snatched up her handbag, preparing to use it as a weapon, and scrambled backwards towards the front door. Her heart thudded in a frenzy inside her as if trying to escape.

He mirrored her movements, also rising rapidly. 'Don't let the door hit you on the way out, you cheap tart.' As he rose, his shorts slid down to reveal a large, dark red birthmark on his hip that was roughly the shape of Australia. Bev stared at it. She recognised it.

'Go to sex parties, do you?' she shouted.

The door was within reach — her escape almost made good, now.

He'd already turned his back on her, thankfully, and was making his way to the kitchen, empty glass in hand. But he turned around, wearing a menacing grin. 'What did you just say?' His feet slap, slap, slapped hard on the parquet as he blundered back towards her. Murder in his eyes. 'Are you threatening me?

Jerry Fitzwilliam was clutching his heavy crystal tumbler like a cosh. Closer, closer, he was almost upon her . . .

CHAPTER 23

Angie

Am going to meet him again. Will get everything you need.
Get packed. Get you n kids out. Speak when I'm home. Bev

With a shaking hand, her heart racing from a mix of euphoria and dread, Angie deleted the text. Looked over her shoulder, the hairs on her forearms standing on end from the feeling that she was being observed. Yet nobody was there and nothing was out of place in the domestic scene: sideboard, ornaments, paintings, windows facing onto the back garden. The shutters were still open and the garden was in darkness, though.

Angie snapped shut the louvres, exhaling. Cocked her head to listen. The house was silent. The ticking clock on the sitting room mantelpiece showed that Poppy and Benjy had been tucked up for a good few hours.

'Stop being silly,' she whispered. 'Find the suitcases.'

Making every effort to creep soundlessly past the children's bedrooms, Angie climbed the stairs to the attic. Winced when the old wood groaned beneath even her meagre weight. She was breathless, now, not just from the climb but with excitement at the thought that soon she'd be free of Jerry. Able to make her own decisions on where she went, with whom she socialised, how she spent what she hoped would be a considerable divorce settlement. She wondered if she'd get to keep this grand house that she loved so very much. Her divorce lawyer had assured her that there would be no problem in securing the family home for Angie and the children. The divorce lawyer didn't yet know that Jerry had been amassing a fortune through fraud.

Stop being negative, she told herself.

As she rummaged among the packing boxes and trunks for the suitcases, coughing at the clouds of dust that billowed into the air, she thought about her engineered encounter in Carluccio's with Tim. Who'd have thought in a million years that Tim would be friends with Rob? Sophie and Tim had supposedly hated and mistrusted Bev's ex so much that they had effectively severed contact with Bev until she was rid of him. She made a mental note to warn Bev that Rob had seemingly insinuated himself into her circle of trust, which was surely a betrayal of sorts on Tim's part . . . wasn't it? The biggest surprise of all, however was the psychiatrist who had been introduced to her as Mo. Angie had recognised him from the health centre where she secretly received support for her anorexia. She was certain that she'd seen Bev coming out of the group therapy room where Dr Mohammed Ashraf presided, though she'd said nothing to Bev, not wanting to draw attention to her own foibles.

Angie reflected that she had been so nonplussed by this unlikely cabal of United supporters, who had been laughing and joking over their tortellini as though they were best friends of old, she had failed entirely to ask Tim about the pied-à-terre he'd once shared with Jerry. She'd merely said hello, exchanged pleasantries about the weather, United's prospects and the look of their lunches. Then, she'd hastened back to her car, panicking that Rob might have recognised her without the green bobble hat and sunglasses. It wouldn't take much for Rob to tell Tim about Bev's client. And Tim would lose no time in telling Jerry, of course.

'Silly, simpering girl,' she said, opening the medium-sized case and checking there was nothing inside it.

Tiptoeing down the stairs, she lugged three suitcases – one at a time – into her bedroom. With Jerry not back until mid-morning tomorrow, she had as long as she needed to make good her escape. It was finally happening. She would load up the car and drive them to a hotel somewhere along the M6. Tomorrow, she'd speak to her mother and arrange to travel down to her parents' place in Shropshire.

Flinging the cases onto her bed, she assembled a capsule wardrobe that would cover all bases. Found her pristine Hunter wellies at the back of her shoe store in case walks with Granny and Gramps in the rolling countryside beckoned. She crept into the children's rooms, pausing to watch their eyelashes flutter as they dreamed in their toddler beds – Poppy's Cinderella carriage and Benjy's fire engine. The children wouldn't be happy to leave their idyllic rooms and custom-made beds behind, but these were desperate times and temporary measures. She grabbed clean clothes from their wardrobes, sour that without her nanny, the dirty laundry had stacked up and the clean clothing options for Poppy and Benjy were limited. Never mind. She'd find a boutique near her folks somewhere. She was certain there was a lovely place in Shrewsbury.

After packing their things in the cases, Angie emerged from her bedroom, preparing to wake her babies.

'Going anywhere?'

Yelping, Angie clutched at her chest. 'Gretchen!' Her nanny was standing in the doorway to her room, almost invisible in the dark. No light on behind her. Only the glow of a laptop screen on her dressing table that immediately caught Angie's eye. 'You're in Austria!'

'Clearly not.' Gretchen took a step onto the landing, hands dug deeply into the pockets of her jeans.

At this hour, the nanny was still fully dressed. And what was it that she'd been watching on her laptop screen? Couldn't Angie spy the four-way split feed of the nanny-cam? Except instead of the children's bedroom, the play-room and the garden, the footage was of the living room, Jerry's office, the kitchen and Angie's bedroom.

'Jerry asked me to cut my extended leave short and come back,' Gretchen said in her flawless, barely-accented English. 'He thought you needed help urgently.'

'How kind! When did you get back? Why didn't you come and say hello, sweets?' Angie asked, chuckling nervously and taking a step backwards. She was all smiles, but cringing inside. Unable to decide whether to say something about the nanny-cam or not.

'I got back at lunchtime. You were out. I was so tired from the flight that I fell straight asleep.'

'You've been sleeping all this while? Are you spying on me, Gretchen?' She kept her voice light and friendly, uncertain how best to wear this new-found bravery.

Gretchen pulled the door to her bedroom closed behind her. 'Of course not, Angie.' She clasped her into a stiff embrace. 'It's so good to be back. Although, perhaps you are going as I'm arriving?'

Feeling cold sweat erupt along her spine, Angie shook her head, still smiling. 'No. I'm not going anywhere. I was just packing away some old things for the charity shop. How was Austria?'

Yawning, Gretchen retreated. 'I'll tell you in the morning. I'm very tired from travelling. Schlaf gut!'

'Yes. Good night.'

Angie returned to her room, dragging the cases off the bed. She wept silently into her pillow.

CHAPTER 24
Bev

'The train will shortly be arriving at Milton Keynes,' came the announcement over the tannoy.

Idly, Bev stared out of the window at the early evening sky as the train slowed and the utilitarian office-block anonymity of the station and town beyond it came into view. She glanced at her watch. *Come on! Come on!* There were still hundreds of miles to put between her and the car-crash of a meet with Jerry Fitzwilliam.

The beep, beep, beep of the doors opening almost lulled her to sleep. It was already dark outside at this time of year. She yawned, reluctantly moved her feet back under her own quarter of the table, and folded her arms as a middle-aged woman plonked a large weekend bag on top of the newspaper Bev had been trying and failing to read. The woman cast a judgmental eye over the low-cut neckline of Bev's dress, just visible beneath her coat. But after a night spent in Doc's mother's guest bed, having been threatened by a powerful politician who had a penchant for beating his wife, Bev was in no mood for her new travel companion's behaviour. She yanked her *Times* from under the weekend bag, unleashing the full force of her passive aggression.

'Do you mind?'

As the train pulled away, Bev watched town give way to countryside, but her thoughts were on the late-night conversation she'd had with Doc.

'He's been in my place already,' she'd said, cradling a hot chocolate in the dated kitchen of Doc's family home at 3 a.m. 'Well, either him or some bully boy on his payroll, maybe.'

'What do you mean?' Doc had asked, rocking back on the hind legs of his chair. It was at the small, pine breakfast table, shoved against a wall that still bore food-themed tiled wallpaper from the 70s.

'He knew I live in a basement flat, for a start. And stuff's been moved. My origami's been pissed about with or stolen. Doors have been left open, like someone's trying to freak me out. You know? I'm scared, Doc. I'll tell you that for nowt.'

'So am I. Understandable, given the circumstances. But what are you gonna do?'

'I've got enough to give Angie from tonight.' She'd picked up the tiny recording device, rolling it in the palm of her hand. 'He behaved like the beast he is and it's all here. Everything from him trying to shoot me with his big gun to the bit where he comes at me with a crystal tumbler. How I got out of there before he brained me to death or just plain raped me, I'll never know. Well . . . I suppose a punch to his nuts and my sprint to a waiting lift helped.' She'd enclosed her fingers around the evidence, exhaling heavily. 'I know he's got a secret penthouse flat. I know he's an adulterer and a bully. We both need to go home. Right? Show this turd that we're not scared, even if we're filling our pants. Bullies back down.'

Doc had thrown his head back then and had laughed silently; his shoulders heaving dramatically. 'Yeah? Really.'

Sarcasm in his flat delivery. 'I don't know about you, but I'm moving. I'll go to Levenshulme. Disappear. They'll never find me there.'

Bev had run a finger over a knot in the table's honeyed pine surface, contemplating her circumstances. 'Maybe this will turn out to be the kick up the arse I need. I've got to get a suitable place anyway, if I'm gonna set my world back on its axis. And I need to get away from Sophie and Tim. They're doing my head in, big time. But first, I've got to wrap this case up, and I can't move on until I've found out about one last thing.'

They'd made a pact to dig a little deeper into the fate of a young prostitute named Tatjana – to probe the outer limits of the internet, as far as was possible. A forlorn-looking Doc had made her promise not to call him on his parents' landline, saying he'd be in touch when he had a new, clean phone. With their plan agreed, she'd bid good-night to him and had retired to the Tomcat-piss-fragranced guest bedroom.

Another day of writing copy and supervising a photo-graphic shoot of the charity's facilities had followed. Now, finally, she was leaving London and heading home.

If the woman opposite hadn't have blown her nose loudly, Bev might not have stirred from her reverie. She glanced up. Her attention shifted from her fastidiously-coiffed travel companion to the aisle of the carriage beyond her.

It was then that Bev spotted a man staring straight at her.

He was an ordinary-looking man in his thirties, maybe. An Everyman, wearing a grey fleece over grey jeans. But there was something about the direct way in which he'd been observing her, as if mentally taking notes, and the studied way in which his focus moved to a point just beyond her the moment they'd locked eyes. The encounter seemed to chill the carriage.

Standing abruptly, Bev grabbed her overstuffed handbag and shuffled into the aisle. Taking long strides, she started to move away from the man and towards the front of the train. A quick look over her shoulder confirmed that he too had stood up and was now following, just metres behind.

Jabbing at the illuminated button that opened the doors, Bev started to feel dizziness sweep over her in waves. The man was closing on her. Closing . . . and the touch-sensitive button was not, it seemed, sensitive to her touch.

Just as her pursuer was only three paces away, the doors slid open. Bev pushed past a tall, heavyset man who was wheeling a monster of a suitcase across the threshold into her carriage. His girth and the bulk of the case provided a bung for the thoroughfare, leaving Mr Grey stranded.

Get near the end. Lock yourself in a bog in a busy carriage. Leg it out the door at Wilmslow.

She barrelled her way through three packed carriages of business types, students, screaming children with their harried-looking parents, pensioners, and passengers from the four corners of the world, judging by the smorgasbord of languages spoken. Bev finally found herself surrounded by a group of drunken young men, all standing in the no-man's land by the door. They were singing a rousing song that sounded like a football chant. She looked at the identical shirts they wore and the bulky kitbags they guarded between their muscular legs. Ice hockey players. Boys on tour. They were the perfect cover. Mr Grey wouldn't get a word of sense out of them, she prayed.

No sign of Mr Grey. Yet.

Bev slid inside the mercifully vacant toilet and locked the door. The train swayed violently as it changed track, beating its north-westerly path homewards. Shaking with adrenaline, Bev gripped the handles of her bag, ready to clobber anyone who tried to force their way in.

After ten minutes, nobody had come, though she felt like the cloying smell of the cleaning chemicals might dissolve her brain from the inside out. Forced to play the waiting game, she sat on the toilet seat and started to read the signs on the wall, showing where the soap was, where the hand-dryer was . . . Had Mr Grey given up his search? Had she imagined she was being stalked?

Suddenly, she held her breath as the handle was tried from the outside. Insistent knocking on the door, with the ice hockey team still singing their hearts out. Was it him? Dare she shout out? No. Better to keep her mouth shut.

More banging. Would a spy on Fitzwilliam's payroll have a gadget to open a train's locked toilet door? Could he slip inside, strangle her and disappear into the crowd? Anything was possible in this waking nightmare. The door handle depressed again.

'Fuck off!' Bev said beneath her breath.

'Is anybody in there?' Finally, a voice. An older woman's voice, by the sounds.

'Yes,' Bev shouted.

'You've been in there a long time. I need the toilet.' The woman banged on the door again. 'Can you hurry up please?'

Oh, Jesus. Why did this have to happen? Now she's going to draw attention to me! The train lurched. Bev's stomach was in knots. She felt like she might vomit at any moment.

'I'm busy. It's not the only loo on the train, you know.'

'But you've been in there forty minutes and I've got a weak bladder.'

Was she really on the run, having a conversation with a semi-continent old codger through a train toilet door? 'Well, I've got colitis,' she shouted, following the declaration by blowing raspberries – long and low – that might pass as corroborative evidence, assuming the woman could hear her over the drunken ice-hockey boys. 'So, go and find your own toilet!'

The minutes crawled by and still Bev was frightened to come out. Finally, the ticket inspector insisted she emerge, lest she face the wrath of the transport police at the next station.

'Some bloke was staring at me,' she told the proud wearer of the Virgin West Coast livery – a burly woman who seemingly brooked no argument with the bowel-afflicted. 'I was freaked so I got up and headed for the front of the train. But then, he followed me.' Bev felt her eyes glaze over with tears. 'I was scared and it seemed like a good place to hide. I think he was a sex pest.'

Let off the hook, Bev spent the rest of the journey in the company of the sympathetic ticket inspector, in the frontmost carriage of the train. Pulling into Wilmslow, she'd calmed down sufficiently to believe Mr Grey's interest in her had been purely coincidental or perhaps down to her cheap and nasty minidress. She was overwrought, stressed, imagining things. Easy to do. Gathering her coat and her bag, she bid her ticket-inspecting champion farewell and stepped out into the evening drizzle.

As she marched along the platform, she glanced back at the red snake of the train. The handful of passengers who had intended to alight at the small Cheshire station were already shuffling, strutting, jogging their way to the exit. Bev smiled. Glad that home was now within spitting distance. She was about to turn her back on the train when a malevolent smudge of grey caught her eye. There, standing in the doorway of coach E, she glimpsed her fleece-clad pursuer, jabbing furiously at the button on the wall that released the door. He seemed to glare out at her; started to run the length of the carriage towards the open door at the far end . . .

CHAPTER 25

Bev

'Good Lord, Bev! You look terrible. Whatever is the matter?' Sophie asked, holding the front door open for Bev, where she had failed to let herself in.

Bev stumbled over the threshold, practically falling into Sophie's arms. She tried to regain her poise, noting that Tim was standing in the doorway to the kitchen.

'I'm in t-trouble and I . . . I . . .' She had that strange sensation of a plug being pulled within her and her energy being drained away, as if she might faint. She allowed Sophie to wrap an arm around her shoulder and usher her into the living room.

'Come and sit down, darling!' Sophie said, guiding her to the welcoming bulk of her Chesterfield sofa; pushing the door softly closed so it was just the two of them. 'Tell Aunty Soph all about it. What could possibly have happened to make my Bev so sad?' She took a seat next to Bev and placed her manicured hands on her knees, cocking her head to the side, like a primary school teacher awaiting a confession from a traumatised child.

Running her fingers up and down the slate gabardine fabric, praying the repetitive movement would somehow calm her overheated mind, Bev began recounting her tale. She kept her voice to a whisper.

'You *met up* with Jerry? Oh my God! Is that something you'd normally do for your clients? I thought you gumshoes just sat in your car and took photos.' Sophie's eyebrows shot up towards the widow's peak of her hair.

Bev shrugged. 'Look, I'm not going to into the whys and wherefores, right? Client confidentiality and all that.' Realisation dawned on her that she'd made a mistake in confiding in Sophie. Even though Sophie clearly cared for Angie, and had brought her business to Bev's door with the intention of helping her, she was married to Tim. And Tim was Jerry's "brother-from-another-mother". *Not good, Bev.*

'You're shaking,' Sophie said, gingerly reaching out to rub Bev's arm. 'How come?'

'It's a long story.' Sophie didn't need to know the further extent of her chicanery on Angie's behalf. 'Anyway, I needed to meet up with him. For Angie's solicitor. You know? Proving that he can't keep his dick in his trousers.' Shit. She'd said too much.

Shifting in her seat, Sophie's back straightened as though someone had inserted a rod down her top to stiffen her spine. 'Oh. So, you found him in some amorous clinch? Did you confront him? Or were *you* the bait? Is that why you're wearing a leopard-skin stripper's dress?' She snatched her hand away and shuffled several inches away from Bev on the sofa. 'I've hit the nail on the head, haven't I? Isn't that entrapment?'

Bev felt suddenly cheap and full of dishonesty. She snatched up a scatter cushion and placed it over her naked thighs, exposed by this short, short dress. 'Look. Forget I ever showed up here like a gibbering idiot. OK?' She stood, ready to leave and head downstairs for the privacy of her flat, where she'd be able to lick her wounds in peace.

'No, darling!' Sophie's horrified shock abated instantly. She grabbed Bev with a surprisingly firm hand, pulling her back down. 'You *must* unburden yourself.' Just like at college. Squeaky-clean Sophie had smelled some fabulous gossip and was offering empty solidarity in return for the grubby details. 'I insist. What goes on tour, stays on tour, right?'

'Keep it down, Soph!' Bev was mindful of Tim, possibly lurking outside the living room door, eavesdropping. She chose her words carefully, revealing only a fraction of what had gone on. 'I'm not going into details, but I met up with Jerry to clarify . . . things. It was at his club. He got rude. I got confrontational.' She was trying to keep it together but could feel her bottom lip starting to tremble. The lump in her throat threatened to block her words' exit. 'Then, he threatened me.' Bev pressed her fingers to her lips to stem the outpouring of stress and woe.

'I don't believe it. Jerry threatened you? *Jerry?!*' Sophie had that slightly sharp tone to her voice that spoke to scepticism.

'He's hardly a damned teddy bear, Soph. Why do you think Angie needed a PI's help? You're the one who said in the first place that he's a bully.'

Sophie straightened up, blinked hard and folded her arms tightly. 'So, Jerry Fitzwilliam threatened you. In public, in an exclusive members' club. Okaaaay. What did he say? *How* did he do it, exactly?'

'To hell with this cross-examination crap. I didn't sleep a wink last night, thanks to that bullying bastard. I'm knackered out of my skull. I'm going to bed.' This time, Bev hoisted herself from the sofa and refused to be pulled back down. She yanked her hand from Sophie's grip, feeling like she was a beleaguered fat leopard, pulling herself free of quicksand. Tempering her angry words, lest she get evicted from her flat. 'Listen, Soph. It's lovely of you to be so concerned, but please. Maybe I'm just tired and paranoid. I'll be fine after a proper night's kip in my own bed. Just let me go.'

Pulling the door open, she yelped when she found Tim, standing there.

'Oh, hello, Creeping Jesus! Are you trying to give me a heart attack?' She held her handbag high in front of her exposed cleavage. Tugging her hem downwards. Wishing she'd changed back into her stale office wear, no matter how crumpled it had got in her handbag, rather than this horrible micro-mini symphony in polyester.

With a territorial arm placed across the door frame, Tim barred her way through to the hall. 'Why are you really so tired, Bev? Slept in a strange bed, did you? Maybe that was why you couldn't sleep. Maybe my friend, Jerry, is just playing the fall guy for your insomnia. Let me guess . . . Were you out shagging into the small hours?' He looked her up and down with judgemental eyes, as though she'd infected the house. 'Because I think you ought to take a good, hard look at yourself before you go slinging unsubstantiated mud around about my best friend. OK?'

Bev registered that ominous draining feeling again. Shivers were upon her. She'd always felt off-kilter when she was around Tim. *Don't let him talk to you like that, for Christ's sake!* 'Fuck you, Tim!' She poked him in the gut, forcing herself to take a step towards him, rather than follow her instincts to retreat into his and Sophie's living room, where she was on enemy territory. 'What the hell were you doing, listening into our private conversation, you weirdo? And what has my private life got to do with the shoddy behaviour and misogyny of Jerry Fitzwilliam?'

'I think you'd better pack your bags and leave,' Tim said, still standing between her and the staircase that led down to the refuge of the basement. 'We don't want people like you being around the children.'

'People like me?' Bev scoffed, balling her fist whilst fighting tears.

'Slags with no self-control.'

She looked to Sophie for a show of support, but all she got was, 'Oh, Timmy. That's not very nice.' As though big, unpleasant Timmy was no more than a naughty schoolboy who had been caught smearing a bogey on the hem of some little girl's skirt.

'Thanks a bundle, *Aunty Soph*.' Bev glared at her friend. 'Nice show of loyalty.' She pushed past Tim, suppressing the urge to kick him in the shins. 'And *you* can cock off. I've got squatter's rights.' She jabbed her middle finger up at him, almost ramming it home inside his left nostril.

Hastening down the stone steps to her flat, Bev saw that her front door was standing open. She marched back upstairs, clutching her handbag like a threat; fist balled on her hip. Burst into the living room to find Tim and Sophie whispering to one another on the sofa. Urgency in the speed of their exchange.

'You been in my flat?' she asked them, looking for tells in their body language.

'I was heading down there just before you came in,' Tim said, pointing the remote control at the TV and flicking it on as though she were merely an irritating fly, buzzing around the room.

'Why?'

'Checking the condition you're keeping the place in.' He continued to press the buttons, scrolling through the channels.

Bev wrenched the remote from his hand. 'How dare you trespass? That's my home!'

'I think you'll find it's *my* property.' He narrowed his eyes at her; his lip starting to curl into a sneer. 'And as your landlord, I'm entitled to check it's in a good, clean state. As it is, I only got a glimpse of your living room, and then you burst through our front door, so I came back up to see what the hysteria was about. But what I saw was a mess. So, like I said.' He snatched the remote from her hand. Turned back to the TV. 'Pack your bags or face the consequences. I can't tolerate infestations because you can't be bothered to wash your filthy pots. And I won't have strange men coming and going at all hours. You're unfit on so many levels, Beverley. I feel very sorry for you and your family.'

Fury licked up Bev's gullet, manifesting itself as flaming words that shot from her tongue like the jet from a blow torch. 'This is harassment, you big lump of shit, and I'll not stand for it. It's no sodding wonder you're best buds with Jerry Fitzwilliam. You're cut from the same cloth! Don't think you can intimidate me, Timbo, you big, lumbering wankstain!'

'Enjoy your last night here,' he said.

Bev glanced at Sophie for a show of support but her friend's demeanour was stiff and detached. Notably, she didn't meet Bev's gaze.

Fleeing back downstairs, fighting the tears, Bev longed to be able to unburden herself to Doc but he had no phone. She contemplated calling Mo as an emergency measure, but knew he'd be furious at her for disturbing him out of hours. Instead, she realised she would inevitably resort to a mind-numbing binge on Porn Hub. Anything sufficed, as long as she could get out of her head the memory of

Jerry Fitzwilliam charging towards her with murder in his eyes. And the embarrassment of having Tim, of all people, criticise the moral fabric of her being.

She was just searching for her vibrator down the back of the sofa when she realised the air in the basement flat was uncharacteristically fresh. It was cold too. A draught blew through the tiny space.

Feeling the skin on her arms prickle up with goose bumps, Bev prised her sex toy free and walked into her bedroom. The moonlight streamed in, casting long shadows everywhere, transforming her bulky furniture into menacing giant monsters. It took her a moment to work out why the long voile curtains were billowing inside like ghosts in flight.

The patio doors were wide open. If it hadn't been Tim, who else had been inside her place?

CHAPTER 26
Boo

'So, had he been mental for a long time?' Mitch's mother asked, offering Boo a ginger biscuit on an old china plate. 'Your dad, I mean.' She and Mitch's father locked eyes. Silent understanding seemed to pass between them, making the air in the dated conservatory feel even more stifling.

Boo pushed the plate of biscuits away, sickened. 'My dad wasn't, "mental" . . . whatever *that* is.' She placed a protective hand on her burgeoning little bump. Knowing she should keep her mouth shut for Mitch's sake. Struggling. She tried to backtrack. 'He was the greatest dad I could ever have asked for, and I loved him with all my heart.' Her lower lip was trembling. She felt the full force of a tsunami of grief washing over her. Tears started to roll onto her cheeks. Wiping them away, she contemplated just standing up and getting the hell out of there. Only, her mother had warned her to make nice.

Your dad left me with nothing but debts, the drunken old bag had said, chugging on a bottle of cheap tequila. Grabbing a fistful of brown envelopes from the kitchen table and fanning them in Boo's face. *Do yourself a favour and try to make that boyfriend of yours' parents like you enough to help support this brat you've got knocked up with. Do you think you can do at least that?* Way to go, Mother.

'Dad was severely depressed. He was ill, OK? Same as someone with arthritis or . . . or . . . leukaemia.' Right at that moment, hormonally-led or not, Boo wanted to throw her cup of piss-weak tea into Mitch's mother's wrinkly old po-face. The silly cow was sitting there, smoothing down the pleats in her skirt and picking imaginary bits from a fussy floral cardigan, as though she were preparing to receive Holy Communion from the Pope. Why did Mitch's folks have to be so uncool? Why were they alive when her beloved dad was dead? It wasn't fair. 'It was never anything to be ashamed of. *I* wasn't ashamed of him.' She looked to her boyfriend for support, but Mitch was examining his ginger biscuit, nibbling like a damned squirrel around the edges, as if she hadn't just been insulted to the core by his parents. She imagined she could feel the baby kicking her in defiance, though at the sixteen-weeks stage, that was hardly even possible. The baby needed her to be strong for both of them. Boo narrowed her eyes. 'Turds who don't understand mental health issues shouldn't be so quick to slap labels onto good people who just happen to be ill.'

The father snorted with derision. 'That's what papers like the *Guardian* say. All that left-wing, Channel 4 gay nonsense. Luckily, I know all about mental health issues.' He pointed, as if about to deliver a valuable life-lesson. 'Real men don't get depressed. We shoulder our responsibilities with a bit of backbone and a lot of hard graft. Am I right, Mary?'

'Yes, Gerald.'

Neither of them seemed to register the fact that Boo had called them turds. Mary and Gerald Mitchell. The worst in-laws she could have wished for.

She could hear her father's voice speaking to her, then. *They're not worth it, love. These self-righteous twits aren't our kind. Take no notice, Boo Boo.* She imagined his hairy arm around her shoulder. Tried to block out the memory of him swinging from the ceiling. Forced herself to remember him when he'd been alive and relatively well. Strong Dad. Kind Dad. Dad who made a belting curry and who'd willingly painted her childhood bedroom walls black, when she'd nagged him at the age of fifteen.

'I'm sorry,' she told Mitch, standing suddenly. 'I can't do this right now. It's too soon. I'm going.'

'Don't be daft!' Mitch said, barring her way with an outstretched leg. 'You're just being hormonal.'

She tried to force her way past him, irritated that he'd used the H-word, immediately undermining the value of her carefully considered words. 'Pregnant women are allowed to have opinions, Mitch.' The fact that he hadn't stood up for her and challenged the offensive bilge his parents had come out with hurt her deeply.

But he simply stood and locked her in an unyielding hug that felt more like control than comfort. 'We're having a baby. Mum and Dad are offering to help. I know you're grieving. Just hear them out, Boo.'

Barely able to bite back a sharp retort, Boo sat back down again on the rattan chair. Spied a wasp throwing itself against one of the double glazed panes in the roof of the conservatory. It too wanted to get the hell out of there, away from these 1950s-throwback freaks. *Try to make them like you enough to help support this brat . . .* She took a deep breath and reconsidered her mother's cynical suggestion. 'I'm sorry.' She took a ginger biscuit from the plate on the small coffee table as a gesture of truce. Nibbled daintily on it, like the sort of woman would who these small-minded fools might wish the mother of their first grandchild to be. Ruined the effect by talking with her mouth full. 'It's just that my dad and the morning sickness combined . . . Well, it's been a rough first trimester.'

Their hard-bitten faces softened slightly.

Gerald crossed his legs and spread his arms regally on the armrests of his wicker throne. 'Obviously, there's absolutely no question of you having an abortion.'

'No question,' Mary said, nodding vehemently. 'We're Catholics. You know that, don't you? Colin told you, didn't he?'

Boo just nodded. 'Oh, I'm keeping the baby.' She laced her fingers together to form a protective coracle over her abdomen, imagining the infant Moses being hidden in a basket among the tall grasses that fringed the banks of the Nile. Just as Moses had been saved from the evil Pharaoh, she vowed to protect the new life inside her from this saggy-bollocked old prick.

But the two glanced at one another; then, at their son. The muggy air seemed ripe with an indecent proposal.

'Well, we've given some thought to how very young you two are,' Gerald said. 'How much living you've got ahead of you and how having a baby will interfere with your studies.'

Mary nodded. 'I had my eldest at nineteen, and I can tell you now, it was no picnic,' she said. She turned to Mitch. 'I knew the ropes by the time you came along, of course.'

How old was she? Boo wondered. Sixty? She looked sixty. Way too old to be the mother of a Fresher at university. Must have had him on the change, maybe. Boo glanced at the array of family photos that hung on the wall behind the couple. One, two, three, four, five . . . Mitch had six siblings and he'd said he was the youngest. Now, it made sense. *Jesus. The woman must have a twat like a horse collar after all those kids*, Boo thought. *Am I going to end up a dried-up old bone like that at sixty? Is that what motherhood does to you?* She choked back a guilty sob for resenting the fledgling life inside her.

'My own mother did a lot of the parenting when I had my first child,' she said, seeking corroboration from her husband. 'It was a difficult birth, wasn't it, Gerald?'

Mitch's father nodded. 'Very. Thomas was a big baby.'

Mary examined her short, surprisingly grubby fingernails. 'I was . . . in a bad way for a long time. Lost a lot of blood. Anyway, my own mother coming to the rescue was a godsend. It meant I could get back on my feet and ease into looking after Thomas when I was ready. And that's what we'll do for you, when the baby comes.'

Boo blinked hard, looking from Mary to Gerald and back again. Why was Mitch sitting there, impassively, saying not a single word? Unless, they'd discussed it beforehand, presenting it now as a fait accompli. 'No,' Boo simply said. 'This is my baby. I'll raise her myself, thanks.'

This time, when she stood to leave, she managed to topple the table, with its tray holding their best tea set and an opened pack of ginger nuts. The floor became awash with beige liquid, broken floral china and biscuit shards that slowly darkened as they soaked up the tea.

'Oh, I say!' Mary half shrieked. 'Get a cloth, Gerald! The tannin will stain the grout between the floor tiles. Quick!'

'What did you do that for?' Mitch asked above the sound of his fussing parents. He shook his head, screwing up his eyes and curling his lip at her like some bully in the playground. 'I love you so much. All I wanted was for the woman I love – the mother of my unborn child – to come and be nice to my folks. But you couldn't, could you? Not even for an hour. Is this what I deserve, Boo Boo?'

His words bit, but the mess and panic provided just the distraction Boo needed to escape the confrontational confines of the tiny conservatory. Knocking a cactus plant from the low sill with her bag, spilling compost everywhere, cementing her fate as the future daughter-in-law from hell, she barrelled into the gloomy dining room. Had to get out. Had to call a taxi; somehow get back up to Durham, to the peace of her room in college and the autonomy it offered from someone else's controlling parents and her own disinterested mother. 'Forget it. I don't need you – any of you – to raise this baby,' she said, scowling at Mitch. She wondered how she could have thought for a moment that the two of them might work out. Dad was gone. She was on her own.

'Wait!' Mitch called to her down the hall as she donned her coat. 'Think of what my folks are offering, Boo! We can finish our degrees. Take the baby back once we've graduated and found jobs.' He advanced towards her with purposeful strides. Bore down on her. 'What the hell do we know about child-rearing? Look at us! We're kids ourselves.' He grabbed at her sleeve. Whispered close to her ear. 'All those drugs you take? Are you willing to run the risk of the authorities finding out about your lifestyle?'

Gazing at him open-mouthed, Boo absorbed what he was insinuating. 'All the drugs *I* take? Are you having a laugh? You wanna blackmail me into giving our child to your parents so they can play house with kid number seven? And then what?' She wrenched her coat sleeve from his grip. 'You get to trip and drink your way through your twenties, maybe shouldering a bit of fatherly responsibilities when the novelty wears off? What am I in this equation? A visitor? A surrogate? You're tapped. No frigging way, Jose. Mary and Gerald Mitchell are not my kind of people and they're *not* raising my daughter.'

Feeling as though an umbilical cord, attached to her own stomach, was tugging her down the driveway and along the cul-de-sac to the busy street, Boo wept openly. Relieved that Mitch had remained behind, declaring his undying love, beseeching her, and when that didn't work, shouting ultimatums from the doorway of his parents' Barratt home. Let him plead. Let him threaten and cajole. There was no way she was going to give up this precious life inside her to a ploy that sounded suspiciously similar to informal adoption. True, she had nobody in the world now that Dad had gone, but . . .

Climbing into a cab, Boo took the folded piece of paper reverentially from the envelope.

'Station, please,' she told the driver, as she expanded the concertinaed shape so that it made a delicate three dimensional frog.

Heaving silently with the agony of solitude, Boo then carefully unfolded the shape to reveal a piece of notepaper on which had been written a short letter in a small, shaky hand.

Dear Boo Boo

I'm so very very sorry to be writing this farewell letter. Your dad just feels like he's hit a dead end, I'm afraid. You know I've tried for the longest time to find the sunshine. I thought I'd found it the other day when you told me about the baby, but then, I realised a pure little life shouldn't be tainted with my black moods and troughs of despond. I've failed you and your mum over the years. I can't fail the baby, too. It's better this way. There's so much white noise in my head, Boo Boo. I just can't bear it any more. All I want is a little peace and quiet.

*I won't be here to help you with the baby, but I
know you'll be a brilliant mum because you have only
love and good in you. Whatever happens, though,
make sure you finish at university and make a
comfortable, happy life for yourself. You're my baby,
after all and I'll always be the proudest dad in the
world. I love you with all my heart and forever, even
from the other side.*

Love, Dad.

xxx

'You all right, duck?' the cabbie asked, regarding her
through his rear-view mirror. 'You need a hanky?' He
pulled a tissue from the bejewelled box on his dashboard.
Passed it back.

Boo took it, thanking him. Blew her nose hard. Her dad
had wanted her to finish her studies. How the hell was she
going to do that with a baby in tow? On her own.

'Station's not far now,' the cabbie said, trying to sound
encouraging but looking unnerved by the distraught girl
on his back seat.

'Actually,' she said, already feeling regret biting in the
pit of her stomach. 'Change of plan . . .'

CHAPTER 27

Angie

'It's me. Are you safe?' The panic in Bev's voice was audible. She started to babble barely intelligible nonsense at speed about grey men on trains and Jerry getting shirty and origami facing the wrong way. 'Please tell me you're out of there.'

Damn. If she'd realised it had been Bev calling, she'd have sent the call to voicemail. But Angie had answered without checking who it was. A schoolgirl error, since Gretchen was standing right by her in the kitchen, ironing the children's freshly washed clothes while Angie made a shopping list. Now was not the time to be discussing her clandestine plans to escape. It was clear the snooping nanny was eavesdropping, and, as if that weren't oppressive and worrying enough, Jerry was back.

'Esme! How lovely to hear from you!' Angie said, taking several steps away from Gretchen, towards the sink. Ran the tap, lest Bev's words somehow reached unintended ears. 'It's a lifetime since we got together. I've got *so* much to tell you.'

'Is he there?' Bev asked, clearly paranoid as hell. 'If you're safe, say banana. If you're in danger, say . . . earrings.'

As if he instinctively knew she was speaking to her secret ally, Jerry padded in. Thankfully ignoring her and instead making a beeline for the children, who squealed with delight to see Daddy, Daddy, Daddy! Then, Gretchen. Asking about her holiday. *How were the folks? How was the schnapps and the lederhosen? Ha ha ha.* There was definitely some subterfuge going on between those two.

Yes, she was in bloody danger, with Spy Nanny from Hell and her potentially vengeful husband, who was definitely onto her. Mustering as much jollity as she could, she considered her breezy response. 'Do message me with the address of the place where you got those divine earrings.'

Bev sounded like a violin string that had been tightened to snapping point. 'I've got everything you need. Meet me in an hour. Somewhere where people hardly ever go – off the beaten track and impossible for someone to follow you without you knowing it.' There was a pause. 'I've got it! Let's meet at Dunham cemetery. Watch your back!'

The drive out to meet her took Angie along the leafy green tunnel Dunham of Road, past sprawling period country piles and, to her left, the high brick wall that encircled the National Trust's Dunham Park. Breathing too quickly and feeling her heart fluttering inside her like a trapped moth, she had eyes everywhere but on the road ahead.

Is Jerry having me followed? There's almost certainly a satellite orbiting the earth a hundred miles above Cheshire, with me in its sights. Any minute now, I'll be surrounded by government agents and arrested on trumped-up charges as an enemy of the state or a double agent in Putin's employ. Let's face it, Jerry can do anything he wants. He'll take the children and have me committed. I won't even be admitted to the Priory. He'll make darn sure I end up in some godforsaken NHS facility with no Clarins, riddled with C Difficile and

MRSA. Has that BMW been behind me all the way from Hale? It has. It's on my tail. Oh dear.

A honking horn punctuated her panic, and Angie was forced to swerve out of the path of an oncoming dumper truck. She held her hand up apologetically. She had veered into his lane, after all. Glancing behind her, she saw that the BMW was still there. Turning right into the country lane that led to the cemetery would flush the driver out, if he was pursuing her.

She put her indicator on, praying that she wouldn't be followed; thankful that she'd dropped the children at short notice on a playdate at Venetia Crooke's house on Bankhall Lane. But the BMW's indicator also started to flash, heralding a right turn. Trying to catch a glimpse of the driver's face through her rear-view mirror, Angie wondered how she might shake this fiend off, enabling her to meet Bev unmolested. Bev said she had everything, but Angie also had to show Bev what she'd found. It sat in her handbag like nuclear waste, threatening to pollute everything it touched.

The ivory-rendered Axe & Cleaver pub was coming up on her right. Hastily indicating, she turned into the tiny road that serviced the place.

'Please go past. Please go past.'

When the BMW turned into the road behind her, lights seemed to pop all around her and her fingertips and toes prickled numb.

Knowing she could at least yell for help in the pub and stand a chance of some brave stranger coming to her rescue, she determined to park up and sprint inside before the BMW driver had a chance to get to her. If need be, there was a heavy tyre iron in the boot that she could use to defend herself, assuming she could lift the thing. She stalled the Range Rover. It lurched forward, almost knocking the legs from under an elderly man with a giant beer gut, who was clearly off for a spot of lunch.

Slamming her door shut, Angie was about to retrieve her weapon of choice, when she realised that the BMW contained nothing more sinister than a family of five – two harassed parents, two bawling, brawling toddlers covered in magic marker and sick, with a shrieking baby who was so red in the face, Angie thought he might bust a blood vessel at any moment.

'Oh dear. Oh thank you, thank you, thank you,' she said beneath her breath.

Getting back into the Range Rover, leaving the pub behind her, she continued up the winding country lane to the cemetery and crematorium. Bev had insisted they meet in the secluded new Jewish section – no more than a field containing a couple of rows of pristine-looking headstones; handily out of sight of the established, main areas.

Angie stowed herself behind the prayer hall, peeping out periodically whenever she heard footsteps on a path or the rustle of vegetation being disturbed. After about ten minutes, it was clear someone was approaching. Could it be Gretchen, sent by Jerry? Or Jerry himself, if he was tracking the car.

Peeping out from her hiding place, holding her breath, she spied a dishevelled-looking Bev in torn jeans with circles beneath her eyes that said she hardly ever slept.

Sliding her Prada sunglasses on, Angie strode out into the expanse of green, keen to appear like a woman who was holding things together, though the itch of hives at the base of her neck said otherwise.

'Ah! There you are,' she said. She gripped her shoulder bag close to her body; stole a glance around. 'Were you followed?'

'Let's go behind the prayer hall,' Bev said, dragging her back into the shadows of the dark little building.

Clearly Angie wasn't the only one on edge.

'Let's make this quick,' Angie said, unable to keep the waver out of her voice. She checked her watch. 'Jerry and Gretchen think I'm just dropping the kids off at a playdate and taking some dry cleaning to be done. You first.'

Bev reached into her handbag. Spoke rapidly, checking beyond the wall at regular intervals. 'I've got a USB stick containing details of his bank accounts, passwords, the lot. This is the motherlode, and your solicitor will have a field day. It took me ages to go through everything, but I found an Excel spreadsheet where the silly pillock has listed all his passwords. The spreadsheet itself is password protected, but my business associate worked out what it is.'

Angie stared at the stick, feeling like it was some kind of magical key to her future as a free woman. 'And what is it?'

'The date your dog died. Jerry talked about it on Facebook like it was the death of his mother. My business associate put two and two together . . .'

Angie smiled weakly. 'He loved that old Staffie. Elsie. He treated Elsie better than he does his own mother!'

Bev pushed the USB stick into her hand. 'There are video files on there too. Films and audio from my trips to London to honeytrap him. He was a total pig, I hasten to add. He's threatened me, so if he works out that I'm not some marketing PR called Cat Thomson and I wind up dead, you'll know who's to blame. In fact, he specifically mentioned my basement flat, even though I'd never told him where I live, so I'd say that scenario's worryingly likely. Anyway, I've screenshot all the LinkedIn and Facebook conversations that took place between me and him and saved them into a special file. That, plus the film footage prove he had every intention of being unfaithful to you. You've got the lot, including some nasty emails where he orders girls and drugs like pizza to his London flat, which I have an address for. This is as far as I go.' She squeezed Angie's hand in a show of solidarity. 'I'm sorry you'll have to see all this. It's worse than anything you anticipated.'

'No, I'm afraid it's not,' Angie said, shaking her head dolefully. Wiped a tear away. 'You're not the only one with incriminating evidence.'

Bev looked at her quizzically and Angie took out a stick not unlike the one her PI had just given to her.

'What is it?' Bev asked.

'Proof . . .' Angie said, struggling to say the words as tears started to roll onto her cheeks and sorrow threatened to tie her tongue in knots. '. . . Screenshots of emails that show Gretchen is in the pay of Jerry to spy on me. But not only that . . . I think she's blackmailing him, actually.'

'Where did you get this?' Bev asked.

'I went through her things while she was at the park with the children and I found a shoebox at the back of the wardrobe. This was inside a shoe.'

'Have you looked at it?'

Angie nodded. 'Unfortunately, yes. There are some stills on there of . . . sex. The London parties in the flat you mention. Men with girls. Young girls. There's a photo of Jerry being . . . Oh, it's horrible, Bev.' She pulled a sheaf of printouts from her handbag and showed Bev the evidence of five men, naked but for latex animal masks, cavorting with girls. In another photo, her husband was being fellated by a young black girl who couldn't have been more than sixteen. She couldn't stifle the wail that emerged. Pressed the stick into Bev's hands and covered her face with her silk scarf.

Bev glanced at the printouts, grimacing. Looked ponderously at the stick and held it out. 'Your solicitor will need this. Don't give it to me.'

'But I'm frightened, Bev. Take it! I think Jerry's onto me and I'm scared he's going to . . . disappear me. I really do. Whether it be having me committed or having someone hurt me. I'm just——'

'Listen, Angie,' Bev said, grabbing her hand and squeezing. 'You've got to be strong for you and your kids. Get all of this evidence straight to your solicitor. Right now, this minute. And where are your kids?'

'They're at a friend's. They're safe.'

'Get them and leave immediately. Go to your parents. Another relative. Someone trusted and on your side. Go to a hotel. It doesn't matter, but don't arse around packing. Just get out. OK? Today. You have to take that sleaze-bag down!' She released Angie's hand at last. Her eyes were ablaze with fervour. 'And make damn sure you pay me what I'm owed as soon as you get your money, else me and you are going to fall out. Right?'

Angie nodded, pocketing both USBs. Handing the printouts to Bev. 'You've got copies of everything?'

Bev nodded, taking the sheaves of paper. 'Yep. I've texted you my bank details so you can transfer my fee. I need it asap I've got a lot riding on that money. OK?'

Pulling an envelope from her bag, Angie treated her to a half-smile, slightly put out that Bev seemed to care so much about the money. 'There's £500 in there to tide you over. I sold a handbag,' she lied, remembering how she'd taken a wad of cash from a Jiffy bag full of money that had been resting underneath the shoes in Gretchen's shoebox. Feeling strangely guilty that she'd stolen from her own nanny, though it had almost certainly been extorted from

214

Jerry. 'Can't I give you the rest in person? Take you for lunch. It's the least I can do.'

Checking around the corner of the hall that nobody was lurking, her PI shrank further into the shadows, pulling Angie with her. 'I'm not sure where I'm going to be. I've had a falling-out with Tim and Sophie. And things are . . . weird.' She took a deep breath, seeming preoccupied by something other than getting paid. 'Look. Jerry's dangerous and there's one last missing piece of the jigsaw that I'm going to look into.'

The florid smattering of hives on Angie's neck itched to the point of stinging.

'But whatever you do,' Bev continued, '*don't* turn to Sophie for help. Tim's hostile. Him and Jerry are thick as thieves. I know Tim and I know men like him. He'll take Jerry's side over anything you or Sophie say and he'll betray your confidence. Believe me. Get out of the house and don't look for help from Sophie and Tim. You won't be safe.'

Angie swallowed hard. 'Is this it, then?'

'It is for me.' Bev checked the time on her watch. 'I'll be in touch. Good luck.'

Angie was already back in her car, speeding away from the cemetery when she remembered she'd meant to tell Bev that she'd spotted none other than Rob and her psychiatrist in Tim's company at Carluccio's. Damn. She hit the steering wheel, annoyed with herself. But by the time she reached home, the thought had been buried by her own immediate concerns. She had to somehow get packed without arousing suspicion. It was time to make her great escape.

CHAPTER 28

Bev

Sitting on her saggy sofa in the basement flat, Bev cradled her cup of coffee and opened her laptop. Brought up Rightmove's home page, inputting her search details. Although Tim had given Bev her marching orders, Sophie had negotiated a small stay of execution – she had a week to get out. She needed a flat within a couple of miles of WA15, ideally. Two bedrooms.

Scrolling through several pages of overpriced dumps, she lost interest some twenty minutes in and returned to a previous Google search that had become an itch she desperately needed to scratch.

Tatjana. Russian prostitute. London.

Last time, she had managed to trawl through ten pages of bilge before giving up. This time, she persisted. Changed 'London' to 'Ealing, West London', remembering that she now knew the location of Jerry Fitzwilliam's secret London bolthole. Fifteen pages in, she came across a news story from the *Evening Standard*, dated 25 July the previous year. It caught her attention precisely because it was a world away from the porn sites and other trivia that the search had dredged up. The hairs on the back of her neck stood up as she read the headline.

Murder probe after human remains found in Ealing butcher's bin.

The thunderous beat of Bev's heart was almost too much of a distraction to allow her to read the article.

'Focus, Goddammit!'

Dismembered human body parts were found yesterday at 6.25 a.m. in a wheelie bin behind an Ealing-based family butcher's shop. The Metropolitan Police have opened a murder enquiry, appealing to members of the public to come forward with any sightings of suspicious activity in the area over the past three days.

The gruesome discovery was made by butcher, Ryan Sands, who was disposing of unsold offal, just prior to the weekly rubbish collection. He said, 'I saw some black bin liners that I knew weren't mine, and thought the neighbours had been sticking their rubbish in my bins again. I ripped them open to make sure, especially since it smelled really bad, but not what you'd expect from out-of-date meat. That's when I spotted an arm.' Mr Sands said he was very distressed by the find.

Detective Chief Inspector Barry Greene said, 'Our enquiries have established that the victim is a young female, aged between thirteen and fifteen, who had been strangled, dismembered and then dumped. A dangerous individual or group of individuals is at large, possibly in West London in the Ealing locale. A post-mortem revealed that the victim had been killed elsewhere. Somebody somewhere will perhaps be trying to hide or dispose of clothing that is covered in blood. We would urge anyone who has seen anything suspicious or who has any information that they think might be relevant to this investigation to come forward.

Bev pressed her fingertips against her lips as she pictured the scenario of some poor teenage girl being choked to death and then disposed of in the most heartless manner imaginable. A butcher's bin. In pieces, discarded with the other tainted meat. Could this be the Tatjana mentioned in Jerry Fitzwilliam's emails? Surely not. There was no mention of the dead girl's name in the article, so why had it come up in the search results? Was it a metadata thing? Tags, perhaps. She scanned her screen to see if she could find a connection, but her concentration broke up like a bad Wi-Fi connection.

The sound of Sophie and Tim arguing in the hall was drifting down the stone steps, through her flimsy front door to the basement. Ordinarily, she'd be eavesdropping to see what the contretemps was about, so rare was it that the two argued . . . at least, within earshot. But right now, her unsupportive friend and idiot landlord were the last things on her mind.

She walked into her bedroom, closing the door on the raised voices. She'd already restored her origami models to their proper positions, shuddering whilst doing so – trying her damnedest to blot out the thought that a stranger had been rooting through her things with the deliberate intention of playing with her mind. Missing her last couple of therapy sessions only served to heighten her paranoia. She'd checked that all the windows were shut and locked; that nobody was lurking in cupboards or cubbyholes that were large enough to conceal an intruder. The patio doors had been barred shut with an old lacrosse stick she'd liberated from Sophie's garage. The curtains were firmly drawn. Rightmove could wait until the morning. But before stressful, fitful sleep claimed her, she wanted to see if there was more about the girl in the Ealing butcher's bin.

Crawling into her unmade bed, Bev started to look at the stories that were listed in her laptop's sidebar, adjacent to the *Evening Standard's* report of body parts in black bin bags. They had a shared location in common: Ealing. One was a story about pro-life campaigners being banned from an abortion clinic. Another was about a suspect package scare at Ealing Broadway. But the final feature seemed linked to the case that had piqued her interest.

Girl in butcher's bin identified.

'Bingo,' Bev said softly, clicking on the link. 'Come on. Put me out of my misery.'

The photograph of a slightly built girl with pale skin and dark, straight hair loaded onto the screen. Wearing an earnest expression, her bone structure was recognisably Eastern European with high cheekbones and a straight nose. But her deep-set eyes gave her a Mediterranean look. There was no happiness in that small haunted face.

The fine hairs stood to attention on Bev's arms as she read . . .

The Metropolitan Police has finally released the identity of the dismembered girl found in the butcher's bin in Ealing. Dental records show that the victim's name was Tatjana Lebedev, a fifteen-year-old who had been living in temporary accommodation locally. Although she had been trafficked to the UK two years ago and was supposed to be under the protection of social services whilst seeking asylum, Miss Lebedev had not been resident at her registered address for seven months.

In the course of a thorough search by police, Miss Lebedev's clothes and purse were discovered in another bin belonging to a neighbouring business – Café Soleil – in the same back alley that also serviced Mr Sands' family butcher's, where the victim's remains were found. Her purse contained receipts from a supermarket and hairdresser's in Moscow and also a stolen Oyster card.

Detective Chief Inspector Barry Greene said, 'We are certain that somebody knew Tatjana's whereabouts on the day leading up to and the night before her brutal murder. We are hopeful that a member of the public will be able to identify who Tatjana was with at the estimated time of her death – 1 a.m. Anybody with potentially useful information, however insignificant the details may seem, should come forward to their local police station as soon as possible or call the witness hotline.

Blinking back panicked tears, in a shaky hand, Bev wrote the reported date and rough time of Tatjana's murder in her notebook. She then took a USB stick from the zipped pocket inside her handbag onto which she'd copied all of Jerry Fitzwilliam's files, plugged it into her laptop and brought up his email files. After some searching she happened upon the email to Stan where Jerry had mentioned Tatjana.

You're not answering my calls. What did they do with Tatjana? What happened to the film?

Jerry had sent that missive to the dealer-cum-pimp only five days after Tatjana Lebedev's death.

'Oh my God,' she said. 'Why did this have to happen? Why the hell did I keep looking? Why can't I just let things lie? You're a bloody idiot, Bev Saunders.'

She snatched up a brass frame from her bedside cabinet that held two photos, side by side – one each of the man and the girl she loved more than anything. She held the frame tightly against her chest so that the corners dug into her left breast.

'Hope has left the building and is never coming back,' she said, softly.

As if losing the people that made life worth living wasn't enough; as if losing her career and all her worldly goods in an acrimonious divorce wasn't enough, she was deep in the trenches of psychological warfare with an unseen enemy. And now, she'd potentially stumbled upon an unsolved murder where the high-profile and powerful man, who was almost certainly harassing her, was somehow involved. Judging by his surprisingly revelatory emails to Stan, the pimp, he evidently thought himself untouchable, too.

She aggressively wiped away a fat tear that escaped her right eye. *Pull it together, woman. I bet this is just one massive coincidence. Your work for Angie is over. Forget what you've just read. Move on. You're no cop. You're a bob-a-job sleuth who takes pictures of cheating husbands. That's it. Finito. Sort your own life out.*

And yet . . . Bev laid out on her stale duvet cover the printed stills of Jerry and his masked cronies, engaged in gang bangs with suspiciously young-looking working girls. The shadow Science Minister was quite the exhibitionist in front of a lens. Could there be filmed evidence somewhere of Tatjana Lebedev's murder, assuming she and the Tatjana mentioned in Jerry's email were one and the same person? How could they *not* be? Girls were trafficked to the UK from Eastern Europe mainly to work in the sex trade. The Tatjana in Jerry's email to 'Stan' had clearly been a prostitute, and Bev now had the sexually explicit photos that Gretchen, the blackmailing nanny, had been sitting on to insinuate the likely link. She could go to the police and let them do the rest. But then, she'd face being given a hard time by those two arse-clown detectives, Curtis and

Owen. Ever since she'd cornered an unfaithful plasterer in a Travelodge on the M6, resulting in a fracas with the plasterer, a cleaner and the guy on reception, Curtis and Owen had it in for her as an interfering vigilante amateur. Perhaps they'd arrest Fitzwilliam but then drop the case due to insufficient evidence. Then, when Fitzwilliam discovered who had grassed on him, Bev and Angie would attract even more unwanted attention. Was it unfeasible that she too would end her days in the bottom of a wheelie bin, her severed limbs entwined with Angie's?

If she retreated now, the whole thing might go away. But that wasn't necessarily the moral thing to do. Retreat or advance?

'Doc.'

Scrambling to the end of the bed, taking her phone out of her cardigan pocket, she brought up the number of Doc's folks' landline. He'd asked Bev not to contact him using their number, but all bets were off in an emergency like this. At this time of night, he'd either be gaming, masturbating or fiddling with Lego in his attic, she reasoned. But what about his parents? Didn't people of their age go to bed at 9 p.m. with a cup of something warm and milky? *Murder is more important than an early night*, Bev decided. *Come on, Saunders. One last stab at getting to the bottom of this. If it's a dead end, you hand what you've got over to the cops and head for the hills.*

The phone was picked up after a seemingly endless period of ringing, ringing, ringing out.

'Hello?' Doc on the other end, sounding nervous.

'It's me. Bev.'

The pitch of his voice went up by an octave. 'You're calling me on my parents' landline at this time of night? Are you tapped in the head?'

'Yes. We both are. That's why we're in therapy, chuck. Now listen . . .' Bev spoke in almost a whisper. 'I need you to find the film Jerry mentioned. It could be on the Dark Net.'

'I told you,' he said. 'I'm not doing any dodgy Dark Net shit while I'm here. The last thing I want to do is jeopardise the safety of my folks. And if you think—'

'Fine!' This wasn't going the way Bev had hoped. 'I'm only talking about the murder of a fifteen-year-old girl here. But that doesn't matter. Forget we might be able to put a rapist of trafficked girls and a possible killer behind bars instead of in government bleeding office. Fine. Leave it, Doc. I realise you've fulfilled the task I paid you for in Lego that cost me every bean I had. Fine. But I thought we made a pact to keep digging. Have a good evening pulling on your pecker. Careful of your balls . . . Oh, wait. You haven't got any! Silly me!'

Boom. Bev could feel her anger supplanting her fear. It was a welcome sensation. Sleep was ebbing away from her.

'Why are you being a dick?' Doc asked. 'I should put the phone down on you right now, but . . .'

'But what? You haven't got the spine?' She knew her words would sting. She didn't care.

'I'm your friend, Bev. I'm worried about you. You need to get some critical distance from this job – and it is just a job. We both need to take a step back. This is some dangerous shit we've got ourselves involved with. Even I'm not that desperate for money.'

'Because you're still hiding behind your mummy's skirt, Doc.'

'OK. You're using me as a whipping boy because you're frustrated. I get it. But I'm not playing. Go to your sex club, Bev. I'm putting the phone down.'

'I'm sorry,' she said. 'I'm sorry. Right? I'm just upset. I'm scared. But don't cut me off. Listen, if you're not going to help, tell me how to access the Dark Net. I'll do it. I'll look for the film.'

An hour later, Bev clicked on a link that took her down the rabbit hole.

CHAPTER 29
Boo

'I've called the ambulance,' Holy Jo said, rubbing Boo's hand. 'They won't be long. Keep breathing.'

Boo nodded. She tried to answer but her sentiments were swept away on another gust of pure pain. Clenching her bedclothes in her sweaty fists, she dug her buttocks into the hard mattress, praying for the contraction to be over. Three minutes apart, finally, after twenty-four hours of ineffectual agony. Her bag was packed; her papers ready. The maternity ward had told her over the phone not to bother coming in until the contractions were closer together and that time had finally come. Boo was convinced that her waters were going to break suddenly and that the baby would shoot out here, in her dismal student room. Why did the bed have to be so bloody uncomfortable? How had she ended up in halls in her second year, still living next to the woefully unadventurous Holy Jo? She should have been sharing a cool student house, instead of being holed up with a load of freshers; stuck with Holy Jo as her birth partner. Where the hell was Mitch, the infernal selfish jerk?

'You're holding your breath, sweets! Remember to breathe,' Holy Jo said, like she was some kind of goddamned expert. 'In through the nose. Out through the mouth.' She demonstrated by making wafting motions with her slender hands. 'In and out. Breathe.'

Torn apart by the contraction, Boo angled her head so she could see her neighbour. Lithe. Skinny. Beautiful. Not the size of a house, about to shit out a bowling ball. She grabbed Holy Jo's hand as the pain became more intense. '*You* fucking breathe.'

'Now, now. Don't be silly, sweets. I'm trying to help you.'

Boo glanced down at her neighbour's fingers, encased in her own iron fist – turning white as the flow of blood ceased. The stoic sod hadn't said a word.

'The meek shall inherit the earth,' Boo managed as the contraction started to ease off, releasing her from her grip.

'What do you mean?' Holy Jo rubbed her palms, smiling benignly.

'You. You didn't complain even though I'd cut your circulation off. Jesus, man. If I hurt you, say so! I don't know what I'm doing when the pain comes. Don't be a doormat.'

Holy Jo's lips parted in a beatified smile, revealing a string of pearly whites, polished to a shine, perhaps by angels. 'I'm not the one about to give birth at nineteen, Boo. And where's your doting boyfriend, exactly?'

'He's . . .'

'So, who's the doormat?' That smile was still there but Holy Jo's words cut like a cat o'nine tails in an act of told-you-so flagellation.

In the delivery suite, midwives bustled about her, monitoring her blood pressure and heartbeat; handing her a mask, connected by tubing to a giant canister full of gas and air. If nothing else, Boo felt certain this was an excellent opportunity – perhaps, the last for a long while – to get high. She lay on the bed and inhaled deeply. Kept inhaling long after the midwives had told her the gas and air was only meant to be used at the peak of a contraction. Twenty minutes in and she wouldn't be torn from the mask. She was utterly blasted.

An apparition of her own mother manifested itself like the Ghost of Christmas Future in the corner of the room, drinking vodka from the bottle and daubing paint over the door to the en-suite toilet.

'What are you doing here?' Boo imagined that she asked.

'The writing's on the wall for you, girl,' her mother said. 'See?' In red, the brush strokes assembled themselves into words:

SHALLOW END. DEEP END.

'What does it mean?' Boo asked.

The hallucination of Sozzled Sylvia – appearing so very real that Boo fancied she could reach out and slap the old bag – treated her to an unpleasant, patronising grin. 'You've got shitty genetic inheritance, Boo Boo. You and the baby are forever paddling in the shallow end of the gene pool.'

In her peripheral vision, Boo caught sight of her beloved dad. Still alive with good colour in his cheeks. He was wearing only an operating gown. The glint of metal drew her attention from his kindly stubbled face southwards – he was clutching a scalpel.

'Dad, no!' Boo cried, reaching out to stay his hand as he started to draw the blade across his wrists.

She turned back to her mother, horrified as her dad's blood sprayed on the door, covering the daubed words.

'Deep end,' her mother said, gasping as she swallowed a gulp of neat vodka. 'You're drawn to trouble, Boo. Drama

227

finds you. You'll always end up in the deep end. Careful you don't drown.'

'Push!' A stern female voice permeated through the narcotic haze. 'Push now or this baby's not going to make it.'

Boo felt strong hands lifting the mask from her face and prising it from her as she tried to snatch it back with grabby fingers.

Suddenly, her drunken mother was gone. The nightmarish red mess of the painted words and spattered blood were nowhere to be seen. With regret, she realised her dad too had vanished like defeated poltergeist.

'Come on, Boo! The head's about to crown. Push!' Holy Jo had joined in with the midwives' cheerleading and words of encouragement.

Aware of an overwhelming urge to bear down, Boo concentrated her rapidly clearing mind on this one task – to give birth. The tension in the room was punctured finally by the mewling of her newborn child.

The midwife turned to her, cradling the tiny bundle of goo and gore, the purple-grey umbilical cord hanging below like a parachute ripcord. 'Congratulations! It's a healthy girl.'

As her daughter nestled at her breast for the first time, skin on skin, Boo was neither aware of Holy Jo nor the midwives nor Mitch, who had just entered the delivery suite. She had eyes only for her baby and she had never felt such love for anyone in her life.

'So you give her to us as soon as you've got the registration documents and then we take her home with us. Are we agreed? Colin?' Mitch's mother was peering into the back seat of the old man's Rover at her son, failing to look at Boo as though she had merely acted as a surrogate in the production of their baby.

'Listen, Mrs Mitchell,' Boo began, trying to articulate the maelstrom of conflicting emotions that had kept her awake for the past week. 'I know what we said when I was pregnant, but—'

'You signed an agreement,' the old bag said, the furrows around her mouth deepening.

'It was a bit of paper you knocked up on the computer.'

'It's legally binding. Me and Gerald are the baby's legal guardians until you two finish your studies and get married. That's that. There's nothing you can do about it.' There was that piranha grin Boo had seen, time and again, in the course of the last few days. 'And besides, we're her family, and you've got no support at home.'

Fleetingly, Boo thought about her mother, increasingly drinking more than she ate. The doctors had warned her that her liver was enlarged and her kidneys were at risk of packing up entirely, but of course, the stubborn cow wasn't listening. Sylvia thought she was invincible since Dad had gone. And she had zero interest in the baby. No surprise there.

At her side, Mitch absently glanced at his daughter and immediately looked away. 'Mum's right, Boo. The baby's a Mitchell. There's nothing we can do for her that Mum and Dad can't.'

Her stomach was churning; her stitches stinging as though she were being jabbed with hot needles – some kind of karmic retribution for being weak enough to hand her infant child over to strangers. Boo wanted to unstrap the baby carrier at the traffic lights and make a run for it. How far would she be able to waddle before they had her arrested?

'Forget it,' Mitch said, as if reading her mind. 'One day, we'll both be in a position to be good parents to her. But right now? We're nineteen, Boo Boo. Think it through. We've got nothing to offer.'

'We've got love,' Boo said, barely able to push her words past the guilty grief lodged in her throat.

'Here we go!' Gerald said, pulling up outside the registry office. 'Out you get. We'll go for a nice pub lunch when you're done. Celebrate.'

Celebrate? Celebrate my painful nipples and my broken heart while you coo over stealing my baby and I struggle to lactate, you fucking cradle-snatching bastards. 'Nice. Bring the change bag, Mitch.'

'Can I see your ID please?'

The registrar was a sour-faced man in his thirties, Boo assessed. Far older in his dress and hairstyle, though. Should she tell him her baby was about to be stolen against her will by her boyfriend's parents? Would he even care?

They showed their passports and the registrar entered the details on a computer.

'What's the baby's name?' he asked.

'Hope,' Boo said. 'She's called Hope.'

Staring quizzically down at the passports, the registrar peered at the tiny pink bundle in the car seat and then at Mitch. 'Colin?'

Mitch laughed. 'Only my folks call me Colin. Please . . . I prefer my middle name. Rob. Or Mitch. My mates call me Mitch.'

The registrar raised an eyebrow and shook his head dismissively. 'You're not married, Mr Mitchell. Is little Hope taking your surname? Hope Mitchell?' He turned to Boo. 'Or Hope Saunders? Do you want her to have your family name, Beverley?'

Boo nodded. Her guilt at having consented to give away this precious life she'd created, however temporarily, manifested itself merely as throbbing pain in her tender breasts. Unable to articulate anger at being sidelined by a disinterested babyfather and his bullying parents, as though her value in this little family equation amounted to precisely zero. No matter what she had said months ago to Mary and Gerald in a crisis of confidence, she'd changed her mind, now. The bond between her and her baby was everything. Her studies meant nothing. Mitch meant nothing. What her father would have wanted for her mattered not a jot now that he was dead. But Boo was outnumbered and outmanoeuvred; rendered little more than a child herself by having her voice stolen from her. There was nobody coming to save her day. She was on her own. 'Yes. Hope_ Saunders,' she said in a small, rebellious voice.

'No! Mitchell,' Mitch said, pointing insistently at his passport. 'She's a Mitchell.'

Hours later, when her daughter had been wrenched from her bosom and she had been divested of all the baby paraphernalia that reminded her that she was a new mother with purpose in her life, Boo sat on Holy Jo's bed and wept.

'I'm the worst person in the world,' she said, stumbling over her confession as hiccoughs took a hold of her. 'I g-gave my baby away. That makes me the scum of the e-earth.' In her mind's eye, she could see Hope's downy pink cheeks and the miniature feathers that were her eyebrows – a perfect picture of repose when she slept. That tiny rosebud mouth. A face no bigger than Boo's palm which already showed the full spectrum of human emotion whenever she grimaced or yawned or cried. 'I won't see her first smile. I won't be there for her when she wakes up in the night, hungry. I won't wean her onto solids. I won't see her crawling for the first time. Jesus! What have I done?'

Holy Jo moved from her desk chair to the bed, draping a slender arm around Boo's shoulder. She rubbed her upper arm gently. 'Stop punishing yourself, will you? You've just had a baby. Your hormones are all over the place. You're nineteen, Boo.'

'I'm not a little kid. Loads of nineteen-year-olds manage to mother their own children. Face it. I'm weak.'

Clasping her even closer, stroking the side of her head, Holy Jo had an encouraging answer even for that. '*I* wouldn't have the strength to get through what you're going through! I don't know that I'd make any better decisions. And maybe Mitch's folks are brilliant parents and will give Hope the best start. It's not for long. You'll get to see her regularly, won't you?'

Boo studied her neighbour's blemish-free complexion, gleaming blonde hair and sylph-like body. Religion and clean-living suited her. She looked down at her own giant breasts and ran her fingers over her chin – skin that was rebelling against four years of drugs and heavy drinking followed by the stress of an unplanned pregnancy, bereavement and a flake of a boyfriend. Maybe it was time to change her bad habits. Yet, the urge to get high and forget, or to go out and fuck a stranger in a bid to feel wanted, was strong. 'I'll try to see her every other weekend. It's just cash that's the problem.' She slid free of Holy Jo's embrace.

'Can't your mum help?'

She pictured the last time she'd seen the old lady when she'd rolled up at the hospital, stinking like a smashed bottle of vodka, sitting in silence but for the odd desultory outburst of criticism or stinging ridicule. 'Sylvia doesn't give a shit. She told me not to come running to her when

I'm out of nappies. You'd think bringing a baby into the world would be a cause for celebration but—'

'Boo! It's me.' Mitch's voice resounded along the corridor on the other side of the door. He was knocking with some urgency.

Turning to Holy Jo, she grabbed her arm. Barely able to assemble her half-formed thoughts into a coherent sentence. Her desperation tumbled from her mouth all at once. 'Don't let him know I'm here,' she whispered. 'I can't face him right now. He's a suffocating, unpredictable nightmare, and I don't want him around me or the baby. Please. I want to get my Hope back but I don't know how. You're doing law. You've got money. Please. Please! Will you help me? Say you will. Say you'll help.' The sorrow caught in the back of her throat as a desperate gasp.

When no response came from inside Boo's room, Mitch moved onto Holy Jo's door. He hammered on it like a bailiff. 'Sophie. Is Boo there? Come on. Open up! I know she's in there.'

Boo shook her head fervently. Mouthing, 'Don't let him in.'

Holy Jo patted her hand. 'Leave it to your Aunty Soph.' She winked. Ushered Boo to the wardrobe and shut her inside.

Squashed in among the fragrant-smelling designer clothes of a rich girl, for those fleeting moments, Boo imagined she was just like Hope had been inside her belly– cocooned in a safe place with somebody else to fend for her. She could hear the conversation taking place.

'Listen, Robert.'

'It's Mitch.'

'Is it? Well, I'm not pandering to your ego. You think you're Mr Too Cool For School but really, *Robert*, you're nothing more than a junkie and a bully.'

'Cheeky bitch! Hey. What are you doing? Are you filming me?'

233

'Yes. Deal with it. *I* don't have to put up with your nonsense. Now, I've no idea where Beverley is, but if she is in her room and just not answering, I suggest you leave her be. I know what you've done. I know what you've pressured her into and I'm not scared of you.'

Boo chewed the inside of her cheek frantically as she pictured the clash unfolding. She prayed that Holy Jo had Jesus on her side at that moment. Mitch was unpredictable at the best of times and was so cunning in his ability to spin a situation that he always ended up the moral champion, with his opponent defeated and apologetic at his feet.

'Get that fucking camera out of my face or I'm gonna—'

'What, exactly? What are you going to do?'

'I'll report you to McIntyre.'

'Me? Ha! That's a joke. I'm not the one who drives their neighbours potty with anti-social behaviour all hours of the night. You do realise the drugs you take are illegal, don't you?'

'Maybe I'll plant some in your room when you're out.'

'You wouldn't!'

Boo couldn't idly stand by, listening to her boyfriend threaten her neighbour, while she hid in the safety of her wardrobe behind protective layers of cashmere and silk.

She burst out of the wardrobe. 'Leave her be!' she yelled

Powered by pure rage, Boo slapped Mitch's face hard, but he caught her wrist in a vice-like grip, twisting it painfully. 'I'm doing this for your own good, my love,' he said. 'Think about what you're doing, Boo. You go psycho on me and we'll have to get you professional help. They might never let you see Hope again, for her own safety.'

'You wouldn't,' Boo said, aware of the milk seeping beyond the confines of her breast pads to drench her top.

'I'm only thinking of my daughter's best interests.'

CHAPTER 30
The Wolf

Standing in the garden, under cover of darkness, The Wolf feels confident that the whirr and whine of the camera's zoom lens will go unnoticed; drowned out by a noisy soirée that is taking place two doors down. The chattering neighbours won't see him either. Their garden is ambiently lit by fairy lights strung from tree to tree. Their glow won't penetrate the pitch black shadows of the summer house.

Beverley Saunders had shut her bedroom curtains earlier, but now she has drawn one aside to allow her to open the patio door. She stands only ten metres away, smoking a cigarette that she clearly doesn't know how to hold correctly. She doesn't inhale, but The Wolf notices with glee that her hands are shaking. He is getting to her. The endgame is near, and she is in no way prepared for the torment that he is planning next.

As she casts nervous glances into the impenetrable dark of the long garden, it excites him to think that he could rush her right now. Crack her head open on those flagstones and leave her to bleed out. He is the patient crocodile, entirely camouflaged; waiting to sate his hunger and slake his thirst for blood. She is the unsuspecting deer at the water's edge, unaware that a born predator stalks her every move.

Whine. Click, click. He snaps her again at close range.

No change in her movements. Good. The Wolf takes this as proof that she cannot hear him, though she is peering into the darkness in earnest, now. Perhaps she senses his presence. No doubt the knowledge that she has been followed and that her private space has been encroached upon has got her jumpy. Yes. Now she has stubbed her cigarette out beneath a slipper-shod foot, he sees her snatch up a lacrosse stick after she has closed and locked the door and before she draws the curtains again. If she is carrying it around with her, she is clearly beside herself with fear.

Imagining that he can smell the cortisol on the summery night air, he grows hard. In a feat of daring, he moves towards the house, just short of the point at which the security lights will be triggered. He takes out his erect penis. Urgently, violently, The Wolf masturbates in Beverley Saunders' direction, imagining that they are rutting in the garden, him mounting her from behind as any alpha would in the wild. Digging his sharp teeth into her flesh, he imagines that she tastes of salty sweat and smells of stale perfume. He is both repelled and aroused by her propensity to fuck anything that moves when she is under extreme stress. Except now, he remembers again the time when he had come across her at a sex party, clad in only a mask but still recognisable with those pendulous breasts and the light smattering of stretch marks that show she has borne a child, long ago. He remembers how she had failed to recognise him but had rejected him, there in that tawdry gilt and stucco room, where strangers fucked each other indiscriminately. Not her, though. She had the cheek to say no.

Only moderately irritated by the remembered slight, it merely fuels his wrath at the ultimate injustice she has committed against him. He fantasises about squeezing the life out of her. Remembers the Russian whore, Tatjana. Savours the memory of how her diminutive teenage body had grown limp beneath him as he ushered in the end of her days.

He comes with a grunt, spilling his wolfish seed on the perfectly manicured lawn. Beverley Saunders has much to regret in her dysfunctional life and she will regret her treatment of him, and her flagrant lies, bitterly, just before he kills her.

First, however, she must know shame.

Retreating to his den, The Wolf considers the progress of his project and deems that it can now go live. He uploads the photos he has just taken to a folder on his computer, accompanying others he has taken of her in her bedroom – sleeping fitfully; eating like a slob as she watches porn on her laptop; making origami models at her desk with scissors, a ruler and those careful fingers; pleasuring herself on that unmade bed. He even has several of her having sex with men she sneaked into the shared house. She has not been careful to draw those curtains . . . until now.

Once he has Photoshopped some images of genuine porn stars, engaging in acts of bestiality and anal sex, he transposes Beverley's head onto the actresses' shoulders. Then he scans through the legal documents he has acquired. With no small degree of glee, he reads again the grounds for divorce that her solicitor had listed – for these are none other than her divorce papers. It seems ironic that this bitch, who champions the cause of downtrodden, abused women who have been swindled, beaten and cheated upon, should have been such a hapless, helpless victim herself for so many years. Soon, the embarrassment and disgrace she faced less than twelve months ago, when she was ousted from her high-flying job with her name blackened and bridges comprehensively burned . . . soon that cringeworthy experience of being the laughing stock, branded untrustworthy and considered a failure will seem like child's play compared to the exposé he is planning.

'You'll be begging for the end,' he says to the official photo he has clipped from an old annual report printed by her previous employer, BelNutrive. He places it carefully on a flatbed scanner, next to a newspaper clipping that is sure to hurt like a boot in the ribs. 'Your past is coming back to haunt you, Beverley Saunders. The whole world is going to know your dirtiest, darkest secrets. You'll never regain your dignity. You'll never get your daughter back. I am The Wolf and I am going to rip out your heart.'

CHAPTER 31

Bev

'Crank it up to 70 per cent,' the spin instructor shouted at a pitch just high enough to hurt Bev's ears. 'Come on. Out of the saddle.'

Bev pedalled in time to the pop track that boomed through the spin studio's speakers, feeling the burn in her thighs. She had two hours before she met her new client. It was just enough time to melt away a few hundred calories and nip to Tesco for some fruit. She'd found nothing more on the internet about Tatjana. Her freelance contract for Graham's charity allowed her to take on at least one other PI client, if not two. Though she'd determined to keep hunting for the truth about Tatjana if a lead presented itself, it was time to acknowledge that she had to move on professionally and take better care of herself. New job. New flat. New start. At least, that's what she hoped for as she chugged her way up a manufactured hill, grinding through the gears until she was pedalling at 90 per cent of her ability. Feet stinging; muscles in her bottom screaming in complaint.

'All the way up to your maximum!' was the order, barked over the sound system.

Surveying her fellow spinners, Bev wondered if she hadn't imagined the hot pursuit of Mr Grey on the train.

Perhaps he had been the product of an over-tired over-stressed mind. Reflected in the wall of mirrors opposite the two rows of bikes, she studied the man beside her. Even in the semi-darkness, lit only by whirling disco lights, she could see his face was almost aubergine from exertion; his turquoise T-shirt darkened around the chest and pits where he was sweating profusely. He didn't seem in the least bit interested in her.

Behind her, in the second row, the mirror-wall revealed nothing but super-fit gym bunnies, rising and falling above their saddles in unison. The cheap and cheerful local leisure centre was only down the road from Sophie's, yet despite the wish to get fitter and the availability of pay-as-you-go sessions, she'd been only three times, so their faces were hardly familiar. Would she spot an interloper?

Stop it, you silly cow. This is a crappy budget spin class. What are the odds of some spy-stalker paying to watch your fat arse bobbing up and down for forty five minutes? Stop looking for excuses to stay unfit! Exercise is good for managing stress, and if you don't de-stress, you're going to explode. She pedalled on, trying to find the rhythm. Except Bev felt eyes on her.

The man in the corner wearing the glasses. Had he been watching her? Was it possible that he'd turned his attention from her reflection to the instructor the moment she had looked at him?

A sickly pop song with lyrics about blurry-boundaried women wanting it, even when they'd said no, boomed through the speakers. Bev focused on pedalling in a standing position, feeling that her heart might give out at any moment. Half wondering if she should get off her bike in protest at the terrible rapey song. Half surreptitiously observing the corner of the room to see if she could catch the man with the glasses out. He was facing forwards. Pedalling, pedalling.

Now, they were all doing press-ups, pushing against their handlebars, elbows out. The reek of onions and testosterone in the room became even more pungent with all those armpits on show. Like the others, the man bent double over his handlebars but looked straight at her through the mirror while everyone else faced the floor in choreographed unity.

Should she confront him? Bev stared at the sweat-stained floor, feeling suddenly cold, though her sweat-soaked body was roaring hot in this sauna of a studio. Should she just get off her bike and march over to him, kicking him in his Achilles tendon as his feet slowed? No. What if he had just been idly checking her out as a new face among the regulars?

Glancing at him again, he was focused only on cranking up his gear knob.

You're imagining things, you weirdo, she chided herself. *Pack it in. The case is over. You took the hint and you've backed off. Hopefully, that will be that. Focus on salvaging your life and getting your daughter back.*

In the supermarket, Bev stood on the travellator, rising slowly towards the elevated store level. There, she counselled herself that nobody was interested in a sweaty woman with dishevelled hair and grubby trainers. But she clutched her anorak tightly closed, feeling exposed in that open space.

Hearing footsteps pounding up behind her, she turned around to see a man hastening in her direction. Pushing past old ladies who stood to attention on the left, gripping their shopping trolleys like Zimmer frames as they waited to be ushered to the top. Mr Hasty was staring straight at her; gaining on her second by second. At the same time, Bev glimpsed another man, descending on the other travellator, oddly standing on the wrong side so that they would shortly pass within inches of one another. Bev was sandwiched in mid-air between two strange guys, both looking intently at her. Coincidence or an ambush?

Searching out the security guard at the top, she grabbed her handbag, prepared to wield it as a weapon, and sprinted upwards. Gasping for breath, she had a decision to make. Should she ask the security guard for protection from these men, potentially making a fool of herself if it turned out to be a false alarm? Or should she disappear among the cramped carousels and racks of the clothing department, relying on Florence and Fred to conceal her with their acrylic offerings? She opted to hang around by the security guard, pretending to try on unsuitable children's frames in the adjacent optician's department.

Spying the men over the top of her borrowed frames, she exhaled heavily as the descending man disappeared out of the store into the car park beyond. Mr Hasty, who had been coming up fast behind her, gave her not so much as a second glance before he reached the top. He loped in the direction of the café, perhaps late for a date of lukewarm chips and beans with his sister, or perhaps a sexually incontinent mother of three, looking for clandestine, deep-fried kicks in Tesco's eaterie of a mid-morning.

'Are you all right, love?' the security guard asked her.

'I thought some blokes were staring at me funny,' Bev said. 'Following me, like. You know?'

The security guard pointed to her face. 'That why they're staring, maybe?'

Bev took the children's glasses off and studied her reflection in the mirror. Her skin was an alarming shade of red, thanks to her efforts at the gym. She smiled, feeling relief seep from her open pores. 'Jesus, I look like I've been in a fire. So much for keeping fit.'

But the guard was no longer listening. She was just some crazy woman in Tesco with a complexion like tomato puree.

Picking up a basket, she made for the milk aisle and plucked a two litre bottle of semi-skimmed from the cheesy-smelling display. The overhead lights seemed so bright, she felt as though she were being picked out by a searchlight and stripped bare of her suburban post-gym camouflage. Anxiety dogged her every footstep as she made her way round the store, collecting baked beans and tinned tuna, all the while thinking of her tampered-with origami collection and those open patio doors, framed by ghostly billowing curtains.

'Hello.'

As she peered into the meat reductions cabinet at yellow-stickered chicken breasts, the voice at her side took her by surprise. It was the man from the spin class who had been sneaking glances at her. He was standing so close, she could feel the heat of his breath on her cheek; could see the broken veins on his blob of a nose.

'You!'

'I was watching you earlier.'

Snatching a tin of baked beans out of her basket, she brandished it like a cosh, whacking him squarely in the chin so that his head snapped back.

'Bastard!' Bev yelled. 'Help! Help me, somebody!' Again, she treated him to a good baked-beaning, this time on his upper arm.

'Jesus! Ow!' he yelped. 'What the hell's wrong with you? I was only trying to be nice.' He grabbed her wrist to stem the blows of a Heinz variety, forcing her to drop the tin.

243

Bev swung around, ninja-like fearlessness suffusing her body like a shot of triple espresso – the result of weeks of being on edge. She grabbed at a large yellow-stickered chicken and clonked gym-guy squarely on the side of the head with it. Dropped her shopping on his foot and ran.

An hour later, she sat in Mo's consulting room, hugging herself tightly and rocking in his easy chair. Finally acknowledging that missing two group therapy sessions had led her to this point where she needed one-on-one attention if she was going to avoid meltdown.

'I've just got this terrible feeling all the time,' she said.

Mo crossed his legs and laced his fingers together over his right knee. His face, impassive, as usual. 'Oh? A terrible feeling about what?'

'That something bad's gonna happen. That I'm being followed. That death is waiting for me, just around the corner. Know what I mean?'

Raising an eyebrow, Mo's nostrils flared. He cocked his head to the side, thoughtfully. 'Beverley, are you sleeping?'

She shook her head. 'Not really. Not very well. Broken sleep. I don't feel safe in my own place.'

'Have you been indulging in origami again? Sex with strangers?'

'I told you I didn't want to discuss that in therapy group. It's off limits.'

'We're not in therapy group, Beverley. There's just me and you, and this is a problem area you definitely need to work on. It impacts on your suitability—'

'No! No! No! OK? No sex with strangers.' She blushed. She knew he'd realise she was lying.

'Any other compulsive fail-safes that you rely on when you're stressed?'

'No!' Bev said, deliberately omitting to mention the origami dinosaur that she'd sat up folding until 3 a.m. in a bid to calm her overwrought mind and racing pulse. 'Look! I finished the job I was working on, so I'm going to have good money coming in very soon. I'm meeting a new client after this. But . . .'

'You've filled out your form, putting a three next to "Are you worried that something terrible might happen?"' Mo cast an eye over the questionnaire she'd filled in on arrival, where she declared how crackers she was feeling that week on a scale of one to three. 'All of your levels are up.'

Bev thumped the arm of the easy chair. 'But I'm getting better, not worse. This is nothing to do with my mental state. You wouldn't believe how stressful and *dangerous* my last job was. I'm talking threats from powerful men, being followed, someone turning my place over . . . That's why I'm here! That's why my anxiety's through the roof. And I want my daughter back. I've done everything that was asked of me to make the judge happy. I got my own place. I've set up in gainful self-employment.'

'And yet, you're here in one-on-one therapy with me, Beverley. You've taken a step backwards from the group sessions. You're becoming more anxious, more paranoid and you've been lying about your addictions.'

She threw her hands in the air. 'Bloody origami and the odd one-night stand. It doesn't make me an irresponsible mother. That piece of crap, Rob, won't even let me have my supervised visit this month. He's given me some cock and bull story about Hope having chickenpox and feeling rough.'

'It sounds fair to cancel a visit if she's got chickenpox.'

'She had it already! She had it when she was five. He's a liar. A dirty, rotten liar.'

Mo was writing in his notebook. She hated it when he did this, falling silent so that she didn't have any inkling as to what he thought of her or anything she said. Was she digging herself in deeper?

Finally, he stopped scribbling and studied her face, as if trying to see the quality of her soul and the true state of her mind, beyond her skin and sinew and bone. 'I've known you for a very long time, Beverley. Don't forget, I conducted your couples counselling when you and Rob first got married; when you finally took Hope back from his family and started to parent her yourself. I understand your predicament. I do. I can see the toll that your life, your losses and your choices have taken on you. It's OK.'

'Don't patronise me, Mo! I want you to sign me off. I want Hope back. I'm only here because . . .' She searched for an explanation as to why she was there. She'd requested these extra sessions because the perils of the Fitzwilliam case and her X-S club relapse had put her chances of getting custody of Hope in jeopardy. A chaotic lifestyle, coupled with her anxiety and obsessive compulsions spinning out of control, would never cut it with a judge. Additional therapy had seemed like a good idea at the time. Now, she looked at Mo's smooth, inscrutable face and the slick front he put on with his crisp shirts, open at the neck, and the expensive watch and cool designer jeans. She wondered if his professional supportiveness and soft encouraging voice wasn't all a front. Was he really helping her here? Thinking about it, he'd always seemed more sympathetic of Rob during their couples' therapy in the past. Was there some boys' club collusion in play? 'Are you sabotaging me?' she asked, shuffling forward on the chair. 'Are you deliberately making it look like I'm regressing so Rob can keep Hope indefinitely?'

'Do you think, Beverley . . .' Mo said, writing in his book. His lower eyelid started to flutter. A vein was now prominent on his shining forehead. He was rattled though his voice remained even – almost hypnotic, '. . . that you're displacing your anxiety about your personal situation and taking it out on me? Do you feel you could withstand the stresses of soloparenting? Given the circumstances . . .'

'Yes! I damn well do. There's nowt wrong with me. All of my symptoms have a bloody good explanation. Imagine how you'd feel if someone broke into your home and rearranged things just to freak you out! Imagine if some guy . . .' She bit her tongue, then, realising paranoia about being stalked would not help her case.

'Beverley, you're clearly *very* stressed, and my main concern is your well-being. Perhaps your state of mind and your personal circumstances just aren't conducive to having a child around. Not yet.'

'You saying I'm making it up?'

Mo retrieved his iPad from the coffee table and swiped the screen. He clicked on a tab, bringing up a website. Its name was redhotslut.com. The homepage showed a crystal clear close-up photograph of Bev, straddling some guy in the reverse cowboy position. It seemed genuine and looked as though it had been taken through the patio doors of her flat from the garden. A fortnight ago when she'd picked up some guy in a Hale wine bar. Beneath the photo was her burner phone number and the invitation to:

Call Bev Saunders, now! Fuck her hard. Beat her black and blue. She loves it!

Bev pressed her hand to her mouth, swallowing down a choking glob of bile.

'Oh my God,' she said. 'This isn't how it seems. This isn't me.'

Mo smiled though there was no sympathy in his eyes. 'Really? It sounds like you. It certainly looks like you. You want to appear before a judge to contest Rob's custody order and demonstrate that you are a fit mother. And I've got to give my report as an expert witness. I'm being honest, Bev. I don't think the judge will be very impressed by redhotslut.com.'

CHAPTER 32

Doc

'Are you decent?' his mother said, barging into the attic regardless of what his answer might have been, had she waited for it.

Doc lay on the floor in just his pants, trying and failing to do a sit-up whilst lifting a kettle bell he'd found in the garage. 'Jesus, Mum!'

'Don't blaspheme, James. It's not nice.' Humming tunelessly, his mother stepped over him, carrying a blue plastic basket full of fresh laundry. She set it on his unmade bed and started to take the items out. A pile of pants. A bundle of paired socks. Vests. Did he even own vests? 'I've ironed your jeans. Daddy wants you to go with him to the garden centre to get some manure for the borders.'

'I'm busy,' he said. He got to his feet, scrambling to his desk where he pulled a faded terry towelling dressing gown from the chair, slipping it over his semi naked body. 'I've got research to do.'

His mother handed him a pair of stonewashed jeans, treating him to a knowing look over the top of her rhinestone studded glasses. 'Erm. Young man, while you're staying here, you'll pitch in.'

Sighing, Doc took the jeans. Held them up. 'Mum, for God's sake! Why have you ironed a crease into these?'

'It's smart. You need to start dressing better, James. Get a proper job, not this research nonsense. You didn't go to Oxford to play on the interweb on *our* computer for some private investigator. I don't even remember giving you permission to use our computer. It's *very* valuable.'

'It's seven years old, Mum. It takes about half an hour to boot up.'

'Anyway, Daddy says he's had a word with Derek Forsythe from the golf club.'

'Who the fu – flip is Derek Forsythe when he's at home?' Doc pulled the jeans on under his father's faded spare robe. Reached inside the terry towelling to daub his armpits with roll-on deodorant.

'He's an accountant. He runs a chain of small firms in Bucks. Very well thought of, by everyone. You should see the size of his conservatory.' His mother's sallow, ageing complexion had started to glow as though she was rather more impressed by the size of Derek's appendages and outbuildings than she should be, Doc assessed. 'And guess what? He's looking for an IT manager. Daddy's lined you up with a job interview. This coming Friday, I think. He knows more about it than I do. Ask him.'

Doc felt over-burdened by gravity as though his father was standing in the room directly below, pulling him down, down, down with a strong oedipal magnet, designed to bring adult sons to their knees. This wasn't the getaway Doc had envisage when he'd fled the wilds of Sale and his life as an independent adult, with only his most prized possessions in a bag. *I've traded one oppressor for another – a politician armed with a computer virus for Action Dad with his high-waisted slacks, composting fetish and Five Year Family Plan. Brilliant. Just brilliant. I've got to get the hell out of here. I wish I could talk to Bev.* 'Yeah. I will. Cheers, Mum.'

'Good boy. Ten minutes. Be in the hall, waiting. He's ready for the off in ten. And put a nice shirt on instead of one of those ungodly T-shirts.'

He kissed his mother on the cheek and ushered her out of the attic with her shitty laundry basket and good intentions.

Switching on his new phone, which he'd persuaded the old man to register in his name, he brought up his brand new email account. Apart from the odd communique regarding some lame-arsed social arrangement with Steve and Jakey, he wasn't expecting any correspondence in his inbox beyond spam. Sighing deeply, he saw there was indeed nothing except a solitary, fatuous one-liner from Jakey about, 'pulling some fillies on quiz night'. He'd never felt so cut off from the world.

'Now, James, I'm going to tell you what happened when I was a young chap like you and looking for work,' his father began, reversing the Volvo out of the gravel drive and onto the road. He draped his arm over Doc's passenger seat, pressing on his shoulder with a gnarled hand clad in part-leather, part-Aertex driving glove. 'Like you, I found myself at a crossroads after university . . .'

Doc switched off as the tedious lecture began, idly noticing how his dad had hardly any facial hair these days, as if the rigours of age had proven too much for his follicles and caused a mass shutdown. How long before he started quizzing him about Bev? How long before he started trotting out the usual teary-eyed stories about his own father not having left him with a single photograph from his childhood?

They pulled into the garden centre, parking badly in a disabled space. His father slapped a blue badge onto the dashboard.

'And I don't know if I've told you this story, son, but you know? Your grandfather – my father – never left me a single photo. Not a one. Stop me if you've heard this, James.'

'Yes, Dad.' *When's the pissing the bed story coming?*

'And it didn't help that whenever I stayed at my cousins' – your Great-Aunt Irene's house – I used to wet the bed and they . . . well, they were very nasty about it.'

'Good job you didn't have any photos of that, then,' Doc muttered under his breath, dragging a flatbed trolley round to the compost and manure section.

'What?'

'Horseshit.'

'What?' His father started to tamper with his hearing aid until it whistled.

'How many bags of manure do you want, Dad?'

In the long queue for the till, that was peopled with sprightly white-haired retirees and the odd young mother, juggling a pushchair and pot plants, Doc noticed that he had a Google alert in his inbox. Enjoying respite from his father's verbal diarrhoea whilst he chatted to some old battleaxe from the parish council, he read the latest search result for Beverley Saunders. Any guilt at cyber-stalking his friend and business associate was overridden by biting curiosity as he read the headline of a *Guardian* article, posted onto a public Facebook page, claiming to represent, 'The Real Beverley Saunders'. It was dated just over a year ago and was illustrated with a photo of Bev, topless with her nipples pixelated out and wearing a leather thong. It looked as though it had been taken in the X-S Club or somewhere like it.

Wholefood marketing guru lacks moral fibre

Scandal shook the health food world yesterday as Beverley Saunders, the Marketing Director of BelNutrive was ousted from the blue-chip company for embezzling tens of thousands of pounds in unauthorised expenses. Husband, Rob Mitchell had exposed his wife after he learned that she had enjoyed an accelerated career-path, shooting from administrator to a board position within only five years, because she had slept her way to the top. He had learned that she had regularly offered sexual favours to non-executive board members and then subjected the men to blackmail in return for her silence.

Saunders, well known among her friends for a rampaging sex addiction and poor mental health, had recently filed for divorce from Mr Mitchell, citing his infidelity and controlling behaviour as grounds. Mr Mitchell reported that it was, 'rich, coming from such a lying slag and a manipulative social climber, that she should accuse me of the very things she's guilty of.' He remarked that her theft was evidence of a lack of moral fibre in Saunders, ironic and utterly inappropriate, given her status as the woman in charge of promoting a global leader in wholesome health food to the public.

The police are investigating the case, though it is clear that her instant dismissal is warranted and that it is absolutely right that her daughter, Hope should be taken away from her.

'Fucking *heck*!' Doc said aloud.

'James!' His father clipped him around the ear as though he were seven. 'Don't use language like that in front of Mrs Tench. Whatever's got into you, boy?'

Almost dropping the phone through trembling fingers, Doc apologised, breathed deeply and re-read the ghastly article. Now, he took his time to study the layout and language used. With some cunning click-throughs to check its provenance, he quickly ascertained that the piece wasn't from the *Guardian* at all, but a spoof. It certainly read like a spoof, though at a glance, in terms of layout and branding, it looked authentic. It had clearly been knocked up by someone who knew their stuff. Though it was dated a year earlier, it had been published only yesterday.

Dialling Bev's number, he was frustrated when her voicemail kicked in straight away. Unwilling to leave a message, he hung up, considering his next move. Wheeled the flatbed trolley to his father's Volvo and heaved the five bags of manure into the boot. Bev was going to hit the roof when she saw this. Was this the work of a vengeful Jerry Fitzwilliam? Had Bev stoked up an almighty shit-storm since they'd last talked?

'I'm never going home,' he said, staring forlornly through the windscreen at the hedgerows and semi-rural fuck-all that whizzed by.

'What?' his father asked.

'Nothing,' Doc said, thumbing out a message to Bev.

Somebody's doing a hatchet job on you online. D.

He was poised to send it, but texting her was the last thing he should be doing if somebody had the knives out for her. It stood to reason that a person who was savvy enough to have a defensive virus rigged on their computer, and powerful enough to pay for a faked broadsheet article, might easily be monitoring Bev's phone too. And if he texted her, rather than called, changing to a new phone and laying low at his parents would be worthless.

As he prepared to dial her again, another Google alert popped into his inbox. This time, it was from Twitter. He clicked on the link that took him to the brand new Twitter feed of @Beverley_Saunders. Breathed in sharply when he read what was posted there, how many followers she had and how many times the tweets had been retweeted around the globe.

'Shall we stop off for a nice bacon sarnie?' His dad asked, punctuating the sheer horror of what Doc was reading with inane old-guy snack suggestions. 'Don't tell your mother. It can just be us boys. I'll buy you a pop.'

'Shush, Dad. I'm on the phone.' Doc dialled Bev once more, praying she would pick up.

'I like ketchup on my bacon sarnie. Your mother hates ketchup. Says it's the devil's condiment.'

Doc turned to his father. 'Dad. Just shut the fu – heck up a minute, will you? I'm on the fffflipping phone.'

This time, Bev answered just before the phone went to voicemail.

'It's me,' he said. 'Have you got a Twitter account?

'No.' Her voice sounded edgy and uncertain. 'Why?'

'You have now. And you're not going to like it one bit.'

CHAPTER 33

Bev

'Pick up! Come on, you bastard. Pick the bloody phone up.'

Bev was already climbing in the loaned Ford Fiesta, her mobile pressed to her ear. All this while, she had been certain that Jerry Fitzwilliam was the man who was making her life a misery. Right now, though, a mental image of her ex-husband, rubbing his hands in glee as he watched her world fall apart, blocked out everything else.

Rob. Colin Robert Mitchell, the duplicitous gaslighting piece of crap was trying to ruin her and destroy the chances of her ever getting custody of their daughter.

Running her finger over the recent, pocket-sized school photo of Hope that she'd slid into the inside flap of her purse, she whispered, 'Mummy will get you soon, my love. Mummy's going to be strong.'

In an ideal world, she would just head straight for Hope's school. Fallowfield was not far from here. The headmistress knew that she was only allowed supervised visits thanks to Rob's legal chicanery, but surely she could wing it. If she said that her mother had died . . . Except one of those damned tweets contained a jpeg of a genuine newspaper article from the time when her mother *had* died. Two years after Dad had hung himself.

Local artist mourned, two years after husband's tragic suicide.

That's what the headline said. Bev snorted with derision at the photograph of her mother, posing next to her latest canvas, with a cosmopolitan in a posh glass in one hand, paintbrush in the other.

'Screw you, Sylvia.' Bev willed the anguished, guilty tears to dissipate at the backs of her eyes. Her mother had been the architect of Bev's lifetime of emotional trauma. She had blamed twenty-year-old Boo's wayward behaviour and inattention for every minor mishap and epic tragedy that had ever befallen the Saunders family, rather than drying out and stepping up to her role of grandma. Not once had the old lady conceded that it had been more important for Boo, the Bev of old, to forge a bond with her baby – a child who had been snatched from Boo's leaking milky breasts by in-laws who behaved like outlaws – rather than waste her weekends travelling home to watch her mother drink herself to sclerosis of the liver, kidney failure and an early grave.

No. There was no using Sylvia's passing as an excuse to get Hope out of school. Telling a flagrant lie like that would show she was impulsive, irresponsible and dishonest. First, she had to disprove the slanderous filth that was appearing online.

All thanks to Rob.

'Redhotslut! I'm gonna deck the arsehole,' she told the hand car wash by Southern Cemetery. 'I'm going to snip his balls off and stuff them down his throat,' she told the funeral home in Moss Side.

Bev eventually found a parking space in one of the cramped back streets behind the Manchester Metropolitan

University where Rob now worked in marketing. She made for the Faculty for Humanities and the Arts. The bleak brick bulk of the Geoffrey Manton building contained a maze of small lecture theatres and offices, rising in tiers that wrapped around a giant central white atrium.

'Where can I find Robert Mitchell?' she asked the receptionist, a girl with badly bleached hair, topped by a giant false bun. She barely looked older than the students themselves. 'I'm from . . . the Arts Council. I'm late for a meeting with him.'

The girl clack-clacked on some gum she had wedged in her cheek. She looked Bev up and down. 'Is he expecting you?'

'I've just told you.' *Chill out, Bev. Losing it will only slow you down.* 'We've got a meeting. I'm *really* late. Can you just point me in the right direction and I'll find him myself?'

The girl stopped chewing momentarily. 'He's in the caff.'

Marching across the giant atrium and into a cafeteria that looked like a gaudy staff breakout area for some new-age advertising company in Hoxton, Bev spotted the balding back of Rob's head immediately. Mitch, the fun, perpetually horny junkie who had wanted to rebel against his stifling, disapproving parents, had morphed over the course of eleven years into a carbon copy of them. Now, he was a thin-lipped, line-towing corporate shitkicker, whose only concession to fun involved affairs with a string of younger women and the odd recreational coke binge.

'You!' Bev said, growling the single syllable across the space like a tiger's war cry.

She grabbed him by his shirt collar before he had the chance to turn around. The people he was conducting a meeting with straightened up in their chairs, open-mouthed at the intrusion. They instinctively grabbed their paperwork from the table, holding it before them like ineffectual admin shields. They rose and edged away amid scraping chair legs as Bev yanked Rob backwards, pulling him clean out of his own seat.

'Security!' Rob yelped. 'Get security!' He wriggled against her grip like a fish trying to escape the hook of an angler, hell-bent on making a catch.

Brandishing her phone only millimetres from his face, she brought the screen to life. Tweet after sordid tweet illuminated his pallid complexion.

'You did this, didn't you?' She poked at the screen until the website Mo had showed her appeared. '*Redhotslut? Beat her black and blue. She loves it!* Are you kidding me?' She was a pressure cooker whose weight had been yanked off too quickly, blasting boiling air over her ex. 'Not enough that you circulated false accounts to the board of directors in BelNutrive? Me and you work together for years. Years! And there was me, thinking it was happy families. But no! You make it look as though I've been fiddling my expenses to the tune of ten grand! It wasn't enough that you lit a fire under the gossip mill, saying I'd been sleeping with the old CEO? Then, you spread rumours that I'd been sleeping with the young lad on my marketing team? And for a fucking encore, you financially ruin me by taking all the equity in our house and denying me maintenance, even though you managed to destroy my livelihood as a marketeer. Because let's face it, Robert, shit sticks so very, very well.'

He tried to interrupt at this point, but Bev ploughed on, shouting over him, relishing the fact that his colleagues were still within earshot.

'And it's not enough that you did all this just because I'd confronted you about your affairs with junior members of staff. You didn't bloody like that, did you, Roberto?

259

No! Aw, diddums. So, you use my shot-to-bits – under-standably – mental health to cast doubt on my ability to mother my own child safely, just so you can control my access to Hope. The apple didn't fall far from Gerald and Mary's fucking tree, did it? And now, you're intimidating me and doing that crazy-making shit from afar. Because heaven fucking forfend I should get back on my feet and lead a normal life. What a cunt you are, Robert Mitchell.'

Finally, she released her ex-husband, allowing him to stand and face her. The pallor was gone now, replaced by thunder.

'Have you finished causing a scene in front of my visi-tors?' He kept his voice calm and even. His thin body was rigid with indignation.

Bev balled her fist, wondering how she could have ever found this prick attractive. 'It was you. Admit it!' She forced herself to maintain eye contact with him, though she could see the alarmed expressions on his colleagues' faces in her peripheral vision. 'You put all this filth on social media.'

'No!'

'Do me a favour. It's got, "*Mitch on a bad trip*" written all over it. Bitter. Snarky. Perverse. Well thought-out. Who else knows that much about me? Divorce grounds? All that stuff about my parents. Who do I know that can knock up a belting website in a matter of hours?'

'Well, that creep you hang out with, for a start. What's his name? Doc? A criminal record for phishing? I'm sure putting up a spoof website's not beyond—'

'Bullshit! Does Doc stand to benefit from making me look like an insane nymphomaniac? Eh?'

'Out!' he said, pointing back towards the atrium. He exchanged a glance with a fat man behind the cafeteria servery. 'Security's on their way. I'd leave sharpish, if I were you, before they call the police.'

'Not the first time you'd have tried to discredit me though, is it? Funny this should happen just as I'm in with a fighting chance of getting Hope back.'

A burly security guard was making his way over to them. With one nod from Rob, he grabbed Bev's arm and wrestled her towards the exit.

'Get off me. This is assault.'

The security guard spoke in gentle tones as if he was escorting a lost elderly lady to the toilets. 'You're harassing a member of staff, madam. We take security of the people who study and work here very seriously. I'm sorry.'

Rob was following in their wake, only a couple of paces behind. Harsh words spoken through tight lips. 'Coming here and attacking me in my workspace, Bev! Unprovoked? And you think the judge will give you custody? You're dumber than I thought.'

Bev craned her neck around and spat at him. A glob of mucus hit him squarely on the nose. 'Wanker.'

As the security guard held her, poised to expel her into the vortex of the revolving doors, Rob spoke through gritted teeth into her ear. 'I had nothing to do with that disgraceful . . .' He was clearly searching for a word that wasn't an obscenity. Because the last thing Rob would want nowadays would be for the world to know he had ever been anything other than a law-abiding arbiter of good taste. 'Filth you just showed me. But I tell you what. You try to come near Hope without my prior consent and a social worker in place, I'll make your life a misery. You try to accuse me of trolling you, I'll do you for slander. Whatever money you've got left, I'll take. And you'll never see Hope again, I swear.'

She was pushed through the heavy doors into the street and, with a flash of sunlight reflected in the glass, he and the security guard were gone.

Bev stood on the flagstones outside, staring at the entrance to the faculty, trying to make sense of what had just happened. She walked towards her car.

Unpick this. Ignore the willy-waving. What are you left with?

Rob was Machiavellian, selfish to a fault and cruel but he had denied involvement in redhotslut.com and her other online torments vociferously. Had he been for real?

Making her way back to Hale, Bev's mind was a-whirr as she picked over what had come to pass in the university's cafeteria; the defamatory bilge that had appeared online about her. *Somebody* was making her life hell. Somebody was trying to harm her custody case. Was it was time to get the police involved, or at least, her solicitor, Eve?

Bev rummaged in her bag to find her burner phone, which she hadn't checked since she'd abandoned her persona of Cat Thomson. *Eve first. See what she says about involving the cops.* Ignoring the lights popping behind her eyes thanks to stress, Bev flicked the phone into life and waited for the latest call information to load. Within a minute, the phone was pinging incessantly with missed calls. She swerved to avoid a school minibus, intent on seeing who had so persistently been calling this temporary number. Of course, it could only be one man. Jerry Fitzgerald.

'Cat, it's me. Call me. I'm sorry.'

'Cat, it's Jerry. I didn't mean to threaten you. Please get in touch.'

'Cat, I can't believe you're overreacting like this. It makes me think that you do have something to hide.'

The tone became progressively more hostile in later messages.

'It's me. I know what you are. I know what you're after.'

'Don't ignore me, you stupid tart. Don't you know who I am? I've got more resources at my disposal than you can imagine. I'm onto you.'

Dare she listen to the rest of those messages?

Jerry is *behind this torment, after all. How could he not be? He knew.*

Ignoring the angry horn-honking of a bus, whose path she had crossed doing forty with only a millimetre margin for error, she thumbed through the contacts tab on her usual phone. Brought up Angela Fitzgerald – only half watching the road; accelerating to run a changing light. She had to warn Angie.

'Come on! Pick up!'

Angela answered on the third ring. 'Bev? What do you want?' The reluctance to take the call was audible.

'Did you get away? Did you get safe?' Bev asked, tugging on the car's steering wheel to veer right back onto Princess Road.

'Yes. I'm staying with my aunt for now.' Angie's voice sounded stilted, as though someone else were within earshot.

'Good. Good. Look, we've got to meet. I'm sorry. I know your life's complicated enough as it is, but I've got major hassle with Jerry and both of our lives are in jeop—'

Bev had just pulled into the fast lane, heading out towards the M60 and beyond. She only registered the heavy goods vehicle in the nearside lane when it was too late. The Fiesta bounced off the wheel arches of the juggernaut, careening into the central reservation; lifting into the air and spinning twice before it hit the ground on the wrong side of the carriageway, landing on its roof in a soupy cloud of debris.

CHAPTER 34
The Wolf

Standing over the unconscious bitch, he's questioned by nobody about why he should be there among the monitoring equipment and rhythmic beeping. He's wearing the blue scrubs he's pilfered from a side room down the corridor that had stupidly been left unattended. Only his fine leather shoes would give him away as an interloper, if anyone were even there to question his authenticity. No trainers or crocs for The Wolf.

The hospital, normally infested by the local scum who come to have the cancer and clap excised from their disease-ridden bodies, is a ghost town, peopled only by those who mark time with medicated, fitful sleep. It is the small hours of the morning, after all. Even the nurses at the main desk for this ward read their magazines and eat their chocolates in silence. He will not be disturbed. He is stealthy because he is The Wolf. Checking that the door is firmly shut, he pulls on his mask. Now, he is a wolf in doctor's clothing. He smiles at the thought.

They've put her in a side room that smells of blood and bleach. Only a night light shines at her bedside. It is enough to illuminate her battered and bruised face. Though her arm is plastered and in a sling, and she wears a dressing on the side of her head, her pulse seems strong. Good. He is enjoying this game. How disappointing it would have been had she died in that crash, just as the hunt was getting really entertaining.

Taking a seat beside her, he watches the movement of her eyeballs beneath those purple and yellow lids. He knows she is dreaming, though it is definitely not of him. He imagines she will be reconstructing scenes from her nightmarish life in a jumble of fear and despair. If she opens her eyes now and looks at him, she will see a man dressed as a doctor, wearing a latex wolf mask. That waking nightmare will be the last terrifying thing she will ever see because clearly, if she wakes, he will have to kill her.

'Sleep,' he whispers, stroking her lacerated cheek.

He leans over her, pausing with his face directly above hers. Through the ventilating nose holes in the mask, he inhales her sickly breath. He exhales, knowing she will take in the expelled matter from his body. Now, they are part of one another. Predator and prey, locked fleetingly in a symbiotic dance.

Squeaking footsteps approach, though this room is on an isolated spur off the main ward.

The Wolf moves silently around the bed and retreats into the dense darkness of the unlit en suite, pulling his mask off and stashing it in the waistband of the pilfered blue trousers, covered by the baggy top. His skin and hair are wet with cold sweat from the latex. He takes a clean, fluffy towel, intended for her and dries himself with it.

He can hear the door opening. The squeak squeak of the visitor's footsteps grows louder. Trainers. Is this a doctor who could surely identify him as an impersonator, should he be discovered behind the door? Will he be unmasked?

There is a sharp tang of perspiration in the room now and the musk of a man's unwashed body. This is surely no doctor, prowling in the long shadows cast by the room's night light. The agency night-shift nurses would bustle in and slam the main fluorescents on like interrogators. *Wakey wakey, Beverley. Time for your painkillers.* He knows the drill in this underfunded NHS dump.

Peeking through the crack in the door, he can see it is her friend – the lanky 1980s rocker throwback with the greasy blond ponytail. He is carrying a large rucksack and wears a red anorak several sizes too big for him, looking dishevelled as though he has just arrived after some long journey. This is not a man. This is an overgrown boy.

The greasy boy takes the seat at the side of her bed. Does he feel that the already depressed seat pad is warm from another man's body? It would appear not. He merely rummages in his rucksack and takes a half-drunk bottle of Coke out. Swigs from it. Sits there, staring at Beverley with a crumpled look on his sallow face that heralds the onset of silent weeping. Sure enough, his shoulders start to heave and he begins to wipe his eyes on the grimy sleeve of his anorak.

It is 5 a.m. Somehow, this loser has slipped in, unnoticed. The way that he settles back in the easy chair indicates that he has no intention of leaving for a good while, as long as he remains undisturbed.

The Wolf has a decision to make. Should he remain in the en suite or reveal himself? Is it likely that he will be recognised by the loser she calls 'Doc'? If he stays behind the door, it is inevitable that a visitor drinking Coke will eventually need to use the toilet? Then, his concealment will certainly be discovered. Either the alarm will be raised or he will be forced to murder this fool.

He has made his decision.

As he emerges from the en suite, the boy jumps.

'Jesus. Where did you come from?' he says, slapping his hand over his heart. He is out of the chair now.

'I was washing my hands,' The Wolf says, picking up the clipboard from the end of the bed. 'Beverley's last on my round. Graveyard shift. You know?' He chuckles. Intently examines the notes on the clipboard. Glances over to the boy. 'Sit! Sit!' Anticipating that the boy's relief at the out-of-hours visit being sanctioned by none other than a doctor will trump any suspicion.

'Cheers. How is she?'

'Are you family?' The Wolf asks, slipping the clipboard back onto the bed. Glancing down to check that his latex mask is still safely stowed in his waistband and hidden from view.

'Business partner. Friend.' His smile is weakened by having been caught in the unmanly act of weeping. 'They called me. She's got no next of kin, see? Not really. I was one of the last people she'd spoken to on her phone. I came as soon as I could.' He swallows hard. 'I can't believe it. One minute, I'm speaking to her. The next . . . Will she be okay?'

'What did she say to you?'

'Eh?'

'On the phone before she crashed.'

The boy's brow furrows. He cocks his head at a questioning angle. 'Why?'

The Wolf can feel sweat starting to roll down his back. Is the boy studying him, wondering where he has seen this slightly familiar doctor before? How might he kill him quietly if it came to it? Garrotte him using the wire from the oxygen clip? Beat him swiftly to death, perhaps. But what with? Anything that might serve as an impromptu cosh is bolted to the walls. 'It was a bad crash,' he says. 'I'm just interested to know her state of mind at the time.'

This visitor shrugs. His eyes dart away, towards the heart monitor. If he knows anything, he is not willing to share it. 'I just want someone to tell me she's gonna make a full recovery.'

The adrenaline that had kicked in starts to ease off as The Wolf notices how everything about this chump's body language is evasive and defensive. The shifty gaze. The folded arms. The staccato way in which he is speaking. It is a comforting thought that the boy might be too unnerved by having entered the bitch's room without permission, and outside visiting hours, to consider that this doctor's presence might also be unsanctioned; his credentials, spurious.

The boy she calls 'Doc' is no threat. Though it would give him pleasure to snuff out his miserable low-rent life, The Wolf makes the decision to leave before the two of them attract unwanted attention from the battleaxe agency nurses on the desk.

Before the endgame comes, The Wolf has plans to turn Beverley Saunders' torment dial all the way up to ten. It will serve her right for all she has done and the terrible lies she has told.

CHAPTER 35

Bev

Instead of the sirens she'd been expecting, the wail coming from the police cars had sounded more like a child crying. They'd been chasing her for the best part of a mile now, their blue and neon green livery vying for her attention as she'd glanced in her rear-view mirror. Trying to ascertain if they were gaining on her, with their blue lights flashing.

'Go faster, Mum!' Hope had said, sitting in the passenger seat at her side.

Bev had glanced down at her daughter's small body. 'Where's your booster seat?' she'd asked, panic pushing her blood ever faster around the tangled network of her arteries. 'Why haven't you got your seatbelt on? Buckle up, baby!'

'Weeeee!' Hope had yelled, rolling the window down and sticking her skinny arms out, fingers trailing the cold, damp air. 'I can fly.' Then, she had leaned out so her head and shoulders had only just skimmed the sides of the traffic in the next lane.

Bev had reached out to grab her. 'Get in! Get back in.' She'd pulled hard on her daughter's fleece but the fabric had slipped through her fingers. 'I can't protect you, Hope. Get back in!'

The glancing blow from the heavy goods vehicle at her side had hit Hope, yanking her out of the passenger seat and through the window. The car had shot into the air. Rolling, rolling into the opposite carriageway. When she'd hit the asphalt, Bev had woken with a start.

'Jesus, no!' she'd cried, trying to propel herself into sitting position but realising her left arm was in plaster, suspended from a rig-up above the bed.

'Are you OK, Mum-Mum?' a small voice had said.

Bev had glanced blearily to the visitor chair at the side of her bed and burst into tears at the sight of Rob, slouching to the side as though he'd been sitting there for a long time, wearing a bored and resentful expression with just a hint of smugness about it. Their daughter had been perched on his knee.

Bright-eyed Hope had leaned towards Bev with childish concern on her delicate features. 'Were you having a yukky dream?'

'Hope! You're OK. You're OK. Oh, my love. Come here. Give your mummy a kiss.' Her speech had been morphine-slurred but her relief had been acute.

Hope had leaped up from Rob's lap and had covered Bev's battle-scarred cheeks in a flurry of wet kisses. Bev had winced at the pressure of her lips on the emerging bruising and the deep cuts that the doctor had taped, but she'd said nothing. Had just revelled in the knowledge that her daughter was by her bedside and unharmed. That particular nightmare had been merely that.

Hope's fingers had wrapped around her hand – warm and clammy and thrumming with vitality. 'Sorry. Am I hurting you, Mum-Mum?'

'No, love.' Bev had felt sleep and heavy medication trying to pull her back to the depths of slumber. Her heavy lids had started to close of their own accord, rebelling against her wish to keep them open so she could drink in the sight of her beautiful girl; ignoring the sulky wanker who held her on his lap. Even as she'd drifted back to the blackness, she'd silently bet that Rob was loving every minute of this. Surprised that he had deigned to visit, though they were at war. Perhaps he'd heard disapprobation in the doctor's voice when he'd refused to visit the gravely injured mother of his only child. That narcissist had always set an inordinate amount of store in being thought well of by strangers.

'I'm so glad you're not going to die, Mum,' Hope had said.

Bev had felt those skinny fingers tenderly stroking her hair. 'No, doll. It takes more than a car crash to kill your . . .'

She woke many hours later to find Doc standing by the bed. 'Bev! You're awake!'

Disorientated, Bev now blinked hard in the grey dawn light. It seeped in through the hospital room's tall windows, making out the hollows and highlights in Doc's angular face, rendered ghoulish by the night light's directional beam.

'How long have I been asleep?' she said, smacking her lips. Not waiting for an answer. 'Hope and Rob the Knob came to visit. I'm not sure I didn't dream it.'

Doc shrugged. 'Who knows? I'm here now, though.'

'I crashed the car,' she said, appraising her exhausted-looking friend, glad that he was back in town. Acknowledging the searing pain in her head when she spoke.

'I know. I heard. Do you want a glass of water?' Doc picked up her plastic jug and marched around the bed to the en suite, not waiting for her response.

'Get me some painkillers before I die, will you? I feel like my head is falling off. My arm's itching like a bastard under this cast.'

Gingerly trying to sit up, Bev allowed Doc to fuss around her and give her ibuprofen that she was certain the nurse wouldn't allow on top of the codeine she'd taken hours ago.

'What made you come back?' she asked, recalling all that had led up to this point.

'They got in touch with me on my burner. The cops. Traced my number through your phone. Are the police on your case?'

Bev nodded. 'It's all Rob's fault. And that douche, Jerry Fitzwilliam.' She closed her eyes, uttering a silent prayer of thanks to whoever was listening that she'd been the only person hurt in the accident, beyond the odd bit of whiplash suffered by those who had performed emergency stops.

Doc raised an eyebrow. 'Were Rob and Fitzwilliam behind the wheel?'

'Piss off, Doc. If you've come back to Manchester with the sole intention of making me feel bad, just sling your hook back to Chalfont St Bollocks. OK? I've got Rob trying to prove I'm an unfit mother, Fitzwilliam leaving me threatening messages. Mo thinking I'm self-sabotaging by publishing some masochistic sex site called redhotslut. com or some shit. Jesus. I might as well just bloody give up if you're not on my side.' She remembered then, what Rob had said about Doc's possible involvement in the slanderous website. 'Are *you* behind redhotslut?'

Peeling the wrapper aggressively from a Mars bar he'd taken out of his bag, Doc took a huge bite of the chocolate bar and chewed in morose silence. Finally, he swallowed noisily. 'Is that what you think of me? Is that the extent of the trust between us? Think it through, for God's sake! I'm the one who warned you about this online shit. I trek all this way overnight to visit you, and you think *I'm* your stalker? Seriously?'

Bev realised that Rob had merely been twisting and stirring things, as usual. ''Course not. I'm just tired and in pain and sick to the back teeth of my crappy life.'

He offered her the Mars bar, with the caramel dangling like tiny stalactites from the place where he'd bitten.

She waved him away and sighed heavily. Closed her eyes until the flashes of pain forced them back open. She focused first on the large utilitarian clock on the wall. 'Who the hell eats that crap at 5.30 a.m.?'

'Breakfast, innit?'

'Not for me it isn't. They leave you lying like a dog in a manger in this place. All I wanna do is call my baby girl and tell her I love her and that I'm going to fight 'til I get her back. I bet Rob won't bring her in to see me again. Maybe I did dream she was here. He's such a dick. Anyway, then I've got to get hold of Angie and see if Jerry really has sussed I'm Beverley Saunders and not Cat Thomson. It certainly sounded that way, judging by his messages. If it's not my ex, it's got to be that nutter. Rob has the motivation, but Jerry's the only one with the resources to get my place turned over and dig up enough dirt about me to put all that shocking crap up online. If he knows I was cat-fishing him, he's going to be angry. Though he must have a tech-savvy nerd on the payroll, because he never struck me as some computer whizz.' For the briefest of moments, Bev scrutinised her friend and wondered again if she was missing something; if Doc could possibly be behind the trolling and stalking she'd fallen victim to.

She squeezed her eyes tightly shut. *Stop being ridiculous. Doc's not capable of having men follow you on a damned train. He wouldn't harm a fly!*

'Well, we both saw how Fitzwilliam killed my computer,' Doc said. He took a swig from his Coke bottle. Narrowed his bloodshot eyes, pointing. 'I saw how aggressively he behaved towards you in his secret shag-pad. How long before he has one of us or his wife bumped? You've got to take him down.'

Though it even hurt to grimace, Bev shuffled herself up the hospital bed using her good arm. '*We*, Doc. *We've* got to take him down. And Tatjana, the girl in the bin . . . she's the key. It proves what he could be capable of. I've not come across the "film" mentioned in his email to the pimp. The Dark Net's a giant and grim place. But if we find it and it's incriminating, we're home and dry.'

'Jesus. That's a big, "if", Bev. In the meantime, we're in over our heads.'

Doc rubbed his face and ran his hands through his hair. As he did so, he gave off a pungent whiff of stale marijuana and damp, and an earthy tang of compost. He smelled of neglect. Bev could see that, though he'd spent the last couple of weeks in his parental home like some overgrown teen, he'd somehow aged. Despite the dire situation she found herself in, she was surprised by the pang of pity and wave of overwhelming affection she felt for him. Here, in the midst of her hard, lonely, chaotic existence that was marbled with danger, addiction and poverty, she realised she had a friend.

'You really care, don't you?' she asked.

Doc nodded. Opened his mouth to say something, but only breath came out. Then, when the moment had passed, he smacked his lips and slapped his knees. He stood. 'Let's get you out of here. Get you in your own bed. Then, we can sit and eat Jaffa Cakes and look for this Tatjana film properly. OK?'

274

She shook her head. 'Look at the bloody time, James! They're hardly going to let me out at the crack of dawn.'

'We'll see about that.' Doc flashed her a mouthful of yellowed teeth and winked.

Ten minutes later, Bev was being pushed through the double doors at the end of the ward by Doc, dressed as an orderly.

'Where are you going with that patient?' the staff nurse shouted from the comfort of her padded typing chair, stationed behind the main desk.

'X-ray,' Doc said, tapping at the face of his watch as though he was late for an urgent appointment. 'Can you release the doors, please?'

The staff nurse rose to her feet and started to waddle towards him, her dark blue A-line skirt swishing from side to side in her wake. 'Who are you? I don't recognise you.'

CHAPTER 36

Bev

Doc flashed the lanyard around his neck to the inquisitive sister. 'Jim. I'm new from the agency.'

She seemed to consider his explanation. Nodded. Returned to the desk and buzzed them out.

He pushed the wheelchair into the corridor, saying, 'Yesssss' under his breath.

'Where the hell did you get this get-up?' Bev asked, cradling the cast on her broken arm. For a moment she was so amused by their getaway that her her pain was momentarily forgotten.

'Nicked it out of a dirty laundry cage,' he said, taking his backpack from her and swinging it onto his back. 'Amazing what people leave lying around big hospitals in the early hours of the morning.'

'And the lanyard?'

He grinned, illuminating that dismal place with its shiny, bumpy vinyl flooring far better than the unfriendly glaring strip-lighting overhead. 'Iron Maiden backstage pass. 2004 world tour!'

When the taxi pulled up outside Sophie and Tim's, Doc helped Bev up the stone steps, holding her elbow as if she was a frail, elderly woman. Dithering with each step she took, thanks to the agony of the bruising – outside and in – and the hangover-like effects of strong codeine, Bev bit back self-pitying tears.

'Come on. You can do it. Only three more steps,' Doc said, speaking softly.

She shook him loose. 'Sod off, Doc. You're making me feel like an invalid.'

'You *are* an invalid! Jesus, Bev! Would it kill you to accept a little help off someone who cares?'

Stopping on the penultimate step, panting with the sheer effort required to propel her towards the front door, she glared at him. 'I'm standing here with my arm in a sling and my arse hanging out, still wearing a hospital gown, for Christ's sake. I've lost—'

'I'm helping you to get up the stairs after a serious car crash,' Doc said. 'Not stripping you of your dignity. Stop looking for the bad in people, and give me your arm.'

'Shhh! Keep your voice down, gobshite.'

Inside, everyone was still sleeping. With a heavy heart, she unlocked her damp basement flat. The sharp whiff of mildew stung in her nostrils immediately. She sneezed four times in a row.

'Ow. My ribs.'

'This place is a dump,' Doc said. 'Even by my standards. You've got to get out of here.'

'I've got no option. They're chucking me out on my arse, anyway. Believe me, I'm working on it.'

She allowed him to help her onto her bed.

'I'll make some tea,' he said, disappearing off into the kitchenette.

Bev was relieved to see that her doors and windows hadn't been breached in her absence, at least. But as she lay there, listening to the tinkle of a teaspoon inside a ceramic mug in the kitchen, she realised that the laundry basket full of clean towels and T-shirts, that had been wedged up against her chest of drawers for days, had been moved. Or had it?

Ignoring the twinges from her battered and broken limbs, she struggled to her feet and approached the heavy hand-me-down piece of oak furniture.

'I could have sworn this basket was . . .'

Tugging the top drawer open with her one good hand, she peered inside at her underwear. Blinking hard, she registered the mess. A slattern elsewhere in the home, Bev always kept a clearly compartmentalised undies drawer: knickers on the left. Bras stacked neatly on the right. Socks and stockings balled in a line at the front. What she beheld now was lingerie pandemonium.

'He's been back,' she said. 'How the hell has he managed that?'

'What's wrong?' Doc asked, standing in the doorway bearing two steaming mugs.

Clinging onto the chest of drawers, Bev gasped as something else struck her. 'The deadlock. The deadlock on the front door.' She felt as though ice were seeping out of her every pore. 'I always put the deadlock on the Yale, but it wasn't on, just now.'

'Were you in a hurry when you left?'

'Yeah, but it's muscle memory, isn't it? I always, always deadlock it. When we came in, it just took me one turn of the key to unlock. I've only just sussed it. And someone's been through my undies drawer. Either Fitzwilliam's been in, or he's paid someone to rifle through my things. I'm telling you, Doc. Wipe that incredulous look off your mush, because I'm not going nuts.'

'I never said that. This is how I normally look. I'm the last person to judge.'

'Well, I'm telling the truth.' She stumbled over to her computer, switched it on and put her own name into Google's search engine. Her spoof Twitter account was the first thing that appeared in the listings. 'Look at this! It's a disgrace.' She pointed to the latest in the Twitter feed of @Beverley_Saunders. 'Constant, too. One tweet every fifteen minutes, dead on. Look!' The blush crept into her cheeks, momentarily melting the icy sensation of dread, replacing it with searing embarrassment. Picture after picture loaded up onto the screen of some porn star in an almost yogic pose, either being screwed by a well-endowed beefcake or entered by some projectile or other. In some photos, there were two or more men, making full use of every available orifice. Bev's head had been Photoshopped onto each image convincingly. 'Only consolation is, at least the world will think I'm super bendy and have a damned thigh gap.'

'He's using a programme like Hootsuite to time the tweets,' Doc said. 'Wow.'

'Search for that film of Tatjana, Doc. Angie showed me some snaps her nanny was using to blackmail Fitzwilliam. If those are anything to go by, the men in the footage will be wearing animal masks, and I'll bet it was filmed in a posh penthouse. Find it now, and we can end this. Or else I'll force you to look at my new porn makeover for the rest of the day.'

Doc flushed red, shunting her out of the way. His fingers started to fly across the keyboard. 'Get back on the bed and drink your tea. I'm going in.'

An hour later, Bev woke to find Doc standing over her. His colour had drained almost entirely away.

'What is it?' she asked, almost forgetting why he was in her bedroom while she'd been asleep . . . until the pain kicked back in, bringing crystal clear recall with it. 'Why are you standing over me like an avenging bloody angel?'

'I've found it,' he said. 'The footage of Tatjana's death. I had to get behind the paywall on a snuff site to access it. It's had more than five thousand hits, too.' His mouth was downturned; his eyes bloodshot as though he'd been crying or had seen something disturbing enough to make his capillaries pop. He chewed the inside of his cheek. 'It's really not pretty. Wanna see?'

Levering herself into the typing chair, with Doc standing behind her, they watched the gruesome home video together. The action took place in the living room of Fitzwilliam's secret apartment. Wooden floors and leather sofas. There were five men, all naked but for latex masks that covered their heads entirely – a pig. A bulldog. A horse. A cockerel. And a wolf. The men from the stills that Gretchen had stashed in her shoebox. Their voices were muffled and eerie.

In the footage, the naked girl lay on one of the sofas as each of the men took turns.

'It's definitely Tatjana Lebedev,' Bev said. 'Same girl as the photo in the *Evening Standard*. Poor little bleeder.'

Bev watched on, feeling her heart quickly shattering on this girl's behalf. Stomach churning with revulsion at the sort of gang bang she'd taken part in before, though she had, importantly, been a consenting adult and had made it out sore but happy, as opposed to dead.

In the film, Tatjana was clearly passive, her speech heavily accented and slurred. It was clear she'd been plied with drugs and alcohol. The Wolf took centre stage only fifteen minutes in, forced her to wear an SM ball gag and began to strangle the girl, mid-coitus.

'Hold it!' Bev said, her voice wavering, barely able to make herself heard above her thudding heartbeat. 'Scroll back a little and freeze the frame.'

Doc rewound the film. 'What is it?'

'There!' Bev said. She pointed to the hip of the portly pink-skinned man wearing the pig mask. On it was a birthmark she had seen before. A red blotch, roughly the same shape as Australia. 'There he is. *That's* Jerry Fitzgerald.'

They watched the grim recording to the end, to the finale where Tatjana's head lolled to one side and the men began to argue over what had come to pass; watched to the point when The Wolf returned from the kitchen bearing a meat cleaver and roll of black bin bags.

Bev inhaled slowly and sighed long and hard. In Russia, there dwelled a distraught and ruined mother who had also lost a daughter. Except unlike Hope, Tatjana would never be going home.

'Well, if Jerry Fitzwilliam didn't kill her,' Doc said, pointing to the savage canine face that filled the screen, hand outstretched towards the camera, 'who the fuck is he?'

CHAPTER 37

Bev

'Just keep reading the plaque. Pretend to be interested,' Bev said out of the corner of her mouth. She stole a glance at Angie from over the tops of her sunglasses. 'You look better, anyway. You've got colour in your cheeks.'

At her side, a smile flickered on and off Angie's gaunt, perfectly made-up face as she wheeled her daughter's pushchair back and forth, back and forth. Her semi-feral son was a way off, climbing onto and jumping off a bench, just where the museum's famous tyrannosaurus rex presided over the gallery, skimming the ornate stucco ceiling with his giant bony head. 'That'll be the gin I had at lunchtime,' she said. 'Dutch courage. Every time I go out, I'm worried Jerry will be there, watching and waiting for me.' It was suddenly apparent that her eyes were glassy with sorrow or, more likely, fear. 'He keeps sending me horrible emails.'

'Listen,' Bev said, scanning the space for eavesdroppers and suspicious-looking types who were clearly not at Manchester University Museum simply for something constructive to do with their toddlers on a rainy Wednesday morning. 'I wanted to see you to give you the heads-up.'

'About what?'

'You need to find a way to get as much money as you can from Jerry, as fast as you can, and get it hidden, because it's gonna get seized.'

'What are you talking about?' A florid rash sprang up on Angie's neck. She started to scratch at it with pink shellac nails.

'I'm definitely going to the police about Jerry. He's involved in . . . some very nasty stuff. And I'm getting continual grief.'

'Hang on. Nastier than the cash for questions? Has this got something to do with those ghastly photos Gretchen had ferreted away?'

Bev nodded and squeezed Angie's hand. 'You and your kids need to stay as far away from him as you can. That Gretchen's bloody lucky she's still breathing.'

'Those two had a tit-for-tat agreement. I'm sure of it,' Angie said, shaking Bev off. 'She was getting cash out of Jerry and spying on me in return. I don't care what happens to the lying little brat! She'll have got the first flight back to Austria the moment I was out the door, I'll bet. Her sort always looks after number one.'

'Well, she's been playing with fire, because this is the sort of thing someone would kill to keep under wraps. At best, the press are going to be on your backs if this breaks.'

Angie pushed the trolley back and forth with such alacrity that her daughter began to scream. 'Shush, Poppy! Mummy's talking.' She spoke to the child in a sing-song voice. 'Look at the dinosaurs, sweetie.' Lowered her voice to a near hiss for Bev. 'I'm sorry you're being pestered by him. I can assure you I didn't breathe a word about your involvement in the divorce. He never heard it from me where I got all the information on his finances from. And

283

I haven't yet shown him the footage from your catfishing date. I'm keeping a stash of just-in-case dirt.'

Bev took several steps towards the dinosaur. Waited for Angie to catch up. 'Well, the cat's out of the bag whatever you have or haven't said, because he's making my life a waking nightmare. And I'm telling you now, you're going to have a problem when I go to the police with what I've dug up. It may well get Jerry off your back for good, but the paparazzi . . .'

'Oh my gosh, Beverley! What has he got involved in? You need to tell me.'

'Accessory to murder. A teenage prostitute was found dismembered and discarded in a butcher's bin in London.'

Coming to a standstill in the middle of the gallery, Angie's disbelieving voice was audible above the interested chummer chummer of the other visitors. 'Oh come on! I know he's a rotter and a bully . . . and even a thief. But *that*? No way!'

'Yes, way. I've seen the evidence. There's filmed footage of it doing the rounds online in the sort of places normal people don't visit.'

'Rubbish. A shadow cabinet minister? Murder? That's so far-fetched, it's—'

'Is it far-fetched?' Bev raised an eyebrow. Spoke so quietly that Angie had to lean in to hear her. 'I've seen the film with my own eyes, Angie. Five men in animal masks, just like the stills you stole from Gretchen.'

'Oh, well if they're wearing masks, it could be anyone! I realise Jerry's a sexually incontinent pervert . . . but murder?!'

'Gretchen's photos, Ange!'

'Maybe there's a trend for men wearing animal masks. The internet's a very strange place.' Her tone was unconvincing;

her voice, thin and squeaky. The horror of this revelation was evident in her anguished expression.

She could deny Jerry's involvement all she liked, but sometimes, two plus two simply equalled four. 'In the same flat I've been in and fled from,' Bev said. 'And how many men do you know with birthmarks the shape of Australia, eh? That's what the police would call an anomaly. It's how they identify suspects. Tattoos, disfigurements, scars, birthmarks.'

'Are you certain?'

'Ninety-nine point nine per cent. Sorry.'

Angie fell silent for a moment. Swallowed hard several times and then grabbed Bev unexpectedly, her bony fingers closing around her arm like pincers. 'The police are in his pocket. He's their golden boy; Jerry Fitzwilliam, the great white budgetary hope for law enforcement. He fancies himself as a future Justice Minister if Labour gets into power and he's promised them the earth.'

Bev could feel the sweat from her client's hand coming through the fabric of her top. 'Go easy, Angie.' She pulled her arm free. 'What are you saying?'

'If you think he's a thorn in your side now, wait until you've tried to frame him for murder.'

'Accessory to murder. And I don't need to frame anybody, thanks. He *did* do it! The camera doesn't lie.'

'They'll cover for him, Bev. You'll end up arrested on trumped-up charges yourself and they'll throw away the key. Be very, very careful.'

Climbing out of the taxi, Bev took in the Stretford vista – the busy main road into town, the old brick-built police station. The car park was rammed. This was a place that saw plenty of action. The only station for miles with a counter that was open to the public.

Wincing from the sheer effort of walking, she climbed the stairs to the reception area. Inside, the seating was bolted to the floor. Crime prevention and grassing hotline posters had been dotted around liberally on the walls. Bev imagined she smelled desperation and defiance on the air, still lingering after the drunks and those gunning for a bust-up had been flung in the cells of a Friday or Saturday night. This was where the victims and relatives waited, side by side. The yin and yang of the UK's most violent city.

'What the hell am I doing here?' she muttered. Pausing by the heavy door to the counter. Wondering if she should just leave before she said things that could not be unsaid about a democratically elected MP of one of the most powerful nations on earth. *You're nuts. Call another Uber before it's too late,* her internal voice of reason advised. But the need to put back together the shards of her shattered world sliced through any apprehension. 'Come on, Bev. Do the right thing. Not just for you. Be the mother your girl can be proud of.'

She pressed the bell and waited, peering beyond the bullet proof glass. A powerfully built policewoman emerged from the area closed to the public and buzzed her through. No going back.

'I've come to report . . . I've come to give evidence of . . .' she stuttered.

Bev couldn't take her eyes off the woman's officer number on the epaulettes of her shirt or the sheer size of her shoulders.

'Go on, love.' She scrutinised the cast on Bev's arm, positioned across her body in a sling. Narrowed her eyes at the cuts and bruising to her face. 'We're here to help.'

Bev reached into her handbag and withdrew the small Jiffy bag that contained several USB sticks. 'This is one for CID. It's evidence of a murder that was in the papers a while ago. He was involved. You can see it in the footage. And there's evidence of fraud and trolling. I'm a private investigator, see? I'm being stalk—'

'Hang on, madam,' the policewoman said, raising a hand. 'Who are we talking about here? Is it a man known to you?'

Swallowing hard, Bev inhaled deeply, willing the tears to stay firmly behind her eyes. She was a professional, possibly committing career suicide. But a pro and a woman with a functioning moral compass, nonetheless. Even if her statement might ultimately lead to her never getting Hope back, she couldn't knowingly let a thief, a rapist and an accessory to murder walk free. 'Jerry Fitzwilliam. The shadow cabinet Minister for Science.'

The policewoman straightened up, regarding Bev and the Jiffy bag as though they were both other-worldly exhibits from Area 51, incomprehensible to the average sane human. She paused briefly, seeming to consider what to do with dastardly revelations of national importance, that bore no relation to the usual Stretfordian reports of pockets being picked or nuisance neighbours cobbing rubbish onto the streets. Then, she almost snatched the package from Bev. Speaking rapidly, it was clear she too was flustered. 'I'll need this, if you don't mind. Oh, and I'll have to take some details. Name. Address. Date of birth.'

After Bev had reluctantly revealed her identity, knowing there was now no way back, the policewoman pressed the buzzer to release the door. 'Just go and take a seat, please, madam. We'll be with you in a minute.'

CHAPTER 38
Bev

'Tell us how you got hold of this information,' Curtis said, tapping his finger by the evidence bag that now contained the USB sticks.

The confrontational way in which he pushed the baggie towards her bristled with aggression; testosterone seeming to evaporate off his sweaty forehead in waves like those fuel mirages that surrounded the petrol nozzle whenever Bev filled up her car. On the couple of occasions she'd gone to this arse-carbuncle with a tale of shocking domestic violence, child abuse and some class A criminal activity well worth reporting to the cops, he and his pal, Owen had delighted in ridiculing her. They'd made it pretty clear that they considered private investigators to be low-rent facsimiles of the real enforcers of the law. Today was no exception to that rule. 'Assuming it actually is what it appears to be.'

'You know full well I'm a PI,' she said, wishing that waver in her voice would abate. Wondering if she ought to call her solicitor in a bid to break free of the net of cheap polyester suiting, stale coffee-breathed suspicion and labyrinthine bureaucracy that she seemed to be caught in. 'I was hired by Fitzwilliam's wife, Angie to put together some information—'

'But catfishing an MP and hacking into his bank account goes a bit above and beyond the call of a PI's duty, don't you think, Beverley?' The timbre of Owen's saccharine-sweet voice grated on her ears. She couldn't have been more than twenty-seven. A graduate fast-tracker, perhaps, with everything to prove in a man's world. 'That kind of activity is against the law. You must realise that. If every Tom, Dick and Harry started—'

'Angela Fitzgerald came to me after he'd tried to throttle her,' Bev explained. 'Covered in bruises, she was. I know a desperate woman in mortal danger when I see one and that danger's only escalated since he knows that she's realised what a morally bankrupt fuck-stump he is.'

'Did you personally hack Mr Fitzgerald's bank accounts, Beverley?' Curtis asked. 'Or did you pay someone?'

Wishing she could just get the hell out of that claustro-phobic interview room, Bev closed her eyes. *Stand up for yourself, woman. Don't let them push fault onto you. They're playing the same shitty trick Rob always did. Switch the tables back on them.* 'Never mind how I get my information. Right? On those USB sticks, you'll find hard evidence of a public servant squirrelling away millions of undeclared cash that he got from companies he's pushing to give government contracts to. OK? You'll find screenshots of the filth that's been appearing online about me since I took this case on. Defamatory stuff, inviting randoms to visit me at home, rape me and beat me up. You want illegal activity? I'm giving you this. And the biggest coup for you guys, is that this stick . . .' She pointed to the baggie placed by Owen's hands. 'Has Tatjana Lebedev's final moments on it.' Saw the ambition in the woman's eyes. 'Don't you fancy being the detective who solved the murder of the dismem-bered Russian girl in the butcher's bin? Those southern softies in the Met are going to be twisting their melons if a Manc brings home the bacon on a big case like that, and it turns out to be a bent politician and his mates behind it. Underage Russian prostitute. Trafficked, at that. Drugs. Murder. Eh? An email trail that proves Jerry Fitzgerald organised it all, like he was planning some lads' night in with a few tinnies and the match.'

Curtis produced some printouts, fanning them out on the battered table's surface and sliding them within her reach. 'You've got mental health problems, haven't you, Beverley? A judge deemed you unfit to parent your daughter.'

Bev's insides twisted into tight knots she would never untie. She pressed her lips together, breathing heavily through flared nostrils. 'I'm addicted to origami. That doesn't make me a liar.'

'And you've been in a car crash recently.' He gestured towards the cast on her arm. 'My colleagues are investigating you for dangerous driving.'

Standing, leaning as far into the detective as she could, Bev mustered every last shred of molten anger that welled within her. She jab-jabbed her good index finger towards him. 'Listen, pal. Check your CCTV footage for Princess Road. The HGV at the side of me wandered into my lane.' She turned to Owen. 'And I've got a copy of all this shit. Maybe you'd prefer me to go to the press with it. Because if I do that, and it goes national, suddenly, this is all prejudicial evidence and you can't admit it in court. No medals for you, chuck. Is that what you want?'

Returning to the house, Bev circumnavigated her inquisitive landlords by skirting down the side access. There, the wheelie bins stood to attention in a line. Desperate to slip into her flat via her patio doors, where she'd be able to debrief Doc, she noticed that her bag of paper recycling, that she'd put out only days earlier, lay behind the bin for bottles and tin cans. It had been slashed open. The rain-sodden contents were strewn across the paving, like soggy stuffing spilling from a bust sofa that had been fly-tipped and left at the mercy of the elements for too long.

'Of course he's been through my rubbish,' she said, trying to scrape the disintegrating documentation back into the bin.

'Yoo-hoo!' Above her, Sophie was calling. 'Just the girl! Can I have a word?'

Bev looked up to see her friend dangling out of the window to the guest bedroom at the side. The tone was jolly, but Sophie's face was inscrutable, bordering on clearly pissed off. Not good.

Unable to make the case that her need to repair to her sickbed was a matter of urgency, Bev found herself being corralled into the kitchen to discuss, 'The Twitter Thing'. She was summoned not to the island in the middle of the room, where wine was normally drunk and convivial conversations were had, whilst Sophie pottered about, arranging pre-washed salad leaves on her favourite Cath Kidston crockery. Instead, she was bidden to sit at the dining table in a straight-backed chair, with Sophie at the head. She felt like she'd been summoned to the boardroom by the boss of BelNutrive all over again. Damp rings quickly bloomed beneath her armpits, making the fabric of her T-shirt unpleasantly wet and cold.

'Feeling better?' Sophie asked, wearing a smile that was more of a grimace.

'Not really,' Bev said. 'I'm still—'

'Good. We need to talk.' Sophie was screwing a piece of kitchen roll in her hand. She sipped a smoothie while Bev was left with no drink at all.

'Oh yeah?' Bev said, chuckling nervously. Wondering how her morning could possibly get more stressful. 'You've already given me the order of the boot once this week, so it can't be that.'

Sophie examined her beautifully manicured hands and touched the discreet diamond cross that hung around her neck as if she sought the guidance of Jesus. Ever-forgiving, cheek-turning Holy Jo was still waiting to inherit the earth – didn't even realise that she already had.

'I've seen it,' she said. 'The revolting Twitter account.'

'It's not me,' Bev said. 'How could you think—?'

But her friend wasn't listening. She merely closed her beautifully made-up eyes and held her hand aloft. 'I knew your . . . problems were escalating. And the crash was an awful thing to happen to you. But when Tim showed me that outrageous . . .' Focused on Bev, now with a hard, blue-eyed stare. 'Well, I couldn't believe you'd be so reckless. Posting nude pictures of yourself. Inviting dirty men into our home to abuse you.'

'OK. Enough!' Bev shouted, rising from the uncomfortable seat. Clutching at the cast on her arm, she fantasised fleetingly about swinging it into Sophie's judgemental face. But scratch beneath the defensive layer of bluff, and Bev acknowledged that her friend's disapproval bit deep. 'I didn't post any of that stuff and need I remind you that I'm a mother? I resent you believing that I would—'

'What?' Tim's voice, now. 'Bring strange men to the house for sex? The house where our children live.'

Bev turned to the doorway to see him standing there, arms folded like a man-mountain of stone. There was nothing but disgust etched on that flinty face with its broken nose and cauliflower ear. The jaunty pastel colours of his polo rugby top were at odds with the ominous dark cloud that seemed to hang above him like a brewing storm.

'Listen, pal,' Bev said, marching up to him and pushing him in his over-developed pectoral muscle. 'I've just about had enough of you, doling out judgement. Who the hell do you think you are? You charge me an exorbitant rent to live in your basement flat – a mildewed stinking pit that you can't even be arsed to maintain properly.'

'Well, actually it's a long time since you paid—'

'Need I remind you that I've got my own front door with my own lock, and that I can bring whoever I want home? And if you must know, if I have guests, I make them come in through the patio doors, so they don't have to walk through your precious family home.' She was standing on her tiptoes now, shouting up at him. Feeling nothing but festering resentment power her every word. 'What I do in the privacy of my own place, as a consenting adult, is absolutely fuck all to do with you. Just because you're not getting any, Timbo, don't take your jealousy out on me.'

She tried to push past him but his shovel-like hand closed around her shoulder.

'You're hurting me,' she said, trying to wriggle free. Wishing Doc were there to witness this affront. 'Sophie! Are you going to let him manhandle an injured woman like this? Say something, will you?'

But her friend was looking at a flower arrangement on the island with studied disinterest, plucking the pollen-laden anthers from the stamens on some white oriental lilies.

'Sophie nagged me into letting you stay until you've got a place,' Tim said. 'But I've changed my mind. You've got forty eight hours to get out. You're a malign influence on my family.'

Digging deep within to mine the most hurtful thing she could say to him, Bev came up with the perfect retort. 'No need to keep repeating yourself, *dear.*' Patted him on the head. 'I already got that you're evicting me. That's okay. I need to get away from this dump anyway. Because when the press get a whiff of the incontrovertible evidence I've just handed over to the cops about your "brother-from-another-mother", they'll be crawling all over here to see if you've got the same murderous, perverted, swindling DNA as that twat, Jerry Fitzgerald.' Not allowing the agony of wrenching her shoulder free of his iron grip to surface in her eyes, Bev finally made a break for the freedom of the hallway. 'An abusive father? Seduced by your own mother's best mate? Yeah, Soph filled me in on anything I didn't already know! You're no choirboy, Tiny Tim.'

His face had crumpled. Sophie was gasping like a carp, plucked from a pond by a feral cat.

But Bev was enjoying herself. 'So, it wouldn't surprise me if this forest fire spreads, Timbo. Don't expect all your friends and colleagues and your boss to keep the love for you when they read in *The Times* that your elective "brother" is going to prison for being an accessory to murder, grand theft and trolling a wrongly-maligned origami addict called Beverley Saunders.'

Tim's mouth hung open.

Sophie balled her bony fist and punched her in her good arm. 'Don't speak to my husband like that, after he's been so kind to you. You're a horrible person. I know why Rob dumped you now. With friends like you, who needs enemies?'

'I don't believe a word that comes out of her foul, lying mouth, Soph,' Tim said. 'Nobody in their right mind would try to pin such heinous crimes on an upstanding member of the shadow cabinet like Jerry. She's certifiable!'

Outside, there was the rumble of a diesel engine, coming to a standstill. Through the leaded lights of the front door, Bev saw the neon chequerboard of a police van. Footsteps up the stone stairs. The click and hiss of a police radio springing to life on the officer's shoulder. There were two men, both uniforms, by the looks. Had they come to arrest her for dangerous driving or was there news about Jerry?

'Am I? Well, we're about to find out.'

CHAPTER 39

Bev

The two burly uniforms – one Asian, one white stood in Sophie's hallway, making the generous space seem suddenly cramped; the ceiling too low for comfort. Behind them, though the sun streamed in through the stained glass of the door, Bev felt the chill of the long shadows that they cast.

'Go on. Out with it.' *Please don't arrest me*. The handcuffs glinted at their waists, threatening like miniature gallows. *Please don't say I'm going to end my days sewing mailbags in Styal women's prison*.

'We're just here to inform you that our colleagues are right this minute placing Mr Fitzwilliam under arrest,' the Asian officer said, his walkie-talkie going into overdrive on his shoulder. 'We'll need you to come down the station tomorrow to make a statement. Detectives Curtis and Owen are leading the investigation. They asked us to let you know as a courtesy, like.'

Bev waited for the words to soak in. She slouched against the newel post of the grand oak staircase, exhaled heavily and smiled. Pressed her hands to her lips. 'Brilliant.' Shot a glance towards Sophie and Tim. Both were grey-faced, seemingly with shock. Wide-eyed and staring at one another. This was a told-you-so moment Bev would savour for a long while. 'Jesus, what a relief! That's great news. Thanks for keeping me in the loop, guys. I was glad to be of help.'

The second uniform pointed to her arm in its cast. 'And you'll be happy to hear there'll be no charges brought against you for the accident. Our specialists have examined the CCTV footage and the HGV driver was at fault. In fact, he's admitted it. You're in the clear, love. Let your insurance know.'

Tears welled up in Bev's eyes. For so long, she'd been running like a blind rat through the dark maze of life, hitting only dead end after dead end. This news felt like a turning point where she could finally change tack, heading for the sunshine. 'That's smashing. Thank you. Thank you.'

When the cops had gone, Bev opted to say nothing to Sophie and Tim, ignoring their awkward, 'Good news about the crash' comments and their shit-eating, 'Seems the police believe you about Jerry' remarks. She hastened down to her flat and slammed the door. Dialled Angie straight away.

'Have you heard?' she said as soon as Angie answered, breathless and audibly trembling.

'I know! I know! They called.'

'We won!' Bev grinned.

'I know it sounds awful, but . . . Let's celebrate!' Poppy and Benjy were chattering away in the background, oblivious to what was about to befall their father. But Angie sounded relieved now. 'Am I a terrible person?'

'Not at all, Angie. But don't be so quick to toast the downfall of your husband. They'll have to try him first. You'll be investigated too. It's not going to be a picnic by a long stretch.'

'But the hard work's behind us, Bev. I owe you. Come on! Get your glad rags on. I'll leave the children with my aunt. Let's do lunch. On me.'

Feeling that she really needed to get out of Sophie and Tim's house at that moment, Bev agreed. 'Where?'

'Meet in the middle? How about Crewe Hall?'

'It's a bit of a schlep, isn't it? My arm's buggered. I can't drive.'

'I'm sending you a cab. No arguments.'

Just over an hour later, Bev's taxi pulled up outside the Jacobean towering splendour of Crewe Hall. Busy on a Saturday, with the weekend trade in anniversaries, weddings and spa-users, its spires rose above her, pointing to the blue, blue sky. The only thing that marred the scene was a giant, dense cloud that moved over the sun as soon as Bev's cabbie drove off. It seemed to threaten so much more than just heavy rain. The elegant specimen pines that studded the immaculate green velvet of the lawns felt like an encroaching, dark forest, full of terrible secrets.

Pack it in! Bev counselled herself. *Jerry's under lock and key. You're going to get paid, move flat, get your daughter back. Be positive, for God's sake. You're not even stumping for lunch. Order steak! Don't get pissed.*

Hoisting her handbag onto her good shoulder, she wended her way through the dark panelled, almost ecclesiastical foyer that was a temple to four star provincial luxury. Made her way to the restaurant at the back, which was modern and less exciting than anticipated. It smelled good, though.

'Bev!' Angie was already sitting at a table. She rose to meet her. Kissed her on both cheeks. 'My saviour!'

Feeling progressively less awkward about socialising with her client, the more she worked her way through a large glass of cabernet shiraz and her rump steak, Bev leaned back in her chair, smiling. Slapping her stomach.

'Thanks for this. I've been through the mill. We both have.' The man who had appeared at the door to the restaurant remained in both the periphery of her vision and her subconscious mind.

Angie, who had eaten only half of the dressing-free salad on her plate set down her cutlery. 'Actually, I've got another surprise.'

'I don't like surprises.' Bev wiped her peppercorn sauce from the sides of her mouth with a napkin.

'Let's pamper ourselves rotten! I've booked spa treatments. You can borrow one of my bikinis. Will that be OK, with your injuries?'

Stifling a groan, Bev arranged her reluctant lips into a smile. 'Lovely. I'll be fine.' She hated spas with a passion. Would Angie understand that she didn't like to be mauled by strangers who weren't physiotherapists, some other medical practitioners or sexual partners? *Can it! She's being nice. Go with the flow.* 'I'm not sure your bikini will fit, Angie. I'm a twelve and you're what? A size zero?'

'A twelve? You're never that fat, Bev! You'll be fine!'

'Thanks.' *That fat? I could lose a few pounds, but since when was a twelve, 'that fat'?*

In the changing rooms, Bev stared at Angie's jutting hips and shoulders, from which hung an expensive looking bikini. Wincing, she pulled the borrowed swimwear over her own badly bruised, dimpled flesh, ignoring the sniggers and stares of the other women.

'Great! It fits like cheese wire,' Bev said, looking down in horror at the straps that were so tight, they simply disappeared into the folds of her accommodating flesh. 'I think a tiny triangle of fabric up your bum-crack is going to be the new, "thing". Don't you? Don't worry. I'll wash it after.'

Angie pointed to her chest. 'Your nipples . . .'

The miniscule cups of the strangulating top wouldn't quite sit in the right place over Bev's substantial breasts. If she pulled right, her left was exposed. If she pulled left, her right was exposed.

'Just put a dressing gown on, darling. Nobody will notice.' Angie handed her a fluffy robe.

'Thanks.' *This is a mistake,* Bev thought.

A few minutes later, she followed a middle-aged woman in a lavender uniform into a darkened room, where she made Bev lie on a vinyl massage table and proceeded to cover Bev's face in something that smelled and felt like mortar. Then she scrubbed Bev's lower legs and feet hard.

'Jesus, what are you doing? Sanding me down? I'm not a bloody coffee table. Take it easy! And don't touch my upper body. I've been in a car crash.'

Amid a good deal of sympathetic cooing and an explanation about circulation and pressure points and other such spa cod science, Bev heard a scream. She leapt off the table, snatching up the coarse-bristled scrubbing brush the woman had been using on her legs. Ran into the hallway. Where had the scream come from?

'Angie?'

'Help!'

The cry came from two doors down. The door was shut. Bev tried the handle but it was locked. With her bare foot, she kicked the door open. It crashed against the wall. The scene that greeted her was not one she'd anticipated.

'Hello, Cat. Or should I say, Bev? Interesting makeover. Is mouldy a good look for you?'

'You! I thought you'd been arrested.'

Jerry Fitzwilliam had Angie in an awkward headlock up against her own massage table. The beautician who had been tending Angie was out cold on the floor, blood seeping from a blow to her head. Next to her lay shards of glass, a pool of shining yellow liquid and the jagged neck of a broken glass bottle – massage oil, by the looks.

'Well, you thought wrong. It's a lot easier to give the police the slip than you think when they come for you on your home turf. I'm no fool, you know. Angie serves me divorce papers right after some big-titted tart has been trying to get in my pants? Did you really think I wouldn't make the connection between you two?'

'Run, Bev! Run!' Angie shouted.

But Jerry slapped a meaty hand over her mouth and her cries were stifled.

'Let her go,' Bev said. 'You're making things worse for yourself, Jerry. Hand yourself over to the police. Face a trial like a grown-up.'

'I didn't kill that girl.'

Bev knew Tatjana had not died at the hand of the man before her, but she could still see untamed violence in his eyes. Jerry Fitzwilliam stood to lose everything, and now he was hell-bent on revenge. Of that, she was certain. 'Well, if you're innocent, you've got nothing to worry about. Think about it, Jerry. If you hurt Angie, you'll never see Poppy and Benjy again. But if you give yourself up and tell the police what you know . . .'

Fitzwilliam threw Angie to the ground, pushing the massage table so hard into Bev that she stumbled backwards, crashing onto a pyramid display of face creams. Like some villain from a superhero movie, suffused with serum that gave him enormous physical strength, the shadow Science Minister leaped over the table, pinning Bev to the floor, the pain almost rendering her unconscious. The fury inside him twisted his coarse features into a mask of hatred.

'The pig wears the pig mask. Oh, what bitter irony,' Bev said, bracing herself for whatever came next.

Fitzwilliam drew back his fist and brought it down fast towards her face.

Raising her cast defensively, his knuckles met only solid plaster. He yelped. Backed off, clutching his hand – just enough to allow Bev to scramble to her feet. She spied her scrubbing brush, which she'd dropped when she'd plummeted into the face-cream display. Flinging herself to the side, she closed her fingers around it. Rammed it as hard as she could, bristles first, into Fitzwilliam's face.

'Ow! You bitch!'

He lost his footing in a bid to get away from the further blows she rained down on him with the unforgiving brush. 'Bitch isn't a word that loves women, Jerry, dear. Don't call me that.' Bev felt like she had the upper hand. 'Call the police!' she yelled to anyone who might be listening. It felt like triumph was just around the corner.

But Fitzwilliam regained his balance, then grabbed Angie by the hair. Suddenly, he was holding a large splinter of broken glass to her carotid artery.

'I'm going to kill her if you don't get out of my way right now,' he said in a deadly calm voice.

Nonplussed, Bev held her good hand aloft in surrender, allowing him to drag Angie past her and into the hall. She followed him down the narrow corridor. The place was deserted. 'What the fuck are you gonna do, you big muppet? There's nowhere to go! Leave her be.'

'Jerry!' Angie whimpered. 'You're hurting me! Think of the children. Let me go. You're not yourself. You need help.' Her legs marched uselessly beneath her as he heaved her onwards.

With a bewildered look on his scratched and bleeding

face, Fitzwilliam entered the dappled light and instant humidity of the pool area. The handful of staff and spa-users there screamed as they registered the fact that a man had entered their leisure space, dragging a woman by her hair, holding broken glass to her neck. His own hand dripped with livid red blood onto the poolside tiles.

Feeling her bladder might give way at any moment, betraying her panic, Bev looked around. How could she neutralise this terrible threat? She studied the women's faces for signs of bravery or outrage. Might they come to her aid? No. There was nothing but fear there. As ever, she was on her own and would have to bluff it.

'See? You're cornered, now,' she said, shaking her head at him. 'What are you planning on doing? Killing your defenceless wife? Is that going to improve your situation?'

Fitzwilliam grinned nastily. From some Orwellian nightmare, he was a pig more equal than others. He certainly seemed to think so. 'No, but it might make me feel better.' He pulled Angie's head up. Dug the tip of the glass into her skin so that a bead of blood appeared on her neck like a ruby stud.

As if awaiting a reaction from his captive audience, he lowered the glass just enough to give Bev the opportunity she needed.

Grabbing a towel from an adjacent lounger, she followed her body's impulse unquestioningly. She ran it through the pool water and swung the heavy, water-laden fabric into the air like a slingshot. David, facing down Goliath, she flicked Fitzwilliam squarely in the face with it. It was just the distraction she needed. He released Angie. Bev barrelled into him, pushing him into the pool. Kicked out to get away from him. But she was clumsy in her wet terry-towelling robe, her injured arm and bruised ribs making every movement pure torture.

He pulled her down, down, down. She was lead-heavy. Bubbles escaping from her mouth as her lungs felt like they were being crushed in a vice. Felt his hands around her throat.

Instinctively, she jabbed her fist in slow motion but with force into his crotch. Saw through the chlorine-blue blur that he'd opened his mouth and inhaled water. He released her. Was thrashing around now. Jerking. Sinking. Drowning.

Hooking her arm around him from behind, Bev used her powerful legs to propel them both upwards. Gasping, they both surfaced to find two security guards standing over them.

'He's all yours,' Bev said, shedding her robe and clambering out to check on Angie.

As Fitzwilliam was hauled out by the two man-mountains, every woman in the pool area applauded Bev. Caught by at least twenty phone cameras, Bev would forever be the have-a-go hero, rocking the properly nutritioned look in a cheese-wire bikini, with Lycra stuck up her arse and one exposed nipple.

CHAPTER 40
Bev

Large bubbles of dread effervesced in her stomach, curdling with the rubbery scrambled eggs Doc had forced her to eat for breakfast. A night on his sofa hadn't been the best prep she could have had for this. But she'd needed to escape the emotional toxicity that continually leaked down through the floorboards into her basement flat from her erstwhile best friend and Timbo the Himbo.

It had been intolerable since Jerry's arrest, as if she were to blame for the siege at Crewe Hall. Matters had been made worse by not having found a flat, and Sophie having magnanimously though grudgingly insisted she stay until she sign on the dotted line for somewhere new. Bev felt equally cursed and blessed.

Now, though, as she stood in the mid-century county court, that was all cheap office carpet and utilitarian wood panelling, her happiness really swung in the balance. The most important thing in the world was at stake – her child.

'Step forwards, please,' the judge said, studying the faces of the four people, gathered in his courtroom.

Only feet away, Rob kept nervously fidgeting with his cufflinks and his earlobe, though Bev only had eyes for the suspended ceiling panels.

Funny the things you notice when your back's to the wall, Bev thought. *One of those panels has been shoved out of place by some workman, maybe, and hasn't been put back. I wonder if there's a hidden camera up there, watching the petty shenanigans of Trafford's most dysfunctional families? Maybe we'll appear on some reality TV thing. Britain's Most Fucked-Up.*

It was showtime. Eve, Bev's solicitor, explained how Dr Mo, the Duplicitous Dickhead had not declared a conflict of interest in the friendship that had grown over the years between him and Rob.

'That's a pile of crap!' Rob said. 'It's not like that at all.'

His solicitor gripped his arm.

'Please keep your client's outbursts under control,' the judge said to his brief, glancing down to scan the documentation before him.

He was peering at A4 images Bev could just about see from her vantage point below the bench. She smiled, realising these were the cheeky snaps Angie had taken on her phone in Carluccio's when she had tracked down Tim, enjoying his pre-match lunch in the Trafford Centre with his homeboys, Rob and Mo. The last thing Angie had had on her mind was Bev's private life, at a time when she'd been desperately trying to uncover her husband's financial chicanery. But she'd taken the initiative of getting photographic evidence of the unlikely threesome.

'How did Angela Fitzwilliam come across these images?' the judge asked, showing the snaps to Bev and her solicitor. Tim, Mo and Rob, all wearing the latest United strip, shovelling down tortellini. 'How did she recognise Dr Ashraf?

'Mrs Fitzwilliam has an eating disorder, Your Honour,' Eve replied. 'She'd seen the psychiatrist at the same medical centre where Beverley receives group therapy.

Mrs Fitzwilliam attends a support group there too. In the past, she's observed Beverley there, leaving sessions which had been led by Dr Ashraf.'

'It's a set-up!' Rob said.

'My ex is big buddies with my shrink,' Bev said. 'And my shrink is responsible for sending evaluations into court, testifying to my mental well-being and fitness as a mother. And that's not a set-up?'

The judge banged his gavel. 'Silence!'

Bev chewed the inside of her cheek, trying desperately not to smile. Thanks to Angie, she was finally able to chip away at the wall Rob had built around Hope.

'I'm going to allow unsupervised visits,' the judge ruled, after having heard the new evidence and refereed the bickering between the two lawyers. He locked eyes with Bev. 'I think you've been wronged and I'm sorry for that.' His stern expression softened, ushering in a smile. 'I've seen the clip of you in that swimming pool, you know.'

Feeling the heat in her cheeks, Bev bit her lip. Was this a good thing or a bad thing that the judge had seen her in an ill-fitting bikini, wrestling with a grown man? 'Yes. Sorry. It's gone viral on social media. I've got no control over—'

'Don't apologise. You're quite the heroine, Ms Saunders.' The judge turned to Rob, addressing him with the castigatory voice of a head teacher, giving a wayward pupil a dressing down. 'And you, sir, are in contempt of court.' Back to Bev, in a soft voice. 'When you have a fixed address that is suitable as a home for a child and the social worker has been satisfied by it, I will hear your case for a custody application, Ms Saunders.'

Punching the air with delight, Bev only just managed to suppress the urge to flip Rob the bird.

'Get in!' Bev said, hugging Doc, who was waiting for her on the steps of Trafford County Court.

His body was rigid in her arms, but it didn't matter. Mo had fallen into disrepute and doubt would therefore be cast on his evaluations. Rob had been put firmly in his place and was in hot water with the judge.

'I'm taking that bastard to the cleaners,' she said, linking arms with her business partner.

'With what money?' Doc said, treating her to a yellow-toothed smile and presenting her with a Greggs' ice bun.

Bev bit into the bun. Spoke with her mouth full. Relishing the feeling in the pit of her belly of optimism – and it wasn't just down to the icing. 'Dunno. I guess we'd better get some more work in, pronto. One new client and a few hours freelancing isn't going to cut it. Know any more wife-battering politicians?'

Best of all, Bev considered, as she walked through the side streets back to Doc's flat, Jerry was – for now, at least – locked up. No more trolling. No more stalking. Though the murderer of Tatjana Lebedev was still at large, Bev was sure the police would squeeze the relevant information out of a politician who had fallen so very far from grace. Meanwhile, she would be left in peace to enjoy a life that was improving daily . . .

CHAPTER 41

Bev

'Which do you fancy, bum-bum?' Bev asked, peering up at the menu behind the counter. 'Cheeseburger or a classic with everything on?' She put her arm around her daughter, savouring the scent of her hair. It smelled of cocoa butter; felt like satin.

'Ooh, can I have a double decker with fries? I'm starving,' Hope said, her eyes reflecting the backlit multicoloured Perspex of the menu as rainbows.

When her daughter put her arm around her, Bev felt like a missing piece of her being had been found. 'You can have whatever you like, my love. You need it, anyway. You're growing tall like a beautiful, willowy tree.'

'Nearly as big as Dad, now!'

Bev pictured Rob in her mind's eye. Dad. What a joke. A college dropout-turned-short-arsed dictator who didn't even have the genes to qualify him for his reign over Hope's life. Fuck him. 'This is our treat,' she said. 'Our girls' weekend away with no interruptions and solid fun. High five!'

Hope giggled, slapping her mother's hand with a palm that was almost as big as an adult's. 'Yay! Hurray for holidays. Can I have a milkshake too, please?'

Setting aside for a moment her concerns about how little money she had in her bank account until Angie settled up in full, she nodded. 'Just this once. But no more sweet stuff for the rest of the day. I don't want your teeth to drop out.' She kissed her daughter on the forehead, savouring every detail of her face: those large, doe-like eyes; her bow-shaped lips; the pixie chin with a dimple in the middle. Her build and her bone structure were all her father's. Her facial features were miniature Bev. She said a silent thank you to the universe for having reached this place, where she had time alone with her daughter.

They sat at a table with their motorway-services feast. Bev tried to make conversation about the latest pop bands that turned out to be old hat, and the latest toy craze that turned out to be yesterday's favourite Christmas present.

'Oh, Mum!' Hope groaned, shovelling a pile of French fries into her mouth but talking nonetheless. Fidgeting in her seat like the excitable ten-year-old she was. 'You're *so* uncool!' Cheeky laughter, followed by a flurry of heartfelt apologies.

Bev placed her hand on top of Hope's. 'It's been so hard being apart from you,' she said. 'I feel bad that I don't know all your favourite stuff. But I'll make it up to you. I promise.' *Don't bad-mouth Rob. Don't bad-mouth those shits he calls parents.* 'Things are going to change, my love.'

Nodding, Hope frowned. She licked her ketchup-smudged lips thoughtfully. 'How come we're allowed to do this, then? Has Janice gone forever?'

Smiling, Bev imagined pushing the social worker on her polyester-clad, interfering arse. 'Mummy just solved a big case at work and helped the police to catch a terrible criminal. Dr Mo — remember Mummy told you how he's been a bit like a school pastoral teacher for Mummy and Daddy over the years?'

Hope nodded. 'You said he has breath like bad eggs and makes you talk about your paper models in front of strangers.'

Bev chuckled. 'Yes, well Mo said some nasty things about Mummy and had to eat what's called humble pie.' She bit into her burger, relishing the news that she'd been assigned a new, impartial psychiatrist for the court's psychological evaluation. And if her solicitor had anything to do with it, the ongoing assessments and therapy would be dropped entirely. The grounds for Rob's insistence upon them had been spurious, in any case. 'So, that's why we're going to spend lots more time together, and when I get a new place, you'll come to live with me. You'll see Daddy loads, but you belong with your mum, pickle.'

Seemingly oblivious to the high drama that had been playing out between her parents since the time of her birth, Hope merely nodded, grinned and slurped on her mortar-thick milkshake. 'I love you Mum. I've missed you so much.' She blew Bev a kiss with those rosebud lips. 'It's not the same with Daddy. Best Mum!'

As she cleared the spent packaging onto the plastic tray and carried it towards the bin, Bev's attention was drawn to a television bolted to the wall of the restaurant. On it, the news flashed up with images of a police crime scene that fluttered with blue and white tape. There was something familiar about the house that the forensic pathologists, clad in their white jumpsuits, stood outside, along with the uniformed constables in their Kevlar vests.

'Angie,' Bev said.

She watched the silent footage, open-mouthed, that showed her most recent client, hurrying through a crowd of baying, bulb-flashing reporters. Angie wheeled her push-chair, with Poppy strapped into the seat and Benjamin standing on a buggy-board, at high speed down the tree-lined road, away from the sprawling house. The cameras followed her progress towards her Range Rover. Bev noticed that despite the mayhem, and drawing the world's attention for the wrong reasons, Angie looked happy. Pink in the cheeks. Shiny-eyed. And was that the hint of a smile that played on her glossy lips?

But the real focus was on Jerry Fitzwilliam. The feature flashed back to the news that had made headlines only two days earlier, when Fitzwilliam had been arrested. Bev watched the snippet she had since seen countless times, on every channel, of Angie's abusive husband being led in cuffs from the grand entrance of Crewe Hall to a waiting squad car.

'Ha,' Bev muttered, grinning up at the screen. 'Look at that face. Sick as the proverbial parrot, aren't you, you big lump?' Fitzwilliam's colour had drained from his usual pink to a sickly greenish hue. It seemed her old GMP adversaries, Curtis and Owen, had had an axe to grind against Labour's golden boy and self-proclaimed saviour of the underfunded force. The BBC had been tipped off before any public statement had been issued, triggering a press free-for-all. She felt certain that Jerry Fitzwilliam wouldn't be liking it one little bit. 'Serves you right.'

'All finished?' Bev asked Hope, cradling her velvety soft face in her hand.

'Can we get a rowing boat when we get there?' Hope asked, allowing her to spit on a serviette and wipe the red ghost of ketchup from her mouth.

'You bet. I'll let you have a go.'

Bev held her daughter's warm, clammy hand as they walked out to the car park, returning to her repaired Polo. With bruising skies above them, it was no surprise when fat beans of rain started to bounce on the bonnet of her car almost the moment they crossed the invisible border between Lancashire and Cumbria. As they sped down the M6 with the undulating peaks of the Lake District on the horizon, with the soporific hee-haw of the windscreen wipers counting down the metres covered, the weather seemed inconsequential.

She started to sing. 'We're off, we're off. We're off in a motor car. Sixty coppers are after us and we don't know where we are! We're off, we're off . . .'

With Hope singing along in the back seat, Bev's lack of funds and painfully stiff arm, now that the cast was off, mattered not a jot.

Settling into the Brackenrigg Inn – the modest black and white B & B that was perched by the banks of Ullswater – Bev was able for the first time in a long while to notice the birdsong; breathe in the fresh scent of the unsullied air. The light was beginning to fail but the rain had abated. The lake shimmered as though God had spread out a giant sheet of foil, anchoring it to the earth with trees and stapling it fast with tiny white dots that were sheep, scattered across the hills on the far shore.

'Come on,' she said to Hope. 'It's a bit late to take a boat out. Let's skim stones. I'll show you how.'

They found a perfect spot along the river's shoreline and started to search for the flattest pebbles.

'My dad showed me how to do this,' Bev said, flinging her first pebble almost horizontally across the water's surface with a practiced flick of her wrist. It bounced.

'One, two, three, four . . .' Hope counted. 'Five! You got *five* bounces!' She jumped up and down, clapping her hands together. 'Clever Mum-Mum.'

'Here. You try.' Bev gave Hope the finest stone she had in her collection and encased the girl's hand in her own, showing her the slick movement of the wrist that was required to flick it out onto the water like a Frisbee. 'You're a quick learner,' she said, when Hope had had success, skimming the dead calm of the lake like an old hand after only a few tries.

As twilight started to nudge daylight from centre stage, they were the only people left by the lake's edge but for a man, standing some two hundred metres away, watching bats swoop and dart from the trees through a pair of binoculars. It was so peaceful. Too tranquil to imagine for a second that that man might be pointing his binoculars in their direction.

CHAPTER 42
Bev

Bev yawned. 'Bedtime,' she said, gathering her daughter in her arms and planting a smackeroo on her forehead.

How wonderful it was to tuck her little girl into bed in the chintzy family suite – the only place that had been available, thanks to a last-minute cancellation.

Stroking her brow, Bev drank in the smell of Hope's freshly showered skin and her clean winceyette pyjamas. 'I see Daddy's changed the washing liquid,' she said, wrinkling her nose at the unfamiliar fragrance. Not explaining to her daughter how it hurt that even her own motherly washing detergent preferences had been swept aside by Rob, in a bid to expunge her from Hope's childhood. 'Lovely smell.' But this weekend was not a place where bitterness belonged. This was the beginning of the end of the nightmare and a time for quiet celebration. 'Na-night, my bestest love.'

'I love you, Mummy. You're the best, too. Na-night.'

Exhausted, Bev turned out Hope's light, repairing to her adjacent room where she checked that the door to the courtyard and windows were all locked. However chintzy the décor was, and the loose lampshade on the bedside lamp notwithstanding, it was a relief to climb into a freshly made bed, in a place that didn't smell of mildew. *Tomorrow, if it's dry, we'll go out. If it's raining, I'll teach her how to make an origami sheep,* she thought, remembering the kit she had brought with her, secreted in the zip compartment of her case. She smiled at the thought and drifted off into a shallow sleep; jerking, twitching, then finally relaxing, falling deeper, deeper . . .

With no idea of how much time had passed, Bev awoke in the dead of night, roused by a cracking noise. Still half in the clutches of an intoxicating dream, she opened her eyes, wondering where she was. Then she remembered that she was in the main bedroom of a family suite at the Brackenrigg Inn; Hope in the adjacent room. There was the rectangular outline of the wardrobe. There was the glimmer of the dressing table mirror, dimly reflecting the moonlight outside. But there at the end of the bed was a silhouette she couldn't place at first. Then, suddenly, she realised she was looking at a giant of a man, dressed all in black, wearing a balaclava. She tried to scream but he threw himself on top of her, slamming a hand over her mouth.

'Keep your mouth shut,' he said.

His voice was muffled by the fabric covering his mouth, almost drowned out entirely by the blood rushing in Bev's ears. A vaguely familiar timbre to his voice nevertheless which she couldn't place.

'One word and I'll kill her – your daughter. And then I'll kill you, you interfering piece of shit.'

Bev lay perfectly still for five seconds, allowing the terror to flood in. The crushing weight of him on top of her compressed her lungs as though she were at the bottom of the Crewe Hall pool again with Jerry Fitzwilliam. What did he want? To rape her? To kill her? Whatever his intentions, she had to get her attacker far, far away from Hope.

With all the strength she could harness, Bev brought her knee up fast between his legs, mashing it into his groin. He cried out, rolling off her, onto the floor. Doubled up, now.

Bev leaped off the bed on the far side, sprinting over to the en suite. *Lock yourself in? No. You can't leave Hope defenceless. You've got to neutralise this threat. Think! Think!* She snatched up a can of body spray that she'd unpacked and left above the sink. Leaped back out of the bathroom and over the open suitcase on the floor. But as she kicked at her attacker's head, hoping to knock him out while he was down, he grabbed her ankle with one of those shovel-like hands, trapping it in a vice-like grip.

Bev grunted as he unbalanced her and she hit the deck awkwardly, sustaining a glancing blow to her head on the edge of the bed's divan base. Writhing for all she was worth, she broke free just long enough to expel a cloud of fragrance from the can of body spray directly into his face. Warm vanilla engulfed the room.

'My eyes!' He started to cough violently, pressing his fists to the balaclava's eyeholes.

'Shut your face and get the fuck out of here!' she half-whispered. The fury rose within her like a wall of flames, snuffing out her cold dread. 'If you dare wake my daughter—'

But her half-baked threat was an empty show of bravado. The intruder was on his feet again. He trapped her from behind in a painful arm lock she simply didn't have the strength to free herself from. He bent her over the bed, pushing her down onto her knees.

'Who are you, you bastard? Do I know you? Are you some perv who read that website?'

'No,' he said.

'I don't really like to be raped and beaten, for Christ's sake! I didn't publish any of that.'

'I know.'

He clearly knew of redhotslut.com, though. 'Then, why are you doing this to me?'

'I'm The Wolf. And I'm here to teach you a hard lesson in what happens when you lie and cheat and treat men like dirt.'

She could feel him rummaging behind her, pulling at the waistband of her pyjamas with one hand. The other hand, he shoved beneath her chest, squeezing and kneading her breasts as though they were spongey corporate stress balls.

'I'll scream.' Bev tried to free her left arm. If she could only reach the bedside lamp . . .

'No you won't,' the man said, his mouth so close to her ear that she could feel the heat from his breath through the knitted balaclava. He roughly shoved her legs apart with his knee. 'If you scream, she'll wake. And if she wakes, I'll do to her what I'm going to do to you. I'll make you watch. Then, I'll kill you both. I swear.'

Clenching her eyes shut, Bev suddenly saw the footage of Tatjana Lebedev's last moment playing in her mind's eye. The star of the gut-wrenching snuff video had been a large man wearing a latex wolf mask. Not Jerry Fitzwilliam – the pig. A wolf. And her attacker had just identified himself as 'The Wolf'. This must be Tatjana's murderer.

Realising that when he threatened to kill her and Hope, he meant it, Bev bucked upwards. She rammed herself with all the brute force she could muster against The Wolf's erect penis.

He shrank back, giving her just enough leeway to snatch up the bedside lamp, still plugged in at the wall. She flung her arm backwards, smashing the lamp's marble base into the side of her attacker's head. Scrambling onto the bed, she turned to face him.

He shook his head momentarily, as if stunned, then flung himself at her. But his size made him cumbersome and slow.

Bev managed to switch the lamp on, wrenching the wonky shade off and ramming the blazing filament bulb into the exposed flesh of his muscular neck. The electricity buzzed as the delicate glass shattered. When the current made contact with The Wolf's skin, there was a loud crack. He jolted, as though he'd been punched.

They were plunged into darkness again. The smell of burnt skin and wool made Bev's nostrils sting.

Buoyed by adrenaline, she was just about try to wrap the cord around his neck when there was a knock on the glazed door.

'Everything all right in there?' A woman's voice. A neighbour perhaps.

Bev could see a stout, middle-aged woman in her dressing gown, squinting in the bright white shaft from the security light.

'Help!' she yelled. 'Help me!'

The Wolf leaped to his feet and bounded towards the door, wrenching it open and pushing past the neighbour. By the time Bev had pulled her pyjama bottoms back up and stumbled into the courtyard, there was no sign of him.

'Oh, my word!' the woman said, touching her lips, then laying her hand on her chest so that her wedding and engagement ring glinted in the light. She spoke quickly and with a tremulous voice. 'Are you OK, lovey? You don't expect that, do you? Not round here. I'll get my Des up. He'll call the police.'

'Mummy. What's wrong?' Hope was standing in the doorway to the suite in her onesie, wiping sleep out of her eyes. Her brown hair flowed over her shoulders. She was pale and looked frightened, but she was unhurt and none the wiser. That was the main thing.

'No need to call the police,' Bev said, straining to pick Hope up so that she wrapped her long legs around her middle. 'It was just some chancer breaking in to nick my handbag, I think. I'll barricade the door. I need my little girl to get her sleep. We're fine. Honestly.'

The concerned neighbour seemed reluctant to take no for an answer, but eventually retreated to her own room, still shaking her head.

'What are you doing, Mummy?' Hope asked once they were alone again.

Bev started to empty the drawers, flinging clothes into the suitcase. 'Get dressed, honey. We're going on a late-night adventure.'

'Where? Who was that man?'

Bev took her daughter's face into her hands. 'What did you see?' Hoping that she hadn't witnessed a failed sex attack by a masked intruder.

'Just him running away. I heard noises. They must have woke me up. It sounded like when you used to fight with Daddy.' She bit her lip. There were tears in her eyes. 'When I felt brave enough to open your door, I just saw that guy pushing past the lady next door. Did he hurt you, Mummy?'

Examining her daughter's delicate features, and feeling her evident bafflement as physical pain in her own chest, Bev swept Hope up into a protective embrace. 'No. Not at all, baby. I tripped over, but that was just clumsy me. I'm so sorry you had to see that man,' she said. 'But he was just some nasty burglar. And that's why we're going to move to another hotel.'

'Now? In the middle of the night?'

Hope had a point. Even if there was a B & B with a free twin room nearby on a Bank Holiday weekend – highly unlikely – there would certainly be nobody around at 2.45 a.m. to take her booking.

'In the morning, lovely.'

'Are you going to call the police?'

'Probably not, dolly.'

As she tucked her daughter back in, Bev knew she was taking an enormous risk in not reporting the attack and staying put. But the last thing she needed was a formal record of her one night alone with Hope in a year, ending in a violent break-in and attempted rape by her own personal troll, followed by an emergency bivouac in a freezing cold car. If a judge got wind of that, she'd never get her baby girl back. Most importantly, though, the last thing Bev wanted was her daughter absorbing the anxiety and drama that was part and parcel of her crazy mother's life.

After extinguishing the main light, she picked her way to her own bed, lighting the way with the flashlight on her phone, being careful to avoid the place where the broken pieces of bulb had fallen. She knew she'd never be able to sleep now, but at least she could mull over what had come to pass. Had Jerry Fitzwilliam been behind the attack? The shadow cabinet minister was in a police holding cell or possibly even on remand, awaiting trial by now. Perhaps he'd been in cahoots with this 'wolf', planning their terror campaign as a two-pronged attack. At least the online trolling would have stopped now that Fitzwilliam was out of the picture and her solicitor had issued take-down notices for all the spoof sites.

Bev couldn't resist checking Twitter, just to be sure that the @Beverley_Saunders account had gone.

'Thank God for that.'

No such feed had come up in her search. But just as she was about to switch off and maybe close her eyes, just for a second, she noticed a new account she'd not seen before, already with over one thousand followers. She read the most recent tweet for @BevSaundersLies1.

> I know you'll read this, Beverley. I follow you everywhere.
> I'm coming back for you & this time, I will kill you.
> #TheWolf

CHAPTER 43

Bev

'Why couldn't we stay for breakfast, Mummy? I'm starving,' Hope said.

Speeding down the motorway, pushing the Polo to reach ninety, the road seemed to undulate beneath them. *Keep your eyes open, Bev. Stay alert. Make a mental note of the cars behind you.*

'I'm sorry, sugar puff. I'll take us to a café when we get back to civilisation, I promise.' A red saloon in the fast lane. A white van in the slow lane. A little silver hatchback hogging the middle. At this godforsaken hour of the morning, the roads had not yet started to build up with Saturday shoppers, travelling to their local DIY warehouses or supermarkets.

'But you promised me we'd go boating.'

Bev studied Hope's reflection in her rear-view mirror. The girl's complexion looked as though it had been bleached of all colour, like vibrant silk left in strong sunlight for too long. And that was her fault. *You're a shitty, shitty mother, Beverley Saunders. This is why Rob got custody of her.* She could hear the judge's proclamation resounding in her ears as though she were still in that empty county courtroom: unfit; mental health issues which make you unable to provide a stable environment; anti-social behaviour.

'We will, my love. I promise. Mummy just wanted to get you to a safer place because of the weirdo last night.' She checked her mirror again. The red saloon had overtaken her now. The van had been left far behind. The hatchback was still on her tail, though. Would a murderous troll, calling himself 'The Wolf' drive a small silver hatchback? Was he coming to run them off the road? He'd said on Twitter that he followed her everywhere. How the hell was he doing that? *Don't pass your angst onto Hope*. 'I tell you what, I'll take you to Heaton Park in north Manchester. Yes. We'll go there. They've got a massive lake and rowing boats.'

Finally, her wan daughter smiled, bringing some of the colour back to her cheeks. 'Really? Yay! Can I row the boat?'

Bev nodded, not even knowing if the rowing boats were still a thing any more. Rob had taken her there once when they'd still been students. He'd dropped an oar in the water because he'd been off his tits on super-skunk. Hypocritical idiot. The giant in the black get-up had certainly not been Rob. But Bev wondered momentarily if Rob had somehow been involved in this conspiracy to break her. She resolved to probe him about the attack and gauge his reaction next time she saw him. Was it even possible that Rob had been one of the men in the recording of Tatjana's death? Rob in a cockerel mask? Maybe Mo in the horse? No. Neither men's skin tones or body shapes matched those of any of the men in that film clip. It didn't follow on that because they had a clandestine friendship with Tim, they would have anything to do with the extra-curricular interests of Jerry Fitzwilliam.

She shook her head, clearing the notion from her over-taxed, under-rested mind. 'You bet. Course you can. You'll be a perfect captain! And after that, how about we find a nice hotel by Manchester airport? Finish our weekend there. I'll take you swimming and plane-spotting. You'll love it!

'Ooh, I can show you my front crawl. I've just gone from purple cap to blue cap in my swimming class. I'm the fastest. Are there double-decker jumbos?' Hope held her arms out like a plane, replicating the rumble of take-off at the back of her throat. 'They're dead noisy, aren't they? Will we see one?'

The silver hatchback was drawing ever closer. Gaining, gaining. She tried to push the Polo harder, but with a 1 litre engine, it wouldn't budge and started to shake. Bev felt light-headed suddenly. Her fingertips were hot and clammy. Prickling in her lips. Stabbing pain in her newly healed arm. Freezing cold beneath her heavy winter anorak. *A panic attack. You're kidding me. Not here. Not now.*

'You sure will. Are you strapped in?' She asked Hope, glancing at her in the rear-view mirror.

'Yes.'

'Good. Good.' She had to breathe like that prick, Mo, had taught her. In for four, hold for two, out for six. Repeat.

When the hatchback was close enough for her to make out the driver in the mirror, she felt normality flooding back into her body.

'It's just some old guy in a pork-pie hat,' she said, chuckling.

'What?'

'Nothing. Take no notice of Mummy.' *Thank you, universe. Thank you.*

*

'What do you mean, you had to leave the Lakes?' Rob asked as he put a territorial arm around Hope.

Bev stood on the doorstep to the grand house Rob had bought from the proceeds to their old marital home in London, wondering how the hell she'd let herself get into a situation where he had staged a raid on everything of value in her life, like a greedy magpie. The place smelled different from her old house. It had a strange floral smell to it. 'Don't you think Hope should go to the loo and switch the telly on while us grown-ups talk?'

She tried to cross the threshold but Rob barred her entry, pushing her back to the edge of the step. His touch felt like a punch, and for a second, she was in Angela Fitzgerald's Gucci loafers.

'Go inside, Hope, lovey,' she said, trying to neutralise the acid before it reached the tip of her tongue. Her daughter didn't deserve to get sucked into in her parents' emotional black hole. She looked her ex-husband in the eye. 'Let her go, Daddy.' Spitting out the consonants through gritted teeth.

As soon as Hope had disappeared off to the living room in search of *Horrid Henry* on the TV, Rob rounded on her.

'So, you couldn't even make it through the weekend without messing up?' He wore a supercilious smile on those thin lips that she hadn't thought quite so mean when they'd first got together. Arms folded tightly as though he didn't want to let her near his heart.

'It was a brilliant weekend, if you must know,' Bev said. *Stand up for yourself for God's sake. What kind of an example are you setting for Hope if you let him talk to you like you're dirt? Why are you strong for the likes of Angie but not yourself?* 'We just had a change of plans because someone broke into the hotel where we were staying and I

326

didn't think it was wise to hang around. Me and Hope had a wonderful bonding time. And it's none of your fucking business what I do with my daughter while she's in my care. That's what your solicitor agreed with my solicitor, and the judge OK'd it.'

Out of the corner of her eye, Bev spied his neighbours, twitching their vertical blinds to get a good look at the familiar spectacle of her arguing with Rob. She was sorely tempted to turn around and flip them the bird. That would get the whole of Didsbury's senior population talking for a week. But Hope was smiling and waving at her through the living room window of the large Edwardian terrace, hanging onto the vintage-style curtains Bev had picked for their London home. Kneeling on the flea-market find swivel chair she'd bought in a British Heart Foundation shop in Croydon. *Her* daughter with *her* stuff in what should have been *her* house, following their relocation up north after the divorce.

'You've paid someone to intimidate me, haven't you?' She hadn't meant to say it out loud, but the burden of curiosity had been too great. 'Because if it's not Jerry Fitzgerald who's been trolling me on social media and having me followed, you're the only one left with good motive.'

Rob retreated into the hallway. 'This *again*? You're tapped. The social worker's going to have a field day when she hears this. And my solicitor's going to be interested in that kind of slander and harassment too. Nice one, Bev. Maybe I should be calling into question if you disclosed all your assets honestly. You seem to have a lot of money sloshing around for trips to the Lakes.'

'Go fuck yourself, Colin.'

'You shouldn't be swearing around Hope. And don't call me that. I hate it.'

She smiled sweetly, keeping the anxiety and sorrow out of her voice. Maintaining a deadly, cheery air. 'Yeah. I know. See you next week. And the week after that. And the week after that, until Hope comes home with her Mummy permanently. Because I'm not scared of you.' She reached beyond the door and poked him in the chest. Nothing but venom in her delivery, now. 'You're like a verruca. I never wanted you but I ended up stuck with you. You're an unsightly, shitty parasite. But even the most stubborn verrucas shift in the end.'

With Hope safely delivered, Bev hastened to Doc's place.

'We've got to find out who's posting this crap,' she said, scrolling on her phone through the pornographic smut that had sprung from the new Twitter feed. 'I think if we can work out who's posting this, we'll know who attacked me. We'll find Tatjana's murderer.'

Pulling another Jaffa cake from the half-empty box that sat among the flotsam and jetsam on his crumb-strewn desk, Doc rammed the biscuit into his mouth whole and opened a tab on his new computer. His long, slender fingers were a blur of movement, putting Bev in mind of a concert pianist who had lost his way.

'I can't believe this,' Doc said, mouth full of half-masticated biscuit. 'I thought when Fitzgerald got arrested that we were safe. That was the whole bloody reason I moved back in and forked out for new gear. All that time spent at my folks, bored stiff in the land that time forgot . . .' He turned to Bev with accusation in his bleary eyes. 'I got burgled while I was away, you know.'

Perched on a scuffed up PVC footstool at his side, Bev laced her hands together in her lap. Looked at her knees, feeling her cheeks blaze with mortification. 'What did they nick?'

'That's the weird thing,' Doc said. 'They didn't. But the place was a mess and there was the obligatory burglar's turd on the lounge carpet.'

Bev turned to look at the stained beige carpet and realised for the first time that a small square had been cut out. She wrinkled her nose. 'Sorry to burst your bubble, Doc, mate, but the place was a mess to begin with. How the hell did you know the difference?'

Doc glared at her. 'I didn't shit on my carpet before I left. And I certainly *didn't* smash all my Lego to smithereens. And I *don't* make a habit of breaking in through my back door. I thought it was kids.' There was hard frost in his delivery. 'But now I come to think of it . . .' He suddenly turned a sickly shade of putty. 'Maybe it was this guy. The Wolf.'

The silence and dawning dread that passed between them made the air thick.

'Did he look like the kind that would do a shit on someone's carpet?' Doc finally asked.

Shrugging, Bev looked at Doc and saw he was little more than an oversized vulnerable kid. Close to her in age, no doubt, but a small-town boy nonetheless, whose only street smarts involved selling the odd bag of home-grown, computer hacking and picking litter from motorway sidings. Her own life had always been chaos and loss and continued to be a struggle of epic proportions. But she had put a man-boy, who cared only for junk food, heavy metal and Lego, in this situation. 'He said he was going to rape and kill me and Hope, so I'm guessing that puts him in the, "likely to take a dump on the Wilton" category. Yeah.' She remembered the most recent tweet, intended for her. 'I don't like this, "I follow you everywhere" bullshit that he tweeted, either. What do you think of that for arrogance? He knew exactly where to find me and Hope, right in the middle of nowhere.'

'Phone.' Doc held his hand out. 'Give it here.'

'No! You don't think, do you . . .?' Bev unlocked her screen and handed her mobile phone to her friend. Tugging at her braid.

Frowning, Doc thumbed his way through several screens. Found an app on his computer and downloaded it via a USB cable to Bev's phone. 'This can identify well-hidden spyware on your phone, yeah? If he's tracking you, I reckon you've been hacked. And if it's an app on your phone, there's a good chance he's had access to it. I mean, physical access to your device. You left your phone unattended?'

Bev blushed, recalling the countless times she'd jealously guarded her drinks in nightclubs to lower the risk of being spiked, but had been laissez-faire in the extreme about leaving her phone lying around in cafés, bars, sex-clubs . . .

Moments later, Doc held her phone up. An app icon she'd never seen before shone on the screen. 'Yep. As I thought. Some Trojan shit.'

'Jesus! Get rid of it. Get it off!' The words almost caught in Bev's throat.

'Yes, ma'am.' Doc's raised eyebrow finally softened into a half-smile. 'There. It's gone. I've uninstalled it and done a scan. No more spyware. Now, let's shut this moron down.'

Bev scrolled through the photos she'd taken of Hope over the lost weekend, and the myriad selfies of them grinning into the lens of her phone like buffoons – in the car; at the service station; by Ullswater. Then, on the boating lake in the sprawling municipal mess of funfair, woods and topless thugs that was Heaton Park on a Bank Holiday, where they had narrowly missed colliding with a flock of Canadian geese. As she did this, Doc brought up tab after tab of coding she couldn't possibly begin to understand.

'What are you doing?' she asked.

'Infiltrating Twitter's database,' he said, opening a bag of Monster Munch, which he started to devour noisily. 'I'm trying to see what email address this spoof account is registered to. If I can then hack the email provider, I should be able to get to the truth.'

Eight hours later, the sun had gone down and Bev had made three origami shapes – a duck, a frog and a carp – with some paper she'd pilfered from Doc's printer. Now she stood in his basically equipped kitchenette, trying to avoid looking at the mess of cornflakes strewn across the worktop, while she stirred boiled water into two plastic Pot Noodle containers.

She was just pondering the nutritional value of her chicken and mushroom flavoured reconstituted meal when Doc appeared in the doorway, even more wan-faced than usual, wearing an unconvincing half-smile.

'You look like someone puked on your best keyboard, James Shufflebotham,' she said. 'You want soy sauce in your chow mein?'

'Never mind that,' he said. 'It was an absolute nightmare tracing the owner of that email address. I hope you appreciate my talents, Beverley Saunders.'

'Get on with it. What have you found out?'

'I know who's behind your trolling, and it's not Jerry Fitzgerald or any identifiable spook, doing it for a backhander.'

'Yes! Yes! Spit it out!'

Bev could sense the hormones rushing around her body. Adrenaline and cortisol, mainly, but with just a small dollop of dopamine at the thought that they'd perhaps finally got to the bottom of a sinister mystery. Lord knew, she'd slept with enough crazy men to shorten the odds of attracting the wrong sort of attention from a dangerous psychopath. Would it be anyone she knew?

She wasn't prepared for Doc's answer.

CHAPTER 44
Bev

'Good luck!' Doc had said as she'd left his place with a stomach full of butterflies.

The Mancunian sun had just reluctantly started to rise, like a teenager trying to drag herself out of bed. The down-at-heel street where Doc lived was empty but for the odd stolen car and some weeds, swaying in the stiff breeze.

Bev had instinctively grabbed him into a bear hug, wondering at the pang of grief that permeated her tired body. It had felt like a goodbye. 'I'll call if it gets sticky.' Slapping him on the back had seemed the easiest way to end that uneasy intimacy, especially when he'd seemed reluctant to let go. Slapping was matey. Non-committal. But part of her had acknowledged that Doc meant something to her – entirely different to a throwaway lover; much more than just a friend.

'You should call the pigs first if it gets sticky. I wish you'd let me come with you.' The furrows in his brow had spelled out just how concerned for her safety he'd been.

She gave a brief, mirthless laugh. 'Oh, yeah. You'd really be a tonne of use against a man-mountain with murder on his mind. No.' She'd patted her cardigan pocket. 'You've rigged me up. I know you'll have my back remotely, and that makes me feel a damn sight better about what I'm doing. If I'm gonna stop this lunatic, the main thing is that I get concrete evidence. I want him on record, admitting to what he's done. If I've got you in tow, he'll clam up or kill us both.' She'd taken a step down the path towards her car. Then another. Reluctant to leave the relative safety of Doc's marijuana and Pot Noodle-scented dump. 'Let's just see how this plays.'

Now, she stood on the driveway of the house with a heartbeat so thunderous, she was sure she'd wake the entire family and trigger the street's burglar alarms. But apart from the odd builder, passing on his way to some big job in Bowdon, Hale was still sound asleep.

Steeling herself to traverse the gravel driveway as silently as possible, she opened the side gate and crept along the utility area where the bins were stored. Time to turn the tables. Opening the lid to the blue bin for paper recycling, Bev leaned right inside to rummage through the discarded junk mail, not really knowing what she was looking for. There was nothing but leaflets for overpriced plantation shutters, advertorial brochures for some frozen organic food, letters from the children's private prep school . . . Nothing whatsoever that might help Bev.

When she got to the back garden, however, she immediately spied something out of place in the normally pristine manicured scene. A steel drum had been set next to the summer house – the sort that the homeless burned firewood inside in a bid to keep warm. Where had it come from? She crept forward, looking behind her to see that there was nobody peeking from the windows above. All the curtains were drawn. The only company Bev had were the birds and the heady almond scent of a giant mock orange bush that was in full bloom.

Feeling the blood leech away from her face, Bev peered inside the drum. Was she too late? Were there ashes in the bottom that would provide the proof she sought? Maybe it was inside the house. Maybe she was wasting her time entirely.

'Let's try your little man cave,' Bev muttered under her breath.

At a glance, she could see that the summer house was padlocked. Except on closer examination, the combination lock that hung from the door of the cedar-clad outbuilding was open. Stealing another glance around the garden, she let herself into her attacker's home office. How was it that he had left the place unlocked? Had he been at the pinot grigio before downing tools for the day? Had he been distracted and in a hurry? On the desk, however, there was nothing of interest save for a family photo. The drawers were locked shut.

'I bet you've got the laptop inside, haven't you?'

Bev drummed her fingers on the desktop, wondering what to do next; drinking in the expensive smell of his leather desk chair and the rich musky aroma of the cedar. As she mulled over her options, she peered at the walls on which hung several old team photos from the Durham University Rugby Team.

There was Tim in the front row, wearing his kit – the beefcake Bev remembered bedding her in her first year, on a night when she'd been so very desperate to get away from a tripping Rob. Back in the days when she'd been Boo and he'd been Mitch, and Tim had just been a poorly chosen exit-strategy that had turned into date rape. Bev knew it for what it was, now. The dirty little secret that neither of them had acknowledged or ever talked about. Not a week later. Not a month later when he'd started to see Sophie. Not years later, when he had married his Holy Jo.

Remembering that there was a black CCTV orb on the front of the summer house, in addition to the one on the back of the main house, which would certainly be watching her movements like the all-seeing eye of Tolkien's Sauron, Bev slipped out, replacing the padlock.

She was just about to give up the ghost and repair to her basement flat, when she caught sight of the compost bin. The lid was slightly askew as though it had been recently disturbed. Except that the gardener came on a Friday and today was Tuesday. Feeling like the pungent smell of the mock orange was sharpening her senses, Bev approached the bin. Held her breath. Had a sudden inkling of what she might find there. Yes, it was a good hiding place.

She lifted the lid; looked inside. There, beneath a thin layer of grass clippings was a pair of black jogging bottoms, a black long-sleeved T-shirt and a black balaclava. She picked up the balaclava and held it close to the tiny camera concealed in her cardigan.

'This is it, Doc,' she whispered. 'Bingo.'

She lifted the garment to her nose and inhaled. It reeked of her vanilla deodorant.

Letting herself into her flat through the patio doors, she slowly examined the layout of her furniture, her things, even her bedding. She'd left the duvet messily arranged. It was now much neater. She'd been careful to leave her typing chair abandoned at an angle in front of the desk drawers. It had been rolled neatly into the aperture where her legs went. She'd righted all of her origami on the shelves and had laid her latest folded work-in-progress facing northwards. Those too had been disturbed. Yet again, it was clear that someone had been in the place, not least judging by the lingering smell of aftershave – Creed, if memory served. It had a distinctive lemony smell to it, and Bev recalled Sophie boasting that she'd bought Tim a £200 bottle for Christmas so that he'd smell like a proper Hale man. The Wolf clearly liked to smell right, even when he was rifling through his tenant's home. Or perhaps he'd deliberately left signs of his intrusion this time to freak her out. She calculated that if he'd dumped his clothing from the Lakes in the compost bin, and the place still honked of his overpriced party-perfume, Tim must have broken in after the attack.

'All this time, I'm wondering how the hell Jerry Fitzwilliam or one of his cronies had got into my space,' she said, shaking her head whilst filling the kettle in her dingy kitchenette. She switched it on. Opened her cup cabinet to find it empty. Retrieved a dirty mug from the sink and rinsed it out absent-mindedly. 'You had a key, didn't you? Of course you did! You're my landlord! How frigging convenient. I bet you planned this from the moment you heard I was getting divorced and heading north.' She mimicked him, adopting a high-pitched mewling voice. '"Why don't you move into the basement flat? You can keep Soph company while I'm working in London. You girls will have such fun." Yeah, so you could have your fun at my expense, you psycho dick.' She shuddered. Wiped the cold sweat from her top lip.

Sitting stiffly on the edge of her sofa, cradling her coffee as though it might turn out to be her final drink, Bev contemplated her next move. Call the police or confront him? As if she'd been thinking aloud, her phone buzzed. There was a message from Doc.

*

U getting on wiv it then?

She texted back.

It's still early. Not so easy either. Thinking of calling cops but don't want a big scene with Sophie & kids in house. Use proper grammar!

Moments later, as she'd gone back into the kitchen to make some toast, deciding that she'd do better to confront a man who murdered and stalked on a full stomach. She slipped two slices of bread into the toaster – a hand-me-down from Sophie. Knew enough by now to be swift in depressing the lever, stepping back as the little white sparks made it fizz and crackle white like a sparkler. Some bloody housewarming present! Charity like that, she could do without.

Her phone buzzed again.

Got bad feeling. U can't handle this on own. Either call pigs or I come over.

'I can't handle this on my own?' she said aloud, knowing Doc would pick up her voice on the tiny microphone that was incorporated into the spy-standard camera. 'Cheeky sod! You think I'd let a rapist and a murderer threaten me and my child in our beds and not have the guts to face him down on my own? Then, you don't know the ferocity of a mother when she's cornered, mate.'

Her friend's lack of faith had switched on her inner heroine. Abandoning the toast, she made her way up the narrow, damp stone staircase to Sophie and Tim's house above, being careful to leave her door on the latch in case she needed to beat a hasty retreat. Not really knowing how she would corner Tim in a way that

338

wouldn't endanger her, or what she would say to him when she did, she padded through the pristine interior. Drank in the smell of furniture polish and the top note of Sophie's favourite Jo Malone room spray that gave the place a wealthy aroma.

In the living room, she noticed that one solitary coffee cup still sat out on the coffee table. No lipstick around the rim. There was no evidence of Sophie or the children in there, though Sophie often cleared up once they were in bed. In the kitchen, there was one spent wine glass on the island with red wine dregs at the bottom. A half empty bottle of Shiraz next to the Nutribullet. A copy of *Men's Health* on the centre island, open at a page where the reader was told how to cultivate the perfect six-pack.

Bev's skin puckered into goosebumps. She glanced at the oversized clock on the wall. It was approaching 6.30 a.m. Cocking her head to one side, she wondered that she couldn't hear the children thundering around at this hour, since they always woke early. Sophie continually complained that Tim wouldn't allow them into their bed, and that they had to be placated in the playroom by *CBeebies* and beakers of milky tea.

Moving like a wraith around the house, she entered the dining room and saw the family photos, standing to attention on the stylish Danish rosewood sideboard. She hesitated. This was trespass. Even though her profession now demanded snooping into people's business, and Tim had given no such thought to invading her own privacy, nosing around her friend's house like this added to her unsettled feeling, making her skin crawl and her stomach flip. It was so uncharacteristically silent that Bev wondered if the curtains hadn't just been closed to give the impression they were home, when in fact they'd gone away.

None of this felt right. Had Tim bumped off his own family and then absconded? Bev felt sickened by the thought. Imagined a scenario where Sophie had uncovered his terrible secret and had confronted the man she'd thought was her loyal husband, but who turned out to be a philandering, sadistic Wolf. *Don't talk rubbish,* she castigated herself. *Maybe they're just having a lie-in for once.*

Heading back into the kitchen, Bev sought out the pinboard – the only place in the room where Sophie allowed mess. Among the church family fun day and Sunday school notices, as well as the long receipt for an overpriced shop from Booths, she spied the National Trust calendar. Read what was written on the preceding and today's date.

Sophie & kids to Mum.

The floorboards creaked directly above her. Tim. She was alone in the house with him. The creaking moved rhythmically away from her but then became audible through the open kitchen door as he started to descend the stairs. Squeak, squeak. The wood complained beneath the considerable weight of a rugby player gone partly to fat.

Bev held her breath, tiptoeing at speed to the utility room in the far corner of the kitchen. In there, there was no place to hide apart from behind the door or else the tall cupboard, where Sophie's cleaner stored the ironing board, mop and bucket.

Squeak, squeak.

Tim was near the bottom, now. Bev tried to squeeze next to the ironing board, one foot in the mop bucket, but found the cupboard simply wouldn't accommodate her. She opted to stow away behind the door to the utility room instead.

Pad, pad, pad. Tim was in the kitchen, now, bare feet slapping on the porcelain tiles. There was that smell of his aftershave again, lingering around him like a cloud of persistent gnats in summer. From her hiding place, Bev could hear him fill the kettle and put it on. He took something out of the dishwasher, judging by the rattle of crockery as he pulled the basket out. The clink of metal on glass. He was making coffee. If only he would go. Better still, if only she was brave enough to step out and take him to task over his terrifying misdeeds.

She could hear Rob speaking in her imagination: 'You're a wimp, Bev Saunders. You catfished an MP but you can't hold your own landlord to account for murder? Pathetic. No wonder you don't have custody of our daughter. You don't warrant that privilege.'

But she wasn't ready yet. And her breath came short. Bev doubted she'd be able to speak at all.

When Tim's footfalls grew closer, she closed her eyes, praying he wouldn't sense an intruder. *He's clearly going to the fridge for milk*, she counselled herself. *Calm down. I hope Doc doesn't call or text.*

Suddenly the door bounced off her chest as Tim bumbled into the utility room, flinging open the door to the very ironing board cupboard that she had tried to stand in. He couldn't have been more than thirty centimetres away. If her stomach growled, it was game over.

Go back in the kitchen, for Christ's sake!

His aftershave tickled her nostrils as he pulled out the ironing board and the iron, setting them up in the utility room. A basket of freshly laundered shirts stood at her feet. She bit her lip, waiting to be discovered. Tim's arm was visible suddenly as he pulled a pale blue shirt from the basket. His head bobbed into view only a hand's breadth away. If he looked sideways, he'd spot her. The iron clicked off, fully heated. Bev reasoned that death by scalding iron was not the way she'd hoped to go.

But his mind was clearly elsewhere and he didn't notice her at all, standing in the shadows, holding her breath and digging her nails into the palms of her hands.

Time passed improbably slowly but once his shirt had been ironed, he padded back into the kitchen, humming tunelessly to himself. As he creaked back up the stairs, Bev emerged from the utility room. Listened carefully as the sound of falling water came from above. He was running a bath. She would wait until he'd got in, and then what? Should she take the Scandi-style candelabra from the dining room and threaten to club him to death with it if he didn't explain himself? No. He was too big and strong. He could easily wrench it out of her hand and turn it on her. How about a knife? No. Same problem. She would only be endangering herself. Then, the perfect plan occurred to her.

Descending the stone stairs to her basement flat, she hurried inside and retrieved the second hand malfunctioning toaster. Leaving a trail of crumbs in her wake from the rarely emptied crumb tray, like Little Red Riding Hood with Hansel and Gretel pretensions, she climbed Sophie's grand mahogany staircase to The Big Bad Wolf, ready to play her role in one fairy tale that would forever give her nightmares, assuming she survived.

Careful to tread only on the sides of the stairs where the hundred-and-fifty-year-old wood was at its strongest, she crept towards the master bedroom. Suddenly realised that the taps had stopped flowing now. She froze outside the door. Was he still in the bedroom, laying his clothes out for the day, perhaps? Had he heard her approaching?

Was he lying in ambush in the wardrobe, ready to spring out and finish what he'd begun in the Lakes?

A mental image of Hope flashed before her and Bev realised the lunacy of what she was risking. Her daughter needed her alive. Why was this so important for her to solve alone? *Stop doubting yourself, you silly cow. This is personal. This is your chance to stand up for yourself and to get justice for a murdered girl. This is you, taking on Holy Jo's monster of a husband – the man who date-raped you as a first-year student.*

The outrage propelled Bev into the bedroom. No sign of Tim, but there was a reassuring sound of splashing just behind the door. Good. He was vulnerable, and now he was all hers to deal with how she saw fit.

She plugged the toaster into the socket just outside the en suite. Flipped the switch. Pushed the door open, holding the live appliance above her head.

Tim was submerged in a full bath. Eyes closed; bubbles drifting upwards from his mouth, his penis floating and bobbing above the bulk of his body like a parachute on the back of a braking racing car. His eyes opened, dazzling blue beneath the water. His brow furrowing as he made sense of the bizarre scene unfolding above the water's surface.

'Who's the Big Bad Wolf now?' she shouted, loud enough for him to hear.

He sat up swiftly, water draining from his muscled shoulders in a gleaming torrent, sending a tidal wave of bath water scudding around the tub. He gripped the sides of the bath, his knuckles white with the effort and the cords of sinew in his giant ham-like forearms standing proud. 'You.' He laughed, his lip curled upwards in derision. 'You think I'm frightened of you?'

Though the sheer size of his body and the testosterone that leeched from his pores seemed to suck all the oxygen out of the room, as it had done all those years ago in his college room, Bev steeled herself to take a step closer. She dangled the toaster precariously over the bath. 'Think you're fucking clever, don't you? Hounding me so I'd leave your, "Brother-from-another-mother" alone. Was that it? Or did you have some other cockamamie motive in mind? Well, see your shitty old toaster that Sophie palmed off on me? It's temperamental as fuck. Sparks all the time. And guess what, Timbo? It's plugged in!'

'You're bluffing,' he said.

'Am I? I want some answers, you animal. Start talking or I'll fry you alive.'

CHAPTER 45

The Wolf

At last, his prey has walked right into his den, and now, he imagines he can already taste her flesh on his tongue. She is holding the old toaster aloft, as if that will have him quaking. Does she not realise that she is nothing more than a vulnerable rabbit within striking distance of The Wolf's salivating jaws?

'I'm glad it's come to this,' he says, watching with delight as she squirms. 'If you don't already know why I hate you and want to ruin you, I guess it's about time you found out.' He can see that her arms are starting to shake with holding the appliance in the air. 'But first, put the toaster down, Bev. You're too flabby and unfit to hold that up much longer. You'll do yourself an injury.'

'Shut your face, you knuckle-grazing tit,' she says, edging further over the bath. There is hatred in her eyes. 'I know what you did to Tatjana Lebedev. You butcher!'

He leans back in the bath, the hot water splashing around him. Wonders if she would electrocute herself to death if he threw water into one of the toaster's slots. But maybe the current would travel back down to him, like throwing a flaming torch on a trail of fuel. Putting his arms above his head, he takes satisfaction in his burgeoning erection, knowing she is checking him out.

His father would be proud of him now. He is no longer the weakling boy who took those thrashings from his Alpha; who allowed himself to be ridiculed by his peers at school; who endured sexual molestation and the theft of his innocence at the hands of his mother's friend. He is now the Alpha; the pack leader. He is the sexual predator.

'Are you remembering our night together at college, Bev?'

'What? The one where I said, "No!" and you fucked me anyway? Are you remembering that, Timbo? Is that the only way you can get it up? When you're screwing helpless young women who don't want you.'

He takes hold of his penis and starts to massage it, watching the disgust curdle her expression. 'Want to climb on? Sophie's not here.'

'You're deranged. I wouldn't sleep with you if you were the last man on earth. You make me sick.'

Her words have an unexpected effect on him, then. Instead of arousing him, he finds he is reminded of the time at the sex party in London where he had spotted her by chance, tongue-deep inside a fat woman's vagina, being taken from behind by a skinny weed of a man who'd had greying chest hair. They'd all been wearing masks – the party organiser's rule of engagement in order to preserve anonymity – though he hadn't been The Wolf that night. He had identified the large mole on her bottom immediately, however, and had recognised her distinctive northern accent among the received English or local twang of the Londoners. But she hadn't known him. He recalls it now. The rejection still stings, even as he lies now in the bath, years later.

'No thanks, mate. You're not my type.'

In a room full of sexual opportunity and permissive decadence, where everyone had been fair game, she'd eschewed

346

a perfect specimen like him publicly, preferring instead to couple with the physical dregs of the barrel. The memory floods him with a toxic melange of anger, embarrassment, sorrow. He lets go of his penis.

'What gives you the right to judge a man like me? What gives you the right to keep secrets from me?' And now he comes to the crux of it, he can feel resentment and rage trumping the embarrassment and sorrow.

'Secrets?' she asks, frowning. 'What the hell are you on about?'

At that moment, he understands that she doesn't realise he knows. 'You're a lying bitch. All these years, you've pretended.'

'I don't know what you're talking about. You're deranged and you're a killer. Admit it.' Despite her show of bravado, she's swallowing hard. He can see it. There's panic in her eyes. He can smell it along with her stale armpits and the grease in her hair and her unwashed cunt. Nothing like his precious Sophie. Sophie who is so perfect and untouchable, that he'd happily keep her in a cabinet under lock and key. Bev reeks like the whores that Stan brings for Jerry when they have a boy's get-together in London. She smells of sex and desperation like Tatjana Lebedev.

'Does Rob know? Does Rob know I'm Hope's real father and that he's been bringing up another man's child all these years?' His erection may have waned but his bloodlust has been piqued as he dredges up the real source of his pain. 'How could you keep that from everyone, Bev?'

She sticks out her chin like a defiant teen, the toaster really wobbling above her now. She's flagging – a threat ripe for neutralisation.

'What I do with my body and my baby and my life is nothing to do with you, Timbo. Hope was the product of date rape by a meathead who had no interest in me beyond something to shag after a night down the student bar. Do you want me to tell her that? Do you want me to tell Sophie that?'

'You wouldn't.' He rises from the bath like the Greek god, Poseidon, water pouring from him, spilling onto the floor.

She instinctively takes several steps away from him. The toaster is now suspended above the dry floor. 'Why are you like this, Tim? Why did you kill that teenage prostitute and cut up her body and dump it in a butcher's bin? I've read the newspaper articles. I've seen the snuff film. Why? And why in God's name do you think you can get away with it?'

'You stole my child.'

'And aren't I glad I did?' She's smiling wryly. She's off her guard. 'You make Rob seem like a prince. The only reason Sophie's still with you is that she doesn't have the first clue what kind of man you are. You're a frigging monster.'

Gambling that she'll drop the toaster where she stands, he jabs at her gut with a right hook that is hard enough to fell a grown man. Sure enough, the toaster drops to the side. White sparks fly from the lever.

Clambering out of the bath, his hands are around her neck before she can catch her breath. He's pinning her down beneath him, his erection returning as they slip and slide together on the damp floor. His shame and those hurtful memories have all been washed away. He is The Wolf, and the kill is within reach.

She thrashes beneath him, her eyes popping. This is the perfect death for the perfect bitch. He has no interest in raising the daughter he has fathered – and he is absolutely certain the girl *is* his. He's known from the start that the dates matched; that he was a likely candidate when the college bike fell pregnant. Years later, the girl had visited her bitch of a mother in the basement, accompanied by a social worker. He had taken one look at the child's build and her bone structure and had realised she had to be his, though he'd itched to prove it. It had been child's play to break in and steal her drinking glass, once she'd gone. The internet is awash with companies offering DNA analysis from a saliva sample. The results that came back from the test were irrefutable. Now, he only wants revenge on the mother who rejected him and lied. When she is dead, he will fuck her hard in celebration. Then, he will take her spoiled body out to the shed and set to it with the chainsaw. He must remain undiscovered as the murderer of the Russian whore. Bev is the most dangerous loose end and she's easily tied up. The tree surgeon is coming on Monday. Nobody will notice if he throws pieces of her meat into the wood chipper.

'Doc! Help!'

These are the only words she says before she stops moving.

CHAPTER 46

Bev

Just play dead. It's the only way to stop him, Bev managed to think through the oxygen-deprived fug of horror and disbelief.

How had she been so stupid as to believe that she could confront a psychopath, without backup, getting him to confess to all manner of violent crimes? And why had she thought he would never realise Hope was his? Hope was built just like Tim – far too tall to be Rob's daughter, though Rob had been too arrogant to consider another man may have fathered his child. He'd always just congratulated himself for having passed on some dormant long-limbed gene from his great-grandfather. Hope had Bev's eyes, mouth and colouring, which had kept suspicions at bay, but her daughter's nose and the shape of her face had been all Tim's. If anyone had known of Bev's ill-fated liaison with Tim and had thought to ask the right question, it wouldn't have taken a DNA test or a genius to put two and two together to make four. Idiot.

Bev was dimly aware of the gravel crunching outside. A car's engine rumbling. A key in the front door and the sound of three sets of feet – one big, two small – clattering on the wood floor of the hall.

Lying as still as she possibly could, sprawled across the threshold between the bedroom and the en suite, she held her breath and stared into the distance. Knew Tim had not yet registered the fact that his family had walked back in the door. He was too engrossed in yanking her trousers and knickers down, and shouting triumphantly, the prick.

Where was the toaster in relation to where she lay with her arms, splayed above her head? The appliance was still plugged in just within reach, on the bedroom side of the study wall. If nothing else, she could surprise him and cosh him over that boulder of a head with it.

Finally, just as he was about to force himself inside what he believed was her corpse, it seemed to dawn on him that Sophie and the kids were home. He scrambled to his feet, slipping on the wet tiled floor.

Bev seized her chance. Snatching the toaster, she caught him on the temple hard enough that he was momentarily dazed. Horrified disbelief in his eyes.

'You're dead!'

'Nope. Think again, dickhead.' She hit him again.

With wet hands, he clawed at the toaster until he got a purchase on it. They were caught in a tug of war, each trying to gain dominion over the appliance. Wearing trainers with a good grip, Bev knew that she now had a physical advantage over him, despite her trousers and knickers still hanging round her ankles. And she sensed panic in her opponent.

'Timmy, darling! We're home! I'm coming up.'

She tried to hook her leg inside his to destabilise him. But just as Tim prised the appliance from her hands, he lost his footing, slid and fell over the side of the bath with an almighty splash, taking the toaster with him. There was a loud bang. Bev fell backwards, landing by the toilet.

'Timmy! Are you OK!' Sophie at the top of the stairs, now.

Hastily yanking her trousers back up, Bev peered over the side of the bath, aghast. Tim's body twitched and shook as the electricity cracked and fizzed around him. Rushing to the socket, wiping her hands on her top, she yanked the plug out.

'What's going on?' Sophie asked, perplexed, advancing into the room.

'I'm afraid there's been an accident.' Bev's voice was hoarse. Her throat ached from the attempt made on her own life. She approached Sophie, holding her hand out.

'An accident? What kind of accident?' Sophie pushed her away, running into the en suite. She dropped to her knees by the side of the bath. Her high-pitched scream rent the air when she saw her husband, face down in the water, still clutching a toaster with blackened, blistered hands. 'Oh my good God.'

'It's not how it looks,' Bev said, wishing at that moment that she were anywhere but in a bathroom with the naked dead body of her best friend's spouse. 'I can explain.'

CHAPTER 47

Bev

'You have the right to remain silent. You do not have to say anything but . . .'

Bev stopped hearing the female detective who was cautioning her. The words of warning became a confused jumble of legalese as she stared at the heavy metal cuffs on her hands. Of all the dreadful things that had happened to her of late, this was perhaps the worst.

'It was an accident, you know,' she said, searching for a glimmer of sympathy in the cop's flinty face. Then she recognised that it was Owen. 'He throttled me. We started scuffling. Next minute, he's in the bath.'

In the en suite, a team of forensic pathologists wearing white jumpsuits were busy about the crime scene, photographing the alarming tableau of the large man in a small bath, still clinging to a toaster. She'd been arrested for murder by a detective who was irritated by her at best. Bev knew she was never getting Hope back. Even if she could somehow clear her name, this was all Rob needed to put a permanent kibosh on any claim she might have had to custody.

'He's a killer. Was, I mean. Tim. I can prove it.' Squeezing her eyes shut, she tried to push away the memory of Sophie, screaming at her that she was evil; keening over her husband's lifeless body, magnified beneath the electrified water. 'If you look in my cardigan pocket, you can see I'm wired.'

'You never learn your lesson do you, Beverley?' Owen said, a glimmer of satisfaction lightening an otherwise disapproving scowl. 'You're just an amateur, love. Not the police. You should never have tried to tackle him alone.'

'I'm not an amateur! I was trying to get him to confess.'

'With a live electric toaster? In a bathroom?' the policewoman asked. 'OK, let's take this down to the station, shall we?'

'I need to call my solicitor,' Bev said, trying to expel the strange tightness in her stomach and gullet.

Her attention shifted back to the forensic team, grunting with the effort of lifting Tim's body from the bath. The water was pouring everywhere as they manoeuvred his dead weight into a black body bag. Bile rose in her throat at the sight of his face, already showing a strange blue tinge around the lips and along his jawline. Almost overcome with pity and guilt, it was as though the contents of her stomach were rising on a bubble of her anxiety.

'Oh. Oh, I'm sorry.' She vomited on the cop's shiny court shoes.

As she was escorted down the stairs, the sound of Sophie's wailing, and the children's apoplectic screaming in the living room, left her feeling crumpled and defeated.

'Get out of my house,' Sophie yelled as Bev trudged past the doorway. She flung a *Homes & Garden* magazine with such force and accuracy that it hit Bev squarely in the chest. 'I'm going to throw your stuff out and change the locks, you heinous bitch. I hate you.' She was shrieking now, hammering her fists on her knees. The bawling children, red-faced and woeful beyond redemption, froze and fell silent, staring at their Mummy with startled eyes as though she had transformed into a crazed beast that might eat them whole.

'I'm so sorry,' Bev whispered. 'If it's any consolation, Tim—'

'Out!' Sophie was on her feet now, prowling with intent to where Bev stood in the hall.

Bev couldn't remember ever seeing her friend looking so human. Her hair was dishevelled. Her eyeliner had melted into panda-like rings on her lower eyelids. Her normally flawless complexion had taken on a satanic florid fury, and the vein in her forehead, normally so delicate beneath her translucent skin, lending her an apparent vulnerability, throbbed blue like a warning signal.

'You killed him. You witch. You fucking . . . fucking . . . bastard.'

She hadn't heard Sophie swear that prolifically since Rob had visited them in his Mitch days, during one of those times when he and Bev had only been in contact to arrange visits to his parents in order to see Hope. Rob had showed up at 3 a.m., drunk as a lord, hurling stones at Sophie's bedroom window at the front of the little terraced student house they'd shared. As an encore, he'd pissed on her plaque in the little front garden that had declared, 'You're nowhere closer to God than in the garden.' Sophie had been incensed, then. Now, Bev had finally crossed a boundary she'd never be able to retreat behind again.

'You'll see, Soph,' Bev said as one of the uniforms restrained her friend, ushering her back to her armchair and her coffee table full of tear-sodden tissues. 'This wasn't my fault, and Tim was telling you terrible lies. I'm sorry for your loss. I really am. But he wasn't who you thought he was. And I'll be here for you when you need me.'

'Need you? You've ruined my life!' Sophie had started to weep. Her face contorted and puckered up. Her words came out in grief-distorted bursts of rage. 'I'll never need you. I'll see you rot in prison for the rest of your cursed days.'

As Bev was carefully installed in the back of the squad car, she saw the body bag that contained Tim being carried on a stretcher by the forensics people into the garden; ushered with some difficulty into a van, whereupon presumably he'd be transported to the morgue for autopsy.

It seemed ironic that The Wolf should be eviscerated and carved up on a slab, given how he'd carved up a teenage girl, perhaps on the kitchen floor of that Ealing flat. Except Tatjana's remains had been dumped, whereas Tim's would receive a proper burial.

The squad car pulled off the gravel drive. Bev sniffed, observing the nosy neighbours, all gathered in a huddle just outside the garden gates, speculating on what this to-do might possibly be about.

What *had* it been about? Bev examined her feelings for the dead man who had fathered her most beloved daughter. If she was convicted of murder or manslaughter and sentenced to a long stretch in prison, Tim would have effectively ended her life too. *No. There's no sympathy there, she decided. I hated him and I'm glad he's dead. I wish I could console Sophie, and being the cause of her husband's death will always haunt me. But right now, I'm just crapping my pants that I'll lose my baby girl forever.*

'All right, back there?' the officer in the passenger seat asked, glancing over his shoulder.

Bev fought back a sob of desperation. 'Fine.'

*

Days in a holding cell came and went as Bev awaited the police's verdict as to whether Tim's death could be described as having mitigating circumstances or not – compelling enough to get her off the hook. Could they believe that she'd only intended to threaten him with electrocution so that she would extract the truth about Tatjana's murder? Would the post-mortem reveal what had actually come to pass in that en suite?

'They'll prosecute you for "Threat to Kill",' her defence lawyer had said. '*Kandice with a K*' had been sent from the same solicitors' firm that had originally botched her divorce. Not some hotshot legal eagle from the top 500, but a £130 an hour hump from a local firm that had offices above a barber's shop in Wythenshawe. Marginally better than the Legal Aid she didn't quite qualify for. The best she could afford, since Angie's assets had been frozen, and still too costly, at that. Kandice with a K had spelled her prospects out for her: 'That's very serious, Beverley, and carries a pretty muscular prison sentence if you're found guilty. It's not as if you didn't have other options. You should have just called the police.'

'But I already explained—'

'I know! I know! We'll make the best case for you we possibly can.' Kandice had placed her hands authoritatively on the table top, in the interview room that smelled of sweat and impending doom. 'But first, I need to know how you'll be paying for my services.'

Bev had sighed, closing her eyes, wishing that when she opened them, this nightmare would be over. 'I've got sod all money at the moment. Until I get paid for my last job. You know. Things are difficult for me since my divorce.' She'd shaken her head sorrowfully, hoping for sympathy but getting none; observing the stiff body language of the solicitor. Bev had pondered whether Kandice, with her out-of-date suit and her plastic beads, would be worth her fee.

'I'll sell my car. It'll be fine as long as you can get me off quickly.'

Kandice's shoulders had returned to their normal position. 'We'll see. You can demonstrate how Tim had been stalking you, so that will help. That woman at the Brackenrigg Inn. We'll be able to get her witness statement for the break-in. The balaclava and black outfit he wore have been retrieved by forensics. All of that can be proven. We'll see what the police find on his personal computer equipment and in his office at home, too, with regard to the fake website and Twitter accounts in your name. If your little recording bears out your statement that he attacked you in the bathroom and that you had a scuffle, I may be able to get some leniency.'

'I didn't bloody well kill him!'

Kandice with a K treated her to a sarcastic smile that cracked her heavy make-up. 'No. But the live toaster doesn't look good for you, Beverley. That's premeditation and you had a demonstrably good motive for murder. As I said, "Threat to Kill" is what you'll be prosecuted for at best. But you've got no criminal record and you having your daughter to consider means you're unlikely to be a flight risk. I think I can get you bail. That's assuming someone will pay it for you . . .'

'How can this be happening? How? Why does my life always go to shit? I solved a cold murder case, for God's sake, and now, I'm facing prison! How is that fair?' Bev slapped the scuffed tabletop. Felt the urge to throw her chair across the room and understood then why the furniture was bolted down.

'Life isn't fair, I'm afraid. Good things happen to bad people and bad things happen to good people. You shouldn't have tried to take the law into your own hands, should you?'

'No.' *Fuck off, Kandice with a K, you sanctimonious heifer.*

Bev's only other visitor during that dark time had been Doc. She'd not been allowed to see him during questioning, though the policewoman who had arrested her had told her that he'd showed up later on the day of her arrest to give evidence. Her heart had lifted slightly at the thought that she had an unlikely hero, but a hero nevertheless.

She'd been dozing on the narrow bed in her cell when her fortunes had started to change. The door had clanged open and the custody sergeant had marched into her cell, displacing the air of desperation with his detached authority.

'You've been bailed,' he'd said. He'd surprised her by smiling warmly. 'Come with me and I'll process your release.'

Her muscles screaming in complaint from the thin mattress, Bev had levered herself up and had looked at him quizzically. 'Who? Eh?'

'Bail. Your friend, James Shufflebotham. He posted it. He's waiting for you.'

In the foyer, now, Doc was leaning against the counter, legs crossed awkwardly, fingers laced together. She overheard him, chatting to a uniformed officer as though they were old friends, showing the guy his Metallica tour T-shirt that had faded from sheer age and regular use. His hair hung lank on his shoulders. His trainers were grey with dried-in mud.

'You look terrible,' Bev said, clasping him in a fleeting, awkward hug. 'And you smell of bacon.'

Doc grinned a yellow-toothed grin. His Adam's apple pinged up and down in his scrawny neck. 'I know, right? The smell in here really clings.' He turned to the officer he'd been chatting to, winked and guffawed with laughter. 'Sorry, mate. Only joking.' Turned to Bev, whispering. 'Not really joking.'

Seeing her friend, standing there, smiling as if the world were still turning, drumming a tattoo on the counter with his long, long fingers as though his head was full of rock music and Lego dreams, Bev felt optimism surge inside her for the first time since she'd been allowed to take Hope away for the weekend. She took her personal effects from the plastic box that the uniform pushed towards her. Hot, fat tears started to fall as she struggled to do up the buckle on her watch.

'Here, let me help,' Doc said, taking her dry hand into his clammy palm and nimbly fastening the watch. 'Don't be sad, man. It's going to be OK.'

'I'm not sad,' Bev said. 'I'm tired. I'm frightened. And I'm wondering why my knight in shining armour is a metalhead wearing a four-day-old T-shirt and stonewashed drainpipes.'

CHAPTER 48

Bev

'Rob! Wait!'

Though she'd followed her ex right across Manchester's city centre, trying to engage him in a conversation about the apocalyptic solicitor's letter that had landed on her doormat, Rob had spent the last twenty minutes walking briskly away from Bev, as though he had neither seen nor heard her.

'I want to talk to you, bastard! Stop!'

Her words had no effect whatsoever. Rob just shuffled on in those too-tight shiny grey trousers that he wore to work.

Finally, some two hundred yards ahead, he slowed, coming to a stop outside the King Street Townhouse Hotel. He went inside. Bev followed, momentarily nonplussed as daylight was swapped for low-level lighting and boutique hotel glamour. She caught a glimpse of him as the lift doors ahead closed. He was heading for the roof terrace, she calculated.

Taking the stairs two at a time, she eventually reached the summit to find him, sitting at a low table on the large veranda, facing a blonde woman, whom Bev could only see from the back. The woman wore her hair in a chignon in just the same way that Sophie wore . . .

'Oh, for God's sake, Bev!' Rob said, leaping to his feet, causing the steaming coffee on the table to slop from the two cups into their saucers.

But Bev's attention had been caught not by Rob's scowl, or the stunning view of Manchester's vertiginous rooftops beyond the glass railing but by the woman. She had turned around and wore a look of dismayed surprise on her beautiful face, as though she'd seen a ghoul made from cack.

'Sophie,' Bev said, neither shouting, nor questioning but simply stating her friend's name, as if her betrayal was a foregone conclusion in Bev's shitty life.

'You? What the hell are you doing here?' Sophie had that frost and bitter edge to her voice that she'd had in her early Holy Jo days, when Bev had been nothing more than a problem neighbour named Boo. 'You're supposed to be emptying my basement flat. You agreed you'd be gone by lunchtime.'

'I've not come to pick a fight with you, Soph. I'm here to ask Rob why the hell he thinks it's OK to get his solicitor to file for a restraining order against me, so that I can't come within 150 yards of my own daughter? Just at a point where I was about to gain custody.'

'Security!' Rob shouted over her head to the waitress. 'Can you call them, please? We've an unwanted visitor, here. She's on bail for murder.'

'I am not on bail for murder, you slandering tit.' Bev looked at the glazed barrier that was the only thing separating Rob from a rapid death by pavement. She realised with some regret that pushing him from the roof terrace of a tall building was not a practical solution for her woes. Not currently. 'It was self-defence.'

'With a live toaster!' Sophie said, her eyes already glassy with tears. Balling her fists.

'Don't do this, Rob. Please,' Bev said. Trying to remain dignified. Failing, unable to keep the desperation out of her words. 'For Hope's sake. A girl needs her mum.'

Sophie had started to back towards the adjacent table, wrapping her arms around her slender body as though she was in mortal peril. 'I don't blame Rob,' Sophie said. 'You're a danger to everyone you meet. I thought I could help you, but there's nothing but bad in you.'

Though there was a large part of her that ached inside for Sophie's lot, Bev's fatigue won out. She took four steps towards her friend so that they were nose to nose. Looked into her bloodshot widow's eyes, that she'd still managed to adorn with eyeliner and mascara. 'Listen, you. Your husband was worse than all the Jerry Fitzwilliams put together. I'd take a look at that snuff video of Tatjana Lebedev's final minutes before you start pointing the finger at me, you sanctimonious twat.' She poked Sophie in the arm. 'And you can work your mouldy basement up your bony arse. I'm out of there by twelve. Stick it. Stick your fucking Christian charity and your faulty toaster and all, while you're at it. All right for me to blow my tits off with it, but not Tim's. The meat-cleaver-wielding Wolf? Fucking hypocrite!' Turning back to her ex-husband, Bev could feel her anger being rapidly supplanted by sorrow. It wouldn't do to cry in front of these two. 'I'm going to fight you, you know. You don't know how my trial will play out.' She thumbed herself in the chest. 'I was backed into a corner and I did what I could to defend myself. I'm innocent. And I'm getting my Hope back. And you can fuck the fuck off.'

Get out. Get out now. She could see the security guard emerging onto the veranda at the far end. *You're going to blub. Don't cry.*

'I'm going to prison,' Bev said, placing her origami creations carefully into the compartmented box she'd fashioned from a Sainsbury's veg crate and Sophie's discarded

Amazon packaging. Sneezing when the dust tickled her nose, blowing the debris of crumpled up, tear-sodden toilet roll across the coffee table and onto the floor. 'I don't know why I'm even doing this. I may as well just leave the lot and let that cow clear it out.'

Doc took four books from the bookshelves above her desk and dropped them into an old cardboard box that didn't entirely look sturdy enough to bear the weight. 'You won't be going to prison, for Christ's sake. You're like Wonder Woman or some shit. You've gone viral, wrestling Fitzwilliam in that ridiculous bikini. You, pushing him in the pool is the biggest trending "angry GIF" on Giphy!'

'Rubbish. Everything I touch turns to stone. You should keep away from me.' She picked up a photo of Hope from her desk, polishing it carefully with the sleeve of her fleece. Among the dusty artefacts that she had in her possession, this silver-framed school portrait of her baby girl, at a time when she'd just lost her first front tooth, was always dust- and fingerprint-free. The shine of her daughter's smiling eyes caused despair to lodge uncomfortably in her throat and an ache to snake around her already breaking heart, squeezing tight. She clasped her hand to her chest, admiring her child; saying a silent prayer that she would not become but a confusing, painful memory to Hope Mitchell.

Doc took the photo from her, wrapping it carefully in two-ply newspaper and setting it carefully on the top of an almost full box. 'Stop it. You can't see into the future. You're catastrophising. Gordon the Klepto would rip you to shreds in group therapy.' He took some strapping tape, severing a strip from the roll with his teeth, and started to seal the box.

Bev forced a smile. 'You can't see into the future either, Doc. How do you know the cops won't work out who did the hacking for me? We're gonna be waving to each other through barred windows.'

'Are you finished, you big pessimist?' Doc said, crouching. 'Just chill your boots and stop worrying!' He picked the box up with a grunt, the muscles taut in his long skinny arms. The bottom of the box gave way suddenly, spilling the contents all over the floor.

'No!' Bev cried, spying Hope's photo as it scudded to a halt by the sofa – the wrappings open and shattered glass scattered around it like the fragmented memories of happier times. She picked the remnants of her precious keepsake up. 'It's a sign.' Cut her finger on the jagged edge of the glass that still clung to the frame. 'That's it. It's over. I've ruined everything.'

She sucked the blood from her thumb. Doc stood, still clutching the collapsed box with her wrapped effects covering his trainers, opening and closing his mouth as if seeking words of comfort that just wouldn't take shape on his tongue.

'Look. It's not like—'

Bev's phone rang shrilly, interrupting his explanation. She glanced at the screen. Kandice with a K calling. Closed her eyes. 'What now? What final nail in my coffin is this?' Pressed answer and listened . . .

'I've got news. Are you sitting down?'

CHAPTER 49
Angie

'Of course, I didn't have a clue what Jerry was up to. None of it. I'm as scandalised by this as anyone else,' Angie said, her voice just the right side of tremulous. 'Jerry kept me in the dark about all of it. He made sure he kept me compliant and unquestioning.'

'And how did he do that, Angela?' the prosecution asked, treating her to an encouraging smile.

Angie looked over at her soon-to-be-ex-husband, standing in the dock, looking very much like he'd spent two months on remand. That high colour, typical of a man who enjoyed too much fine red wine and sirloin steak, had drained, giving him the porridgey complexion that she had seen in the other inmates, on the one occasion she'd visited him in prison. Maybe that was why they called it porridge, she mused. Even the bespoke tailored suit didn't detract from the air of despondent resignation that now dogged his every move like a lingering fart.

The judge cleared his throat. Peered at her through his bifocals, looking somewhere between a sheep and the modern-day Pharisee that he was with that ridiculous long wig and those red robes.

Angie snapped out of her meandering reverie. Realised the judge, the barristers, the jury, the court artist, the entire gallery of this grand Old Bailey courtroom . . . they were all watching her expectantly, awaiting more of her tale of woe and subterfuge.

She toyed with her pearls, happy that her rash had crawled up her neck. The bruises were no longer there, but let the jury see how her hand shook. Let them see how easily she wept. 'He beat me, of course. He strangled me. He forced me into sex.'

'Objection!' Jerry's barrister was on her feet, her legal outrage ringing loud and sharp in the lofty, mahogany-panelled space.

Angie could see the artist, beavering away, glancing up at the no-nonsense ball-breaker in her short wig and black gown. Sketching, etching a snapshot in time of this long, long trial, capturing the drama, the disapprobation and the national bafflement, that the Labour party's number-one son should have gone quite so off-piste. Jerry was going to plead 'not guilty' of course. Cunning that he'd got himself a female defence, clearly in a bid to bamboozle the judge into thinking he wasn't a wife-battering misogynist. Maybe he'd actually pull it off. He was quite the charmer until he let his guard drop. His odds weren't good, though. Thanks to Bev, Angie knew exactly what evidence the prosecution had up his billowing sleeves.

As she relayed the tale of her domestic nightmare, she weathered the drubbing that the defence inevitably subjected her to. She revelled in the warm feeling in the pit of her stomach where the primordial soup of anxiety, bitter experience and expensive legal advice was coalescing into cautious optimism.

'You'll get to keep the house,' her divorce lawyer had said, ensconced in her tower of steel and glass in Manchester's Spinningfields. 'Obviously, his assets will remain frozen until the trial's over. They'll confiscate anything that's been embezzled or acquired illegally. But once that's done and dusted, you'll still be comfortably off. And more to the point . . .' The sharp-suited hard-ass of a woman who charged £350 per hour – a fee commensurate with twenty years spent at the top of her game – had patted her hand. 'He'll be in prison and you'll be safe.'

With another day at the Old Bailey endured, Angie pulled her coat tightly closed against the September wind and hastened through the paparazzi. Battling to conceal her smile, lest the red tops indulge themselves in a hatchet-job portrayal of her as being in cahoots with a dirty politician. Bad enough that they had got wind of her having employed Bev's services. Catfishing and hacking: she and Bev had agreed to keep those nuggets to themselves. If the press knew the full extent of how the police had come about the evidence against the mighty Jerry Fitzwilliam – fraudster, abuser and accessory to murder – they'd have a field day, and Angie would be done for perjury.

'What's life like, living with a man who stole millions of the public's money, Angela?' one reporter asked her, shoving his recorder too close to her face. 'Did you know he was planning drug-fuelled orgies for his pals? Did you know about Tatjana Lebedev?'

Of course I didn't bloody know, you berk, she thought, ploughing past the persistent little oik with his angles and his deadlines and his ridiculous haircut. *Just keep moving, Angie. Hail a cab.*

As she clambered into the back of a taxi on the opposite side of the road, she saw Bev standing outside the grand white stone façade of the Old Bailey. She appeared dwarfed beneath the building's towering dome with Lady Justice, armed with her sword and her scales, presiding metres above, over the motley band of reporters and photographers that had gathered around.

'Oh dear,' Angie whispered, catching Bev's eye as the taxi doubled back before peeling off down towards the river. 'She hates me for dragging her into this. I can tell. Even after I begged Dad to lend me all that money so I could settle her bill.'

Turning away in a bid to switch the guilt off, Angie forced herself to focus on what awaited her in her London Bridge hotel. There, her new nanny, Klaudia waited with the children, having been on a lovely riverside walk that Angie had planned meticulously, taking in HMS *Belfast* and Tower Bridge. Even though she had to endure the scrutiny of the High Court where her character, her morality and her honesty seemed to be on trial, just as that duplicitous fiend she'd married faced judge and jury, it was important not to let her mothering standards drop. The children needed improving activities, after all, and Klaudia needed managing as much as the gardener or the ironing lady or the cleaner. Tate Modern tomorrow, with lunch in the cafeteria. A trip on the London Eye, the day after. They'd love that.

Angie congratulated herself on holding it all together and managing to bring her A-game in the wardrobe department. That trip to New Bond Street had not been wasted. The new black dress looked a treat. Just the right amount of demure with the correct degree of panache. Her dad didn't need to know that eight hundred of the three grand he'd lent her for Bev had gone in Burberry's till. A lady had to have her things, didn't she?

She tittered at the thought as the taxi bounced down towards Blackfriars. Angie felt some of the tension leech from her shoulders as the glittering band of the Thames came into view. Open space, at last, quickly supplanted by the congested, claustrophobic Upper James Street that led them among the recently built monoliths in the City of London – Jerry's old stomping ground.

In the back of the cab, she shivered with distaste at the thought. Right now, there was no escaping the dreadful legacy of Jerry Fitzwilliam's misdemeanours. No matter, though. She was playing the long game. Very soon, Angie would be free. And she'd owe that fresh start entirely to Beverley Saunders.

CHAPTER 50
Bev

Gazing dolefully at the scuffed vinyl tiles on the floor, and the bars on the windows, Bev tried to imagine what life would be like somewhere else – a place with gleaming wooden flooring and whitewashed walls covered in quirky art. Stylish sofas where clients could flick through magazines in a waiting room. Sipping a latte from one of those Gaggia machines, before she summoned them into her office for an initial consultation, describing how she could help them to get even . . . for an hourly fee. She visualised the effort it would take to make this dump that idyllic workspace.

'I think it's got potential,' she said, noticing that the ceilings were high – always something she'd loved about period properties. 'What do you think?'

Doc shrugged. 'It's all right. I still don't think we need an office.'

The shiny-faced estate agent's rictus grin dimmed slightly. He started to toy with the brightly coloured plastic tags on his jangling giant bunch of keys. 'Oh, I think you'll find this space offers the best value for money in Altrincham. You can't underestimate the importance of decent business premises.' He checked his giant gold watch as though he had a more lucrative appointment to attend elsewhere.

Bev wondered briefly if estate agents practiced their lines in a mirror at home every night before bed, rubbing a slick veneer onto their faces in the morning, after they'd showered. 'I think calling this "decent" is a bit of a stretch, love.'

'I've got another interested party coming to look this place over in a few minutes. It's going to get snapped up today. No doubt about it.'

The image in her mind's eye of the airy workspace with the beautiful floor was fading fast. The butterflies in Bev's stomach had taken flight and were being rapidly displaced by apprehension. She didn't want to let her dream slip away on the cusp of it becoming reality. 'Do you mind giving us a minute to have a little snoop round and talk it over?'

The estate agent nodded and left. Bev and Doc were alone.

'Look, this is a great opportunity,' Bev said, wandering through to the functional but tired kitchen. Her footsteps echoed through the space. 'Two offices and a big reception area. A kitchen. A bloody shower room! But it's a real shithole.'

'Precisely. You're not in the sort of game where you need an office, Bev.' Doc bypassed the kitchen, heading for the offices beyond. His expression was inscrutable. 'And I'm certainly not.'

Bev tried to turn the shower on in the tiny bathroom. It sputtered and spat as air worked its way through long-disused pipes. Eventually, a dribble leaked from the grubby plastic handset. She shrugged. 'I think we could breathe life into this place for a couple of grand, tops. Think about it, Doc. I need a space where abused and frightened people can come. A neutral space that's got privacy. I also need a home.'

Doc was standing behind her, now, chewing on his bottom lip. Frowning at the brown bowl of the toilet. 'Jesus. That's grim even by my standards.'

'Nothing Harpic can't clean, James. And you need somewhere to lay your head too, or had you forgotten that your place was done over while you were at your folks'?'

'Yeah. I know Jerry Fitzwilliam has gone down for a ten-year stretch, but I still don't feel safe knowing his little spy friends know where they can get to me. Moving into office space that will have our names on the contract is hardly lying low, is it? And I bet there's something in the small print says it's not for residential use, anyway.'

Bev pushed past him and stood in the middle of the empty office she'd already mentally called dibs on. A barred window with a view of some bins. Shredded carpet tiles. Peeling paint. It wasn't prison. It wasn't Sophie's mildewed basement. It was perfect. 'This is just a temporary stopgap, though, isn't it? Now Angie's paid me, I'm flush. It's the right time to invest in my business, and you, my friend, are my business partner whether you like it or not.'

'Silent partner.'

'You say potato, I say chips. Whatever. I've had a lucky escape. I could be behind rather different bars right now. If Kandice with a K hadn't have turned out to be such a Rottweiler—'

Doc threw his head back and laughed. 'Rottweiler? She was a joke! You need to get better legal representation, Bev, man. The only reason the charges against you were dropped was down to Westminster wanting to cover their arse.'

'It's always a conspiracy theory with you, isn't it? You're such a paranoid—'

'The last thing they wanted was a prominent politician getting done for boning an underage sex slave and then helping to dispose of her body parts. Man alive! You think MI5 didn't put two and two together when they saw that video with those masked wankers and make ten?'

'Eh?' Bev peered outside at the grey skies, smiling at the sliver of blue that had broken through the thick blanket of cloud. Better times ahead.

Kicking at a frayed and curling carpet tile, Doc shoved his hands awkwardly into the back pockets of his stone-washed jeans. Today, he wore a *Los Pollos Hermanos* long-sleeved T. Ever the corporate dresser. 'They're thinking that, apart from Tim, who we know was The Wolf, maybe the other guys in that film are all high-ranking politicians like Fitzwilliam. Right? Stands to reason. Maybe they know them! Distinguishing marks on their body and such like. So, the last thing they need is it coming out in a further investigation that there's a cabal of paedos in parliament, getting off their faces on coke and bumping young girls off. *That's* why your case was dropped. Didn't she say – that solicitor of yours? Didn't she say, "It's not in the public interests to try your case"?'

Suddenly, Bev felt that sliver of blue go back behind the clouds as the turmoil of the last few weeks loomed like a spectre in that hopeful space, ushering in darkness and sucking all the oxygen from her optimism. Rob's threats that she'd never see Hope again. His solicitor's letter, applying for a restraining order against her. Sophie's complete rejection of their friendship. The prospect of losing her liberty as well as her child and her reputation. It was an end-of-days apocalypse that she never wanted to repeat.

'When Kandice asked if I was sitting down, I thought they were going to go for the maximum sentence or actually go the whole hog and charge me with murder,' she told Doc. 'But yeah. They dropped the case like a hot stone. She said it was because I was the only witness and that there was a tonne of mitigating circumstances. But thinking

374

about it, you're right. It was a cover-up. It wasn't Tim's death they were interested in at all. It was the probable identities of the cockerel, the horse and the bulldog. I did wonder why Jerry's trial at the Old Bailey was all about the fraud and not the murder.'

When Doc placed a supportive hand on her shoulder, the spectre vanished and the blue sliver reappeared.

'You're in the clear. Forget it now. And your phone's not stopped ringing with potential new business. You're like some kind of revenge-ninja for the country's fucked-over underdogs and bullied women.' He made a devil's horn sign with his hand and mimed an air-guitar axe-lick. 'All's well that ends well, Bev.' He strode purposefully through to the adjacent office and walked back again, nodding. 'Sod it. Let's go for this place. We can move all our crap in here – just as an interim measure. Take a six month lease, yeah? Get sofa beds. Keep quiet about it.' He jerked his thumb backward, grinning. 'There's even a storeroom in there for my Lego.'

'Great. Let's do this.'

The trepidation that now jangled in Bev's belly was the right sort. For the first time in many many years, she felt in control. And for the first time since her girlhood, when she looked at the beams that spanned the ceiling, she didn't see her father, grey-faced and hanging by his neck; didn't visualise her mother in a corner of the room, glass of vodka and paintbrush in hand, telling her how she was too clumsy and ill-fated to walk life's tightrope without falling. The office was empty. It was a blank canvas, ready for Bev to paint as she saw fit.

Epilogue

'Will the nasty man break into our room again?' Hope asked, her small, pale face wrinkling up with curiosity.

Bev smoothed down her daughter's silken chestnut hair, blown into cotton-candy wisps in the stiff Lakeland breeze. 'No, darling. Course not. Forget all about him. We're here so I can make up for that weekend. And we're gonna start the way we mean to go on.' She enfolded Hope in a bear hug, drinking in her sugary scent of childhood and sweetness and innocence. It was the finest smell in the world. 'Ready for some fun?'

'It's always fun with you. Best Mum.'

'Best girl.'

Once they'd checked into the beautiful Victorian hotel on the edge of Ullswater, Bev led Hope by the hand to the children's play area. She relished the sight of her little girl clambering up the steps of the slide, squealing with delight as she shot back down to Bev's waiting arms.

The sun had come out in earnest and had turned the lake into a giant sheet of blue foil. The sound of bleating fluffy white sheep was carried to them on the wind and the woolly white clouds scudded through the blue, blue sky as if the heavens reflected the earth in perfect symmetry. Bev drank in the clean air, feeling that this was a fresh start and that she was somehow renewed by what she had endured of late.

'Push me, Mummy!' Hope cried, leaning back and forth on a swing, clutching the thick chains in her little fists.

As Bev obliged, she considered her decision to keep the identity of Hope's father to herself. Yes, if she'd had a DNA test performed before his burial to prove Tim's paternity, she'd be able to get Rob out of her life, once and for all. She'd even be able to take back the family home, since Rob would have no claim on it beyond that of a childless party in a failed marriage. Her needs for Hope would take priority over his. She'd even be able to lay claim to some of Tim's considerable estate on Hope's behalf. But Bev had opted to keep her secret as exactly that, preferring not to break Hope's heart with the knowledge that the man she'd loved as her daddy for all of her ten years was nothing more than another of her mother's past lovers; that her true father had been a monster; that embedded in the fabric of her being was genetic material that marked her as flawed and impure. No way did Bev want to saddle her precious child with the same emotional burden that had been bequeathed to her by her own suicidal father and alcoholic mother – the burden of being made to believe that she possessed a congenital tendency to failure.

'Come on,' Bev said, wrestling Hope from the swing and running her down the path to the glittering lake. 'Race you to the rowing boats.'

Easing the oars back and forth in the crystal clear water, Bev listened to her daughter's excitable chatter about school and her friends and her favourite food and how she'd like a kitten one day. She watched her dip her skinny fingers into the freezing cold lake as Bev manoeuvred the boat out to the island in the middle. They were surrounded by the majesty of the steep, rocky hills that encircled Ullswater for miles. The only sound apart from their laughter was the bleating sheep. The warmth of the sun lit their faces, banishing the shadows cast by strife and separation. Danger felt a million miles away in that glorious unspoiled place. And Bev knew that for now – at least until she took on her next job – she'd climbed down from the tightrope to feel the good earth and all its solid possibilities beneath her aching, tired feet.

THE END